To Dance with the Earl

A Regency Historical Romance

Brighton Seasons Series

Evie Fairfax

Copyright © 2025 by Evie Fairfax

All rights reserved.

No part of this book may be reproduced in any form or by any electronic or mechanical means, including information storage and retrieval systems, without written permission from the author, except for the use of brief quotations in a book review.

This is a work of fiction. All the names, characters and events portrayed in this novel are fictitious. Any similarity to actual persons, living or dead, is entirely accidental.

Cover photograph © Mary Chronis, VJ Dunraven Productions, and Period Images

Cover Design © 2025 Evie Fairfax

Chapter One

London, Early July 1794

Gabrielle woke to daylight streaming between the curtains. Dawn came early this close to the summer solstice. Most likely the only other people awake in the house were the servants.

Charlotte, the little girl Gabrielle cared for, was still asleep on the other side of the room.

After two years as a governess, Gabrielle was as familiar with the daily routines of her new life, as she'd once been with the rhythms of her old life.

She had no control over where she and Charlotte lived. That decision was always made by Charlotte's mother, Lady Henderson. But wherever they were living, Gabrielle's first task of the day was always the same—she checked Charlotte's collection of snail shells.

She slid out of bed and crossed the room to perform the essential inspection. She'd have preferred not to keep the precious collection in their bedchamber, but it was the only way to be sure it was safe from Charlotte's older brother.

Gabrielle counted herself fortunate that Lady Henderson had employed her to be only Charlotte's governess.

Augustus, the Hendersons' son, was educated separately from his sister. But occasionally he came into the two-room suite that comprised the nursery.

It was always an unpleasant experience when Augustus visited them. Last time he'd made a disdainful comment about one of Charlotte's paintings and flicked it onto the floor.

On a previous occasion, he'd picked up the piece of linen Gabrielle had been hemming, ready for Charlotte to make a sampler. Augustus had run his fingers up and down the cut edge, worrying away at the loose threads until he'd created a ragged fringe the length of the piece.

"I suppose such poor-quality stuff is adequate for Charlotte's first attempts," he'd said, tossing it aside.

Gabrielle had responded with cool courtesy rather than drawing attention to his poor behavior. The only time she'd tried to exert her authority over Charlotte's brother, she'd been reprimanded by Lady Henderson and threatened with dismissal if she repeated the offense.

Augustus was the reason Charlotte insisted on keeping everything she truly valued in their bedchamber—including, and especially, her collection of snail shells.

Charlotte adored snails. She painted pictures of them. She made up stories about them, and she collected their empty shells.

Except—sometimes the shells weren't empty.

Gabrielle didn't care for snails, so she approached the wooden box warily. The night was usually when those apparently vacant shells suddenly turned out to be occupied.

Three paces away from the box, a thin, silvery gleam caught her eye. She stopped dead, her toes curling against the floorboards, as her gaze tracked the shimmering trail down the side of the box, across the tabletop and over the edge.

Where had it gone?

She bent to pull her nightgown tight around her ankles, and then studied every inch of the floor surrounding her bare feet.

Nothing.

Still holding her nightgown close, she crouched without moving from her spot, trying to see if the snail was clinging to the underside of the tabletop.

"Mademoiselle?" Charlotte said in a sleepy voice.

"A snail woke up in the night," Gabrielle replied.

"Ooohhh." Charlotte padded over to join her, and then fearlessly approached the table. "I'll find it."

"We're only supposed to be collecting empty shells," Gabrielle reminded her.

"I did," Charlotte said, not looking at Gabrielle. "But sometimes it's hard to tell. And it was so pretty—oh, it's not the prettiest one that's escaped! Which one is it? Don't run away little snail, I'm not going to hurt you."

Gabrielle smiled ruefully at Charlotte's crooning tone. Her own instinct when confronted by a snail was to make a brisk retreat, her skin crawling—not to address it like a friend.

But two years ago, Charlotte hadn't spoken to anyone. She'd been a silent, suspicious child of five when Gabrielle had become her governess. With no experience as a teacher, and no easy way to seek advice, Gabrielle had tried to engage Charlotte's interest in the plants they saw on their morning walks.

Her plan had worked—but not quite as Gabrielle had anticipated. Charlotte had indeed developed a passion for some of the things they found in the garden, but not the flowers. She loved little creatures—beautiful-winged butterflies, ladybirds, crawling beetles, worms...and snails.

She'd also grown into a happy, talkative—at least with Gabrielle—seven-year-old. Gabrielle considered the presence of the snail shell collection in their bedroom a small price to pay for its part in Charlotte's transformation.

"Shall I check around the water jug and wash basin for you, mademoiselle?" Charlotte asked.

"Thank you, that's thoughtful of you." Gabrielle retreated to sit on the side of the bed while Charlotte carefully carried out her self-appointed task.

The little girl had a kind, generous heart and she was a delightful companion. Gabrielle had grown to love her—and she worried about what the future might hold for both of them.

"It's all right, mademoiselle," Charlotte's deep little voice broke into Gabrielle's thoughts. "You can wash now while I find the snail."

∼

As soon as they were ready, Gabrielle and Charlotte went out for their regular morning walk.

Gabrielle carried an old ceramic pot containing the leftover crumbs from their meals the previous day. Charlotte carried the recaptured snail in the small bag Gabrielle had made for the purpose of transporting little creatures.

To Dance with the Earl

They weren't going far. Their destination was the private garden in the center of Grosvenor Square. Gabrielle had been told the oval-shaped garden covered an area of about six acres. It wasn't comparable to the expansive grounds of the château where Gabrielle had grown up, but it was large enough for them to take brisk walks. There were also plenty of fascinating creatures for Charlotte to find along the paths, and in the grassy areas, trees and shrubs.

They made their way through the bands of alternating sunlight and shadow to their favorite small lawn. Gabrielle sat down on the bench overlooking the grass. Charlotte opened her bag and delicately took out the snail, which had long since retreated to the safety of its shell.

"There you are, little snail." She put it down behind the bench. "When you wake up, you'll see you're safely home again. Do you dream of going home, mademoiselle?"

"Sometimes." Two years ago, Gabrielle had fled revolutionary France with her papa, the Duke de la Fontaine, and her younger brother, Felix.

They'd arrived in England with little more than the clothes they were wearing. Her papa now earned his living as a fencing master and Gabrielle was Charlotte's governess.

Apart from the death of Gabrielle's mother, which had occurred shortly before their escape from France, Gabrielle's memories of her old life were happy. And her most joyous memories included the time she'd spent with Quin, the Earl of Hanwell —the man she loved.

She'd met Quin on his first visit to France when she was thirteen and he was fifteen. She'd fallen in love with him as they roamed the parterres of the château and the local countryside. But it was more than three years since she'd last seen him, and she missed him every day.

"Now you're home with me." Charlotte smiled at Gabrielle, claimed the breadcrumb pot, and turned to scatter a fistful of greasy crumbs onto the grass.

Within seconds, sparrows fluttered down for their breakfast, while pigeons arrived with noisier wing flaps.

It didn't take long for Charlotte to empty the crumb pot. "All gone." She brushed her palms together and wiped her fingers on the cloth kept in her bag for that purpose. "We'll bring you more breakfast tomorrow, birds."

Gabrielle stood and they continued their walk through the garden. Charlotte ran ahead and back several times until she was breathless, and her cheeks glowed with healthy color.

Gabrielle strode along briskly, resisting the urge to break into a run herself. Whenever she was in public, she was always conscious she should behave with utmost decorum—as befitted a governess.

Charlotte turned her attention to searching the grass and plants for anything of interest, and soon came back to Gabrielle with one of her hands cupped over the other. "Look what I've found, mademoiselle. It's not a snail, I promise."

"I know you'd never torment me with one." But Gabrielle couldn't help feeling a little uneasy—until Charlotte lifted her hand to reveal the shiny, rounded red back of a ladybird.

"Isn't he pretty?" the little girl said.

"Very." Gabrielle relaxed. She was comfortable with ladybirds. "So bright and cheerful. Perhaps you should paint him later?"

"Can we take him home?" Charlotte asked hopefully.

"No, sweetheart, he might need to go about his duties of caring for his children," Gabrielle said.

"Not if he's a papa." Charlotte held up her hand to study the black-spotted red beetle more closely. "Only if he's a nurse or a governess. But then he'd be a she. How can we tell if he's a she?"

"I don't know," Gabrielle admitted.

The ladybird opened its red casings and whirred into the air on its inner wings. Charlotte watched it fly away.

"Shall we go in for breakfast now?" Gabrielle asked.

Charlotte nodded. "I'm hungry. What are we doing this morning?"

"We'll begin with your multiplication tables, and then we'll practice our watercolor painting." Gabrielle would paint the sprig of leaves she'd collected, think of Quin, and hope for his speedy return.

∽

THE MULTIPLICATION TABLES were a necessary chore for both of them—though more so for Gabrielle than Charlotte, who took an unexpected pleasure in the ordered logic of numbers.

Then they dedicated an hour to the ladylike activity of watercolor painting. They were still engrossed in their work when Lady Henderson's maid, Ethel, came into the nursery.

"Good morning, mademoiselle, here are the newspapers Lady Henderson has finished with," the lady's maid said.

"Thank you, Ethel." Gabrielle smiled as she took the papers.

Apart from Charlotte, Gabrielle had only one certain ally under the Hendersons' roof, and it wasn't Ethel, but she considered it prudent to remain on courteous terms with everyone in the household.

Ethel lifted her chin and looked down her nose at the paintings lying on the table. Her gaze passed over Gabrielle's leaves without a hitch, then settled on Charlotte's painting of a ladybird and a snail.

She gave a small but audible sniff.

Charlotte's attention remained fixed on her painting. She began to add another swirl to the snail's shell, but Gabrielle could sense the tension in her slight body.

"Now I've given you the papers I must return to her ladyship at once," Ethel announced haughtily. "She's to attend the Duchess of Morden's exclusive soirée this evening."

Charlotte lifted her head and watched intently as the door closed behind her mother's maid. Her shoulders only relaxed after she heard the firm snick of the latch.

Gabrielle suspected Ethel had treated Charlotte unkindly before Gabrielle had become her governess. But Charlotte never talked about what had happened during the months between the death of the nurse who'd raised her from birth, and Gabrielle's arrival.

Sometimes, Gabrielle wondered if she should ask Charlotte directly about that time, but she always decided not to. She couldn't see what purpose it would serve, and it might even cause a setback in Charlotte's growing self-assurance.

Charlotte painted another snail near the first one, while Gabrielle put the newspapers in date order.

The oldest had been published ten days ago. Gabrielle would have preferred her news to be more current, but she was used to the haphazard way the papers eventually arrived in the nursery.

She moved to an armchair to peruse the first one while Charlotte continued to work on her painting.

HMS Wayfarer…

The name of Quin's ship leaped off the page at Gabrielle.

Her heart started to pound, and her ears buzzed.

Her gaze flew along the lines of text, devouring every precious word.

Plymouth…

She eased out a breath and read the short report again.

Quin had departed England more than three years ago on a Scientific Expedition arranged jointly by the Royal Navy and the Royal Society. But Quin wasn't a naval officer. He was traveling as a civilian botanist.

Gabrielle was infinitely proud of him—and she'd missed him dreadfully from the moment of his departure.

But now he was nearly home.

She read the report a third time. HMS Wayfarer had called briefly at Plymouth, before continuing to London. Packages of letters had been exchanged at the Cornish port. There was every indication the venture had been an outstanding success.

Gabrielle closed her eyes and lowered the precious newspaper to her lap.

Quin was coming home.

Finally, he was on the way back to her.

In an instant of panic, she scanned the report again, looking for his name. He wasn't mentioned, but surely...*surely*, he was safely on board the Wayfarer?

She soothed her spike of anxiety with the reassuring thought that the venture could hardly have been called an outstanding success, if the only son and heir of the Marquess of Appledrum had been lost.

Quin was coming home!

She wanted to jump up and sing with happiness. Only a lifetime of training kept her sitting calmly in her chair.

A frisson of anxiety mingled with her joy. Would Quin still love her the same way he had before he'd traveled the world, and made so many new discoveries without her by his side?

How would he feel about her loss of wealth and status?

The boy she'd watched grow into a man had been calm and steadfast—but deeply passionate beneath his quiet exterior. She didn't believe her transformation from pampered duke's daughter to penniless governess would matter to him—would it?

She took another calming breath and went carefully through the rest of the first newspaper, and then every page of the other papers.

To her disappointment, there was no further mention of the returning expedition. But the newspaper was ten days old. By now, Quin might even have arrived in London. They could be within miles of each other for the first time in more than three years!

A new burst of joy surged through her.

She put the newspapers aside, sprang to her feet and went back to the table.

"Well done, that's a beautiful picture," she said to Charlotte. "Now wash your brushes, please, and we'll practice our dancing."

Chapter Two

"Harlequin!"

Quin's boots had barely touched the cobblestones before he was pulled into his father's fierce embrace.

Despite Lord Appledrum's naturally exuberant personality, he rarely displayed his deepest emotions so openly. At this moment, Quin needed no further words to know how much his father had missed him, and the depth of Lord Appledrum's relief that he'd returned safely.

"I'm glad to be home, father." His voice was rough, and he trusted that the strength of his return embrace would convey how much he meant those words.

"Let me see you." Lord Appledrum held Quin at arm's length with a firm grip on his shoulders.

Quin was an inch taller, but the difference in their height made no difference to his view of his father. Lord Appledrum was still the man he loved, respected, and looked up to above all others—even though he was also capable of causing Quin acute embarrassment.

Now he searched his father's countenance with the same intensity his father was scrutinizing him.

There was a little more gray at Lord Appledrum's temples, and perhaps a few more creases at the outer corners of his eyes. But at the age of forty-three, the marquess remained lean and muscular, and he was clearly still in his customary vigorous good health.

Relief coursed through Quin at finding his father unchanged.

"I'm glad to find you looking so well, sir," he said, his heart in his voice, and turned his attention to the woman standing quietly beside Lord Appledrum.

"Trentie—" he started to greet her. But then she was hugging him as tightly as his father had.

Quin closed his arms around the woman who was the only mother he'd ever known, profoundly thankful she also appeared unaltered by the passage of time.

"I promised myself I wouldn't weep all over you." Her words were muffled by his coat as well as the emotion in her voice. "But I'm so happy to see you again I can't help myself."

She lifted her head and cupped his face between her hands. "I'm so proud of you. And so glad you're home at last."

Her eyes glistened with tears, but her smile was wide and full of boundless love and happiness.

"I'm glad to be home." Quin's own eyes were damp. "Exploration was as rewarding as I hoped it would be." He paused to clear his throat. "But it would have been even more satisfying if all of you had been with me."

In truth, there had been several times when he'd been extremely grateful that the ones he loved were not being exposed to the same dangers he faced. But that didn't invalidate the strength of the emotions behind his claim.

Miss Trent pulled his head down and kissed his cheek. Then she gave her own head an almost imperceptible shake and stepped back.

"Welcome home, my lord," she said in a more formal tone, and dropped her gaze to the reticule she was trying to open.

"Is this what you're looking for, Miss Trent?" Lord Appledrum offered her a beautifully laundered and folded handkerchief.

She flashed a glance up at the marquess from under her tear-spangled eyelashes. "Are you sure you don't need it yourself, my lord?" she asked, even as she took it from him.

He grinned. "I've got more than one. You were most diligent in reminding me we would likely need them this morning." Then he proceeded to prove his words by touching another square of fine linen to his own eyes.

Quin listened to their byplay, the love filling him up far warmer and more enveloping than the July sun above.

These were the two people who'd provided the rock-solid foundations for his growth from child to man. And Agnes Trent's role had been as important as his father's.

She'd been a lowly housemaid when she'd first become his nurse when he was three years old. Now she was Lord Appledrum's principal housekeeper, responsible for the overall management of all the marquess's households.

"Come." Lord Appledrum clapped Quin on the shoulder. "I've reserved a private parlor for us at the King's Head, so we can catch up on our news in comfort. I'm sure you have many duties left to perform on board before you can come home for good."

"Yes, I have." Quin fell into step beside his father. "There were many packages of letters waiting for us at Plymouth—from the Royal Society, the Admiralty—but yours were the ones I was most eager to read. I'm so thankful most of your news was heartening. Not knowing the latest news can be very unpleasant. We only discovered we're now at war with France when a French ship opened fire on us in the Atlantic."

"Oh my goodness!" Miss Trent exclaimed.

"No harm done," Quin assured her, wishing he hadn't illustrated his point quite so graphically.

"Going back to your earlier comment, yes, you're correct, sir," he said. "Among the letters I received were requests for meetings with members of the Royal Society. But my first priority must be making sure the live specimens and seeds we've collected are unloaded safely. One way or another, there is a great deal to do before we can pause to rest."

He broke off. "To be honest, my responsibilities to the expedition are the last thing on my mind at the moment," he admitted. "I'm too eager to hear all your latest news. And Gabrielle, how is she? The duke and Felix?" His muscles tensed and his heart pounded as he waited for his father's answer.

"Gabrielle is not permitted any visitors except her father and Felix?" Quin repeated. "But surely I can deliver a note to tell her I've returned?"

"Only if you're happy for Lady Henderson to read it first," Lord Appledrum said with uncharacteristic grimness.

"That's outrageous! Why has the duke allowed her to remain in such a position?" Quin demanded. "In your letters you said he's now earning a tolerably comfortable income as a fencing master."

It had been a huge shock to Quin when the news of Gabrielle's escape from France had caught up with the expedition.

He'd read and re-read his father's letter beneath the light of a tropical sun, desperately wishing he was back in Europe, where he could be of some help, rather than half the globe away.

But that was the one letter he'd received during his voyages which had contained a few paragraphs in Gabrielle's own hand, added two days after her arrival in Brighton. Reading her message had soothed the worst of his agitation.

Gabrielle had assured him she was well and safe, and that traveling by fishing boat had been an interesting adventure. She'd even included a tiny sketch of the vessel, crammed between the tightly packed lines of script. That letter was now one of his most treasured possessions.

"It's Gabrielle's choice to continue with the Hendersons," Lord Appledrum said soberly. "From what her father says, she has grown attached to the child in her care, and fears leaving might cause harm to the little girl."

Quin looked from his father to Miss Trent, unsettled by what he'd just been told. He'd been anticipating his next meeting with Gabrielle from the moment he'd said goodbye to her three years ago.

In his lowest moments he'd feared she might fall ill while he was away—or worse. And sometimes he'd worried she might decide a man who possessed limited social graces, but an inordinate obsession with plants, was no longer to her taste. But he'd never anticipated anything like this.

"Do you think...do you think she might be so dedicated to her governess duties she won't give them up for anything?" he asked.

"I don't know," Lord Appledrum replied. "I haven't seen her myself since she moved out of my London house to join the Hendersons' household. All I know is the news her father regularly shares with me, but his own meetings with her are less frequent than he'd like."

Quin stood and began to pace restlessly around the small parlor. "I want to hear all her news—and I have so much to tell her. That's true for all of you, of course, but you're here with me now. I never imagined I could be in the same city with Gabrielle and yet unable to meet or even write to her."

His father watched him. "Why didn't you enter into a formal betrothal with her before you left?" he asked. There was no censure in his tone, but there was curiosity. "That's what we all expected."

"We?"

"Gabrielle's parents and I," Lord Appledrum clarified.

"Oh." Quin flushed, though he wasn't surprised his relationship with Gabrielle had been a topic of private conversation between their parents. "I didn't want to tie her to me and then leave her for several years. I feared...." This was difficult to say. "In short, if she found another man she preferred while I was away, I didn't want to cause her the pain of having to break a formal engagement as well as....Anyway, that was my thinking."

Quin's heart hadn't believed Gabrielle's heart would change, but his logical mind knew people's affections did alter with time —and Gabrielle had only been nineteen when he'd set sail with the expedition.

Lord Appledrum smiled faintly. "As far as I've ever been able to tell, Gabrielle loved you from the moment she first set eyes on you."

"Not the first moment," Quin corrected his father. "I don't shine in the salon or ballroom. But after I received your letter about their exile, I did regret the lack of a formal betrothal."

"We tried to persuade her to live under my sister's protection," Lord Appledrum said. "That's what her father wanted, and if she'd been your official fiancée, I'd have had more authority to press for that outcome. But Gabrielle was too scrupulous to accept your aunt's invitation."

Quin's gut tightened and he ran his fingers through his hair. "I made the wrong choice, but I wanted what would be best for Gabrielle. I did promise her mother that, provided you hadn't a greater need for me, we could live in France after we were married."

His father wasn't easily surprised, but now he gaped at Quin. "And you never thought to tell anyone else that?"

Quin shook his head. "It was only because her mother was anxious about the future."

The duchess's health had been precarious in the year before Quin's departure, and she'd died a few weeks before her family's precipitate flight from France.

"She probably told Phillipe, which accounts for why he stopped nagging me to know of your intentions," Lord Appledrum said, referring to Gabrielle's father. "But why didn't you tell me you were planning to live in France?"

"I didn't believe the duchess would hold me to that promise," Quin replied. "And it was made with the clear proviso that we'd only live near her if your need wasn't greater."

"*My* need?" Lord Appledrum murmured. "How were you going to decide that?"

"After proper consultation with you," Quin said. "I did suspect we might end up dividing our time between France and England. I must seek out the duke immediately." He turned toward the door, ready to begin his mission at once.

"Wait, Harlequin." Lord Appledrum's tone lost its humorous undercurrent. "Gabrielle's father isn't in town at the moment. He's gone up to Sinclair's country estate with a mission to make the youngest son a competent swordsman, fit to hold an army commission."

"I don't know the Sinclairs," Quin said impatiently. "Come to that, I don't know the Hendersons, or what manner of people they are to put such restrictions around a young lady in their care."

"You don't know them because you spent virtually no time in society before you left with the expedition," Lord Appledrum pointed out. "From what her father tells me, Gabrielle enjoys her duties as a governess, despite the lack of variety in her routine.

And she regularly reads the newspapers to keep up with the world—though that might be because she's looking for any reports about your expedition."

"Have there been many such reports?" Quin's interest was caught.

"Several. What are you thinking?" Lord Appledrum asked.

"I'm going to put a notice in the newspaper." Quin strode over to the parlor door and called for an inn servant.

A few minutes later, with writing materials procured, Quin sat at the table, Lord Appledrum and Miss Trent on either side of him, both of them shamelessly watching as his borrowed pen scratched across the paper.

"Lord Hanwell presents his compliments to all relatives and friends he is unable to greet in person directly upon his return to London," Lord Appledrum read aloud. "Very formal, referring to yourself in the third person. Nothing like your usual style, but impressively formal."

"Thank you, sir." Quin kept writing.

"He wishes to assure them he is in good health and greatly looks forward to future convivial meetings with them," his father continued reading. "Which he trusts will not be interrupted by any unexpected lupins. *Lupins?*" Lord Appledrum raised an incredulous eyebrow. "I thought you appreciated all plants. When were you and Gabrielle ever interrupted by lupins?"

"Never," Quin replied. "It says lupines."

He crossed out the final word and rewrote it, careful to make sure the 'e' was clearly visible, and then frowned. "I intended it to be a play on words because some plants are called lupines, but perhaps I should put wolves, to make it absolutely clear. Ah, I have it."

"...when he trusts that no unexpected *wolf* will cross their path," Lord Appledrum read out Quin's revised text. "Hmm. That makes more sense—in an alarming kind of way. Am I to understand you and Gabrielle once encountered a *wolf* on your plant-hunting forays?"

Quin flushed. He'd been so focused on his mission to send a greeting to Gabrielle, he'd forgotten he wasn't supposed to voluntarily reveal they'd seen one.

"Ah... I promised Gabrielle I wouldn't mention it unless anyone directly asked us if we'd seen a wolf," he said uncomfortably. "I would appreciate it if you don't tell anyone else. Perhaps I should write something different, but this is something only known to the two of us—or it was." He stared at the notice, trying to think of an alternative which would be equally specific to Gabrielle, but without revealing she was the intended recipient of his notice to the rest of the newspaper's readers.

"Leave it," Lord Appledrum advised. "At this late date I doubt her father will take umbrage, and most people will assume you're referring to an old joke between you and one of your male friends. I can certainly hint in that direction, if anyone asks me. But such redirection will come at a price."

"What price?" Quin eyed his father suspiciously.

"You tell *us* the story immediately." Lord Appledrum exchanged glances with Miss Trent, and then they both turned expectantly toward him.

"There's not much to tell," he began. "It was my first summer in France. It was hot in the open fields and parterres. I thought it might be cooler for Gabrielle in the forest, so I suggested we hunt for new plants there."

"And you encountered a wolf?" His father grinned.

"Yes. I'd forgotten they have living wolves in France," Quin confessed. "It was a magnificent creature. Black fur and glowing golden eyes. If not for Gabrielle's presence, I would have been pleased by the opportunity to observe it so closely."

"What did you do?" Miss Trent asked.

"Gabrielle saw the wolf first. She addressed it with great courtesy." Quin closed his eyes, the better to remember that day.

In his mind, he returned to the hot August afternoon in the drowsing forest. The sun's rays had filtered through the leaves and branches, creating a mosaic of greens and browns, light and shadow.

Vivid butterflies had danced in pools of hazy sunshine, and he'd heard the buzzing of insects and the occasional burst of birdsong. Everything had seemed utterly safe and peaceful, until Gabrielle had come to a dead halt ahead of him on the path. He'd looked over her shoulder—and seen the wolf.

"Gabrielle remained perfectly calm." Quin opened his eyes. "With great courtesy, she said, 'Bonjour, Monsieur Wolf. It's been an honor to meet you this fine afternoon, but now we must depart your kingdom.' She took a step back to me, I took her hand, and we began to walk backward along the path."

"She was between you and the wolf?" Lord Appledrum said.

"Yes. If I'd realized that was a possibility I'd have taken the lead, but it might have turned out for the best," Quin admitted. "Gabrielle's better at making conversation with strangers than I am."

His father chuckled. "Strangers...and wolves?"

"It wasn't the least bit aggressive," Quin said. "And her papa had told her what to do if she ever encountered a wolf. She was scared, so was I, but we both agreed it had been an interesting experience."

"And she made you promise not to tell anyone about it?" Miss Trent said.

"She was afraid she might be forbidden from going on my plant-hunting walks with me if her mother knew," Quin explained. "She also made me promise not to go back and search for it on my own."

"Which you no doubt found a much harder promise to keep," Lord Appledrum said.

"I did. How do I go about getting this notice into the newspaper?" Quin picked it up and looked enquiringly at his father

Chapter Three

Gabrielle sat beside a candle, mending a tear in one of Charlotte's dresses. This task would be more comfortable in daylight, but Gabrielle couldn't set it aside. She needed to pack the dress with the rest of Charlotte's clothes, ready for their departure to Brighton in the morning.

Now Gabrielle knew Quin was on his way to London, she'd have preferred to remain there too. But Lady Henderson had decided she wanted to spend the rest of the summer in the fashionable town of Brighton.

In Brighton, Lady Henderson would attend assemblies and balls. While Gabrielle and Charlotte's daily routine would continue as usual—except they'd take their morning walk along the sea front, not in Grosvenor Square.

Gabrielle finished her repair, and was snipping the thread when she heard a gentle tap on the door.

She tensed at the unobtrusive sound. Even though she

believed she knew who it was, unexpected knocks always made her feel a little uneasy. Perhaps that was how exiles often felt? The sound of banging doors had been the prelude to her family's flight from France.

She put the dress aside and rose to open the door. As soon as she saw her visitor she relaxed.

"Good evening, Mrs. Whittle," she greeted the housekeeper. "Come in. The house has been in such a bustle today you must be very tired."

"I am somewhat tired, mademoiselle," Mrs. Whittle acknowledged.

She was carrying a tray which contained everything necessary for two people to enjoy a well-made cup of tea—and a folded newspaper.

Gabrielle quickly cleared space for the housekeeper to set the tray on the table and stepped back, even though her fingers itched to pick up the paper. But she couldn't help twisting her head around in an effort to read the visible portion.

Mrs. Whittle laughed. "Why don't you look at the newspaper while I pour the tea?"

"Thank you so much." Gabrielle seized it, ready to turn the pages in a focused effort to spot any mention of the expedition.

"It's right on the front page!" she exclaimed. "Mrs. Whittle, the Wayfarer has docked in London. It's right on the front page."

The housekeeper's lips twitched. "So I saw. You'd better read the whole account."

The report on the return of the scientific expedition occupied several column inches, and its tone was both pompous and congratulatory. Gabrielle scanned the paragraphs quickly, eager for any mention of Quin. Her gaze skimmed over the much shorter notice immediately below the main report—

She gasped.

"*Lord Hanwell*...Lord Hanwell presents his compliments," she murmured, totally lost to everything except the notice Quin must have had inserted below the main report.

It didn't sound exactly like him, and for a second she wondered if someone else had given it to the newspaper on his behalf.

But then she saw how it ended.

"He's sent me a message! He's sent me a message."

She leaped up and began to dance to the rhythm of her joyous heartbeat, the newspaper still hugged to her chest. She'd never feared Quin would forget her—they'd meant too much to each other for that. But in her darkest moments, she had feared his feelings for her might dwindle while he was touring the world.

The housekeeper placidly finished pouring the tea and sat back to watch Gabrielle's excited twirling.

"How can you be so sure it's a message for you?" she asked, when Gabrielle finally paused.

"Because of the wolf." Gabrielle hurried back across the nursery to show the notice to Mrs. Whittle. "Look, he says he hopes at our next meeting no unexpected wolf will cross our path. He must have thought of me and sent this notice to the newspaper the moment he arrived in London. He's so clever to have found a way to communicate privately with me."

"Very clever and determined." Mrs. Whittle smiled. "It never occurred to me he might bypass Lady Henderson's restrictions on your correspondence by putting his message for you on the front page of the newspaper."

"He's always been clever and determined." Gabrielle swirled away, her plain muslin skirt flying out around her legs. "If only Papa wasn't far away with the Sinclairs."

In her exuberance she misjudged a turn and stumbled against a chair. The rear legs banged against the hearth and the sound jolted her back to awareness of her surroundings.

She froze, looking anxiously toward the bedroom where Charlotte slept.

Fortunately, though the little girl was sometimes slow to fall into a sound sleep, once she did, she was difficult to rouse.

"Charlotte," she whispered.

Several locks of her hair had escaped their confining pins. She pushed the tendrils back from her face with a trembling hand, her initial joy now shot through with painful uncertainty.

How could there be a way forward for her and Quin, when she couldn't leave Charlotte without breaking the child's heart?

Worry clouded her happiness, but nothing could truly diminish her excitement that Quin was back, and that one of his first actions had been to put a message in the newspaper for her.

"I'll keep this paper forever." She hugged it against her, and then decided to check the date. "Oh, it's today's. Is it Lady Henderson's?" She bit her lip as she looked at Mrs. Whittle.

"No, it's mine," the housekeeper said cheerfully, "and you may keep it with my goodwill, mademoiselle. I decided to buy it because I thought I might as well be up to date on the latest news before we leave the capital."

"Thank you." Gabrielle smiled tremulously at the older woman. She was certain Mrs. Whittle had bought the newspaper entirely for Gabrielle's sake, not her own.

"Come and sit down before you wear yourself out dancing," Mrs. Whittle recommended. "It's going to be a long day tomorrow, even for an energetic lady like yourself."

Chapter Four

Brighton, South Coast of England

Gabrielle walked through the moonlit darkness, her heart beating fast. It was the first time in her life that she'd gone out alone at night. The experience was both exhilarating and unnerving.

She was following a cart track along the edge of a field. On one side of her was the high wall which surrounded Lord Appledrum's gardens. On her other side was a hayfield—and beyond the field were the rolling hills of the Sussex Downs.

Over the last decade or two, Brighton had become one of the most fashionable destinations for British high society during the summer, but it was still a small town, surrounded by fields and downland.

Gabrielle focused most of her attention on the grass at the foot of the wall, but now and again she glanced across the field, and sometimes even looked behind her.

Her gaze skimmed over the field again—and glimpsed a creature slinking behind a haystack. Her stomach lurched. Was it a wolf? A second later, she recalled there were no wolves in England.

It was just a hunting fox.

With renewed resolve, she continued her progress along Lord Appledrum's wall. Tonight, Quin's father was hosting a masquerade ball in his grand mansion.

Of course, Gabrielle hadn't received an invitation. But she knew Papa had told Lord Appledrum about the restrictions on her correspondence. The marquess wouldn't do anything which might damage Gabrielle's relationship with her employer. Besides, governesses didn't attend the grand balls of the nobility.

But Gabrielle meant to attend one tonight.

She didn't even know if Quin would be present. He'd never liked this kind of event in the past. But perhaps he'd changed? No, his personality couldn't have changed beyond recognition, or he wouldn't have put the notice in the newspaper for her.

She exhaled a shaky breath, kept walking—and looking out for the ladder Mrs. Whittle had told her she'd find waiting.

The housekeeper had offered to accompany her, but Gabrielle had asked her to remain in the nursery in case Charlotte woke—though she hoped the little girl didn't rouse. And she hoped even more desperately that Lady Henderson never discovered her illicit activities this evening.

At the very least, she'd receive a severe reprimand for leaving the house without permission. Most likely, she'd have her wages docked for her transgression. In the worst case, she might be dismissed.

To calm herself, she remembered her exchange with Mrs.

Whittle just before she'd left the Hendersons' house through the kitchen door.

"You won't be recognized," the housekeeper had declared confidently. "The turban and the mask will ensure that. You can enjoy the music, dance a few dances, and slip out again well before the unmasking at midnight. I'll expect to see you back at the house by one o'clock at the latest. Make sure you pay attention to the time."

Gabrielle had promised not to forget. "But if I do make a mistake, at least my clothes won't turn to rags on my body, like the real Cinderella."

On that thought, she glanced down at herself.

She was wearing her dark winter pelisse over her gown. It was far too warm for the July night. But here on the edge of a hayfield, there was no one to notice a young woman wandering about in a blue silk gown. A gown that had never fully recovered from its rough treatment during her escape from France. But it was the only one she had that was remotely suitable.

She put down her carpet bag, tucked the broom she was carrying under her arm, stripped off her gloves and unbuttoned the pelisse with determined fingers.

As soon as she felt the mildly cooling effects of the night breeze on her hands and body, the worst of her anxieties eased.

She found the ladder only a few yards further on. She put on her gloves again and lifted the ladder. She'd never had to maneuver one before. She was glad to discover it wasn't heavy, but it was unwieldy.

On her first attempt to raise it she got the end caught in the honeysuckle cascading down the wall a couple of feet to her right.

She stepped back, almost lost her balance when her heel hit the ridge of a rut and dropped the ladder.

It scraped down the brickwork until it returned to its former resting place in the long grass and wildflowers at the foot of the wall.

Gabrielle flinched and cast a nervous glance over her shoulder, but the usual soft sounds of the night continued without a pause, and she neither saw nor heard any response to the grating noise she'd just made.

She drew in a deep, honeysuckle-scented breath in an effort to quiet her thudding heart and jangling nerves and tried again.

∽

Quin was studying a specimen of *lonicera periclymenum*, also known as common honeysuckle, in the moonlit orchard—but he knew he ought to go back into the ballroom.

Even though his father hadn't explicitly said he was throwing this party for his son's benefit, Quin was certain he had.

Lord Appledrum always loved the theatricality of a costume ball. But on this occasion, Quin believed his father had decreed all the guests should also wear masks because he hoped the anonymity would enable Quin to enjoy himself.

Quin certainly hadn't enjoyed the one and only other ball he'd attended since he'd returned to England. Before arriving at the party, he'd wondered whether he'd encounter the thinly disguised boredom he'd so often experienced whenever he'd spoken of his botanical interests in the past. It hadn't occurred to him that he'd be the main focus of interest for nearly every young, unattached lady in the ballroom.

Too late, he'd discovered that his status as one of the most eligible young bachelors in London, combined with the romance and mystery associated with his long absence circumnavigating the globe, had made him an object of fascination to almost every lady he met.

He'd been less shaken by almost crossing paths with a bad-tempered bull elephant in Africa, than he had at finding himself backed up against the elegant paneling of a London drawing room by a cluster of society maidens.

To Quin's chagrin, he hadn't managed to extricate himself from his predicament without help. His cousin, Marcus, the Duke of Candervale, had rescued him on the pretext of presenting him to an old friend.

"Next time, make sure you're standing near an open door," Marcus had said.

"Is that your primary strategy for avoiding such situations?" a ruffled Quin had asked.

"No, I've also cultivated a reputation for being the most boring man in London," Marcus had replied.

"I thought I was boring too."

"You *were* boring—until you turned yourself into a mysterious and romantic traveler. You should start spouting tedious botanical facts every time you open your mouth," Marcus had advised.

"I already do that—don't I?"

Marcus had grinned. "Do it more."

But spouting dry, botanical facts at his father's masquerade ball would be a big clue to the identity of the man behind the mask, so Quin couldn't take his cousin's advice tonight. In truth, he didn't want to waste any time on attending a ball.

He had two immediate goals. One was to make speedy progress writing an account of the scientific expedition with his friend and fellow botanist, Lord Duncan Waring. Duncan had been the ship's surgeon on HMS Wayfarer.

Quin's second important goal was to see Gabrielle. He'd only left London after learning from Miss Trent that Gabrielle had traveled to Brighton as part of Lady Henderson's household.

He'd even taken a stroll past the Hendersons' house in the hope of encountering Gabrielle. But he couldn't loiter outside for too long without arousing attention that might rebound unfavorably upon her.

It was an unsatisfactory, deeply frustrating situation.

In the meantime, he had a ball he was supposed to be attending. Unfortunately, the moment he'd walked into the ballroom earlier, he'd discovered he hated not being able to see the full expressions of the people he spoke to. He was at a complete loss as to how to start a conversation with an elegantly dressed, masked stranger.

Feeling like a fugitive in his own home, Quin had made his escape onto the terrace. From there he'd beaten a swift retreat through the garden and into the orchard.

A moth fluttered past his face and alighted on the honeysuckle flower he'd been studying, immediately capturing his interest.

According to Quin's observations, it was moths rather than day flying insects which pollinated the honeysuckle at night—

Something banged and scraped loudly against the other side of the wall.

He froze.

More sounds followed. Quin glanced up and saw the honeysuckle fronds on the top of the wall were trembling in a way that owed nothing to the breeze.

Whoever...or whatever...was on the other side of the wall was tugging on the parts of the honeysuckle which cascaded into the field.

The honeysuckle fronds whipped wildly one last time and settled again.

There was another, more controlled thud, as if something had been placed against the upper part of the wall.

More soft sounds of scraping and wooden creaks.

Frowning, Quin tried to decipher them.

Was it a *ladder*?

Hard on the heels of that thought came another one.

Burglars!

New energy pulsed through his veins.

Foiling an attempted burglary would be a *much* better excuse for absenting himself from the ballroom than observing moths pollinate the honeysuckle.

He stepped back into the shadows of a large apple tree and watched the wall intently. He didn't have the stout stick and machete he'd carried with him on exploration trips with the expedition—but he did have the element of surprise on his side.

He bounced lightly onto his toes and then settled into a

poised, relaxed stance, ready to take any action necessary to protect his father's house. Curiosity and anticipation filled him with a far more rewarding thrum of pleasure than the champagne his father's guests were enjoying.

A head finally appeared over the top of the wall. The first things Quin noticed were the three feathers sticking up jauntily into the moonlight. Followed by a masked face and the pale puffed sleeves of a lady's gown.

He watched in disbelief as the young woman rose high enough to drop two objects over the wall. One looked like a carpet bag of some kind, but the other…

He squinted in the darkness. Had his eyes deceived him, or had she really tossed a broom into the orchard?

He remained motionless, puzzling out the oddity of a well-dressed lady climbing over the wall.

Most of Brighton's social events occurred in public locations, such as the assembly rooms, accessible to anyone who could afford to pay the subscription fee. At those balls, the daughter of a prosperous shopkeeper and the daughter of a duke could, conceivably, rub shoulders. But only those who'd received a personal invitation could attend a ball in a private house.

Quin knew his father's servants were on watch to prevent the admission of any uninvited guests through the front door. Was he witnessing the antics of a particularly determined social climbing young lady, trying to get in through the back of the house? At least this lady didn't hunt in a pack, like the group who'd cornered him in London.

She climbed higher to sit astride the wall. Then she leaned down and away from him. With her skirts bunched up to her knees, he had an excellent view of one shapely, stocking-clad calf—and the stout, workaday boot she wore on her foot.

When she straightened up, he saw she was holding a ladder. Not just holding it—lifting it over the wall! Of course, if she intended to enter the garden that would be her next step. Quin had been so startled by her appearance he hadn't thought ahead to what she'd do next.

As it was, he barely managed to resist his gentlemanly instinct to rush forward and help her. Ladies, even lady burglars or uninvited party interlopers, should not be balancing on eight feet high walls, and manhandling ladders.

Fortunately, she didn't seem to be having any difficulty with her unconventional activity. Quin eased out a breath, and consciously relaxed his tense muscles. If it looked as if she might fall, he'd run forward to catch her, but now his curiosity had returned in full measure.

As soon as her feet touched the grass, she picked up the ladder and laid it on the ground beside the wall. Next, she stripped off her gloves. Quin blinked, and then realized they were dark gloves that, like her boots, didn't match her gown. She must have worn them to protect her hands from the ladder. Illicit entry to a ball obviously required as much forethought as planning an expedition into unknown territory.

Fascinated, he watched her take dancing slippers from her capacious bag. She braced one hand against the wall to change her footwear, put her boots and workaday gloves in the bag and tucked one handle under the ladder. He surmised that was a precaution against it blowing away.

Then she pulled on long white gloves, carefully smoothing each one up her forearm until it was past her elbow.

The deliberate way she put on the evening gloves reminded Quin of a knight, donning his gauntlets before taking part in a joust. And when the young lady picked up her broom, he could almost imagine it to be her battle lance.

She turned her back to the wall. Her head bobbed down, and then her chin rose again.

That subtle movement was unexpectedly familiar.

She visibly took a breath, and then marched straight across the orchard, heading for the picket gate which led to the garden.

Quin stared after her, his heart pounding in his chest.

Gabrielle?

Was it *really* Gabrielle, sneaking into his father's ball? She didn't need to sneak—

His thoughts shattered.

Quin knew Gabrielle hadn't received an invitation. Not because his father wouldn't welcome her, but because there was no possibility of her attending while she was working for Lady Henderson.

She was here without a chaperone.

Her mother, the late duchess, would be appalled. But then, the duchess would also be appalled that her daughter was now working as a governess.

The masked lady disappeared through the picket gate. Quin stared at her, his gut a churning mass of excitement and nerves. Could she really be Gabrielle?

The girl who'd calmly confronted a wolf all those years ago undoubtedly had the courage and determination to climb over a wall. He should have guessed the moment her feather-adorned head had appeared in the moonlight. But it hadn't occurred to him she'd do something so unconventional.

In his mind, even though he knew how drastically her circumstances had altered, she was still the cosseted daughter of a duke.

He wondered how much she'd changed in the three years since he'd last seen her. He'd held the memory of their last meeting close to his heart, and he'd thought of her every single day while they were apart.

But the realization that she was, most likely, only yards away from him now filled him with both joy—and unexpected anxiety.

Would she still like him after all this time?

Would he still like her—or had both of them changed too much since he'd set sail on HMS Wayfarer?

Galvanized into action by his chaotic emotions, he followed her toward the house.

Chapter Five

Gabrielle's heart beat out an excited rhythm as she looked across the formal garden closest to Lord Appledrum's house. The moonlight illuminated an elegant layout of paths and flower beds, all arranged around a marble fountain.

She descended the three low steps from the picket gate to walk along one of the paths. Ahead of her, the fountain sent silvery arcs of water into the night sky.

She cut a little too close as she turned a corner, and her skirts brushed against a low shrub in the flower bed. The scent of lavender rose into the balmy air.

The familiar fragrance jolted her back to the evening they'd fled from their French country home. She'd been wearing this same dress that day for the celebration of Felix's twelfth birthday. Was it good luck or bad luck to wear it again tonight?

She breathed out the lavender-scented air. Good luck, she decided. She, Papa and Felix were all settled into their new lives.

The blue silk dress was a lucky dress. In any case, it was her only suitable gown, so it had to do.

The great glass-filled doors of the ballroom rose beyond the glittering veil of the fountain. Some of the windows were covered with curtains, but light from the chandeliers spilled unimpeded from others. Beneath the chandeliers, Gabrielle could see couples taking their places ready for the next dance.

The music began again, men bowed to their partners, the ladies curtsied, and the couples began to move through the figures of a cotillion.

It was years since Gabrielle had danced with anyone apart from Charlotte. Was Quin inside, dancing with some other lady? Or was he standing near a wall—wondering how quickly he could make his escape?

Could she rescue him this evening—the way she'd sometimes done before? The fantasy thrilled and charmed her, and she hurried toward the house.

There were several sets of steps leading from the garden up to the terrace, but only one set was concealed by shadow.

Gabrielle ascended the shadowed steps and crept close to the house. In her limited experience, ballrooms in July could be extremely warm places, especially for energetic dancers. Surely there'd be at least one door open onto the terrace...

Yes, there!

Right in front of her a door had been fixed open—and it was behind a closed curtain.

Heart thudding, she checked to make sure her mask was secure, gripped her broom tightly, and touched her free hand to the folds of the curtain. On the other side she could hear music, voices and laughter. Happy people gathered together to enjoy a wonderful party with lots of dancing.

She yearned to find Quin.

And she yearned to dance.

She looked up and saw the heavy drape fell all the way from the ceiling high above. There was plenty of play in the material, but only a few inches between the curtain and the wall.

She didn't want her body to be outlined by the folds for too long in case someone noticed her unorthodox arrival. She took a deep breath, fixed a smile on her lips, and sidled quickly into the room.

∼

As soon as Gabrielle emerged from behind the curtain, her senses were assaulted by light, heat and noise. The curtain had muffled the music, but now it was much louder. And compared to the cool, moonlit garden, the ballroom seemed so hot and bright that Gabrielle was grateful her mask hid her squint of discomfort.

An orchestra played at one end of the room. Several couples danced the figures of the cotillion in the middle of the floor. Other guests stood or sat in groups around the edge of the elegant chamber.

Gabrielle knew a card room would be set up somewhere for those who didn't care to dance, while servants would already be preparing another room for the supper that would be served after midnight. Quin wouldn't be in the card room. The man she'd known would be more prone to take refuge in the library.

Summoning all her poise, she moved a few feet away from the terrace door, planning the next stage of her campaign to find Quin. She'd been an invited guest at every other ball she'd attended, and she'd never lacked for introductions—but there would be no introductions this evening.

She went on tiptoe and scanned the crowded ballroom, seeking out any gentleman who might be Quin—or any lady who might be her employer. She needed to avoid Lady Henderson at all costs.

Her initial attempt to spot Quin was frustrated by the masks everyone wore. Her own mask was an essential protection against discovery, but the fact all the other guests were also hiding their faces made her quest more difficult. She lowered her heels to the ground and decided to make a systematic tour around the perimeter of the room.

Just as some plants thrived in full sunlight, others preferred a shady location. When it came to large parties like this, Quin had always been more of a shade-lover than someone who enjoyed being the center of attention.

She strolled along one side of the room, trying to look as if she was on her way to rejoin her friends, while simultaneously paying particular regard to any of the taller gentlemen who weren't dancing.

Her progress was slow, and she became uncomfortably aware she'd caught the attention of one masked gentleman who was far too short to be Quin. Her gaze resolutely facing forward, she covered the next few feet a little faster—and realized she'd now garnered the interest of another man. The only one present who wasn't wearing a mask—Lord Appledrum.

Her heart jumped into her throat. Her first instinct was to evade him, but he was moving purposefully toward her. There was no easy way to avoid an encounter with Quin's father without also making a spectacle of herself by pushing past the dancers.

She wasn't afraid of Lord Appledrum, nor did she believe he'd consider her an unwelcome guest under normal circumstances.

But the fact remained that he hadn't invited her. If he challenged her on her identity, and Lady Henderson found out she was here, it would be a disaster.

She threw a nervous glance at the nearest dancing couples. Lady Henderson was attending the ball in the guise of Queen Guinevere, complete with a tiara made of real diamonds. Gabrielle breathed a little easier when she didn't spot any lady nearby who fitted that regal description.

Nevertheless, her heart remained in her throat as Lord Appledrum came to a halt before her and bowed with a flourish.

Despite her trepidation, she was mildly amused by his flamboyant attire. Unlike most of the gentlemen present, Quin's father had eschewed almost every aspect of contemporary fashion.

He wore long, flowing robes, reminiscent of a Roman toga, and one of his muscular arms was completely bare. Lord Appledrum might be in his mid-forties, but he was obviously in excellent physical shape. Perhaps because he continued to fence regularly with her papa.

The last time she'd spent a few hours with Papa, he'd claimed he owed much of his success as the most fashionable fencing master in London to Lord Appledrum's unwavering support. The marquess truly was a generous, loyal friend, and Gabrielle couldn't help feeling uncomfortable that she was deceiving him.

This evening he wasn't carrying a fencing foil but a three-pronged trident as tall as himself, and he wore a crown of silver laurel leaves, studded with blue and green gems.

He straightened from his bow. "Good evening, lady enchantress," he said. "Please allow me to present myself. I am Neptune, god of the oceans—and freshwater and horses, as my son reminded me earlier." The outer corners of the marquess's eyes crinkled in evident amusement as he listed his extra responsibilities.

Despite Gabrielle's determination to maintain her outward poise, excitement bubbled inside her at Lord Appledrum's casual mention of Quin.

"My son is very particular about the proper categorization of all things," Lord Appledrum continued. "Now, may I ask if you're planning to bespell anyone in particular this evening?" he glanced at Gabrielle's broom.

"Bespell...? Oh, I'm not a witch!" She belatedly took his meaning. "I'm Cinderella. You can see I still have ashes on the hem of my regular skirt, beneath this beautiful silk gown my fairy godmother lent me." She gestured downward, and the marquess immediately studied the spot she indicated.

"So you have." He looked up and grinned at her with unfettered delight. "What a *clever* idea. I'm delighted to receive a guest who has such a proper appreciation for this evening's entertainment."

"Oh, well, thank you, Lord... I mean, Lord Neptune," Gabrielle said, pleased and reassured by his compliment.

Mrs. Whittle had praised her idea of drawing up the torn part of the blue silk hem to reveal a more workaday skirt beneath it—one that hinted at Cinderella's everyday life before her magical transformation. Gabrielle had hoped it would suffice, so she was relieved as well as flattered by Lord Appledrum's words.

"You're in search of a prince, of course," he said. "Allow me to find one for you."

Gabrielle's breath caught at Lord Appledrum's blunt statement. In the fairy tale, Cinderella married the prince. In real life, everyone knew the fundamental reason why any young, unwed lady attended balls and parties was to find a husband.

But she wasn't here to find a husband—only Quin. Not that she hadn't dreamed many times of marrying him. But her current circumstances were so different from when they'd last met that it was a dream she now tried to suppress.

"Oh, no, sir," she began, as another gentleman came to stand beside Lord Appledrum. "I'm not seeking a prince, only a dance or two. I'm..." She faltered, the rest of her words flying out of her mind.

The gentleman standing shoulder to shoulder with Lord Appledrum was an inch or more taller than the marquess. But his half mask revealed the same square chin and firm mouth.

A mouth she was sure she'd sketched many times—and kissed.

She was looking at Quin. Her heart beat a rapid tattoo behind her ribs. Everyone else in the glittering ballroom faded from her awareness.

Surely—she was looking at Quin?

And he was staring back at her, a smile curving those firm lips. A smile of warmth, welcome...happiness?

Her own lips trembled into a smile.

Her fingers twitched to reach out, touch his mouth, and pull aside the concealing mask.

To be sure it was really him.

But what if it wasn't? What if her eyes and her heart were deceiving her, because she wanted it to be Quin so much?

She became aware Lord Appledrum was still speaking and tried to attend to his words.

"Perhaps it's fortunate you're not seeking a prince," the marquess said, "since there isn't one present tonight. However, allow me to present this admirable young man to you." He clapped the newcomer on his shoulder. "As you can see, he's a tall, well-made fellow, and behind his mask his visage is quite pleasing to the eye—"

The masked man didn't say anything, but his mouth flexed into a different kind of smile, and he tilted his head in a way which suggested he was slanting an exasperated glance at Lord Appledrum.

Gabrielle could hardly breathe with new certainty and anticipation.

How many times had she seen Quin react in a similar way to his father's proud, but mildly humorous, praise? Quin loved and respected his father, but she could easily imagine him rolling his eyes at being called a 'tall, well-made fellow.'

Oh, it was Quin! It *was*!

Everything inside her quickened. She gripped her broomstick tighter and smiled at him as widely as her mask allowed.

He stared back just as intently...

Did he know it was her behind her mask? Perhaps he thought he was being introduced to a simpering stranger?

Her smile faltered.

His mouth moved. He didn't speak aloud, but shaped a single word.

Gabrielle?

The lights in the ballroom glittered like stars in her eyes.

Her own lips parted, but she was too full of joy to speak. She responded with a tiny nod, and Quin's smile somehow became warmer and more intimate.

"This young man is inclined to be distracted by dreams of discovery and adventure," Lord Appledrum continued with his lengthy introduction, "but ultimately he triumphs against all dangers to return home with new wealth beyond measure. I present to you—Jack the Giant Killer!"

"Jack the *Giant Killer*?" Gabrielle's startled exclamation had everything to do with the deluge of excited happiness coursing through her body, and nothing to do with Quin's choice of costume.

"Good evening, my lady." His voice was husky, as if he was in the grip of strong emotion, but it was undoubtedly Quin's voice. "Despite my name, I assure you I'm a very peaceable fellow." He bent in a bow which was workmanlike rather than elegant.

Her papa had teased Quin that his bow was as precise as clockwork, and had tried to encourage him to add a little more panache to his gestures. But that kind of social flamboyance had been alien to Quin's retiring nature as a youth, and it seemed he hadn't changed.

In this at least, he was still her Quin.

She gazed at him, her bosom rising and falling in short, shallow breaths, barely aware of the other guests who filled the ballroom, or Lord Appledrum stepping away to speak to someone else.

The music stopped, and the dancers left the organized formation of the sets to mingle in a more haphazard patten, but Quin didn't say another word, just continued to smile at her.

Perhaps she should speak first, the way she often had in the past?

"Are you...are you carrying an ax on your back, sir?" She seized on the first topic that came to her mind. The ax head visible over his shoulder was the only thing about him, except for his mask, that differed from a gentleman's regular evening attire.

"Papier-mâché only," he assured her, a new aura of energy suddenly emanating from him. "For chopping down the beanstalk. If you recall, I rather foolishly exchanged my mother's cow for a handful of magical beans—but then one of the bean stalks grew so large I climbed it all the way to the giant's home and my fortune was made."

Gabrielle's laugh was breathless.

He'd chosen a good costume. Quin would *never* have been so irresponsible with someone else's possessions, but he *had* followed his dreams, and they did involve plants.

"You were brave to climb up so high, Sir Jack," she said.

"One has to take a risk now and then to achieve one's goals," Quin said. "Did I hear you say your goal tonight is to dance?"

Her true goal had been to find him.

She longed to walk and talk with him in the quiet privacy of the garden, the way they had so many times before he'd gone on his travels. But a wave of shyness washed over her.

There had been a few occasions in the past when she'd worried that Quin considered her impulsive behavior to be bordering on improper. After so long apart, she was reluctant to suggest they do something that might be considered scandalous within minutes of their reunion.

"Yes, yes, I would like to dance," she said.

"Then let us take our places on the floor." He offered her his hand as new sets began to start forming.

Gabrielle reached toward him and realized she was still holding the broom. Now it was only an annoyance to her, not a witty prop. "I should have strapped it to my back, like your ax."

Quin stared at the broomstick, apparently as nonplussed by her unusual ballroom accessory as she was. "Ah...why don't we hide it under a chair until it's time for you to fly away later?"

"I'm not a witch," she said. "I'm *Cinderella*."

"Of course you are. My apologies, Lady Cinderella." Quin sounded discomfited by his error. "I'm afraid I'm better at chopping down beanstalks than complimenting ladies."

"It was an understandable assumption to make," Gabrielle assured him quickly. "I was thinking of how I have to sweep the hearth for my stepmother when I decided to bring it—but I can see why you might suppose it belongs to a witch."

"Very clever." The tension in Quin's shoulders eased. "I don't imagine any witch ever wore such a charming gown. But now you've exhibited your credentials, so to speak, perhaps we should set it aside?" His mouth flexed, as if he was regretting the way he'd phrased his comment. "Your broomstick, I mean," he added hastily. "If you'll allow me?"

"Oh, yes." She let him take the broom from her unresisting grip and stow it on the floor between the wall and an unoccupied chair.

He offered her his hand again, and this time she took it.

They were both wearing gloves but, even so, she felt a thrill of joy when his fingers closed around hers.

After all the years spent waiting for him, she was going to dance with Quin again.

.

Chapter Six

Exultation surged through Quin's veins.

Gabrielle was here, in his presence, and he was holding her hand!

While he'd still been trying to find a way to see her that wouldn't fall foul of the restrictions imposed by her employer, Gabrielle had managed to come to him. He was bursting with admiration for her courage and ingenuity.

A momentary doubt assailed him.

He'd assumed she knew who he was—but what if he was mistaken?

His grip on her hand tightened. "Mademoiselle...Cinderella, do you...know the man behind my mask?"

Her smile was as warm as the sunshine had been on that August day so many years ago. "I know he's far too wise to throw a jug at a friendly wolf," she said.

It *was* Gabrielle. Another lady might have read his notice in the newspaper, but no one else would know that detail of their discussion after the encounter.

In a moment of triumphant happiness, Quin almost tugged her into his arms—but then someone jostled his elbow, and he remembered they were in the middle of his father's crowded ballroom.

"I make no claims to wisdom, only ordinary commonsense," he said gruffly, and led her to take their positions among the other dancers.

He had so many questions to ask her.

But he couldn't launch into them, because now he had to concentrate on remembering all the steps of the cotillion. Gabrielle loved dancing, and he didn't want to spoil her enjoyment by getting his part wrong.

The music started and he bowed to her, while she curtsied to him. Then she took his outstretched hand. He was both frustrated by and grateful for their gloves. If they'd been touching bare skin to bare skin, it would be even harder for him to contain all the physical and emotional responses she aroused in him.

They danced together for a few steps. He couldn't see her face, and he didn't like the feathered headgear that covered her glorious hair. He struggled not to feast his eyes on the elegant curve of her shoulder and neck. And he allowed himself only a brief glance at the upper part of her breasts showing above the neckline of her dress.

He wanted to kiss her, and hear everything that had happened to her since they'd last met. But his most urgent desire was to hold her close to his body, not at arm's length. He was intimately familiar with that powerful instinct. Whenever they'd been together before, it had been more normal than not for him to be in a state of semi—or full—arousal when he was with Gabrielle. It was a sweet torment to experience those feelings again this evening.

But, for the first time, he could hope he'd soon be able to satisfy those desires in their marriage bed. He was home and had no plans to go traveling again. And Gabrielle had responded to his notice in the newspaper by finding him at the first opportunity. Surely that signified her feelings for him hadn't changed?

He wanted to haul her into the garden and ask her. But that wasn't how a cultured, considerate gentleman behaved. He gave his lady time to acclimatize to his return—and enjoy one of her favorite pastimes.

With a monumental effort of self-discipline, he wrenched his focus back to his current responsibilities as Gabrielle's dance partner.

There were four couples in the set, and every gentleman was required to dance with every lady many times during the various figures of the dance. Soon Quin was linking hands or arms with each of the other ladies in turn before returning to Gabrielle for a little while before moving on again.

Although the steps weren't difficult, it seemed he wasn't the only one who needed to concentrate, because there was suddenly a kerfuffle on the other side of the ballroom.

Quin looked around to see that a lady and a gentleman had fallen over. He didn't know exactly how they could have tripped, but he immediately felt sorry for the lady, in particular, who was lying on the floor with the gentleman half sprawled upon her.

Most of the people who'd noticed, stopped dancing. But not

everyone had seen, which meant there were one or two awkward encounters in other sets. Fortunately, no one else fell over.

Quin's first instinct was to go to the lady's aid, but then he saw his cousin, Marcus, was already assisting her to her feet, and the next moment his father appeared beside them.

After a brief exchange with the lady, Lord Appledrum lifted his trident into the air as if he were indeed a Roman god. "No harm done," he announced in a booming voice. "Let the dancing recommence immediately!"

Quin turned away at once, far more interested in Gabrielle than anyone else at the ball. But the mishap in the other set was a vivid reminder he needed to mind his own steps to ensure he did nothing to spoil her enjoyment of this dance.

As the music continued, he realized Gabrielle faced another, potentially more difficult, hazard than tripping over her dance partner.

All the young lady guests would have arrived with a chaperone. Sooner or later, Gabrielle would be expected to rejoin her own chaperone. He wasn't sure how he could help her deal with that awkwardness, if it should arise. But by the time the music ended, he'd thought of a way to continue their conversation.

"Lady Cinderella," he said, stepping aside with her as the other couples also moved away. "Did you have any difficulty leaving your house without your stepmother noticing you?"

THE MUSIC and the happy exercise of dancing with Quin had

infiltrated every particle of Gabrielle's body, healing wounds so tiny she hadn't known they existed until they started to mend.

His abrupt question was so out of tune with her thoughts that, at first, she didn't understand it.

"My stepmother?" She looked up at him in confusion. She'd never had a stepmother. Papa hadn't remarried after her mother's death. Why was Quin asking her…?

"Oh!" Suddenly she understood.

He was continuing the game that she *was* Cinderella, even though he knew she wasn't. He was cleverly giving her the opportunity to answer his questions honestly, more-or-less, under the cover of the game.

"My stepmother?" she said, picturing Lady Henderson as she spoke. It wasn't a long step to imagine her employer in the role of a wicked stepmother. Lady Henderson seemed to dote on her son, but barely acknowledged her daughter.

"No, I didn't have any difficulty avoiding her when I left the house," Gabrielle said. "I waited until after she departed for the ball, and then went out by the kitchen door."

She glanced around as she spoke, instinctively looking for Lady Henderson.

"Is she here?" Quin sounded surprised. "Of course she is," he answered himself a moment later, a wry smile tugging at his lips. "This is one of the most important events of the Brighton Season. We will shortly be reading accounts of it in the *Society Columns* of the newspapers. All self-respecting wicked stepmothers must be here."

"Shush," Gabrielle hushed him, barely managing to control

her urge to scan the other guests a second time. She couldn't afford to behave in a way which might attract attention.

"My apologies, Cinderella, I didn't mean to be indiscreet." Quin lowered his voice. "We'll speak of something else—but may I ask if you often attend balls this way?"

"Oh, no, this is my first time," Gabrielle assured him earnestly. She didn't want Quin to believe she made a habit of going to parties she hadn't been invited to. "If you remember, I'm normally too busy sweeping floors to go to balls. But I was well ahead on my chores and my fairy godmother was eager for me to attend tonight."

"Sweeping floors?" Quin tipped his head to one side. "Is that truly how you spend your time?"

"Um..." Gabrielle cast another wary glance around. She didn't want anyone to hear her announce she was a governess. No lady at this ball would ever dream of using a broom in her everyday life, so it felt safe to make jokes about wielding one—no one would believe her.

Claiming to be a governess was different. In this world, there was a bizarre kind of romance about pretending to be a floor-sweeping Cinderella—but none at all in being a governess. It might be a genteel occupation, but it wasn't a comfortable or desirable one.

"My tasks are in the nursery," she whispered to Quin. "Yes, I spend all day and most of the night sweeping floors," she continued more loudly as another couple strolled nearer. For good measure, she mimed the action of sweeping with her empty hands.

"But it's so short, it must give you terrible backache," Quin protested, in apparent seriousness. "I know it still has a fair quantity of bristles on it, but I think you should request a longer one."

Gabrielle blinked. The cut-off broom she'd brought to the party was the last thing on her mind, but Quin had always paid attention to the details.

"Perhaps I will raise the matter with my fairy godmother," she said.

He opened his mouth, no doubt intending to ask her more questions. In her opinion, Quin's curiosity about almost anything was one of his most notable and lovable characteristics. Under other circumstances, she'd willingly explain everything, but not when there was a chance her employer might overhear her.

The other guests were beginning to form new sets for a country dance.

"Let's dance again." She reached out to Quin. "And then you must tell me all about *your* adventures, Sir Jack. You must have seen so many interesting things in the land of the giants. Is it hard to return to the everyday life after experiencing so many adventures?"

"No," Quin said. "Everyday life is turning out to be very interesting and delightful. Exceedingly, wonderfully delightful."

～

Quin had been about to ask if Gabrielle would like to stroll on the terrace with him, but he let her draw him into the dance set forming close by.

Their banter was entertaining, but it was also frustrating. It would be far more satisfying to have a conversation with her where she wasn't revealing the truth about herself under the guise of pretending to be her masquerade character.

And he was desperate to see her face again. He wanted to watch her expressions and see how she'd grown since they'd said goodbye three years ago. She'd been a girl of nineteen then, now she was a young lady of twenty-two.

Already he'd sensed a few changes in her which hinted at the upheavals in her life.

The Gabrielle he'd known before had been completely secure in her position. She'd never flaunted her status as the Duke de la Fontaine's daughter, but nor had she ever doubted her right to attend an event like this. But Quin had detected a genuine frisson of alarm in her when she'd hushed him for speaking too loudly.

His father had warned him Gabrielle's employer had imposed severe restrictions upon her behavior, and now he was witnessing for himself the impact of those restrictions.

The thought of anyone making Gabrielle fearful raised Quin's ire and his protective instincts. He wanted to find out more about her life as a governess, but his curiosity and concern would have to wait until they could speak freely.

The set Gabrielle and Quin had joined included his friend, Lord Alfred, who'd been the first lieutenant on HMS *Voyager*. Unlike Quin, Alfred enjoyed a party, and he'd adopted the very suitable costume character of Sinbad the Sailor.

Alfred's dance partner was a young lady who was wearing an unusual and puzzling headdress.

"You have grass snakes in your hair!" Quin identified them, just as the movement of the dance brought them together.

The lady nodded vigorously, making the wired snakes bounce around her head almost as if they were in search of prey.

"You're the first person to name them correctly," she said cheerfully, as they linked their hands behind their backs and circled around. "One gentleman accused me of wearing vipers in my hair—but I didn't think I should wear poisonous snakes to a ball."

There was no time for Quin to reply before he moved on to dance with the next lady. He didn't have anything to say to the other two ladies, and he had too much to say to Gabrielle, so he remained silent until he was once again with the grass snake girl.

"Are you fond of snakes?" he asked, wondering if she was also a naturalist.

"No, sir. I prefer sheep," she replied, "but I didn't want to come to the ball as a shepherdess. I wanted to be Medusa." She shook her head to make the snakes wave about.

The figure of the dance changed as all the gentlemen moved to the center. Quin lightly touched hands with the other three men as they revolved around in a circle before rejoining their partners.

Later, it would be the ladies' turn to do the same thing.

Quin thought it was odd that a young lady wanted to be Medusa. Surely she knew the story that Medusa was a gorgon who turned anyone who looked at her into stone? Was she daring gentlemen to dance with her?

But Quin's curiosity about the grass snake girl was only superficial. It was Gabrielle he wanted to talk to. He kept hold of her hand when the music ended, intending to lead her toward the terrace door.

But before he'd taken a single step in that direction, Alfred blocked the way, bringing the grass snake girl with him.

"Lady Medusa, allow me to present Jack the Giant Killer to you," he said with a flourish which was almost worthy of Lord Appledrum himself. "Jack, introduce me to your charming companion."

"This is Sinbad the Sailor," Quin told Gabrielle, trying not to sound as disgruntled as he felt at Alfred's attempt to be sociable. He knew the other man was far too generous-hearted to mean any harm. He was probably curious about Gabrielle, since Quin had now danced with her twice, though earlier he'd been reluctant to even attend the ball.

"This is Lady Cinderella," he introduced Gabrielle to the others.

They all greeted each other and commented admiringly on Medusa's snakes. Truthfully, she was the only one of them whose costume did merit praise for its complex construction.

Quin didn't want to talk about masquerade costumes, so he was trying to think of a way to extricate them from the conversation when Alfred said, "Dancing is hot work, ladies. Jack and I will fetch you some lemonade and return forthwith. Come along, Jack."

The last thing Quin wanted was to be separated from Gabrielle. And he could tell from the way her shoulders tensed that she felt the same.

But she immediately changed the gesture into a gracious nod of thanks and turned toward Medusa as if she was at ease with this unexpected turn of events.

Quin couldn't object to Alfred's command without

appearing rude, but he did pause to say, "we won't be gone long, ladies." The reassurance was intended for Gabrielle. He didn't care if Medusa was anxious about how long her lemonade would take to arrive.

"Do you know who Medusa is?" he asked Alfred as they headed toward the refreshment table.

"Of course." Alfred sounded amused. "I met her and her aunt in the library yesterday afternoon. Medusa was disappointed to discover they didn't have any books on sheep management."

"Did she identify herself to you this evening?"

"No, I recognized her voice and her general style. Do you know the true identity of Cinderella?" Alfred asked curiously.

Quin didn't answer. He trusted his friend, but he didn't want to say anything which might increase the risk of Gabrielle being discovered by her employer. A glance at the clock informed him it was already twenty minutes to midnight. High time for him to help Gabrielle slip away before the unmasking.

But when he looked back to where she and Medusa had been standing, neither of the young ladies was in sight. He had to find her again before midnight.

"Let's waste no time collecting the lemonade," he urged. "The ladies must be thirsty."

Chapter Seven

Gabrielle was alarmed when courtesy obliged Quin to walk away with the man dressed as Sinbad.

Between her first encounter with Lord Appledrum and dancing in the same set as Sinbad and Medusa, there'd been no need for Gabrielle to talk to anyone except Quin. Medusa seemed to have a cheerful, friendly personality, but Gabrielle would have preferred not to find herself left alone with the other young woman.

Medusa appeared to be a few years younger than Gabrielle. She'd know the young ladies who'd made their society debut at the same time as her, and those who were a few years older. Among those young ladies would be Medusa's friends, competitors or even enemies. She must be trying to guess who Gabrielle was, but Gabrielle preferred to keep the focus of their conversation on the other girl.

"Your costume is very clever," she complimented Medusa again. The grass snake headdress made her think the other girl had a sense of humor. She wished they could meet under more relaxed circumstances, when perhaps they could be friends.

"I thought it was a funny idea," Medusa agreed. "But it's very hot. I can't take it off because it's wound into my hair. I don't think Aunt M...I mean my aunt, would like it if I finished the ball with my hair looking like a bird's nest."

"Hair is always difficult," Gabrielle agreed. "At least it's no longer the fashion to wear complicated, towering styles. Modern styles are much more comfortable."

"Comfort is important," Medusa said. "That's what my aunt says. Oh look, she's waving at us. Come, I'll introduce you to her."

For an instant Gabrielle considered trying to avoid the introduction by claiming she ought to return to *her* aunt.

But that wouldn't only be rude, it might also ultimately lead to the embarrassing revelation she didn't have an aunt—at least, not here, acting as her chaperone at the ball.

She glanced around in an attempt to locate Quin and instead spotted Lady Henderson's tiara only a few feet away.

"You're *so* outrageous, Sir Lancelot," Lady Henderson said in her familiar arch tone, flirtatiously touching her folded fan to the gentleman's chest. The gentleman wasn't Lady Henderson's husband. Gabrielle knew that because Lord Henderson was nowhere near Brighton.

Gabrielle didn't care who Sir Lancelot was, but discovering Lady Henderson nearby sent a slither of alarm through her.

She turned quickly and followed after her new acquaintance.

It was easy to keep track of Medusa. Even when they were

briefly separated by other guests, the waving grass snakes were almost as good as a flag.

It occurred to Gabrielle that the feathers in her turban might serve the same function for others to identify her, and she wished she hadn't added them. But she'd wanted the turban to look as if it was a fashionable choice, rather than something she'd worn purely to hide every strand of her blonde hair.

The turban was undoubtedly the worst thing about her costume. She'd never worn one before, and she'd already decided she'd never wear one again. Like Medusa's snake headdress, it was hideously hot.

One of the additional benefits of the mask was that it was not only hiding her identity, it was also concealing the unbecoming sweat trickling down her temples and forehead.

Gabrielle was grateful for that protection when she was presented to Medusa's well-dressed aunt. Her stomach jittered nervously, and beneath the mask her skin was covered by a sheen of perspiration. But at least she was able to *pretend* she felt cool and unflustered.

At first sight, Medusa's aunt didn't appear to be wearing any costume at all except for a mask. Her pale cream silk gown was made in the latest fashion, and she wore it with practiced elegance. Only Medusa's slightly breathless explanation that her aunt was the Goddess Diana elucidated the mystery.

"My bow and arrows," Diana said, lifting her arm to reveal a bracelet to which a miniature bow and several arrows were attached.

Gabrielle laughed. "That's very clever, my lady," she said,

hearing the unmistakable note of amusement in the older woman's voice.

It was impossible to judge the age of Medusa's aunt accurately. She had a slim, graceful figure suggesting youth, but she also had the poise and confidence of a society matron. It was also clear she felt no need to curry the favor of her noble host by making an extravagant effort to enter into the spirit of his costume ball.

Diana smiled. "When you've attended as many costume balls as I have, the magic starts to fade," she said. "Now I expend my effort on ensuring I'm comfortable, rather than interesting."

"You're always interesting, Aunt Molly," Medusa assured her earnestly. "I mean, Lady Diana. What is the correct form of address for a goddess?"

"I believe 'lady' is appropriate," her aunt replied. "Good evening, gentlemen." She looked past Gabrielle to greet Quin and Sinbad.

Gabrielle was far more relieved Quin had joined them than she was to take the lemonade he offered, even though she was thirsty.

She forced herself to take ladylike sips, and remembered how he'd given her water after they'd encountered the wolf so long ago. She'd been hot then, but also exhilarated they'd survived unharmed from their meeting with the dangerous predator.

As long as she could escape from the ballroom without detection, she'd be equally exhilarated by her adventure this evening.

A glance at the clock told her it was time to extricate herself from this conversation. But the music started again before she could speak, and Sinbad seized her free hand.

"Please do me the honor of dancing with *me* this time, Lady Cinderella," he begged. "Allow me." He took the glass of lemonade from Gabrielle, put it on the small table beside Medusa's aunt, and then led her out onto the dance floor.

Gabrielle noticed two things simultaneously. The first was that Lady Henderson was in the same set. The second was that Quin and Medusa had somehow been obliged to join a different set of dancers.

For the first time since she'd arrived, Gabrielle began to feel the bite of true fear.

Sinbad bowed to her, and she curtsied to him as gracefully as she could, but her stomach was knotted with anxiety as she stepped toward him.

If the dance wasn't over by midnight, would Lord Appledrum stop the music to order the grand unmasking?

Gabrielle had intended to leave before this—and if Sinbad hadn't requested an introduction after the last dance, everything would have gone well.

Now there was a real and immediate risk that Lady Henderson would discover she'd come to the ball.

Gabrielle wasn't afraid of being forcibly unmasked. She didn't have any friends here who'd think it a good game to tug on the strings of her mask. And she was sure Lord Appledrum, not to mention Quin, would consider it an outrageous assault on a lady, if a stranger attempted to unmask her.

But refusing to reveal her face would be awkward. Perhaps she could explain she needed to take off her turban to remove her mask—which was true—and say she was going to the ladies' retiring room to do so?

But that would attract attention, and some curious females might follow her. What if Lady Henderson was one of them?

A picture of Lady Henderson's expression when she discovered she'd been dancing with her daughter's governess rose in Gabrielle's mind.

It distracted her so badly she turned the wrong way and nearly bumped into the lady who was following behind her. Flustered, she muttered an apology and hurried to catch up with the gentleman she should be dancing this figure with.

It wasn't Sinbad, but an older man who said kindly, "I get confused with the figures too sometimes, but no one cares, my dear. It's all good fun."

"Thank you, sir," Gabrielle said breathlessly. She deliberately didn't glance in Lady Henderson's direction, but she could imagine that lady glaring at her from behind her mask.

The last thing Gabrielle wanted was annoy her employer unnecessarily, so she paid more attention to the dance, particularly when it was time for the ladies to move to the center.

Gabrielle touched her gloved fingertips lightly to Lady Henderson's, her heart beating far faster than the tempo of the music. As they circled around, she tried to sneak a sideways glance at her employer, but the mask limited her peripheral vision.

Lady Henderson didn't behave as if she'd recognized her, but Gabrielle was hugely relieved when she returned to Sinbad.

The dance continued, and as every second ticked by, Gabrielle's apprehension increased. Surely the music should stop soon? As she revolved with Sinbad she managed to catch a glimpse of the clock.

To Dance with the Earl

It was five minutes to midnight...

At three minutes to midnight, the music stopped.

Gabrielle dropped a hasty curtsy to Sinbad and stepped back, murmuring something about returning to her aunt.

There was no time to find Quin. She had to leave the ballroom immediately. She started counting in her head.

One second, two seconds, three seconds...

With every additional number, her sense of urgency increased. She headed toward the curtains concealing the door to the terrace, but checked when she saw a group of people standing in the open doorway.

If she tried to push past those guests, she'd call attention to herself—and she wouldn't get far across the garden before midnight struck.

Gabrielle didn't want to emulate Cinderella and have search parties sent out after her. She didn't want *anyone* here tonight to remember her except Quin.

Frustrated, she changed direction.

She saw Medusa's waving grass snakes ahead and stepped behind a tall man to avoid the other girl's notice. Then she sidled between two groups of people who were laughing and teasing each other about the imminent unmasking.

"Of course, I know who you are, Lord Apollo," one lady claimed boldly.

Gabrielle desperately hoped no one knew who *she* was.

Another two quick maneuvers brought her to the ballroom's grand main entrance. She made it safely out into the hallway, but the front door seemed a very long way away across a gleaming expanse of marble flooring.

Sixty-one seconds, sixty-two seconds...

She was about to risk dashing across the hall, when several footmen emerged from the rear of the house, carrying trays of champagne.

Gabrielle sucked in a breath and backed out of their way so quickly she collided with someone behind her. Heart thudding, she swung round, an apology on her lips—and discovered she'd walked into the newel post at the bottom of the stairs.

Relief startled her into a small laugh, but she wasn't safe from discovery yet. She could hear Lord Appledrum's voice close to the ballroom entrance, and she was terrified he might look out into the hall to round up any wayward guests before he ordered the grand unmasking.

One hundred and one, one hundred and two...

Gabrielle seized her skirts and ran straight up the stairs.

Her decision was driven by pure instinct—her overriding need to get far away from the ballroom as fast as she could.

But by the time she reached the first landing her thoughts had somewhat cleared. She'd been a guest in this house for two weeks, and she believed she could remember the layout. All she had to do was find the more modest stairwell at the back of the house, and she'd be able to make a discreet departure that way.

She stopped on the first-floor landing, breathing quickly as she looked around, trying to get her bearings.

But before she could put her memory to the test, she caught the movement of someone coming up the grand staircase behind her.

Panicked, she dashed through the open door of the music room.

The chamber was lit by candelabras but, to her relief, it was empty of people. She hurried around a sofa looking for somewhere to hide. Unfortunately, the only place she could see was under the pianoforte. She hastily dived into the shadows beneath it and crawled as close to the wall as she could. With any luck, even if someone walked close to the piano, they wouldn't notice her in the darkness.

She held herself completely still and listened intently. The steady chimes of the clock in the ballroom striking midnight echoed up the stairs, and a few boisterous guests took up the countdown.

The noises from the ballroom almost drowned out the light footsteps of the person who'd come upstairs behind her, but she thought she caught a betraying creak from the stairs.

Then there were a few seconds of absolute silence, and she started to think the person had gone elsewhere—until she heard the individual enter the music room!

Gabrielle hardly dared to breathe as the footsteps came inexorably closer. Now her hiding place seemed foolish beyond words. She couldn't think of a single, sensible explanation for why she was huddled under a pianoforte.

Please let it be a servant checking the candles, she begged silently. They'd have no reason to linger once they had fulfilled their task.

But it was a gentleman's evening shoes and stockings that came to stand in front of her hiding place. A moment later he crouched down to peer under the pianoforte. It was too shadowy for Gabrielle to see him clearly. All she knew for sure was that it was one of the most mortifying moments of her life.

Chapter Eight

It took Quin several long, frustrating moments before he could follow Gabrielle. He felt he should probably deliver Medusa back to her aunt when the dance ended, but he abandoned her in a most ungentlemanly fashion when he saw his father ahead.

The last thing Quin wanted was to catch his father's eye immediately before the unmasking. If that happened, he might never get away, so he dodged between the guests with almost as much dexterity as Gabrielle.

Even so, he was only just in time to catch a glimpse of blue skirts at the top of the stairs. If not for that momentary sighting, he'd have assumed she was still on the ground floor.

He started up after her. She'd disappeared by the time he reached the first-floor landing, but the open music room door suggested where she might be.

At first glance, the room seemed empty, but Quin knew

better than to make assumptions based on initial impressions. He strode over to the large pianoforte and crouched down.

And there she was, staring back at him. He couldn't see much of her in the shadows, but he was sure her headgear was now crooked, and he could sense the tension radiating from her hunched body.

He swallowed a laugh. He was sure Gabrielle wasn't finding anything about her current situation funny.

"Well met, Lady Cinderella," he said with grave politeness. "Is there anything particularly interesting to discover under the piano?"

Her breath escaped in an audible whoosh.

"It's you," she gasped.

"Of course it's me." He grinned at her. "Come on, we need to leave while everyone is preoccupied with the big unmasking."

"Yes." Gabrielle crawled out from under the piano and stood up. Two of her crowning feathers were broken but Quin didn't comment.

While she was shaking out her skirts, he removed his mask and put it on a side table, along with the papier-mâché ax. When he looked at her again, he discovered she was staring at him as if transfixed.

"You're more handsome than ever," she whispered. "*So* handsome."

Until that moment, he hadn't felt handsome, only hot and uncomfortable behind his mask. But the admiration in Gabrielle's voice made him feel like an Adonis.

He only wished he could see more of her face than her chin

and delectable mouth. But he knew, without a doubt, she was still the most beautiful lady he'd ever seen.

A particularly loud shout of laughter from the ballroom below reached the music room.

They both started.

Quin cleared his throat. "This way," he said gruffly, and led her back to the first-floor landing.

As they came closer to the main staircase, the volume of conversation and laughter from the ballroom grew louder. At one point, Quin was sure he could distinguish his father's commanding voice rising over the babble.

Gabrielle reached out to him, and he instinctively took her hand. He'd been holding her hand on and off all evening when they danced, but now they were alone this simple gesture seemed far more intimate.

"I shouldn't have come tonight," she whispered, sounding more anxious than she had when she'd greeted the black wolf so many years ago. "Lady Henderson will be furious if she discovers she just *danced* with me."

"She won't find out." Quin was offended by the idea anyone would be furious at discovering they'd danced with Gabrielle—but now was not the time to discuss Lady Henderson. "Come." He walked swiftly toward the rear staircase.

It would be awkward, but not a disaster if they encountered a servant on the way out. This was his home. He'd removed his mask so there could be no delay-causing confusion about his right to go anywhere he wanted in the house. As long as Gabrielle kept her mask on, he'd be the target of gossip if anyone spotted their clandestine exit.

But Quin much preferred to avoid any accidental meetings. He took Gabrielle out through a side door and pulled it closed behind them.

She took a deep breath. "It's so lovely and fresh out here," she said softly.

"It smells much better than in the ballroom," Quin agreed. "Hush now, we need to get back to your ladder before people start spilling out onto the terrace and into the garden."

"They're supposed to have supper first," Gabrielle began. "Wait. How do you know about my ladder?"

"I saw you climb in." He ignored her gasp of surprise and hurried her along the side of the house and onto a path that wound between two neatly clipped box hedges.

The hedges weren't tall enough to conceal them from onlookers, but this was the best way to get back into the orchard without going across the fountain garden next to the terrace.

∽

Gabrielle kept pace with Quin as he ushered her quickly through the shadowy garden. She did her best to tread carefully, but inside she was bubbling with so much joy she wanted to dance.

She'd panicked momentarily on the upstairs landing, when she'd heard Lady Henderson's laughter down in the ballroom. For a heartbeat she'd even feared the viscountess might climb the stairs and discover her.

But she'd known that was a nonsensical fear. Lady

Henderson had no reason to leave the party. She'd been too busy flirting with 'Sir Lancelot'.

Gabrielle dismissed her employer from her mind to focus on Quin instead. He was by her side again. Stronger and more quietly confident than ever. The fact he wasn't at ease in a ballroom signified nothing when he was so accomplished in every genuinely meaningful way.

She threw a sideways glance at him, wishing she could see him more clearly. The moon was lower in the sky than it had been when she'd arrived, and the shadows in the orchard deeper.

But when they stepped clear of an apple tree, she caught a glimpse of his strong, straight nose, and his firm jaw. He had such a perfect profile he'd be a wonderful subject for a cameo silhouette.

He took her directly to the ladder, and she remembered what he'd said earlier.

"You saw me climb in? I didn't see you." She was a little unnerved to discover he'd been watching her. What if less friendly eyes had also witnessed her arrival?

"Hush," he warned her, picking up the ladder. "Some of the guests are liable to go onto the terrace now."

Gabrielle was about to remind him again about the supper, when she realized she could hear voices in the garden. It sounded as if some guests might have wandered out to the fountain. From the fountain it was not far to the picket gate into the orchard.

"Yes, I must get over the wall quickly." It would be awkward for Quin as well as her if he was caught helping her with the ladder.

People might think they were eloping.

The idea should scandalize her. Instead, she wished it could be true. But they both had other claims upon them that would make eloping not only scandalous, but also deeply irresponsible.

And perhaps Quin no longer wanted to marry her. Dancing together for the sake of old times was one thing—marriage was another thing entirely.

She reached to grab a rung of the ladder, while a myriad happy, anxious, and confused emotions tumbled through her.

Her white gloves showed up clearly in the moonlight. She instinctively drew her hands back. Why did seeing her white gloves seem wrong? Then she remembered she'd worn dark gloves when she'd climbed the ladder earlier. And she'd also had her pelisse and bonnet with her.

"My bag." She turned and saw Quin was already holding it.

"Climb up first," he said. "I'll hand it up to you, and you can drop it over the other side."

Gabrielle didn't argue. Climbing over a wall wasn't a ladylike activity to carry out in a gentleman's presence, but she wasn't with any gentleman, she was with Quin. She reached the top of the ladder and carefully positioned herself on the wall. As soon as she was secure, Quin handed her belongings up to her, and she dropped them down into the shadows on the field side of the wall.

She turned back in his direction just in time for him to take her completely by surprise.

One second, he was standing quietly in the orchard, the next he was springing upward to put his hands on top of the wall. After that it seemed to cost him no effort at all to pull himself up to join her. He made it seem as if leaping onto a wall was as effortless as strolling through the garden.

His physical prowess took Gabrielle's breath away. She wished she could watch him do it again.

"Lean back," he said. After giving her that warning, he lifted the ladder over the wall. "Wait."

He dropped into the deep well of shadow on the field side of the wall as soundlessly as a great cat. Gabrielle couldn't see him clearly, but she heard the familiar soft, grating sounds of wood against brick as he made sure the ladder was securely positioned.

"Come down now," he said.

Gabrielle hesitated, momentarily unnerved by what she was about to do. When she'd arrived, she'd been descending into the moonlit garden, and it hadn't seemed so daunting. Now she'd be climbing down into dark shadows. But Quin was waiting for her, and the voices in the garden were getting louder.

She hitched up her skirts and carefully felt with her toe to find a rung on the ladder.

"Take your time," Quin said calmly. "I'm here."

His words gave her renewed confidence, and she descended without any further hesitation. Her feet touched the ground, she wobbled on a deep, sunbaked cart rut—and then Quin's arms closed around her.

She gasped.

He froze. "Should I release you?" he asked, his voice taut.

She shook her head, and then remembered he couldn't see her clearly in the darkness. "No," she whispered, turning and pressing nearer to him.

"Good." His embrace tightened, even as his momentary

tension eased. "I wanted to hold you all evening," he murmured, somewhere in the vicinity of her ear.

She closed her eyes and rested her head against his shoulder. Her mask was digging into her cheek, but it didn't matter because she was finally safe in Quin's arms.

The scent of honeysuckle filled the air, mingling with the faint, lingering odor of Quin's soap, the rosewater she'd sprinkled on herself before leaving her room, and a hint of perspiration. It was hot in the ballroom and dancing was an energetic activity.

Gabrielle wrapped her arms around Quin. She could feel the hard muscles of his back beneath the superfine cloth of his well-fitted coat.

He ran one hand down her back from the nape of her neck to her waist. She quivered at the delightful sensation and a tiny sigh escaped her lips.

His hold on her changed, jostling her a little, even as he kept her pressed close against his chest. He stroked her again, and this time she felt his bare fingertips touch her skin above the back of her neckline.

Her whole focus arrowed to that small point of intimate contact, while new tingling heat coursed through her veins.

She sighed again.

"Does that...please you?" he asked hoarsely.

She nodded—and either the turban or her mask strings pulled her hair enough to make her wince.

He went still. "What's wrong?"

"Not you. My mask pulled my hair," she explained breathlessly.

"Ah." He relaxed again. His gentle fingers tracked around the edge of her bodice to the side of her neck. Pure pleasure radiated through her from his tender caresses.

"Will you take your mask off now?" he asked.

"Yes." She lifted her head.

His fingers followed the line of her jaw and then he brushed the side of his thumb over her mouth.

Her lips parted and her breath quickened.

She tilted her head further back, gazing up at him, though she couldn't see his expression because his face was in shadows.

She felt him explore the edge of her mask and the folds of her turban.

"How do we remove all this without hurting you?" he murmured.

"I'll do it." Reluctant to let him go, but eager to be rid of her masquerade accessories, she pulled her arms forward to remove her gloves.

"You put those on like a knight preparing to go into battle," he said softly. "Where did you get the ladder from?"

"It was waiting for me," Gabrielle admitted. "I think it belongs to the hay makers."

"Your fairy godmother had someone leave it for you?" Quin sounded quietly amused. "I'll lay it down now and take it back to one of the haystacks when I return."

While he did that, Gabrielle tugged off her turban and removed her mask. The warm night air felt almost cool against her sweat-soaked hair.

She threaded her fingers through it, trying to lift the flattened strands from her scalp. Some small sound of dismay must have escaped her, because Quin's arms immediately enclosed her again.

"What's the matter?"

"Nothing. I'm just glad you can't see me looking so...so...hot. My hair must look..."

One of his arms encircled her waist, but his other hand cupped the side of her face and when he brushed his thumb over her lips her words faded away.

"I've seen you looking hot before. You're always beautiful. May I kiss you?" He caressed her lips again.

"Yes." Her eyes had adapted to the shadows, but she still couldn't clearly see his features. She doubted he could see her any better, but a heartbeat later he proved he knew where her mouth was.

She felt his light breath against her skin and then his lips brushed against hers...once...twice...and began to explore with more purpose.

Her whole body stirred into thrilling life. Quin was the only man—or boy—who'd ever kissed her. And she was absolutely certain he was the only one who could ever make her feel this way.

As they'd grown older, she'd often been conscious of him keeping a tight rein over his desires. And sometimes she'd tried to tease him into a greater exchange of passion. Until the day she'd feared she'd pushed him too far, and shocked him with her impropriety.

But he wasn't holding back now. After his first, gentle explorations, his mouth became bolder on hers. His tongue stroked her lower lip and then plunged into her mouth.

Her body tingled. Her breasts felt full and achy. Amid the other sensations, she was aware of the private place between her legs beginning to swell and throb.

This was arousal. And she knew from experience how glorious it would be if Quin caressed her in that most intimate part of her body. But he'd only done it once. Would he do it again tonight? Her heart raced. Her knees trembled. Quin began to press open-mouthed kisses against her cheeks and the side of her neck.

Chapter Nine

Gabrielle whimpered and clung tighter to him. She tasted Quin, and salt, on her lips and tongue. No longer confined by her turban, sweat was trickling down her forehead to sting her eyes, and she didn't care. Quin didn't care.

She felt the flex of his muscles. He pulled her closer, his hand splayed on her lower back. She arched into him and felt a hard pressure against her stomach. She knew what it meant. He wanted her as much as she wanted him.

He shuddered—and went still.

She clung to him, breathless and dizzy with desire.

"Shush," he murmured, his breath caressing the tender skin below her ear. For an instant, she thought he was reprimanding her for her uninhibited response to him—but then she heard voices on the other side of the wall.

A man and a woman. The man offering compliments to the lady, the lady returning the compliments. Ladylike giggles which turned into gasps of...pleasure? Masculine groans. The sounds took on a rhythmical tempo. The lady began to moan in a way Gabrielle had never heard before.

Quin's arms turned to steel around her.

"Lovers," he breathed against her cheek. "The lady seems willing."

Gabrielle's heart raced. The swollen ache between her legs became more insistent. She pressed herself against the hard rod of Quin's arousal. She'd felt it before they'd inadvertently found themselves eavesdropping on another couple in the throes of passion.

She knew it was *her* kisses that had aroused Quin, not the sounds of the other couple's lovemaking. But would Quin like her to respond to him with whimpers and moans, the way the unknown lady was responding to her lover on the other side of the wall?

Gabrielle's legs were almost too weak to support her. She wanted Quin to touch her in every interesting way possible. But she didn't want him to do it where anyone else could overhear them. And she didn't want to lie down on the sunbaked cart tracks either.

"Haystack," she breathed so softly she could barely hear herself. Or perhaps that was because her heart was beating thunderously in her ears. "I mean…we could…lie on…"

Quin started. His arms tightened—then he moved his head in a small, negative gesture.

Mortification flooded her. She'd gone too far again. Shocked him with her lustful urges.

She felt him smile against her cheek and give her a last, gentle kiss before he lifted his head.

He laid a finger against her mouth and released her. She stood trembling, while he collected up her belongings from the ground.

On the other side of the wall, the unknown couple's passion was increasing in tempo. Gabrielle was torn between dismay that, once again, she'd shocked Quin with her forward nature—and yearning to know what it would be like to indulge in the same activity with him.

He took her elbow and began to guide her along the track, away from his father's garden, back toward the town.

His stride wasn't as smooth as it had been earlier. After a momentary unsteadiness caused by the cart ruts, he guided her to walk on the cut grass of the field. But she could still sense the tension in his body.

Behind them, the sounds of lovemaking continued. Not overloud, but still audible—until the lady uttered a long-drawn-out gasping moan, and the gentleman produced a crescendo of grunts which suddenly ended with a shout.

Quin's next step faltered, but he didn't stop.

Gabrielle's body felt as if it was on fire. She couldn't tell how much of her over-stimulation was caused by embarrassment, and how much by her desire the kisses she'd shared with Quin had led them to the passionate intimacies they'd just overheard.

A few yards further on, Quin stopped walking and turned toward her.

"We must set you to rights," he said in a low, hoarse voice.

Shame seared away all of Gabrielle's other chaotic emotions.

"Only with you...I am not wanton...you're the only one I

would want to…" She couldn't force the rest of the words past her lips.

Quin dropped the carpet bag and her turban onto the ground. He put his hands on her shoulders and then slid one round to cup the back of her neck.

He was standing close to her. Not as close as before, but the way he was holding her excluded the rest of the world.

He bent his head until his forehead was touching hers. "You're the only one I want too, my Gabrielle. You have no idea how much effort I'm exerting not to carry you to the nearest haystack."

"Oh." Her hands fluttered against his chest, unsure if she should touch him. "You don't disapprove?'

"How could I ever?" He covered her fluttering hands with one of his, pressing them firmly against his chest. "But you could keep them still…perhaps?" There was a kind of strained amusement in his tone.

She sucked in a breath, realizing he was asking her not to tease him. "I'm sorry…"

He moved his head in that small negative gesture again. "Here is my thinking, so you may consider my reasoning in depth."

"Reasoning?" Her smile trembled. Was there another man in the world who'd talk about reason in their current situation?

"Yes." His lungs expanded in a steadying breath. "Consideration number one—I don't want your primary memory of our first time to be the hours you had to spend afterward, picking hay out of your hair and clothes."

Imagining how they could get themselves covered in hay heated her whole face—and the rest of her body.

"That is...that is a valid consideration," she managed to say.

Especially since Mrs. Whittle was waiting up for her to come home. What would the housekeeper think if Gabrielle arrived with her clothes in a disheveled state? She hadn't even thought of that until Quin mentioned it.

"The second consideration..." Quin paused, and then nuzzled her ear. "All physical activities require practice to perfect one's performance," he murmured. "I'm eagerly anticipating the moment we can start practicing together—but I fear a haystack in a field isn't an optimal location for me to ensure your satisfaction, when..." He was the one who ran out of words this time.

Gabrielle was so distracted by the light kisses he was brushing against her cheek she only belatedly caught his meaning.

She lifted her head. "You haven't done it with any other lady?"

"Why would I, when you're the lady who holds my heart?" he said softly.

It was what Gabrielle had hoped for, but society had different expectations for how gentlemen and ladies should conduct themselves, and Quin had been away for a long time.

On a surge of love and happiness, she rose on tiptoe and peppered kisses on every bit of his face she could reach.

He groaned and wrapped his arms around her. She liked that, but then it occurred to her his groan was more one of endurance than rising ecstasy.

"I'm sorry. I'm not being commonsensical." She reluctantly stepped back.

"I don't want you to change. You're the girl who stood between me and the wolf. The young lady who climbed over a wall to dance with me—didn't you?"

"Yes, of course." She smiled up at him. "Only you."

"But we have some…what shall we call them, challenges, obstacles? That we must navigate now. The first is getting you home looking like a respectable young lady." He picked up the carpet bag again. "Is there a regular bonnet in here? Or must you put on the feathered thing again?"

"That's what you meant by setting me to rights." She belatedly understood Quin's earlier comment. He'd only been referring to her appearance, not her morals.

"Yes." He picked up the turban and dusted it off. "Do you have to put this back on? It's very recognizable."

"No, I wore a different bonnet on the way." Gabrielle crouched to rummage through her carpet bag. Pulling out her pelisse, boots and everyday gloves—

"I must have dropped my white gloves," she realized. "Or did you pick them up?"

"No, only the feathery hat and your bag. I'll find your gloves on my return," he promised. "Make yourself look as unexceptional as you can—I know it's difficult—and I will take you safely home."

"It's difficult for me to look unexceptional because…?" The best Gabrielle could do to reduce her overheated appearance was wipe her face with her handkerchief.

"You're so beautiful and vivacious," he said seriously. "And you knew that would be my answer. I don't know whether I should apologize for my clumsy phrasing or scold you for fishing for compliments."

"You haven't even seen me in daylight yet." The bonnet was somewhat worse for wear, but the wide brim offered at least some concealment for her face, and she tied the ribbons briskly. The dark pelisse was still too warm, even though the night was cooler, but she didn't care because it hid the pale, shimmering silk of her gown.

"It doesn't matter. I've tasted you in the moonlight—" Quin's breath rasped, and he went still.

Gabrielle sucked her lower lip into her mouth and swallowed. She'd imagined running straight into Quin's arms when he finally returned, but then she'd also imagined them sitting for hours just talking.

And she'd also been forlornly aware neither possibility was likely to come true in her current circumstances. Tonight had exceeded her expectations in many ways—and carried the pair of them into uncharted waters.

Quin exhaled slowly, fighting to bring his bodily responses back under his full control. Lusty need pounded through his veins. He was so hard it was painful.

Every raw masculine instinct demanded he seize Gabrielle in his arms and carry her to the nearest haystack—or even down to the ground they were standing on.

He released another breath, consciously making sure

Gabrielle couldn't hear it—couldn't hear how close he was to losing his self-control.

He'd always been physically attracted to her. As they'd both grown older, his response to her had intensified. Other ladies were pretty, but only Gabrielle could arouse him with a single, laughing glance.

He'd had erotic dreams about her for years. Frequently been obliged to take himself in hand, imagining all the time it was Gabrielle's touch bringing him to release. He should have been prepared for the impact her kisses would have upon him, after so long apart.

But he hadn't been. Not for this overwhelming, uncivilized compulsion to claim her and never let her go again. His baser instincts and the rationality on which he prided himself, battled for dominance within him—meanwhile Gabrielle put on a drab pelisse.

She set her boots on the ground and reached out a hand for him to support her as she changed her footwear.

Her silent gesture for assistance was born from years of accepting his help in similar circumstances. Even though he'd warned her he was on the edge of control, she trusted him without question.

Quin was deeply gratified by her continued confidence in him. It was also true Gabrielle had a brave, adventurous spirit—and she was the one who'd suggested aloud they could turn a haystack into an impromptu bed.

Even though she'd subsequently suffered pangs of mortification at her immodest words, Quin didn't believe she'd reproach him if he did carry her off. Or at least, she'd insist on sharing equal responsibility for whatever transpired.

She balanced on one leg, clinging to his hand as she slid her other foot into the boot.

He hoped she'd be a willing participant in their lovemaking not just once, but for the rest of their lives. He was confident that, with regular practice and assiduous attention to what pleased her, he would soon be able to bring her to the pinnacle of joy on every occasion.

"We must be married immediately." His voice was rough, barely recognizable.

She almost lost her balance, tugging against his hand until she regained her equilibrium.

He steadied her at arm's length. "I will obtain a marriage license. We must inform your papa. I will ask his permission, but we don't need it. You're twenty-two."

Gabrielle's hand trembled in his as she changed into her other boot. Her silence threw a cold wash of unease over him.

"I apologize. That wasn't properly romantic. I should—"

She squeezed his fingers and moved closer. "It was wonderful. You're wonderful..." Her voice hitched. "I'm so sorry..."

"You don't want to marry me?" The shock of her apparent rejection was so great he almost staggered.

"I do...but I can't." Her words wobbled as if she was on the verge of tears.

"Can't? Why not? I don't care that your papa has lost his fortune."

"Not that. I know you're too noble to cast me aside for such a reason. I shouldn't have climbed over the wall tonight." A quiet, unmistakable sob escaped her.

Quin had been stunned when he thought she'd rejected him. Now he nearly staggered with relief at this sign that the prospect of *not* marrying him filled her with misery.

"Let us be clear?" he begged. "You would willingly marry me if you could—but for some reason you feel you can't? Did you marry someone else already?"

"What?" she gasped. "No, of course not! How can you think that?"

"I didn't. I never—" He broke off, running his fingers through his hair. He wasn't wearing a hat. A gentleman should be wearing a hat when he was walking about town, but that was something he couldn't mend. "I beg of you—tell me why you can't marry me. If you still love me...tell me your reason."

Chapter Ten

"It would break Charlotte's heart," Gabrielle whispered.

"Charlotte? Who the hell—?" Quin bit off his intemperate exclamation. Anger was an emotion he rarely experienced. Frustration was more familiar, but he was usually able to reason his way into a more productive state of mind.

Tonight, the challenge of responding to Gabrielle's unexpected refusal, hard on the heels of his struggle to control his rampant desire, destroyed his usual capacity to regulate his thoughts and emotions.

He stood in silence, noting, but immediately forgetting, the hoot of an owl in the distance. Tension shimmered between them, so tangible to Quin it almost seemed visible in the silvery light.

Gabrielle bent to shove the feathery headdress into her carpet bag. He didn't offer to help her but, as she straightened, he caught a suppressed sob.

The sound went straight to Quin's protective heart.

"Don't cry, dear heart—tell me about Charlotte." His thoughts had settled enough for him to realize that Charlotte was most likely the child in Gabrielle's care. "Why can't she do without you? I'm certain any child would love to have you as their governess—but surely a new one can be appointed when you give your notice?"

In the moonlight, he saw Gabrielle shake her head. The bonnet, intended to shield her face from the curious gaze of others, also added extra shadows to impede his view of her.

"No?" he said. "But surely—"

Gabrielle came near enough for him to put his arm around her waist, but he didn't know if he should.

"When I first became Charlotte's governess, she hadn't said a word for months," Gabrielle said.

Her revelation startled Quin. "The child's mute?"

"Not now. But it took a long time for me to earn her trust. The first time she spoke to me—it was like a miracle." Gabrielle pulled in a wavering breath.

"There's nothing wrong with her speech organs?" Quin clarified. As so often when he encountered a setback or a difficult challenge, his instinct was to gather more information. And Gabrielle's tearful refusal to marry him was the biggest setback he'd ever faced. "She simply chose to stop talking, and then started again? What event caused her to stop?"

Gabrielle hugged him. "You're wonderful."

Quin experienced a knee-weakening surge of relief. He couldn't remember the last time he'd been so buffeted by different emotions—but he was sure Gabrielle wouldn't be hugging him if she'd said she couldn't marry him because she didn't want him.

"I'm glad you think so. But I don't understand what prompted you to say so at this moment." He couldn't resist returning her embrace.

"Because you immediately asked the reason Charlotte stopped speaking, rather than assuming she's stupid or simply disobedient." Gabrielle still sounded like she was trying not to cry. "You're such a good man."

Quin swallowed. "Strictly speaking, I imagine Charlotte's silence *was* a form of disobedience. But that doesn't mean she didn't have a reason for her behavior that makes sense to her."

Quin himself had rarely been a deliberately disobedient or unruly child—though his single-minded pursuit of his interests had caused Agnes Trent and his father occasional moments of consternation.

Marcus, on the other hand, had rebelled against an injustice he'd suffered—and in a far more physically dramatic way than simply ceasing to speak.

Quin was entirely sympathetic to his cousin's feelings and actions. Marcus's secrets weren't his to share with anyone, even Gabrielle. But remembering his cousin's experiences, reminded Quin of the need to consider what motive Charlotte might have had for turning mute.

"Do you know what caused Charlotte's silence?" he asked. "Does she have difficulties with reading and writing? Did her previous governess punish her for her perceived slowness?"

"Her previous governess remained less than two weeks," Gabrielle said. "I understand she had a nasty argument with Lady

Henderson and was dismissed. But Charlotte fell silent before that."

"How old is she?" Quin asked.

"Seven. She couldn't read or write at all before I started looking after her, but we've been making good progress in recent months." There was an undertone of pride in Gabrielle's voice.

"I know you must be a kind and patient tutor," Quin had no doubts on that matter. "You say she talks to you? Has she told you why she stopped talking before?"

"No." Gabrielle shook her head. "But for the first five years of her life, she seems to have been left almost entirely in the care of her nurse."

"So was I." Quin was thinking of Agnes Trent.

"No, Charlotte's case is not the same. You've told me so many stories about how your father would come and join you in the nursery, or accompany you and Miss Trent on walks. He taught you to ride—" Gabrielle paused to take a breath.

"In the whole time I've been Charlotte's governess, her father has never come to see her in the nursery or anywhere else," Gabrielle continued quietly. "He's never lived under the same roof with us for more than a night or two at a time."

Quin felt an instant surge of mingled indignation, pity—and concern. "Do you know anything to his discredit?" Was Lord Henderson a dissolute reprobate, and it was safer for Gabrielle that he ignored his daughter?

"Only that he and his wife can't seem to be in the same house together without bitter arguments. I would—" she broke off.

"You would?" he prompted. "Do you feel disloyal talking about your employers to me?"

"No. My first loyalty is always to you—and to Charlotte. Charlotte still won't speak in her mother's presence, and for the most part Lady..." Gabrielle spoke even more softly and moved closer to Quin "...Henderson ignores Charlotte."

"It sounds like a most uncomfortable household in which to live." Quin was appalled Gabrielle had found herself in such a contentious situation.

"It's not happy, like the homes we grew up in," she conceded. "But Charlotte and I have our own comfortable daily routine. As she's grown to trust me, she's turned into a d-delightful companion." Gabrielle's voice hitched again.

Quin wanted to wrap her in his arms and comfort her. But he was also trying to come to terms with the profound impact her revelation was having on the future he'd been eagerly anticipating for them.

"Charlotte hasn't told you why she stopped speaking, but have you gleaned any ideas from other sources?" He focused his attention on collecting more information, not his crushing disappointment.

"Mrs. Whittle—she's the housekeeper, and my fairy godmother—told me Charlotte stopped speaking soon after her nurse died suddenly," Gabrielle said.

"Grief." Quin felt another pang of sympathy for the little girl. "Surely it must be grief that caused her silence. But it's extreme response to remain silent for months. She must have an exceptionally strong will."

Gabrielle uttered a small sound that could almost be a tiny snort of laughter.

"Yes," she said. "Since I've been looking after her, Charlotte has never thrown a tantrum. Apart from her silence, she's not usually disobedient. But she's not weak, and she's not slow-witted."

"She must be a challenging pupil," Quin said.

Perhaps grief wasn't the only reason for Charlotte's silence? In Quin's experience, the emotion which could most commonly rob a person of the ability to talk was fear. Once during the expedition, he'd seen a man temporarily struck dumb with fear in the face of immediate danger.

What was Charlotte afraid of? Or who? Quin remembered Gabrielle's fear she might be discovered by her employer at the masquerade ball.

"Are you afraid of Lady Henderson?" he demanded.

"What? No, of course not." Gabrielle's startled response was breathless.

"You were so anxious to avoid discovery at the ball you hid under the pianoforte," he reminded her.

"Only because I will be fined, reprimanded, or even dismissed if Lady Henderson ever finds out she danced with me," Gabrielle said. "I'm not supposed to leave the nursery without permission. I'm not afraid of her. I'm afraid of her dismissing me."

If Gabrielle lost her position, there would be no impediment to her marrying Quin. No sooner had the thought crossed his mind than he banished it. It would be dishonorable to force Gabrielle to go against her conscience. Or even to allow her to be dismissed because he took no steps to protect her from that fate.

"Come, we need to get you home before your absence is noticed." He picked up her carpet bag. "Tell me all about your daily activities. I'm hungry to hear everything that's happened to you since we last saw each other."

"Not as eager as I am to hear about your adventures." She took his arm. "You jumped over the wall so easily. Did you spend a lot of time leaping over things on your voyage?"

"No, but I spent a lot of time climbing the rigging to maintain my fitness while we were at sea." Quin shared a few details of his life on board the ship. But he was more interested in learning about the woman beside him, than in recounting his overseas adventures.

"How did you encourage Charlotte to begin speaking to you?" he asked.

"I didn't know what to do at first," she replied. "I had no experience as a governess, and none with a child like Charlotte. But Mrs. Whittle helped by telling me about the death of Charlotte's nurse."

"She must have felt a daughter's affection for the nurse." Quin understood Charlotte's feelings well, because Agnes Trent had filled the same role in his childhood.

"Yes," Gabrielle said. "After I discovered how close Charlotte had been to her nurse, it made me think that, in some ways, her situation was not so very different from my own. The secure foundation of her life had been destroyed by the death of her nurse, just as the foundation of my life was shaken when we had to leave France. I decided I should begin by showing her I'm trustworthy and reliable."

Quin swallowed a sudden constriction in his throat. He found Gabrielle's unadorned description of how she'd gone about her new duties profoundly moving.

She must have been as bewildered and heartbroken by her change of circumstances as Charlotte. But instead of surrendering to her feelings, she'd used them to help her better understand the little girl.

"I'm sure it didn't take Charlotte long to realize you're utterly worthy of her trust," he declared, a husky note in his voice.

"Thank you," Gabrielle said. "Thank you... um." She paused and glanced away, as if seeking to compose herself.

"Anyway, Charlotte talks to me now," she continued. "It was so wonderful when she spoke for the first time—though I tried not to reveal how emotional I felt. I didn't want to frighten her into withdrawing from me again."

"You make me think of how one tames a wild animal," Quin said. "When it finally approaches you, you can't make any sudden moves or get too enthusiastic petting it, or you will scare it away."

"Something like that," Gabrielle said. "Charlotte didn't say much at first. But gradually she's come to trust me, and now we talk all the time."

"She must be devoted to you," Quin's voice cracked. The more Gabrielle explained, the more he understood why she was torn in her loyalties between him and Charlotte. He'd loved Gabrielle longer, but Charlotte was a vulnerable child. One who, by the sound of things, continued to be in profound need of Gabrielle's loving care.

They walked slowly through Brighton's streets, Quin doing his best to spot and avoid other nighttime wanderers before their paths crossed too closely.

Now they'd arrived at the shadowy bulk of the Hendersons' house. It overlooked Marine Parade, and Quin could hear the distant roll of the tide to his right.

"We've arrived," Gabrielle whispered. "I never told you—you already knew where I'm staying."

"Yes. Gabrielle—"

"Thank you so much for escorting me home," she spoke across him. "I shouldn't have climbed over the wall—but I'm so glad we've been together tonight."

"Is father correct that it will cause you harm if I call upon you?" Quin asked. "If we announce our betrothal...?"

"We cannot." Gabrielle shook her head. "You're an earl. If I marry you, I would outrank...she would never let Charlotte see me again. I'm so sorry. Goodbye, Quin." She flung her arms around him, hugging him tightly for a few precious seconds.

He barely had time to return her embrace before she stepped back, claimed her bag from him, and hurried into the shadows at the rear of the house.

For a heartbeat he remained motionless, still feeling the warm press of Gabrielle's body against his. Then he turned, strode down to the railing at the top of the cliff, and walked away along Marine Parade.

The last thing he wanted was to encounter Lady Henderson when she returned home from the masquerade ball.

Ahead of him, a noisy group of well-dressed gentlemen spilled out of the Ship Inn. Quin pivoted on his heel, went back the way he'd come, and took the next street leading inland.

At this moment, he should be the guest of honor at his

father's ball. The fact that tomorrow no one would remember seeing him at the event wouldn't be particularly remarkable.

But gossip about him roaming the streets of Brighton instead of attending the ball would be much more interesting. Especially if his name was connected with a mysterious lady carrying a carpet bag.

Once he'd checked he was going in the right direction, his thoughts turned wholly to his reunion with Gabrielle. In some ways it had exceeded his hopes. In other, crucial ways, it had been deeply confounding and painful.

In dark moments, Quin had worried Gabrielle might find another man who suited her tastes better than him. But until his return to England, it had never occurred to him that she'd be so dedicated to her duties as a governess that she'd refuse to wed him.

The last time Gabrielle had said goodbye to him, they hadn't seen each other for years.

He wasn't going to let that happen again. Somehow, he had to find a speedy solution to the present, profoundly unsatisfactory situation. He clenched his jaw and strode on over the cobblestones. There had to be a way forward for him and Gabrielle, and he was going to find it.

Chapter Eleven

Tears blurred Gabrielle's vision as she groped in her bag for the key Mrs. Whittle had given her. To keep it safe, she'd attached a string to it and tied the other end of the string to one of the bag handles. Now the key was buried under her turban. Finally, after a few moments of increasing frustration, she pulled it free.

Finding the keyhole was easier, because she could see a dim, keyhole-shaped glow of light part way down the door. The glow looked fuzzy through her tears, but she managed to get the key into the lock.

Then she paused to dry her eyes. She didn't want Mrs. Whittle to see her crying. The housekeeper had encouraged her to go to the masquerade ball to enjoy herself dancing. She'd be dismayed if Gabrielle returned in tears. This heartache hadn't been part of the plan.

But now Gabrielle couldn't understand why she hadn't realized from the beginning how painful it would be to see Quin again—and then have to say goodbye again. Perhaps it was because she'd only half-believed they *would* meet at the ball.

The time with him under the stars had been more than a magical interlude. She'd been so joyful to be with him after so long apart. So full of passionate need when he'd held her and kissed her. Only Quin's protective streak had prevented them from emulating the lovers they'd overheard in the orchard.

More tears flooded Gabrielle's eyes, even as her body heated at the memory. She knew it was for the best she wasn't returning to the house covered in hay. But she wished with all her heart that the first time Quin had envisaged for them could become a reality. That they could learn to be lovers in a comfortable, private place belonging to them.

But that couldn't happen. Not while Charlotte needed her. Gabrielle wished she could discuss with Quin the ways she was trying to help the little girl. He'd instinctively understood there must be more to Charlotte's behavior than slow wits or incorrigible disobedience.

There had been so many evenings when Gabrielle had gone to bed and stared at the ceiling half the night, worrying about whether she was doing the right thing. Even now, she sometimes had misgivings.

No one in Gabrielle's family had ever had any difficulty spouting forth a torrent of words when the occasion called for it. But Quin wasn't like that. He spoke fluently when he was at ease. But even at the ball tonight, she'd been the one who'd spoken first after Lord Appledrum left them alone together.

She didn't care Quin was sometimes awkward in society, because in every way that counted, he showed, and told her, how much he cherished her. But perhaps he would understand some aspects of Charlotte's behavior better than Gabrielle did?

More often than not now, Charlotte acted like any other little girl—or at least, a typical little girl who liked snails. But she had no friends of her own age. And no one else to talk to except Gabrielle, and occasionally Mrs. Whittle.

Gabrielle had no idea how she could widen Charlotte's social circle without running afoul of Lady Henderson. And how would Charlotte ever cope with the challenge of making her debut in society, if she'd never talked to anyone apart from her governess and the housekeeper?

Gabrielle knew it would give her so much comfort if she could regularly discuss her concerns about Charlotte with Quin.

But that couldn't be.

As long as she remained Charlotte's governess, it wouldn't be possible for her to see Quin again.

Lady Henderson was a viscountess who enjoyed the cachet of claiming her child's governess was the daughter of a duke. And she never missed an opportunity to make sly references about Gabrielle's loss of fortune and status.

But if Gabrielle married Quin and re-entered society, the tables would be turned. She'd be the Countess of Hanwell, and the future Marchioness of Appledrum.

Lady Henderson would be furious that her former employee now took precedence over her. And she wouldn't be agreeable to any continuing communication between Gabrielle and Charlotte. But Charlotte would need Gabrielle's love and care for many more years.

The summer night was still balmy, and Gabrielle's winter

pelisse was still too warm for the season, but a strange kind of cold calm settled over her limbs as she fully embraced that uncompromising certainty.

She even managed to summon a half smile to her lips as she opened the door, though she didn't expect to find the housekeeper on the other side.

The hinges squeaked faintly. Gabrielle winced, but she was relieved to discover the kitchen was empty. The only sign the household wasn't entirely asleep was the lamp burning on the kitchen table. Mrs. Whittle must have left it for her, and that evidence of the housekeeper's kindness almost destroyed her hard-won composure.

She gave her head a small shake and resolutely tamped her emotions down again. Her evening's adventure wasn't over until she'd reached the safety of the nursery.

All the public reception rooms in the house were on the ground and the first floors. Those two floors were designed to impress visitors, and they were connected by the main staircase.

Gabrielle had no intention of going up those stairs. Not when she knew one of the footmen was waiting in the hallway for Lady Henderson and her attendant to return home. But he was probably dozing in his chair right now.

Gabrielle made sure the kitchen door was locked, picked up the lamp, and started up the backstairs to reach the second floor. This was where Lord and Lady Henderson each had their own bedroom and dressing room, and Lady Henderson had a sitting room. Augustus, Charlotte's older brother, also had rooms on the second floor.

There was only one flight of stairs from the second floor to the top floor, so Gabrielle had to leave the safety of the servants' stairwell to cross in front of Lord Henderson's rooms. The lamp threw strange shadows on the walls and floors, and she unconsciously held her breath as she trod lightly over the carpet.

The flame suddenly flickered, despite the protective glass of the lamp. At the same time, Gabrielle felt a light breeze ruffle her hair. Her pulse jumped. She threw a quick glance over her shoulder, but she couldn't see anything unusual.

Lady Henderson was still at the masquerade ball, she reminded herself. She didn't know where Lord Henderson was, but he certainly wasn't in Brighton. And Augustus's rooms were at the other end of the hall. She looked uneasily in that direction, but Augustus's door was firmly shut.

Just a draft, then. She wasn't used to walking about on this floor during the night, but she'd noticed the window in her room was drafty. All the same, she quickened her pace as she climbed up to the top floor. The nursery was here, and Mrs. Whittle's bedchamber was on the same floor.

The rest of the servants, including the butler, were relegated to rooms in the attic.

As soon as she reached the nursery floor, Gabrielle's tension eased. Now all she had to do was put on a good show for Mrs. Whittle, and then she could retire to the privacy of her bed.

She scratched lightly on the door of the nursery to warn the housekeeper she was outside, and eased it open.

Mrs. Whittle was sitting beside the unlit hearth in a shabby chair, her head resting against one of its wings. A light snore issued from her mouth as Gabrielle closed the door.

Gabrielle smiled, put the lamp down on the table, and started to unbutton her pelisse. She turned to hang it up, and when she turned back, she discovered Mrs. Whittle's eyes were open and she was smiling expectantly.

"You're home," the housekeeper said softly. "I knew you wouldn't be much longer. Did you have a good time?"

"It was *wonderful*." Gabrielle untied her bonnet strings. "I danced *three* dances." She took a few light steps across the room, arms positioned as if she was dancing another cotillion.

"Three dances?" Mrs. Whittle repeated, her expression alight with interest. "Who with?"

"One was with Sinbad," Gabrielle said. "And...and Jack the Giant Killer." Her voice caught, and she looked away.

"Jack the Giant Killer?" Mrs. Whittle leaned forward. "Oh, you mean a man who went as Jack. Do you know who he really is?"

"Um...it was Quin," Gabrielle admitted.

Mrs. Whittle nodded with satisfaction. "Very good. Did he live up to your memories of him?"

"Yes." Gabrielle hoped the lantern light was obscuring the burning intensity of her blush. "And he recognized me! Just from the tilt of my head as I walked across the orchard."

"He saw you walk across the orchard?" Mrs. Whittle said quizzically.

"He saw me climb in over the wall, but first he thought I was a lady burglar," Gabrielle explained. "I expect he was waiting for me to steal something before he apprehended me—but then he recognized me even in my mask."

She danced another few deliberately buoyant steps, focusing

on a happy part of the evening, not on her sad realization at the end of it.

"From all you've told me about him, he's a very observant gentleman," Mrs. Whittle said. "And he's known you for years. It must be gratifying to know he was able to recognize you so easily."

"It is—but I hope Lady Henderson didn't recognize me from the tilt of my head." Gabrielle felt a renewed flicker of worry.

Mrs. Whittle gave a genteel snort. "I doubt it. Unless she fell over you, she'd have no reason to pay any particular attention to you."

"I hope not." Gabrielle dropped onto the dining chair by the table. "One poor lady *did* fall over. She must have been mortified. I felt so badly for her. But Lord Appledrum intervened and of course he managed everything in the most kindly, good-humored way."

"I've heard Lord Appledrum is a true gentleman," Mrs. Whittle said. "But what of his son? Now that Lord Hanwell has returned from his travels, do you judge his character to be as refined as his powers of observation?"

"Yes," Gabrielle said without hesitation. "Quin is the same as he was—but also…also *more*. More experienced, confident, stronger. He climbed the rigging every day."

"Hmm." Mrs. Whittle hummed dubiously. "That's an odd thing for a marquess's son to do. Are you sure he hasn't developed eccentric tendencies? I mean, in addition to his existing eccentricities."

"He's not eccentric!" Gabrielle said, indignant on Quin's behalf. "He's a scientist. He explained that climbing the rigging was a good way to maintain his physical condition during the long weeks at sea. Has Charlotte woken?"

"No. I peeked in on her a couple of times and she was always sleeping soundly." Mrs. Whittle pushed herself up from the chair. "Well, we should both get to bed before too much longer. I've left you a few slices of bread and butter in case you're hungry." She gestured to a covered plate on the table.

"Thank you," Gabrielle said. "Oh, thank you for helping me to go to the ball." She put her arms around the housekeeper and hugged her tightly.

"You deserved to spend one night dancing." Mrs. Whittle patted her back. "Now eat your supper and go to bed or you'll have trouble keeping your eyes open tomorrow."

"I will," Gabrielle promised, even though she knew sleep would be a long time coming after she laid her head on her pillow. "Oh, I'm sorry, the broom is still in the ballroom, under one of the chairs. I forgot all about it until this minute."

Mrs. Whittle laughed softly.

"Don't worry about that," she said. "I don't think Sally would like it if she had to bend nearly double to sweep the floors. Good night, mademoiselle."

Chapter Twelve

Breakfast in Lord Appledrum's household took place earlier than was fashionable among the upper ranks of society—even the morning after he'd played host to a grand ball. But when Quin entered the breakfast room, his father was the only one present.

"Duncan has already eaten and gone out, and Alfred hasn't appeared yet," Lord Appledrum said cheerfully. "Of course, he was the only one of the three of you who actually attended my wonderful masquerade ball for its full duration. It's not surprising he's tired this morning."

"I would have stayed, but I was being a gentleman," Quin said. "What was Duncan's excuse? Now I come to think of it, I don't recall seeing him in the ballroom at all." Even though most of Quin's attention had been on Gabrielle, he was sure he'd have noticed his friend's Minotaur mask towering above the heads of the other guests, if Duncan had been present.

Lord Appledrum grinned. "Duncan apprenticed himself to the confectioner for the evening."

"What?" Quin paused in the act of spooning some scrambled egg onto his plate to give his father an incredulous look. "Duncan doesn't know anything about confectionery—does he?" Was this an additional interest his friend hadn't mentioned during their three-year voyage?

"Presumably he knows more now than he did before he began his apprenticeship," Lord Appledrum said. "In any event, the confectioner seemed pleased with his assistance. Good morning, Miss Trent." He smiled as the housekeeper came into the breakfast room.

"Good morning, my lords," she replied, smiling at both of them. "Are you discussing the ball?"

"Yes, come and sit down," Lord Appledrum said. "I'll pour you a cup of coffee."

Miss Trent hesitated, throwing a quick glance at Quin. He smiled and waved her forward because he had a mouthful of toast. "Yes, come and join us," he said, as soon as he'd swallowed.

He'd been a little surprised when he'd first returned home and discovered Agnes often sat down at the breakfast table with his father, though she never ate, and only occasionally accepted a cup of coffee. She hadn't joined them at breakfast before Quin's departure with the expedition but, in his opinion, the change in routine was a welcome one.

Agnes had played an important part in the household for as long as Quin could remember. Twenty-one years ago, Lord Appledrum had walked into the nursery to find his son's real nurse, Bridget, dozing by the fire. Agnes, meanwhile, had abandoned her true, menial chores to help Quin arrange his collection of interesting leaves and berries.

Another man might have berated both servants for failing to carry out their designated duties, but Lord Appledrum wasn't most men. He'd immediately appointed Agnes to be assistant nursemaid, and the new arrangement had pleased everyone, including Bridget. The older woman had previously been nurse to Lord Appledrum's late wife. She'd cared for Quin, but she'd found it difficult to look after the energetic little boy. She'd also been bewildered, and sometimes horrified, by his fascination with the natural world.

Fifteen-year-old Agnes, on the other hand, had thrown herself into her new responsibilities with enthusiasm, undaunted by the challenge of managing a curious, adventurous child.

Quin had many happy memories of exploring the Appledrum estates with Agnes by his side. She'd plucked him up from muddy puddles when he'd fallen down, cleaned his scraped knees, been delighted by every new discovery he brought her— and made sure he never ate anything they hadn't clearly identified was edible.

Lord Appledrum had often accompanied them on those explorations. And when the time had come for him to hire a tutor for his son, he'd decreed Agnes should also receive lessons. So the future marquess and the nursemaid had learned the basics of reading, writing and arithmetic together.

Agnes had embraced her lessons as eagerly as Quin. She'd turned out to be extremely good at numbers and fascinated with the practical application of arithmetic.

Quin could still remember the occasion his father had given

Agnes his household account book, so she could see a real example of what she was learning. Agnes had studied the book for several hours—and then astonished Lord Appledrum by pointing out several discrepancies. Discrepancies which had led to the discovery that the house steward had been stealing a little every month for years.

"Miss Trent, you're just in time to hear how Lord Hanwell followed a mystery guest in from the garden last night," Lord Appledrum informed Agnes. There was a gleam of humor in his eyes when he glanced at Quin, but he didn't actually break into his familiar grin.

"You *did* know it was Gabrielle!" Quin exclaimed. "I was sure you must have when you approached her so determinedly."

"Ah, no," Lord Appledrum confessed. "Not when I first saw her sneak in round the curtain. There are a lot of visitors to Brighton who stay in the boarding houses and go to public assemblies. No doubt quite a few of them would like to attend a private ball. When I first saw Cinderella, I suspected she was a particularly enterprising young lady from such a background."

"Were you intending to throw her out?" Quin asked.

"Not necessarily. Gabrielle wasn't the only guest last night who hadn't been invited," Lord Appledrum revealed. "The masquerade ball was a triumphant success—in my opinion."

"Because you had uninvited guests?" Quin would never understand some of the things that gave his father pleasure.

Lord Appledrum grinned. "Tell us about Gabrielle," he ordered. "Before her arrival, I was half-convinced I would find you at dawn, still scouring the garden borders for some hitherto unknown species."

Quin flushed guiltily. "I would have come in after I'd finished watching the moth on the honeysuckle."

Lord Appledrum's grin softened. "I missed you when you were traveling. No one else would make such a comment to me at the breakfast table, or anywhere else, for that matter."

"Duncan probably would," Quin said, but he knew it was the first part of his father's remark which was the most important. He'd missed his home, his family and Gabrielle too while he was away. At times, he'd been achingly homesick for all of them.

But the excitement of his adventures and new discoveries had occupied most of his thoughts and his energy. For those waiting at home for him, it must have been different.

"I am fortunate indeed that you're my father," he said.

"You certainly are," Lord Appledrum agreed. "What prompted that announcement?"

"You could have refused your permission for me to take part in such a long, hazardous expedition," Quin said, knowing it was true. Most men in Lord Appledrum's position would not want their only son and heir disappearing on a journey into little known territories for an unknown length of time.

"You were of age when you left," his father countered.

"But you paid for my place on the ship," Quin said. "And gave your full support to the enterprise. No man could have a better father."

Lord Appledrum blinked, and then picked up his coffee cup to take a couple of sips. "Thank you," he said, a few moments later as he lowered the cup. "No man could have a better son."

His sincere words brought a lump to Quin's throat and for a

while silence reigned in the room as father and son concentrated on eating their breakfasts, and Agnes quietly drank her coffee.

If Quin had looked at her closely, he'd have noticed her eyes were shinier than usual, and a small smile played on her lips. But he was too busy cutting his ham into precise pieces to pay attention to anything else.

"Gabrielle!" Lord Appledrum suddenly exclaimed. "We're still on tenterhooks to hear more about her. How did she get in? I had all the gates except the front entrance locked, because a masquerade ball always seems to be an irresistible temptation for some people to sneak in uninvited."

"She borrowed a ladder from the hay makers to climb over the orchard wall," Quin replied. "I saw her, but she was already wearing her mask, and I only recognized her when she was walking across the orchard away from me. When did you realize who she was?"

"When you both lit up like small suns in my ballroom while I was introducing you," Lord Appledrum said. "We could have doused all the candles in the chandeliers and still had enough light to see by."

"No." Quin was taken aback. "It's true Gabrielle was dazzling. I wasn't."

Lord Appledrum laughed. "You were quivering like a hound who's seen the hare and is desperate to be free of the leash."

Quin's jaw dropped. He closed his mouth and swallowed. "I believe I conducted myself appropriately at the ball," he said stiffly. "In point of fact, I was not the first to speak after you left us alone. It was Gabrielle." Then he wondered whether, in trying to counter his father's description of himself, he'd shown

Gabrielle in a less than flattering light. "As you know, she's far more at ease at such events than I am."

"I presume she found a way to attend the ball, because she saw your notice about the wolf in the newspaper," Agnes said. "She knew you wanted to see her."

"Yes. It was very brave of her. She's as brave and kind and generous as ever." Quin's throat constricted. Her reason for not marrying him and her final 'goodbye' rang in his memory, almost over-setting his resolution to find a way forward.

He stared at the tablecloth, trying to bring his unruly emotions back under his control.

"What's wrong?" Lord Appledrum asked quietly.

"She said 'no'," Quin replied.

"No?" Lord Appledrum repeated. "To what?"

"Marrying me." Quin didn't lift his gaze, but he heard his father's intake of breath, and sensed Agnes move. From the corner of his eye, he saw her lay her hand over his father's hand.

"Did she give you a reason?" Lord Appledrum asked.

"It would break Charlotte's heart."

"Who…?"

"The little girl Gabrielle cares for," Agnes answered his father's question.

"This is not what I was expecting," Lord Appledrum said, after several seconds had passed. "You must know that both Gabrielle's father and I would welcome a union between you."

"The duke mustn't order her to go against her conscience," Quin insisted. "That would be cruel. I think…I believe her decision is breaking her heart too."

"But a child's heart is a more fragile thing," Lord Appledrum said.

"Yes." Quin finally looked up, and saw a composure-shattering degree of understanding in his father's eyes.

He glanced away again and noticed Agnes's hands were now folded together before her on the table. Had he imagined her reaching out to his father a few moments ago?

"I need to know more about the Hendersons," he said. "You told me almost the moment I set foot in England again that Gabrielle isn't permitted to correspond with anyone except her papa and brother. Last night, Gabrielle told me that Lady Henderson wouldn't tolerate her daughter's governess being betrothed to an earl—even a courtesy earl. And that if Gabrielle and I marry, Lady Henderson will never let Charlotte see her again."

"Spiteful, self-defeating behavior." Lord Appledrum stabbed his knife into the butter. "She would be better off befriending the future Marchioness of Appledrum, not turning all of us into her enemies."

"You don't have enemies, sir." Quin was honestly startled by the venom in his usually affable father's tone.

"I don't have many." Lord Appledrum frowned at the butter dish. "I'm sorry, Miss Trent. I've made this look like a plowed field."

"Never mind, my lord. We'll use it to make your favorite fruit cake," Agnes said.

"Rewarded for my temper tantrum. I'll spread some on my toast now." Lord Appledrum suited actions to words. "You want to learn what I know about Lord and Lady Henderson—and my opinions?"

"Yes, please."

"Let's begin with Lady Henderson. I don't like her," Lord Appledrum said bluntly. "She's the daughter of a City merchant who bought a bankrupt viscount to be her husband—"

Agnes sat up straighter, and subtle signs of tension appeared at the corners of her mouth.

"It's not Lady Henderson's birth I object to, Miss Trent," Lord Appledrum said quickly. "It's her behavior. When she first entered society, she was thrilled by her newly elevated status. But as time has passed, she seems to have come to the view that she made a bad bargain by settling for a viscount. But it was too late for her to marry a duke, so she tried to push Henderson into taking a more active part in politics."

"Why? Oh." Quin understood what his father meant. "She wanted Henderson to be rewarded for his services to the country with an earldom."

"At the very least." Lord Appledrum nodded. "But Henderson's not interested in politics, he's obsessed with returning his estates to their former prosperity. So Lady Henderson's machinations on his behalf came to nothing, and now they're rarely seen together. I don't know where he is at present, but it's not Brighton."

"Why did you invite her to your ball?" Quin asked. "Gabrielle was anxious when she found herself dancing in the last set with her. I hope she didn't recognize Gabrielle."

"I'm sure she didn't," Lord Appledrum assured him. "She

was far too busy flirting with Stallmouth—who attended in the character of Sir Lancelot."

"Did they remain in the supper room?" Quin asked. He assumed Gabrielle would have recognized Lady Henderson's voice if she'd been one of the lovers they'd heard over the wall, but he wouldn't mind more certainty on the matter.

"Yes. The flirtation continued somewhat more discreetly after they unmasked," Lord Appledrum said. "I invited Lady Henderson because it would have drawn more attention if I hadn't, considering which members of society are currently here in Brighton. Also, it seemed impolitic to snub the employer of the young woman I anticipated might soon be my daughter-in-law."

Quin forced a smile and let out a long breath.

"Charlotte didn't speak for several months before Gabrielle became her governess," he said. "And it took weeks before she talked to Gabrielle. The death of her nurse seems to be the precipitating event. But even severe grief doesn't usually lead to silence—does it?" He looked at his companions.

"If it caused an extreme lowering of the mood, perhaps," Lord Appledrum said slowly. "I've known of people falling into such a dark and melancholy state of mind they can barely rouse themselves to do anything. Children are as capable of feeling intense emotions as adults, so...perhaps?"

Quin nodded, adding his father's observation to his store of information. "I was thinking fear, not melancholy," he said. "I don't like the idea of Gabrielle living in a place of fear—but she assured me she doesn't feel unsafe in the Hendersons' household.

Just beset by petty rules." He glanced at the clock on the mantelpiece.

"What are you planning?" Lord Appledrum seemed to come to a new level of alertness.

"How do you know I'm planning anything?" Quin asked curiously. "I only checked the time."

"I'm your father. I know the expression you wear when you're weaving plans in your head."

"I have been making some plans," Quin admitted. "Which, in the future, may principally depend upon Miss Trent's assistance?"

Agnes smiled and nodded.

"But my plan for this morning depends upon your help, Father."

Lord Appledrum's eyes gleamed with anticipation. "I'm always willing to be of assistance to my dashing, but thoughtful, son. What do you require of me?"

Chapter Thirteen

"I see a ship," Charlotte said in French.

"I can see a seagull," Gabrielle replied in the same language.

They were standing side-by-side in front of the railing that ran along the cliff-side of Marine Parade, looking out across the beach below.

"I see ladies." Charlotte gripped the top railing and peered down. Two females were walking unsteadily over the pebbles toward a bathing machine.

"I can see them too." Gabrielle noticed that one of the ladies didn't appear enthusiastic about the prospect of being dunked in the sea. A reluctance Gabrielle entirely understood.

She and Charlotte watched as the ladies climbed up a short ladder and entered the bathing machine by the rear door. As soon as they were inside, an attendant closed the door and removed the steps.

At the attendant's shout, the bathing machine began to

trundle forward. It was being pulled into the sea by a horse which would be unhitched when the surface of the water was level with the floor of the hut. The tide was high this morning, so the bathing machine didn't have to travel too far.

Two fully dressed women were already standing waist deep in the sea, waves buffeting their braced bodies. It was their job to hold on to the lady bathers when they emerged from the front door and 'dip' them in the sea. That was Brighton's famous sea bathing cure, and the sturdy women standing in the water were Brighton's almost equally famous 'Dippers'.

"I wonder what it's like to go in the sea?" Charlotte said in English.

"Chilly, I should think, judging by the shrieks we sometimes hear," Gabrielle replied, her thoughts flashing back to her own nerve-wracking crossing of the Channel in the fishing boat. Sea bathing didn't appeal to her any more today than it had on the morning of her arrival.

After Mrs. Whittle had left the previous night, Gabrielle had checked on Charlotte and found her charge sleeping soundly. Relieved her brief absence had caused the little girl no distress, Gabrielle had climbed into her own bed, but she hadn't slept at all.

She hadn't allowed herself to cry aloud in case her sobs disturbed Charlotte, but tears had filled her eyes and constricted her throat.

She'd curled on her side and tried to accept that she and Quin couldn't be together for the foreseeable future. Perhaps never, because he had a duty to set up his own nursery, now he'd returned from his travels. Even though he wanted to marry her, he might feel obliged to marry another lady to help him carry out his family duty.

That possibility hurt so badly she almost wished she hadn't gone to the masquerade—and hadn't stirred up her longings for things she couldn't have. She'd been so careful over the past two years not to dwell on what she'd lost, and to count her blessings for what she did have. Now she must start the process all over again.

"I see the blue sky," she said in French. "It has no clouds in it."

"I see a blue sky too," Charlotte replied, in her surprisingly deep voice. "It is a sunny morning."

"Yes, it is. Let's sit on the bench and talk about what we saw yesterday," Gabrielle said.

"I'd rather talk about what we might see tomorrow," Charlotte replied.

"We can do both," Gabrielle said. "As long as we do it in French."

Charlotte heaved a theatrical sigh. "All right. But will you draw three pictures for me this afternoon?"

"If you talk in French until that shadow has moved from there to there, I will draw three pictures for you," Gabrielle agreed.

She'd had a beautiful little timepiece in France, but it had been left behind in their precipitate flight. Now, when she was out of the house, she relied on the movement of the sun, shadows on the ground or sundials to indicate the passing time. In truth, she rarely had a need for more precision.

"If we talk until the shadow is *there*, will you draw *four* pictures for me?" Charlotte bargained.

Gabrielle laughed at the mischievous twinkle in the little girl's eyes. The sight of Charlotte's cheerful expression made her heart swell with love. It had taken many, many months for Charlotte's sense of humor to emerge. Even now, she was inclined to be silent and watchful in many situations.

"If you talk in French for the rest of the morning." Gabrielle accepted the bargain.

Charlotte nodded. They both turned so their backs were to the sea and they were looking across Marine Parade toward the Steine. The Steine was an open area, something like a park or a town square, which served as a fashionable meeting place for Brighton's visitors.

On the west side of the Steine, to Gabrielle and Charlotte's left, they could see the Castle Hotel and Tavern. Public Assemblies were held at the Castle every Monday evening during the Season. Further ahead, also on the left, was the Prince of Wales's famous domed Pavilion, while Donaldson's library was located on the right side of the Steine.

By the afternoon, the paths crisscrossing the grassy area would be full of elegantly dressed visitors enjoying their daily promenade. But this early in the morning there were more gulls than people to be seen.

The Marine Parade was the thoroughfare which ran along the Brighton seafront from west to east. Its route took it past the oldest part of the town, the bottom of the Steine, the new houses on the right of the Steine, and then up onto the sea cliffs on the east side of Brighton.

Gabrielle didn't usually walk too far east along Marine Parade, because the beach below the east cliffs was where the bathing machines reserved for gentlemen were located.

Now that Britain and France were at war, several army regiments camped outside Brighton during the summer. The officers and men often bathed in the sea, and they didn't always confine their activities to being tamely dunked under the waves by the bathing machine attendants.

Gabrielle had seen several men swimming some distance from the protection of the wheeled huts. Inevitably, there were occasions when they behaved in ways which would not be appropriate in a lady's drawing room. Since Gabrielle always walked alone with Charlotte, she'd quickly deemed it best to avoid that stretch of Marine Parade.

"I see our favorite bench," Charlotte said in French. "No one is sitting on it. We will sit on it."

"Very good," Gabrielle praised her as they crossed the road. Initially, she'd started giving Charlotte simple language lessons as an undemanding way to keep the little girl talking. She hadn't expected her idea to be so successful.

"I see a..." had quickly become Charlotte's favorite game, and she could remember an astonishing number of French nouns. After a while she'd wanted to learn how to say different sentences, so Gabrielle had expanded the lessons. She hadn't yet begun to teach Charlotte to read and write in French, but she intended to do so soon.

"I see the horizon and the white fence. The white fence stops us from falling down the cliff," Charlotte said, once they were sitting on the bench.

"Yes, I'm very glad it's there," Gabrielle agreed. A light breeze blew across the cliff top, tugging at her skirt. She smoothed it down and tucked some of the excess material under her thighs to prevent it fluttering up. She enjoyed being in Brighton and coming out to look at the sea, but there were times when the sea breezes could be inconvenient.

"I see two gentlemen," Charlotte said. "I see two gentlemen walking. I see two gentlemen walking *toward us*!" she finished triumphantly.

"Very—" Gabrielle began, lifting her head.

The instant she saw the gentlemen in question, every thought vanished from her head.

It was Quin and Lord Appledrum striding toward them along Marine Parade. They were both handsome, energetic men, but Gabrielle had eyes only for Quin.

His gaze met hers, his eyes devouring every aspect of her appearance as eagerly as she was studying him. She'd seen his face briefly in the candlelight last night, but he'd only seen her in the moonlight. No wonder he was so intent on looking at her—and he liked what he saw!

Pleasure illuminated his countenance.

An answering smile sprang to her lips. The invisible clouds which had been obscuring the sun disappeared. Now, instead of just telling herself it was a beautiful summer day, she *knew* it was.

"They are tall!" Charlotte said in French. *"Oh!"* she emitted a small squeak as Quin and the marquess came to a halt in front of the bench.

Both men smiled down at her. She edged closer to Gabrielle when Lord Appledrum addressed her directly.

"Our friend Lord Duncan is taller," he said in a friendly tone. "He's six feet five inches tall. That's five inches taller than me." He raised his high-crowned hat and put his free hand on top of his head, palm facing forward with his thumb against his hair. He wiggled the little finger of his gloved hand to demonstrate those extra inches.

Charlotte's mouth fell open, and she stopped trying to move nearer to Gabrielle. "Is he a *giant*?" she gasped.

"It sometimes seems so." Lord Appledrum smiled. "But he's a very kind, well-mannered giant."

"He's a botanist and a doctor," Quin said mildly. During his father's description of their friend, he'd managed to drag his gaze away from Gabrielle and adopt a composed expression suitable for regular social encounters. "Duncan is a tall *botanist*," he repeated. "But he's certainly very kind and well-mannered."

Lord Appledrum's smile widened into a grin. "My son prefers precision over poetic fancy," he explained to Charlotte. As he was speaking, his gaze shifted from her to Gabrielle and his eyes widened in apparent surprise.

"Mademoiselle Rousselle!" he exclaimed. "Is it...? Yes, surely it *is* you. How do you do, mademoiselle?"

"Very well, thank you, my lord," Gabrielle said, with as much serenity as she could muster. Like Quin, she'd tried to regain her equilibrium during the distraction created by Lord Appledrum's description of his tall friend. "I trust all is well with you also?"

"Excellently well, thank you," Lord Appledrum replied immediately. "Let me see. It must be two years since I last had the pleasure of speaking to you. But I recall your father telling me you're now a governess."

"Yes, I am," Gabrielle said, grateful for his verbal cue. Her thoughts were flying all over the place. She very much wanted to look at Quin again. Surely he was responsible for this outwardly chance encounter? She was thrilled to see him again so soon—but worried about how Lady Henderson would react if she found out.

She took refuge in the etiquette of introductions. "My lord, may I present to you Miss Charlotte Sedgemore, the daughter of Lord and Lady Henderson," she said. "Charlotte, this is the Marquess of Appledrum."

"Good morning, Miss Sedgemore, it's a pleasure to make your acquaintance." Lord Appledrum raised his hat again and bowed his head politely toward Charlotte.

Charlotte stared at him wide-eyed for a few seconds. Then a tiny smile appeared on her lips, and she slid off the bench. She dropped into a deep, somewhat wobbly curtsy and came up speaking.

"Good morning, my lord," she said. "Marquesses are more important than viscounts. That's why I must curtsy *very* low to you. My father is a viscount. Our surname is not the same as his title, which is why my name is not the same as his. It's confusing."

Gabrielle stared at Charlotte in astonishment. She'd never heard the little girl say so much at once to anyone she didn't know. What magic had Lord Appledrum wrought to elicit such a loquacious reply?

Charlotte had repeated information every young lady was supposed to know when entering society. Gabrielle had discussed it with her, but she'd never intended Charlotte to explain it all out loud the first time she was introduced to a gentleman. Fortunately, Lord Appledrum didn't look either startled or amused.

"I don't tend to stand on ceremony," he said. "But you're right, titles are confusing. My surname and title are different, too. To make things even more muddlesome, I have more than one title, so it's customary for my oldest son and heir to use one of them. This is my son, Lord Hanwell. Harlequin, my boy, allow me to present Miss Charlotte Sedgemore."

"Are you a marquess too?" Charlotte peered up at Quin.

"No, I'm the Earl of Hanwell," Quin replied.

"An earl comes between a marquess and a viscount." Charlotte nodded with evident satisfaction at being able to properly categorize him. "That's right, because you shouldn't be more important than your papa." She gave Quin a slightly less deep curtsy than she'd given his father.

Gabrielle saw Quin's lips twitch, as if he was trying not to laugh, but then he glanced at his father and gave Lord Appledrum a slight nudge with his elbow as he directed a meaningful gaze at her.

"Oh, my apologies, Mademoiselle Rousselle," the marquess said, an unmistakable twinkle in his eyes. "I've been remiss in completing my introductions. May I present to you my son? As we've already established, he's the Earl of Hanwell. Harlequin, this is Mademoiselle Gabrielle Rousselle. She's the daughter of one of my oldest friends, the Duke de la Fontaine. You may remember we were frequently his guests in France several years ago?"

"I do indeed remember." Quin lifted his hat to Gabrielle, and stepped forward, holding out his hand. "It's a pleasure to meet you again, mademoiselle."

"It's a pleasure for me also, my lord," Gabrielle said breathlessly, taking the hand he offered her. He squeezed her fingers and smiled into her eyes, and she was so happy she felt almost lightheaded.

Quin didn't say anything else, just held her hand for longer than courtesy required, and she couldn't think of another word to say. At least, not in the present circumstances. But if they'd been alone, she'd have had *so much* to say.

"So, you're practicing your French, eh?" Lord Appledrum asked Charlotte.

Quin started almost imperceptibly, reddened, released Gabrielle's hand and stepped back.

"It sounds to me as if you have a good accent," Lord Appledrum continued speaking to Charlotte. "You must be a rewarding pupil for Mademoiselle Rousselle to teach. Do—"

A feminine scream pierced the morning air.

Alarm speared through Gabrielle. She leaped up from the bench.

Quin and Lord Appledrum reacted even faster. Both men pivoted and rushed to the railings, seeking to locate the frightened woman who'd cried out.

Quin arrived slightly ahead of his father. He already had one hand on the fence post, about to vault over, when Lord Appledrum gripped his arm.

"It's all right. There's no need for you to scramble down to the beach," the marquess said. "The lady is scared, but she's not drowning. The dippers have her safely in their care."

Her heart still racing, Gabrielle peered down at the tableau in front of the bathing machine. It did indeed seem as if there was no cause for serious alarm, though the lady bather looked even more bedraggled than was customary. Her hair straggled around her shoulders in a very woebegone way. She was clinging to the two dippers, and sounds of her coughing reached them on the cliff top.

"She's safe. We'll not intrude upon her discomfort anymore." Lord Appledrum turned his back on the beach.

"Why did she scream so loudly?" Charlotte asked, her eyes huge and her voice a little wobbly. "They don't usually do that. Did a fish in the water *bite* her?"

"No." Lord Appledrum smiled down at Charlotte. "The lady can't see well, and she usually wears spectacles. Unfortunately, they were broken yesterday morning. But even if she still had them, I daresay she wouldn't wear them to bathe. I imagine not having a clear view of the oncoming waves made the whole experience of being in the sea more alarming for her."

"You *do* know everyone, sir!" Quin exclaimed.

"I've only recently made this lady's acquaintance,' Lord Appledrum replied. "She was the one who tripped up during a cotillion last night. I don't think she meant to dance, but then Percy Dashthorpe pulled her out onto the floor. It wasn't her fault she fell. I doubt she could see well at all between her missing spectacles and the mask over her face."

"Poor lady." Charlotte looked over her shoulder. "I think she should come out of the water now."

"She has," Quin said. "She's safely back in the bathing machine. How do you know her spectacles were broken, sir?"

"Ah." A smile tweaked Lord Appledrum's lips. "I've heard a rumor that a small person sitting on a runaway donkey shouting 'tallyho' could have been involved. Possibly. Marcus has already made arrangements for the spectacles to be replaced."

"A small person?" Quin stared at his father. "You mean Nancy? *Nancy* broke the lady's spectacles?"

"No, no," Lord Appledrum said. "The lady's brother pulled her out of the way of the donkey. In the confusion, her spectacles fell off and tumbled over the railings. Nancy happened to be sitting on the back of the donkey at the time, shouting 'tally-ho'—according to your aunt, who was an eyewitness to the incident. Marcus wasn't there."

"Nancy is a little girl?" Charlotte asked.

"Yes, she's my great-niece," Lord Appledrum said. "She's a few years younger than you."

"Oh." Charlotte's focus on the marquess was so unwavering it might have daunted a lesser man. Lord Appledrum remained at his ease and smiled.

Gabrielle looked at Quin and discovered he was gazing at her as intently as Charlotte was gazing at the marquess. Her heart yearned for him. Seeing him this morning when she'd been steeling herself not to see him again for months—if not years—was a bittersweet joy. Why had he engineered this meeting? What could come of it beyond an opportunity for him to meet Charlotte for himself?

"What happened after Nancy made the lady's spectacles fall down the cliff?" Charlotte asked Lord Appledrum.

"I believe her brother climbed down to retrieve them—and

discovered they were broken. And then everyone went home to have a calming cup of tea," he replied.

Charlotte's brows drew down. "What happened to *Nancy*?" she asked gruffly.

"I think she probably had a cup of milk or barley water instead of tea," Lord Appledrum replied.

Charlotte's frown became more noticeable.

"You mean, what punishment did she receive?" Lord Appledrum interpreted her expression.

Charlotte responded with a tiny dip of her chin.

"Her Uncle Marcus told her it wasn't ladylike to shout 'tallyho' and gallop along Marine Parade, and asked her not to do it again," Lord Appledrum said. "But he did accept some of the blame. Apparently, he often says 'tallyho' himself when they're riding together through the fields. Unfortunately, he'd neglected to explain to Nancy that she shouldn't do the same when she's riding a donkey through Brighton."

Charlotte's lips parted until her mouth formed a circle to match her wide eyes.

"Lessons were learned by all," Lord Appledrum said. "Charlotte shouldn't have recklessly urged the donkey to go faster where pedestrians could be endangered—but one could also argue that someone should have been walking at the donkey's head, holding the leading rein."

Charlotte's mouth closed, but her attention remained locked on Lord Appledrum.

He glanced over the railing toward the bathing machine and then smiled at Charlotte. "The ladies are returning from their dip. We should walk on to give them privacy when they get up here, don't you think?"

Charlotte looked down at the beach. "They're wearing their bonnets and pelisses, but they might feel cold and shaky." She turned her head away. "We won't watch them. It might embarrass them."

"Good girl," Lord Appledrum said quietly. "Now, I must say, all this sea air and excitement has made me quite hungry. Do you like ice cream, Miss Sedgemore?"

Charlotte stared at him for a few seconds. Then she nodded slowly.

"Excellent, so do I. Let's all go and have some ice cream. Would you like to take my arm?" Lord Appledrum offered Charlotte his elbow.

She hesitated. "Like a grown-up lady?"

"Like a grown-up lady," he agreed.

She looked at his arm, and then up at Gabrielle, her uncertainty obvious.

Gabrielle smiled and nodded. Lord Appledrum simply waited patiently for Charlotte's decision.

At last, Charlotte moved to his side. She reached up to put her little hand through his arm, and the two of them began to stroll back into Brighton, leaving Gabrielle and Quin to follow behind.

Chapter Fourteen

Gabrielle looked at Quin. Her pulse was quick with anticipation—and a hint of something that wasn't quite nervousness. This was how she'd always felt the first time she saw him again after months apart, during the years before he'd left on his travels. Growing up in different countries had always imposed restrictions on how much time they could spend together.

She didn't understand why she was nervous this morning when their true reunion had occurred last night. But last night they'd only had the stars and moon by which to see—and now it was broad daylight. Did he think she'd changed? Did he like the changes?

"Do you like ice cream, mademoiselle?" Quin asked out loud, but his beautiful eyes were saying so much more.

She read affection in his expression, admiration—and simmering desire that reminded her of their moonlight kisses and barely checked passion for each other.

Her skin heated, but not with embarrassment—not when

she remembered Quin's second reason for showing restraint. He wanted to be sure that, when they made love, his performance would give *her* pleasure and satisfaction.

But standing here in the middle of Brighton, imagining Quin undressing her and stroking every inch of her skin, wouldn't do. She dragged her thoughts back to the question he'd just asked her.

"Very much," she said, "though I haven't had any for a long time."

Quin's pupils expanded, darkening his eyes.

"Ice cream, I mean," Gabrielle clarified breathlessly.

The last time she'd tasted the expensive treat had been when she was a guest at Lord Appledrum's Brighton house two years ago.

Quin released a breath. "Of course, ice cream. Shall we follow the others?"

She was about to take his arm when she was suddenly assailed by doubt.

"Gabrielle?" he said softly, his smile fading.

"People will see us this morning," she said. Even though there weren't many people about yet, there was bound to be at least one witness to her and Charlotte's encounter with Lord Appledrum and his son. "Gossip flows freely in Brighton."

"Father and I took a stroll along Marine Parade this morning and unexpectedly met the daughter of one of his old friends." Quin's ready and very reasonable reply suggested he'd anticipated her concern. "It would have been rude of you to give the Marquess of Appledrum the cut direct when he spoke to you."

"Yes, it would." Gabrielle laid her hand on Quin's sleeve,

rather than possessively claiming his arm as she'd done on their walk home last night. "And he spoke to Charlotte first—I've never heard her say so much to a stranger," she said wonderingly.

"She was certainly chattier than I expected," Quin said.

"Me too. She truly isn't usually so talkative." Gabrielle wondered if he believed she'd misled him about Charlotte.

"That's father's magic," Quin said. "He's always had a knack for talking to people."

They walked in silence for a few paces.

"Are you still of a mind that she must be your priority?" Quin asked.

"Yes." Gabrielle could barely force the words past her lips. "For now, at least. But I can't ask you to wait—"

He laid his hand over hers. "You waited for me when I went on my adventures. Encouraged me to make my dreams a reality, even though we all knew that my doing so imposed a high cost on those waiting at home. You lost your home. If I'd been here—"

"We're all safe." It was Gabrielle's turn to interrupt. "We can't rewrite the past."

"No, but we can influence the future. Are the Hendersons aware of our close friendship?" Quin asked. "We never announced a formal betrothal, and we spent more time together in France than England. Father isn't aware of any gossip or speculation about us since my return."

"I've never mentioned you to Lord or Lady Henderson," Gabrielle replied. "Mind you, I've barely spoken or even seen Lord Henderson. Charlotte knows about you, but only as Quin, not your title. She likes hearing about our childhood adventures. She...she becomes anxious if I talk about you coming home."

"I see." Quin said. "She sees me as a threat to her security."

Lord Appledrum and Charlotte were several yards ahead of them as they crossed the Steine.

At that moment, Charlotte looked over her shoulder at them. Gabrielle smiled and waved. Charlotte's expression relaxed into an answering smile, and she went back to chatting with Lord Appledrum.

"I would never deliberately harm a child," Quin said. "I will never ask you to go against your conscience. But I'm not content to say goodbye again for some undetermined length of time."

"I don't want to, either." Gabrielle's voice rose. She drew on all her mother's training to bring her appearance of outward composure back under her control. The emotions churning beneath the surface were not so manageable.

"In caring for their daughter, you're doing Lord and Lady Henderson a great kindness and service," Quin said. "She didn't speak to anyone for months, now she's handling social introductions with aplomb. Even curtsying to carefully calibrated depths."

"I didn't expect her to explain aloud how she was grading you," Gabrielle said ruefully. "I'll need to talk to her about that. But in such a way that she understands I'm not scolding her. It's awkward, because usually I'm trying to encourage her to speak."

"Neither father nor I were offended," Quin said. "From what you've told me, it sounds as if this was the first opportunity for her to put her training into practice. That can be an exciting, and possibly anxiety provoking, occasion. And lots of people, me included, get flustered when they're introduced to a duke, or a marquess, for the first time."

Despite her tumultuous feelings, Gabrielle smiled. "You've never been flustered by high-ranking individuals—you simply weren't at ease in formal social situations."

"Unfortunately, I haven't changed much in that respect," Quin confessed. "Marcus had to come and rescue me at the only ball I attended in London."

"From a duke?" Gabrielle blinked. "Your cousin *is* a duke."

"Yes, I know." Quin cleared his throat. "Anyway, Marcus rescued me from persons who aren't dukes. Then he advised me never to allow myself to be backed up against the wall again. And that's all we need to say on *that* subject. Except...I'm not going to any more balls if I can help it."

Gabrielle wanted to laugh *and* hug him. "My poor earl," she murmured. She couldn't even hug his arm in case anyone noticed her treating him with such familiarity.

"If you were with me, I'd be less daunted," he said. "Now, we must make plans for how we are to communicate over the next... little while."

"I don't know how little," she whispered. "It's hard. Last night I was full of brave resolve, now..." Her voice trembled.

The muscles beneath her fingertips turned to steel. "You choose me?"

"I want to. But I see how Charlotte depends on me...and...I... I can't abandon her." Gabrielle swallowed tears.

Quin's forearm didn't relax. "Then we must make our plans." His voice was uncharacteristically rough. "Someone helped you attend father's masquerade ball—your fairy godmother. I presume that person lives in the same household?"

"Mrs. Whittle, the housekeeper," Gabrielle said softly.

"Very good. You trusted her last night. Would you also trust her to assist us in writing privately to each other?" Quin asked.

Gabrielle's heart leaped at the idea of regularly corresponding with Quin. It would be a poor substitute for being in his company. Walking with him, talking with him—making love with him. When would that opportunity ever come again? She wondered if he was regretting his restraint in the hayfield.

But for years she'd had to make do with reading sporadic newspaper reports about the scientific expedition, and the latest news about Quin that Lord Appledrum had told her papa.

Compared to that, regularly receiving letters from him, written in his own hand, would be truly wonderful.

"I believe Mrs. Whittle would help us," she said. "But I don't want her to get in trouble on my behalf. Going out and moving a ladder for me is not the same as being caught facilitating a clandestine correspondence."

"It wouldn't need to be clandestine if your employer was less petty-minded," Quin said sharply. "You're not a housemaid trysting with the neighbor's footman," he continued in a more moderate tone. "And I'm not sure why that's viewed with such disapprobation if they are both of like mind and the man intends marriage."

"Some people won't employ a married footman," Gabrielle said.

"Ridiculous prohibition," Quin muttered. "Why should a

man be forced to choose between having a job or having a family?"

Gabrielle let out a breath. "Lady Henderson dismissed one of her footmen when she found out he's married. As far as I could tell, he was a good, hardworking man."

"Someone else in the household betrayed his secret?" Quin sounded grim. "We'll proceed with care to avoid arousing suspicion. Miss Trent has suggested she could correspond with Mrs. Whittle—one housekeeper to another—with our letters contained within theirs."

Gabrielle could tell he was unhappy with the situation. No matter how much Quin might believe a footman was entitled to have a family as much as any other man, he was still the son of a marquess. A proud, honorable man who was surely chafing at having to conduct himself like a dissembling rogue.

"I'm so sorry," she whispered.

"The blame is not yours." His voice softened. "I made you wait for me for years. I'm not so unreasonable that I can't now wait for you."

"Thank you," Gabrielle breathed.

"The most difficult part of being away from home for so long," he said, "was being unable to maintain a regular correspondence with everybody. Now I'm back in England I'll ensure I'm in frequent contact with everyone I care about."

The depth of feeling in his voice told Gabrielle that, however curious and adventurous his spirit, the bedrock of his life was his family. And she was part of it.

But there was no time left to exchange further personal confidences because they'd nearly caught up with Lord Appledrum and Charlotte.

The marquess had come to a halt outside a confectionery shop. But instead of entering, he waited in front of the window for Gabrielle and Quin to come level with him.

"See this, my boy!" Lord Appledrum pointed at the display inside. "This little garden is a small portion of the splendid landscape laid out for my guests last night."

Quin stepped closer, so Gabrielle went with him, and they both leaned nearer to the glass to study the pretty display behind it.

Two snow white swans swam on a tranquil lake created from smooth boiled sugar. There was a small waterfall of spun sugar, a bridge over a stream, and low green hills and trees to complete the centerpiece.

Gabrielle knew that everything in the charming little landscape was either created from sugar or, in the case of some of the trees, herbs encrusted with sugar.

"It's exquisite," she said sincerely, sorry she'd been unable to see the full display the previous evening. But that would have meant revealing her identity to all the other guests.

"Indeed it is," Lord Appledrum agreed. "And last night's display was *magnificent*! Miss Bianchetti and Duncan had to work very hard to get it ready in time."

"Duncan the Giant helped?" Charlotte stood on tiptoe to peer in.

"He helped with the display at the ball last night," Lord Appledrum said. "I don't suppose he had anything to do with this garden in the window.

"It's a lovely garden," Charlotte said. "Are the hills made of sugar, too?"

"I believe so," Lord Appledrum replied. "At least, the top layer. I don't know what's under the surface. Probably not cake, it would get terribly stale."

Charlotte nodded. "It would be nice to go there." She turned her head, her attention clearly caught by the large, gilt-edge card at the back of the display. "East …India Sugar," she read aloud slowly. "Not…made by slaves. What does that mean?"

"It means Miss Bianchetti and her family are supporting the sugar boycott," Lord Appledrum explained.

Charlotte peered up at him, her brows drawn down in a slight frown. "Boycott?" she repeated.

"Boycott means having nothing to do with something," Lord Appledrum clarified. "In this case, the sugar boycott was organized by people who want to end slavery. Supporting the boycott means not buying sugar made by slaves in the Caribbean plantations."

Gabrielle looked at the window display with new appreciation. The confectionery made by the Bianchetti family was likely to be more expensive than anything sold by confectioners who used the cheaper Caribbean sugar. They were making a brave business decision, as well as an ethical one. But the display in the window also advertised the high quality of their work. That excellence would enable them to charge higher prices—and attract the custom of wealthy, influential people, like Lord Appledrum.

"Now let's go in and sit down," he said. "Otherwise, Miss Bianchetti will think we're only gawkers, not proper customers."

"What's a gawker?" Charlotte asked.

"Someone who stares at someone or something rather rudely," he explained.

"But aren't we supposed to look in the window?" Charlotte said, as she walked through the door he held open for her. "Otherwise, why is it so pretty?"

"Yes, we are supposed to look at it," the marquess said. "And if we couldn't afford to buy anything, or if we were trying to decide whether we wanted to, it would be perfectly acceptable to walk on after a little while without going inside. But we do want to buy something—several somethings, in fact, which should please Miss Bianchetti."

It pleased Gabrielle too. Even though she knew it was superficial to care about such things, she was looking forward to enjoying her first ice cream in two years.

Chapter Fifteen

Quin followed the others into the confectionery shop, his thoughts and emotions consumed by his all-too brief conversation with Gabrielle.

He thoroughly disliked the situation in which they found themselves. But he also disliked the first way of improving it that had occurred to him. The socially ambitious Lady Henderson would likely grasp with both hands an invitation to one of the Dowager Duchess of Candervale's exclusive soirées.

But Quin recoiled from asking his aunt for that favor—and not only because it would put her in an uncomfortable position. The invitation would only serve a useful purpose if Lady Henderson understood she was expected to reciprocate for her entrance into the duchess's inner circle by allowing Gabrielle and Quin to correspond freely with each other.

Quin feared that revealing their courtship to Lady Henderson might result in her gaining more power to interfere in

Gabrielle's life, not less. That wasn't acceptable to him so, for now at least, subterfuge was their only option.

As the last person into the shop, he was about to close the door, when movement near his feet caught his eye. He looked down and watched a large cat pad around the door jamb and continue inside with all the aplomb of a king entering his castle.

Quin wondered if he'd inadvertently let in a stray. But the cat seemed too self-assured to be a stranger, so Quin shut the door and turned to study his new surroundings.

Despite the large window, it was not as bright inside the shop as it had been outside, but it was very inviting. Everything from the floorboards to the counter at the back of the shop was beautifully clean and polished. And where beams of sunlight did strike the wood, it glowed like rich honey.

The shop was large enough for a few tables and chairs to be set out in the middle of the floor. While stools in front of the counter offered seating for three more customers.

On top of the counter, there was an array of glass jars and bowls. Some of the jars contained preserved fruit, while the bowls displayed heaping treasure created by the magic of the confectioner's art. Quin knew the principal ingredient of the sweets was boiled sugar, but they glowed like jewels in an abundant variety of colors and shapes. He could see twists, ribbons and even bows among them.

The shop was as tantalizing to his sense of smell as it was to his eyes. He easily identified the delicate fragrances of rose, strawberry, peppermint, and many others. Quin didn't have a predilection for eating sweet food, but the aromas of those familiar plants immediately made him feel at home.

As soon as their party entered the shop, a young woman came forward. Her welcoming smile encompassed everyone, but she curtsied to Lord Appledrum. "Good morning, my lord."

"Good morning, Miss Bianchetti," he replied.

Quin studied Miss Bianchetti with what he hoped was discreet interest. She must be the young lady confectioner Duncan had apprenticed himself to last night.

Quin still hadn't had a chance to ask his friend how that had come about, but he was curious to know more. At first glance, he judged the confectioner to be in her middle twenties. In his opinion, her looks didn't hold a candle to Gabrielle's, but he supposed she was pretty. Despite her welcoming smile, she also looked tired.

"How are your sister and her new baby this morning?" Lord Appledrum asked.

Miss Bianchetti's smile brightened, and gratitude now illuminated her face. "They're both well. Sleeping when I looked in on them a few minutes ago. We're so grateful for your lordship's kindness—"

Lord Appledrum lifted a hand. "It was Miss Trent who made the arrangements. She'll be glad to hear that the mother and babe are well. And I hope *you'll* be glad to hear that your confections, and especially your marvelous landscape, received many compliments from my guests last night."

"Thank you, my lord!" The confectioner's cheeks went pink at his praise. "Though I'm afraid I wouldn't have been finished in time without Mr. Waring's help."

"I know he was happy to be of service to you," Lord Appledrum replied, without commenting on how she'd referred to Duncan.

Duncan hadn't used his courtesy title when he was the ship's doctor on HMS Wayfarer, so Quin was used to hearing his friend being called Mr. Waring. He was more curious to learn about whatever arrangements Agnes Trent had made for Miss Biachetti's sister—but he'd save his questions about that for later.

"Despite all the excitements of last night, you've opened your shop in fine order this morning," Lord Appledrum said. "Are we your first customers today?"

"Yes, my lord."

"Good," he said. "Then there is every chance you've not yet sold out of my favorite flavors, and those of my companions, of course. This is Miss Maria Bianchetti," he said, glancing around at Gabrielle, Quin and Charlotte.

"Miss Bianchetti, accompanying me today are Mademoiselle Gabrielle Rousselle, Miss Charlotte Sedgemore, and my son, Lord Hanwell. We would like to sit at the table in the window, if you please."

"Of course, my lord." Maria hurried to pull out a chair for him. She'd just turned toward him again, her hand on the chair back, when she suddenly looked across the room and her brows drew down in a frown.

"Zucchero," she said sharply. "No!"

Quin followed the direction of her gaze and saw her command had been given to the large cat who'd come in with them. It appeared the cat had been about to slip through the half-open door which led to the back of the shop, but Maria's order seemed to have done the trick—at least for now.

The cat sat down and began to lick a front paw, but Quin wasn't fooled nor, apparently, was Maria.

"Excuse me, my lord." She walked over to close the door firmly.

"I'm sorry," Quin said. "I'm afraid I'm the one who let him in."

She smiled at him, and he saw again the weariness behind her pleasant expression.

"There's no need to apologize, my lord," she assured him. "I should have made sure I closed the rear door properly. Zucchero *is* allowed in the shop, some of our customers are very fond of him. But he's not permitted upstairs in the hot and cold rooms. My father would be mortified if a customer found a cat hair in their jelly."

"I can't believe such a thing has ever happened," Lord Appledrum said.

"Not to my knowledge," Maria replied. "But we have to be vigilant at all times," she added with a wry smile.

Quin saw Charlotte tug Gabrielle's arm and then go up on tiptoe to whisper something. From the way her gaze was fixed on the cat, it wasn't hard to guess what she wanted.

"Miss Bianchetti, may Miss Sedgemore stroke Zucchero?" Gabrielle asked.

"Of course." Maria smiled at the little girl. "I'm sure he'd like that."

Charlotte immediately left Gabrielle's side to go and kneel on the floor by the cat, and soon his purr began to rumble around the shop.

The rest of them took their seats at the table. Quin sat next to his father, Gabrielle sat opposite him, while an empty chair awaited Charlotte.

Gabrielle's gaze met his, and he wished there wasn't a table between them. He wished they were alone, but that wouldn't be an option for an unknown length of time. On the other hand, the table wasn't wide, and he was a tall man.

He eased one booted leg forward, gently prospecting until his toe encountered an obstacle. An obstacle that twitched, retreated and then nudged him back.

Gabrielle's cheeks went pink. She lowered her gaze and threw him a reproving glance under her lashes, but she didn't pull her foot away.

Quin's blood surged with the desire to kiss her. He slid his other foot forward so he could capture her small foot between both of his. Her blush intensified. Their view of the empty street was partially impeded by the display shelves in the window, but Gabrielle pretended a profound interest in the lack of activity on the other side of the glass.

Quin was grateful the table concealed the evidence of his growing arousal. He'd never really flirted with Gabrielle before his travels, but this could be an entertaining pastime—if only it could culminate in a mutually satisfying conclusion.

Gabrielle met his gaze again. Her eyes sparkled, but he also detected a deeper concern than simply chiding him for his behavior. If they were officially betrothed, his subtle teasing might fluster her, but only until she could scold and kiss him in private.

But they weren't officially betrothed, and they were trying to make this encounter appear accidental. Gabrielle barely turned her head, but she flicked her gaze meaningfully in Charlotte's direction.

Quin realized his father and Miss Bianchetti couldn't see what he was doing beneath the table, but what if the child kneeling on the floor glanced in this direction?

Gabrielle tucked her feet back. Quin did the same.

"It's a pleasure to meet you again, Mademoiselle Rousselle," Lord Appledrum said blandly, as if he hadn't noticed the byplay between them. "Though, as you probably know, I fence regularly with your father when I'm in London."

"Yes, my lord," Gabrielle replied with almost equal composure. "He has often mentioned in his letters how much he enjoys and appreciates his practice sessions with you."

"That's because he usually wins," the marquess said, with unabated good humor. "Your brother is also developing into a very fair swordsman, but I'm glad to say he hasn't vanquished me yet."

"Felix?" Gabrielle's eyes lit up. "It's so long since I've seen him. Papa said he has grown taller."

"He has indeed," Lord Appledrum said, "though I don't believe he's reached his full height yet. I suspect he's going to surpass your father in that regard—as he correctly predicted my son would surpass me."

"In inches only, sir," Quin said. "In no other way can I surpass you."

Lord Appledrum laughed. "I concede it's unlikely you'll ever throw a better party than I do, but your height is not your only achievement where you've already surpassed me." His words were full of pride.

His father's praise always filled Quin with a deep sense of comfort and happiness. And even now, when he was frustrated by the uncertainty of his future with Gabrielle, his father's support was a dependable anchor in his life.

Maria appeared with their ice creams and jellies and Gabrielle quietly summoned Charlotte to take her seat at the table. From the way her eyes went round when she saw the contents of the delicate serving glass set in front of her, Quin guessed this was a treat she was rarely given at home.

Charlotte was now one of the most important people in his life but, so far, she'd conversed almost entirely with Lord Appledrum. Quin decided he ought to make an effort to engage her in conversation.

She was sitting diagonally to him, directly across from Lord Appledrum. He looked at her from the corner of his eye. He should probably let her enjoy some more of her ice cream before he spoke to her. He waited a few more minutes while Lord Appledrum and Gabrielle carried the conversation with an ease he didn't exactly envy—but he did think would be a useful talent to possess.

"Miss Sedgemore, do you have a cat of your own?" he asked, during a natural pause in the conversation.

Charlotte looked up from her ice cream and stared at him with a disturbingly blank expression. Her mouth remained firmly closed, though the tip of her tongue emerged to lick traces of cream from her inward curving lips. Her gaze wasn't hostile, but it was watchful.

She slowly shook her head.

"When I was a boy, I had a dog." Quin summoned a smile,

while every other conversation opener he could think of drained quickly from his head all the way down his body and out through the soles of his boots.

There was something fundamentally daunting about Charlotte's silence. His admiration and respect for Gabrielle's ability to win the child's affection soared higher. Along with a growing suspicion that Charlotte was wary of him in a way she wasn't with his father. Was that because she considered older men more trustworthy—or because she suspected he wanted to tear Gabrielle from her side?

"Erasmus and I—Erasmus was my dog—had many adventures together," he said. "We went on long walks in the countryside."

A flicker of interest sparked in Charlotte's eyes.

Quin picked the first humorous anecdote he could remember, and sweated through telling it in a way he hadn't when making his presentations a few days ago to the learned members of the Royal Society in London.

His efforts earned a small smile from Charlotte. "Mademoiselle and I like going for walks too. In London, we go for a walk in the garden in the middle of the square every morning."

"Grosvenor Square," Gabrielle murmured. "There's a fine selection of trees and shrubs between the paths. Plenty of places for wildlife to make a home."

"Mademoiselle means snails." Charlotte's gaze sharpened in an indefinable way. "Do you like snails, Lord Hanwell?"

Quin sensed a trap. "I'm interested in all aspects of the natural world," he said cautiously. "I confess, when I was a boy, I did have a collection of empty snail shells—" he broke off when Charlotte's face lit up.

"I've got one too." She patted her chest, but then her expression turned wary, as if she was anticipating disapproval.

"Some snail shells are extremely attractive," Quin said, "and very interesting to study."

Charlotte relaxed. "I think they are pretty. We have collected lots of nice ones, but we don't know the names of all of them, so we arrange them by size—except sometimes we can't tell if a small one is really a different kind, or a baby of a bigger one we've already got."

"Yes, that is the kind of complication that can arise when trying to categorize anything," Quin agreed. "But your current system makes sense. When I was in Africa, I saw snails as big as my hand. One of those shells might need a display box all of its own."

"As big as your hand?" Charlotte breathed, staring at Quin's hand.

He lowered his spoon into the dish, held up his hand for Charlotte's inspection and cupped his other over the top to give her a better sense of scale.

"As big as that?" Charlotte's eyes opened wide with wonder. "I wish I could see one."

Gabrielle shivered.

"Don't worry, mademoiselle." Charlotte patted her arm. "I wouldn't let it near you. Is it like our snails in everything except size?" she asked Quin. "Then it can't run as fast as us, mademoiselle. You'd be perfectly safe."

"I'm not very brave around snails—or slugs," Gabrielle

confessed. Quin already knew that, but he wasn't sure if his father did.

"I...ah...see that snail shells are preferable to the living creatures as collector's items," Lord Appledrum said. "No doubt a great deal can be learned from studying the shells. Also, speaking to the gardener may be helpful."

"The gardeners at Sedgemore Hall donated several fine specimens to Charlotte's collection," Gabrielle said. "All happily unoccupied."

"Sometimes it's hard to tell," Charlotte confided. "And when they wake up, we have to take them back outside."

Quin could *feel* Gabrielle cringing on the inside, even though she was outwardly composed and even managed a wry smile.

"The first thing I do every morning after I get out of bed is check all the shells are where they're supposed to be," she revealed. "Sometimes they aren't."

"Mademoiselle is very good at noticing if one has moved," Charlotte said. "The shiny trail helps. There must be a reason why they leave it behind. I wish I knew what it was."

"I don't know what precise purpose slime serves the snail," Quin said, "but Nicholas Culpeper, a famous herbalist from the past, believed snail water cured consumption."

"Snail *water*?" Charlotte repeated suspiciously.

"I'm afraid the snails don't survive the process of becoming a...um medicinal elixir," Quin said apologetically, wondering if Gabrielle had shared the information that snails were regularly eaten in France. "I believe they're boiled in milk or wine along with other ingredients, and then the mixture is distilled."

"It's been years since I enjoyed this kind of conversation over a dish of ice cream," Lord Appledrum observed. "Harlequin, if you don't know the answers to Miss Sedgemore's questions about snails and their slime yourself, why don't you see if one of your scientific colleagues has more information?"

"Yes, sir, I intend—" Quin began.

Charlotte's gaze locked onto his face. "Harlequin? You're... Quin?" she whispered.

"Yes." He realized she hadn't made the connection before.

All the light went out of her. The transformation was so sudden it reminded Quin of an experiment he'd seen with air sucked out of a glass dome to extinguish a flame.

The revelation of his identity had extinguished Charlotte's flame. She didn't just look shocked—she looked stricken. She withdrew into herself, fixing her gaze on the bowl before her, becoming a small, vulnerable child, not a budding naturalist.

Witnessing her transformation, knowing he was the cause of it, was one of the most painful things Quin had experienced.

Not as painful as leaving his family and Gabrielle behind for years, or having Gabrielle reject his marriage proposal for the sake of this child. But seeing how Charlotte expected his return to destroy her own secure world with Gabrielle shook Quin to the core.

Before Charlotte had dropped her gaze, he was sure he'd seen a kind of bleak fear in her eyes and that was intolerable. He didn't know the root cause of her fear, but he couldn't contribute to it.

"Charlotte," he said.

She ignored him.

There were no other customers in the confectionery shop.

No other sounds to relieve or disguise the buzzing tension at their table.

Charlotte," Quin repeated, making his tone more compelling.

She partially lifted her head, staring at him under her brows. She'd gone pale. Her expression hard, closed and suspicious.

"Mademoiselle isn't leaving you," he said quietly.

By his side, his father was still and silent.

He heard Gabrielle's soft intake of breath. Without her explicit permission, he was speaking for both of them. Perhaps even taking Gabrielle's decision out of her hands, since he'd now made a verbal commitment to Charlotte on her behalf.

He looked at Gabrielle. Her lovely eyes were sad and smiling and she nodded once.

He returned his attention to Charlotte. "Mademoiselle isn't leaving you," he said again. "She will go on helping you with your collections and…whatever else young ladies need assistance with."

Charlotte blinked—then stared at him as if she was trying to pierce his soul. "You're not going to take her away from me?"

"No." Something inside him tore. Was it his heart? "I'm not going to take her away from you."

Chapter Sixteen

Gabrielle and Charlotte proceeded in silence for the first part of their walk home from the confectionery shop. Gabrielle was certain they were both preoccupied by their unexpected encounter with Quin and Lord Appledrum.

For Charlotte, it had been the first extended conversation she'd had with anyone apart from Gabrielle, or Mrs. Whittle, since Gabrielle had become her governess. Gabrielle was certain Charlotte would have needed time afterward to digest everything that had been said, even if she hadn't also had to contend with the emotional impact of discovering Quin's identity.

Meanwhile, Gabrielle was also trying to find a degree of inner as well as outer serenity. Overnight, she'd sought to reconcile herself to continuing unaltered her life with Charlotte. Perhaps even eventually reading a notice in the newspaper of Quin's betrothal to another lady.

But then he'd appeared before her again, strong and determined, declaring he meant to court her via regular, albeit clandestine correspondence. And when he'd been secretly teasing her foot under the table, it had been impossible to imagine not seeing him in person again for an indefinite length of time.

It shouldn't have been a shock when he'd told Charlotte quietly and firmly that he wouldn't take Gabrielle away from her. That was, after all, what she'd told him had to be the case. She loved him so much for respecting her wishes—and she had no idea how she'd managed not to burst into tears at that moment.

It was Lord Appledrum who'd picked up the conversational pieces. Speaking to the table at large, rather than directing his comments to Charlotte, he'd begun to recount some of the things Quin had told him about the scientific expedition.

"Harlequin spent a great deal of time during the voyage checking, and re-wrapping, all the seeds he'd collected," Lord Appledrum had revealed. "He re-wrapped some of the seeds *scores* of times before the ships returned to London."

Quin had summoned a smile. "You *were* listening to my dull recital of my daily duties, sir?"

"To every word, dear boy. Every word." Lord Appledrum's reply had caused more tears to prick Gabrielle's eyes.

"Lord Quin's papa is very proud of him," Charlotte abruptly broke her silence.

"Yes, he is."

"And your papa is proud of you," Charlotte said. "Isn't he?"

"Yes." Gabrielle's throat tightened. Her papa hated the fact that his loss of status and fortune had led to her becoming a governess, but he'd made it plain he was proud of the choices she'd made.

Charlotte's situation was different. Gabrielle had no doubt

the child disliked her mother, and she honestly couldn't fault Charlotte for that. Lady Henderson had done less than nothing to win her daughter's affection, and love couldn't grow without any cultivation.

But Gabrielle suspected Charlotte might hold out greater hopes for her father. Lord Henderson was an almost mythical figure to both of them. They knew far more about him from Mrs. Whittle, who occasionally told them stories about his childhood, than they did from their rare face-to-face encounters with him.

The previous autumn they'd seen him ride up the road to Sedgemore Hall when they'd been out picking hazelnuts. Gabrielle had recognized him from his portrait. Charlotte had spent a long time studying the portrait. Perhaps that's how she'd identified him too.

If *Gabrielle's* papa had arrived unexpectedly, she'd have dropped her basket of hazelnuts and raced to greet him. Charlotte hadn't left Gabrielle's side, and she hadn't spoken, but her gaze hadn't left her father's face when he stopped to greet them.

He'd seemed perfectly amiable, though his manner had been somewhat stiff and distracted. Gabrielle had hoped he'd spend more time with Charlotte. But after only one night at the Hall, he'd departed again the next morning.

Gabrielle had heard the servants gossiping about a dreadful argument between Lord and Lady Henderson. It wasn't hard to guess why Lord Henderson had left, but his lack of concern for Charlotte hadn't improved Gabrielle's opinion of him.

She certainly wasn't going to make any claims on his behalf that Charlotte had no reason to believe.

"My papa is proud of me—and *I'm* proud of *you*," she said.

Charlotte's head jerked around. She peered up at Gabrielle. "*You're* proud of me?"

Gabrielle's heart contracted at the painful yearning in Charlotte's expression. "Very proud."

"Why?" Charlotte asked gruffly.

Gabrielle stopped walking. "Because you have a kind and loving heart."

"How do you know?"

"Because you protect me from your snail shell collection, and you were worried about the lady who lost her spectacles." Gabrielle smiled and cupped Charlotte's cheek. "You have a kind and loving soul."

Charlotte stared at Gabrielle for long moments, and then twisted away to look toward the sea. "So do you, mademoiselle. We have to go back to the nursery now."

"Yes, we do." Gabrielle suppressed a sigh. She didn't think either of them wanted to return to the house.

"We won't tell Mama we had ice cream with Lord Quin and his papa," Charlotte said.

"We shouldn't lie..." Gabrielle didn't want to mention anything about their morning's outing to Lady Henderson either, but she wasn't comfortable encouraging Charlotte to outright lie.

"We won't lie. We just won't say anything," Charlotte said stubbornly.

Well, Gabrielle reflected, not saying anything was something Charlotte was good at.

"It won't matter, because she doesn't listen to what we say

anyway," Charlotte added, with devastating honesty. "But I should write a thank you letter to Lord Quin's papa for my ice cream. That's good etiquette, isn't it?"

"Yes."

"I don't know how we'll send it." Charlotte kicked at the cobblestones thoughtfully. "I don't think we should give it to Roger. I don't like him."

Roger was Lady Henderson's personal footman. Gabrielle didn't like, or trust, him either.

"Perhaps we could walk past their house tomorrow morning and knock on the door," Charlotte mused. "And give it to the butler. Do you know where Lord Quin and his papa live?" She looked up at Gabrielle.

"It *is* good manners to thank Lord Appledrum for our ice cream," Gabrielle said. "It's very thoughtful of you. Unfortunately, it's not good etiquette for two young ladies to knock on the front door of a house where two single gentlemen live."

Charlotte frowned. "*Two* single gentlemen?"

"Lord Quin's mama died when he was a baby," Gabrielle explained.

"Oh." Ahead of them, seagulls were tussling over an unidentifiable object. Charlotte poked her head forward to see it better. "I think it's a fish head. Your mama is dead too."

"Mind your posture, sweetheart." Gabrielle brushed her hand lightly over the upper part of Charlotte's back. "My mama only died shortly before I met you. My papa was proud of me when she was alive, too."

She didn't know if it was right to remind Charlotte her mother had only recently died, but she didn't want Charlotte to believe that fathers were only proud of their motherless children.

"It's easy to be proud of you," Charlotte said. "You're very beautiful and lovable."

"You're very beautiful and lovable too, sweetheart." Gabrielle ached for Charlotte who was treated coldly at best by one parent and ignored by the other. "Anyone who can't see that needs to get a pair of spectacles fitted for their heart."

Charlotte stared at her—and then a huge smile lit up her face. "You're so funny, mademoiselle. Wouldn't it be funny to see people walking around with giant spectacles in front of their chests? You wouldn't need a pair."

"Nor would you."

Charlotte's smile faded and anxiety flickered across her face. "You're staying with me, aren't you, mademoiselle? Even though Lord Quin is your prince, you're staying with me?"

"For as long as you need me," Gabrielle promised.

Charlotte studied her carefully, and then her smile reappeared. "You can help me write my letter to Lord Quin's papa, and we'll ask Mrs. Whittle to help deliver it." Charlotte seized Gabrielle's hand and started towing her toward the house. It was the first time Gabrielle could ever remember Charlotte being keen to return home when her mother was in residence.

∽

GABRIELLE KNOCKED on the front door when they arrived at the Hendersons' house.

"Hello again, Penson," she said to the butler who opened it. "We're home from our walk."

"Good morning, mademoiselle, miss," Penson greeted them both in turn. "I trust you had an enjoyable outing. The weather is very fine today."

Charlotte nodded and tugged Gabrielle toward the stairs.

"Yes, the weather is very good," Gabrielle said to Penson. "I think Miss Charlotte is eager to get out her paints," she added with a small laugh.

"If I had Miss Charlotte's skill with a paintbrush, I would be too," the butler replied.

Penson was a relatively recent addition to the household, appointed after Gabrielle herself had started as Charlotte's governess. She'd half expected him to take his cue from Lady Henderson and Augustus and treat her and Charlotte with barely concealed disdain, but he hadn't. Gabrielle respected him for his professional integrity, but she never shared confidences with him.

"Yes, Miss Charlotte is a good artist." She smiled and followed Charlotte to the stairs.

Charlotte ran up the first flight, obviously impatient to get to the nursery.

"Slow down, Charlotte, and walk nicely," Gabrielle called softly, knowing Charlotte probably wouldn't hear her unless she raised her voice, but not wanting to shout when she was so close to the drawing room.

Charlotte was already on the next flight when Gabrielle reached the landing. She took two quick, silent steps—

The drawing room door opened, and Lady Henderson appeared in the frame.

Gabrielle caught her breath, but instantly summoned a polite smile to hide her dismay.

"Good morning, your ladyship." She curtsied with a downcast gaze.

"Walk nicely, indeed," Lady Henderson said in a sneering tone. "The child sounds like a herd of stampeding cattle. I've ordered you to ensure she behaves with proper decorum at all times, Mademoiselle Rousselle, but you're clearly falling short in your duties."

Gabrielle rose from her curtsy and, with her head still bowed submissively, discreetly assessed her employer's appearance.

One glance at Lady Henderson's heavy eyes and sickly complexion suggested she might be suffering the consequences of overindulging at the ball the previous night.

"I'm sorry we've disturbed you, your ladyship," Gabrielle said politely. "We've just enjoyed an invigorating walk in the sea air. It has put Charlotte in excellent spirits, but I will immediately remind her of the need to behave like a lady at all times."

Lady Henderson's eyes glittered unpleasantly, and a frisson of unease slithered along Gabrielle's spine. There really was something very disturbing about Lady Henderson's smile.

"Invigorating walk?" the viscountess repeated. "Have you enjoyed *many* invigorating walks recently, Mademoiselle Rousselle?"

"Charlotte and I go for a walk every day," Gabrielle said evenly, though her heart rate quickened uncomfortably. Had Lady Henderson discovered she'd also attended the masquerade ball? Had she somehow already learned about their encounter that morning with Quin and Lord Appledrum?

"Come in, Mademoiselle Rousselle," the viscountess instructed. She turned her back on Gabrielle and walked across the room to sink down onto her chaise longue.

Gabrielle followed, taking care not to allow any hint of her unease to appear in either her expression or gestures. The deportment she'd been taught as a child had been intended to allow her to shine in the grand salons of Versailles and Paris.

She'd never had a chance to sparkle at Versailles, but those lessons in self-control and good manners had been equally useful when she'd been unexpectedly confronted by a wolf in the forest —and they were even more valuable to her now she was a governess.

Lady Henderson narrowed her eyes at Gabrielle, and did not invite her to sit down.

"It has come to my attention that Brighton is not a suitable location for a child of Charlotte's sex and tender years," she stated flatly.

Lady Henderson's words were so far from what Gabrielle had expected that, for a few seconds, she almost wondered if her grasp of English had somehow failed her.

"You mean a little girl of Charlotte's age?" she asked, puzzled. "Why not? Brighton is famous for its healthy sea breezes. In fact, I believe several doctors have written—"

Lady Henderson made an impatient gesture. "I know all about the benefits of the so-called sea cure," she said in a mocking tone. "And that is precisely my concern, Mademoiselle Rousselle. It has been brought to my notice that men—we cannot call them *gentlemen*—frequently bathe naked it the sea in full view of promenaders along the Marine Parade. A place where you take my daughter every day."

"I've never taken Charlotte to see naked male bathers." Gabrielle was dumbfounded by Lady Henderson's tirade.

"On the contrary, Mademoiselle Rousselle," Lady Henderson accused her. "I have it on good authority that you've displayed a scandalous and prurient interest in staring at the naked men in the sea."

Chapter Seventeen

Gabrielle had been mentally scrambling to defend herself against the charge of illicitly going to Lord Appledrum's ball. She'd never anticipated an attack on her conduct of this nature, and it threw her off balance.

"I have *never* stared at a naked man," she said, her heart racing with indignation but also trepidation. This was a nonsensical accusation, but Lady Henderson must have a reason for making it. "I don't know who could have claimed such a thing—but I assure you it's not true."

"Don't lie, girl. I know you've been seeking every opportunity to stare at the male bathers because you said so yourself," Lady Henderson snapped.

"No." Bemused, Gabrielle began to shake her head.

"Cease you're dissembling. Ethel *heard* you tell Mrs. Whittle that you enjoyed watching the men," Lady Henderson said.

Understanding, and rising temper, dawned in Gabrielle.

"By your leave, your ladyship, that is not what I said to Mrs.

Whittle." Gabrielle kept her voice low and calm, even though she wanted to issue a counter charge against the spiteful lady's maid. "I'm afraid Ethel misunderstood. I did mention to Mrs. Whittle that I'd noticed some soldiers and officers weren't making use of the bathing machines, but only to explain why I'd decided Charlotte and I should confine our walks to the other direction."

"Pretty words," Lady Henderson mocked. "Belied by your own lurid description of seeing a man's naked torso rising from the waves."

Gabrielle berated herself for not checking they were alone in the kitchen when she'd laughed about the incident with the housekeeper. The only naked male body she wanted to see belonged to Quin—and that might never happen.

"Your blush proclaims your guilty conscience!" Lady Henderson said triumphantly.

Gabrielle wasn't even sure if her cheeks were red or if that was as false as her employer's other accusation. She didn't feel hot, she felt cold. And even though she should feel guilty about going to the ball, anger was the primary emotion pulsing through her veins.

But, for Charlotte's sake, she couldn't afford to have an argument with Lady Henderson it would be impossible for her to win.

"I assure your ladyship—" she began.

"Oh, shut your mouth, girl," Lady Henderson snapped. "Can't you see I'm not well this morning?"

Seething, Gabrielle clamped her lips together and stared at the carpet.

Lady Henderson groaned and pressed a damp cloth to her

forehead. "I'm tired of putting up with Charlotte's sullen face and your fake modesty. First thing tomorrow morning, you're to take Charlotte to Sedgemore Hall, where you will remain until I order otherwise. In the meantime, neither of you are to leave this house again. I will not have my daughter exposed to depravity or impropriety."

For a few seconds, the loudest sound Gabrielle could hear was the pounding of her heart. It was only by force of will that she managed to maintain the calm rhythm of her breathing.

"I assure you that Charlotte has never been exposed to any improper sights or behavior," she said. "But if you think it's best for us to go to Sedgemore Hall, of course we will go."

"Yes, you will," Lady Henderson replied. "I'm the mistress of this household, and I expect absolute obedience from you. Go away, I'm sick of talking to you. Pack all of Charlotte's bags first, before you begin on your own."

"Yes, your ladyship." Gabrielle turned to walk quietly across the carpet to the door.

"One more thing," Lady Henderson said, as Gabrielle grasped the door handle.

Gabrielle paused and looked back at the viscountess.

"Do not attempt to communicate with anyone in Brighton before your departure," Lady Henderson instructed.

Gabrielle kept her expression blank and nodded, as if Lady Henderson's order held no particular significance for her.

She turned the door handle and thought she heard soft, hasty noises on the other side. When she opened the door, she wasn't surprised to see Augustus standing with his back against the banister, staring boldly at her.

He'd put a small distance between himself and the door, but he wasn't even pretending he hadn't been eavesdropping.

"Good morning, Master Sedgemore," she said coolly. "I trust you are well, this fine day."

"Very well, ex-Governess Rousselle," he replied disdainfully, pushing past her to get into the drawing room. The tip of his nose was so high in the air she was sure the only thing he could see was the ceiling.

Gabrielle took a couple of steps towards the stairs, and then registered the way he'd addressed her.

Ex-Governess?

A shriek of outrage emanated from the room she'd just left.

"Why haven't you dismissed her?" Augustus shouted, his fury incandescent. "I thought you dismissed her when you told her to pack. I *told* you I saw her meet a man last night. And she's insolent to me!"

Gabrielle froze. He'd *seen* her?

A memory of the draft she'd felt the previous night when she was crossing the upper landing flashed into her mind. Had Augustus been spying on her through a crack in one of the doors?

"Stop shouting or I'll send you to the country too!" Lady Henderson threatened. "My head hurts!"

"But I *saw* her—"

"I heard you the first time—and I know how much you despise her," Lady Henderson snapped. "You wanted them both gone, and they're going. Be satisfied with that."

"But Mama..." Augustus began.

"Don't whine at me. Pour me some brandy. I don't have time

to find a new governess for Charlotte, and she needs to be at least half-way civilized if we're to marry her off at the first opportunity."

Gabrielle heard movement in the drawing room, seized her skirts, and fled as quickly and silently up the stairs as if scythe-wielding revolutionaries were on her heels.

Augustus had told his mother the truth, and Gabrielle couldn't tell whether Lady Henderson genuinely didn't believe him—or if she was choosing not to believe him because it meant less trouble for her.

Was it simply easier for Lady Henderson to solve the problem Augustus had created for her by making up a spurious accusation that Gabrielle had been ogling sea bathers—and then immediately decree a punishment which partially satisfied Augustus's aims?

All-in-all, the past few minutes had given Gabrielle a great deal to think about. But her current priority was to ensure she didn't do anything before they left Brighton, which might cause Lady Henderson to change her mind about taking Augustus's accusation seriously.

The hateful way the viscountess had spoken of marrying off her daughter at the first opportunity, had made it excruciatingly clear how important it was that Gabrielle remained Charlotte's governess and protector.

Chapter Eighteen

Quin sat cross-legged by the orchard pond. Most of it was in a band of sunlight, and the water lily flowers were open to their fullest extent. As dusk approached, the petals would close to unfurl again tomorrow.

This time yesterday, he'd been working with Duncan on their book describing their voyage of discoveries. Quin had assumed they'd be doing the same thing again today—and he'd probably be arguing with Duncan about the need to include more humorous or adventurous anecdotes rather than only botanical facts.

They were both keen to press ahead to publication while interest in the expedition from all quarters was at its height. In practical terms, the success of their book was most important to Duncan, because he was a younger son who had to make his own way in the world.

But Duncan was also more reserved about including such things as his pen and ink drawing of the tiger they'd encountered.

To Dance with the Earl

Or the elephant. Or his artistic impression of one particularly violent tropical storm they'd survived.

"Those aren't plants," he'd objected. "This is a scientific account of our botanical discoveries, not our adventures with tigers and leeches."

"I agree we needn't focus on leeches in this first book, but we should definitely include the tiger," Quin had insisted. "We want this initial account of the expedition to reach the widest possible audience, not just our fellow scientists. And people are more likely to buy plants from the nursery you're going to establish if they have a chance to meet the man who braved a boa constrictor to collect the original seeds."

Duncan had rolled his eyes, but so far allowed two of his non-botanical illustrations to be in the book.

But Duncan had gone off to London on an unexpected errand, and Quin's thoughts were consumed with Gabrielle, so no progress was being made on the manuscript today.

He'd already written a letter to the Royal Society asking if any of the Fellows had a particular interest in snails. He'd had his father frank the letter and carried it to the post office himself.

Then he'd found himself at a loss. What could he do now, when what he *wanted* to do wasn't a possibility?

He'd wandered around the formal part of the garden and the orchard, looking for empty snail shells, though he wasn't sure how agreeable Agnes would be to passing them to Mrs. Whittle for Charlotte. Agnes wouldn't mind, but Mrs. Whittle might not like it. Were objects like snail shells outside the scope of the correspondence the two housekeepers were willing to facilitate?

Luckily, he'd been distracted by an interesting event in the pond, and now he was trying to capture its progress in a series of sketches. He didn't pretend to have the artistic skills of Duncan or Gabrielle, but he hoped his efforts would provide at least an impression of what he was witnessing.

Movement by the wicket gate caught his eye. He looked up to see Agnes come into the orchard. Hope quickened his pulse—but Agnes's hands were empty. She wasn't bringing him a letter from Gabrielle.

She closed the gate and started to walk toward him. He instinctively lifted his index finger to his lips in the exact same gesture he'd used countless times as a child when she'd been his nurse.

She smiled slightly and circled the pond with soft-footed steps. When she was standing beside him, he pointed at the large, drab-colored insect clinging tightly to the stem of the reed. There was a strange split in its body, and it seemed as if another, much paler, insect was erupting from its back.

"Good Heavens," Agnes murmured, and kneeled beside him so she could get a better look.

"It's going to be a dragonfly," Quin said equally softly.

As he spoke, the pale insect managed to extricate itself from the dark husk of its former self. Its newly emerged form glowed a beautiful clear green in the afternoon sunlight, but its body was curved like a bow, and its wings were nothing more than strange, stunted appendages on its back.

Quin started another sketch on the same piece of paper.

"Your drawing has improved," Agnes noted.

"It's adequate," he said. "Duncan or Gabrielle could do far more justice to the subject. And Duncan's ability to make a rapid sketch at a location and use it to recreate the scene later is remarkable."

They continued to watch and Quin to make new sketches as the dragonfly's body gradually straightened, and its wings unfurled to their full, transparent glory. At last, it started to vibrate, and then launched itself into the air, its wings glittering in the sunshine.

Quin sighed and laid his sketching materials aside.

"That's what you want to do," Agnes said softly. "Fly away. But now you're tied in one spot."

"No," he denied, startled. "I don't want to fly away. I want —" He sucked in a breath. "I will adjust. I'm grateful to be home with you and Father. I have my work, which is of absorbing interest to me. You are kindly going to enable my correspondence with Gabrielle—aren't you?"

"Yes." She smiled at him, and tweaked a lock of his hair into position, as if he was still four years old and not twenty-four. "I'm glad to have you home—and I have a commission for you."

"A commission?" He came alert, ready to leap into action the moment she gave him the details. "What would you have me do?"

She laughed. "Not now, at dawn tomorrow morning. There's no need to rush off now."

Quin's eyes narrowed in confusion. "Where are you sending me at dawn tomorrow?"

When he was a small, adventurous boy, Agnes had often sent him on errands to do such things as buy a loaf from the village bakery, or take a message to the blacksmith. He'd felt proud she'd trusted him to perform important tasks on his own, and only later discovered someone had always followed him whenever he ventured beyond the view of the house windows.

But Agnes had stopped sending him on such errands years before he'd set off on his tour of the globe. This unexpected commission aroused his curiosity, to say the least.

"I'd like you to go and buy some fish for me from the fish market on the beach tomorrow morning," she said.

"You want me to go to the fish market at dawn tomorrow?" he repeated.

"And buy some fish." Her eyes sparkled with affectionate amusement.

"What kind of fish?" he asked.

"Whatever you'd like for your breakfast," she replied.

"I like all fish, so that makes your commission easy," he said, no closer to guessing the reason for her request—though he hoped it might have something to do with Gabrielle.

Two figures appeared at the wicket gate. The taller of them opened it and the smaller one burst through and began hurtling across the orchard toward them.

"Miss Twent…Uncle Haquin," Nancy cried happily—and tripped over a tussock of grass.

"Oh dear," Agnes murmured, shifting her position so she could stand more easily.

But Marcus reached Nancy in a couple of long strides. In one continuous motion, he tossed the miniature cricket bat he was carrying onto the grass near to Quin, and scooped up Nancy with a hand on each side of her torso under her arms.

"Oooo!" Nancy's expression changed from shocked to delighted. "I'm flying."

"Hmm." Marcus deposited her carefully on her feet in front of Agnes. "Nan Bee, make your curtsy to Miss Trent and Uncle Quin."

"Good afternoon, Uncle Haquin," Nancy bobbed up and down.

"Good afternoon, Nancy," Quin replied. "I don't mind if you call me Quin, like everyone else. Uncle Quin," he added, though technically she was his cousin once removed.

"No." She shook her head firmly. "Uncle Appdrum says it's sad he's the only person in the whole *vast* world who calls you by your whole lovely name. Now I will too." She patted her chest.

"Sorry, coz." Marcus grinned at Quin.

"We've come to play cricket with you," Nancy explained, picking up her cricket bat.

"Nancy?" Marcus said.

She squinted up at him.

"We came to *ask* Uncle Quin if he would like to play cricket with us, remember? Not tell him."

Nancy heaved a sigh. "Would you *please* like to play cricket with us, Uncle Haquin?"

"Can I play with you instead of your uncles?" Agnes asked before Quin could speak.

"Yes, you're good at cricket too," Nancy said.

"Nan—"

"Thank you, Miss Twent," Nancy added, before Marcus could finish his prompt.

"Thank you." He gave Agnes a grateful look as he assisted her to her feet. "Call me as soon as you grow weary of the game." He offered her two of the soft balls he used for playing cricket with Nancy.

Agnes smiled and patted his arm. "You're a good uncle, your grace." She'd never been a mother figure to Marcus the way she was to Quin, but she had watched him grow up—and even tossed a few cricket balls for him in the past. "Come on, Nancy, let's leave your uncles in peace for a while." She walked away, juggling the balls.

"You're almost as good as Uncle Marcus." Nancy trotted along beside her.

"Perhaps when you're older, we should form a team of lady cricketers," Agnes mused.

They disappeared through the picket gate. Quin knew they were headed for the lawn beyond the formal fountain garden.

"Thank god for Miss Trent!" Marcus dropped onto the grass beside Quin in a far more dramatic manner than he'd ever allow himself to behave in public.

Quin grinned. "Are you any closer to finding a temporary nurse for Nan?"

At his first meeting with Nancy, she'd explained in more-or-less one breath how her nurse had broken her leg, and her mama was sick so "Uncle Marcus and Grandmama are looking after me now."

"Possibly." Marcus sat up and ran his fingers through his hair. "But she won't arrive for a day or two."

"How's Ceci?" Quin asked.

Cecilia, Lady Daubney, was in the throes of an uncomfortable pregnancy.

"The same." A shadow of concern crossed Marcus's face at

the mention of his sister. "The doctors have assured us she'll feel better soon, and she has strictly forbidden me from writing to Daubney." Cecilia's husband was currently part of a diplomatic mission to Sweden, which was why she and Nancy had moved into her brother's household.

"A stricture you'll ignore if you consider the situation warrants it," Quin said.

"I've plainly told her so. But I didn't come to talk about Ceci."

"You came to finagle me into taking my turn at nursemaid?" Quin guessed.

"No. I came to hear about your reunion with Gabrielle, of course," Marcus retorted.

Chapter Nineteen

Quin stared at his cousin. "Who told you Gabrielle came to the ball last night?"

"No one. I worked it out myself when you danced with the same lady all evening and didn't appear at supper." Marcus grinned, but there was a question in his eyes. "Did it go well?"

"Yes." Quin plucked up a stalk of grass.

Marcus waited.

Quin exhaled. "Ever since last night, I've been swinging between jubilation—and frustration."

"Frustration?" Marcus said in a level voice, but there was a gleam in his eyes.

"Dammit, yes!" The memory of holding Gabrielle in his arms last night, and struggling to control his desire for her, was vivid in Quin's mind. And it took little provocation for his thoughts to reignite his physical reaction to her.

He filled his lungs...and breathed out again, momentarily overcome with a sense of uncharacteristic bleakness.

"It's not funny," he said. "It would be funny if our wedding was to be delayed a week or two—or even a few months. Perhaps. Funny to other people."

The reality of his situation hit him like an avalanche. From the moment he'd seen Gabrielle climb over the wall, he'd had one goal after another to achieve. But they were all done now. All that was left for him to do was settle into a regular, clandestine correspondence with Gabrielle—and wait.

He closed his eyes and felt Marcus's hand land on his shoulder.

"I'm missing some details," his cousin said quietly.

"Gabrielle's sense of duty is compelling her to remain in her position as governess to the Hendersons' daughter." Quin opened his eyes. "Perhaps for years. Charlotte is seven."

Marcus's grip tightened. "Do you fear it's an excuse to avoid marriage?"

Quin shook his head. "No." He swallowed. "I think her choice is breaking her heart. Gabrielle's." He pinched the bridge of his nose.

"And yours." Marcus's hand remained firm on Quin's shoulder.

For a few minutes, the only sounds in the orchard came from the birds, the buzzing insects, and the voices of Agnes and Nancy drifting across from the garden.

Quin swallowed and straightened his back. "Since...well...I don't know since when. When I arrived and put the notice in the paper for Gabrielle? When I saw her climb over the wall? Anyway, I've been going straight from one task to another. But I wrote to the Royal Society this morning to inquire about snails, and now I don't have any more tasks. I must just pick up my routine."

"Snails?" Marcus said.

"Charlotte has a snail shell collection, and what appears to be a scientific interest in the creatures," Quin explained.

"You know this how?" Marcus gave Quin's shoulder another squeeze and dropped his hand.

"She told me."

"She told you?" Marcus repeated.

Quin explained about the encounter he and his father had engineered with Gabrielle and Charlotte that morning.

"You *have* been going from one task to another at a breakneck speed," Marcus said. "You saw Gabrielle climb over the wall?"

Quin explained about that too, though not the most intimate parts of their reunion.

"She told me last night that she couldn't leave Charlotte, but it wasn't until I saw Charlotte myself that I accepted it." Quin rubbed his chest. "I swear, the moment she realized I was Gabrielle's Quin, it was as if all the light had been snuffed out of her. I've never felt like a monster before."

"You're the furthest thing from a monster," Marcus said. "The mere fact you're putting Gabrielle's wishes ahead of your own—and seeking more information on snails for Charlotte—is proof of that."

"I am mildly interested in seeing her collection," Quin confessed. "Though I'm unlikely to have the chance. It bothers me that Gabrielle must help Charlotte with it, because Gabrielle is squeamish around snails and slugs. But it seems Charlotte is mindful of Gabrielle's sensitivity and doesn't tease her about it. It's not reasonable for me to be angry."

"With Gabrielle?"

Quin shook his head. "I left you all. I left Gabrielle to follow my own ambitions. It wouldn't be reasonable for me to come back and expect her to instantly rearrange her life to suit me. I'm angry we're in this situation—but it's my fault."

"I'd dispute that," Marcus said. "And I'd be directing my anger at the Hendersons' door."

"I'm doing that too," Quin admitted.

"When you mentioned Charlotte, it seemed as if you like her. Does that make it easier for you to accept Gabrielle's decision?" Marcus asked.

Quin dipped his chin. "This morning, I promised Charlotte I wouldn't take Mademoiselle away from her." He frowned at the grass. "Something caused her to stop talking for months, and Gabrielle is convinced she would be dismissed out of hand if Lady Henderson discovered we're betrothed. Something is wrong in that household."

"Quite likely. I can't remember the last time I saw Lord and Lady Henderson together," Marcus said. "And we know that even households which outwardly seem well-regulated can have deep-rooted problems."

"What do you know of the Hendersons?" Quin asked.

"Very little. I avoid her and I rarely cross paths with him. Over the past few days, Mother has often been...confounded by Nancy's behavior," Marcus said.

Quin turned his head to study his cousin, certain Marcus had a reason for his abrupt change of topic.

"Yesterday, Mother told me that Cecilia and I were much better-behaved children than Nancy. I struggled to find a response that wouldn't hurt her," Marcus said. "Mother knows as well as I do that when Ceci and I were Nancy's age, she never saw us for more than half an hour a day at most, when we were on our best behavior. It was miraculous for all of us when Uncle John came galloping to our rescue."

Quin nodded. He knew there was no hyperbole in his cousin's grandiose claim. After Lord Appledrum had received news his recently widowed sister's household was in crisis, he had indeed jumped on a horse and ridden through the night to reach them.

Life for Marcus, Cecilia and their mother had improved immeasurably from that moment onward.

"It sounds as if Gabrielle is to Charlotte, what Uncle John was to us," Marcus said. "But without his authority to change the things that are wrong."

"That's what I've suspected since she first told me about Charlotte." Quin closed his hand into a fist and opened it again. "It's infuriating—and worrying."

"I need to further my acquaintance with Lord Henderson," Marcus said. "Although Uncle John might be better suited to the task. Henderson falls between us in age. And your task is to see what you can glean of the situation in Lady Henderson's household from Gabrielle's letters. Short of murder or treason, a peer can get away with pretty much anything he wants under his own roof—but, by the same token, he can order things differently if he chooses. Come on." He clapped Quin lightly on the back. "Let's go and play cricket with Nancy."

Quin stood. "Thank you," he said.

"We'll do what we can to alleviate your situation," Marcus promised. "Meanwhile, are you playing on my team or Uncle John's in our cricket match on Saturday?"

Quin groaned. "I haven't played cricket for years."

Marcus grinned. "All the more reason to get in some practice with Nancy, then."

Chapter Twenty

The sun had begun to tint the dawn sky pink as Quin strode down the Steine. Except for the ubiquitous gulls pecking at a discarded potato skin, there was no one else about.

In the past, fishermen had laid out their nets to dry on the Steine. The need to please Brighton's influential summer visitors, including the Prince of Wales, had ended that practice. But though their nets were gone from the Steine, the fishermen still landed their boats on the beach below the cliff, and sold their catches at the fish market there.

That was Quin's destination. It was only after Marcus and Nancy had left the previous afternoon that he'd remembered he did have another task to complete—Agnes's commission for him to buy some fish for his breakfast.

He was certain this errand was somehow connected to Gabrielle. In his wildest, most hopeful imaginings, he pictured her down on the beach. But that was highly unlikely. Earls and governesses didn't generally encounter each other in fish markets at dawn.

As he drew closer to the railing along the cliff edge, it became easier to hear the voices drifting up from below. Good-natured shouts and laughter carried on the gentle morning breeze. The voices were overlaid by the mewing calls of the gulls swooping overhead, no doubt hoping for an easy meal.

At the top of the steps, Quin cast a comprehensive glance across the beached fishing boats and the people around them, but saw no one who could be Gabrielle.

It was disappointing, but he hadn't really expected her to be here. His body still buzzed with anticipation as he ran down the wooden steps and crossed the shifting pebbles to the market.

He'd been sent to buy his breakfast, so he leaned over to study a basket of freshly caught plaice. Did he want one of those for breakfast? Should he also take some home for Father and Agnes?

A moment later he heard a soft thud a few feet behind him, followed by a woman's exasperated exclamation.

He turned to see an older woman frowning down at an empty basket lying on its side on the pebbles.

"Drat!" she muttered, and looked up at him.

The instant their eyes met, Quin knew this wasn't a chance encounter. The woman studying him with undisguised interest had deliberately dropped her basket to gain his attention. He could tell from her dress that she wasn't a member of the Polite World. She was either one of Brighton's year-round inhabitants —or a senior servant.

"Good morning, ma'am," Quin said, certain he'd correctly guessed her identity.

"Good morning, sir," she replied. "I'm sorry to presume, but my rheumatism is very bad this morning. Would you be so kind as to pick up my basket for me?"

"Of course." Quin bent to retrieve it.

"It would be an imposition to ask you to carry it for me for a little while?" she said in a questioning tone. "But my hands are feeling so stiff and weak today."

"I'm sorry to hear that." Quin kept hold of the basket.

He and Agnes had learned to read at the same time, and together they'd pored over a book of fairy stories. He knew his role in this scene the lady with the basket had initiated. He offered her good-hearted assistance—and she rewarded him with the gift of a comb which would turn into a forest to block the path of his pursuers. Or some other similar magical device.

Though in this case, he hoped her gift would be a more prosaic agreement to help him send letters to Gabrielle.

"Have you come to buy fish?" he asked.

"Yes, sir." She nodded.

"So have I," he said, "but I have little experience with this kind of shopping. Perhaps you could advise me on the best fish to buy this morning, while I carry your basket?"

"I would be honored to do so." She stepped up to survey the catch laid out before them.

"Good morning, Mrs. Whittle," one of the fishermen greeted her. "What would you like today?"

Annoyance flickered across her face. Quin supposed most fairy godmothers didn't have to put up with their identity being revealed before they were ready to make their grand pronouncements.

But Mrs. Whittle's irritation vanished as quickly as it arrived and she began to haggle cheerfully with the fisherman, displaying no signs of pain or stiffness as she did so.

Quin wasn't surprised. Mrs. Whittle might be two or three decades older than Agnes Trent but, according to Gabrielle, two nights ago, she'd been manhandling a ladder in the hayfield. She was a sturdy, active woman.

Nevertheless, when it was time to return across the pebbles to the bottom of the steps, he offered her his arm. She accepted his assistance with a smile.

"Have you come to see if my motives for wishing to write to Mademoiselle Rousselle are honorable?" he asked, when they were several yards away from the throng around the fish market.

"Partly." She stopped walking so she could turn to look up at him. "I trust Mademoiselle Rousselle's judgment, and that of Miss Trent, but I wanted to meet you for myself. They both have longstanding reasons for their partiality toward you."

"They do." Quin nodded. "Your observation is reasonable. I was so young at the time of my first meeting with Miss Trent, I can't remember it, but she has always been an important member of our household. She's bound to speak of me favorably. Mademoiselle Rousselle and I..." He hesitated. Discussing his feelings for Gabrielle with a stranger, even one who'd facilitated their reunion, wasn't easy.

"Mademoiselle Rousselle is very important and precious to me," he said gruffly. "Unfortunately, I'm not cut out for making romantic speeches or grand gestures. I'm a very practical person, but Gabrielle has never seemed to mind that."

Mrs. Whittle looked as if she was suppressing a smile. "You may be doing yourself a disservice, my lord."

Puzzled, Quin shook his head. "I assure you—"

Mrs. Whittle stopped trying to hide her amusement. "You're down on the beach at dawn, humoring an old woman's whim to play fairy godmother," she pointed out.

Quin took a breath of sea air and returned her grin. "When you put it like that...and with the proviso that you appear *far* from old...thank you, Mrs. Whittle, for helping Gabrielle. For the ladder. For...everything you've done to make her comfortable in her position. Thank you."

Mrs. Whittle's expression signaled approval. "I've never known Mademoiselle Rousselle to walk around with her head in the clouds. In fact, I would say she's a very practical person too."

"She does like music and dancing, though." Quin sighed. "I wish she had more opportunities—" he broke off. "I beg your pardon. I was thinking aloud. Now you've met me, do you feel you'll be able to assist us with our correspondence?" A frisson of tension tightened his muscles as he looked at her inquiringly.

After everything that had passed between them, he was fairly confident she'd agree, but he wouldn't completely relax until she confirmed it.

She didn't immediately reply, and as the silence lengthened his fear that she would refuse increased proportionately.

Then she startled him by laughing. "I'm sorry, my lord, I couldn't resist the temptation of putting you to the trial a little more. You've been remarkably patient and kind to a meddling old woman. If I could wave my wand and resolve all your difficulties at once, I would do so."

Quin let out a breath of relief. "You have my undying gratitude, ma'am. How can I repay you for your kindness?"

"Miss Trent has told me that you've brought back all kinds of new seeds from around the world," Mrs. Whittle said. "If you have any plants to spare after they grow, I would be honored to receive one."

"I will select the best for you," Quin promised.

"As for assisting you with your correspondence, I would be more than willing to do so—"

Quin started to reach into his breast pocket for the rather bulky letter which included his dragonfly sketches from the previous day.

"—but I cannot help," Mrs. Whittle said.

A tidal wave of disappointment crashed over Quin.

"Mademoiselle Rousselle and Miss Charlotte are leaving Brighton today," Mrs. Whittle continued. "Lady Henderson has ordered them to go to Sedgemore Hall. Mademoiselle will be able to walk to the village post office to send and collect her letters herself. But here's the one she gave me for you, yesterday."

Quin controlled the urge to seize the note from the housekeeper's hand, instead taking it carefully.

Mrs. Whittle smiled. "I didn't mention I might bump into you on the beach. Mademoiselle assumes you'll receive it via Miss Trent."

Chapter Twenty-One

Only Mrs. Whittle and Penson were present when Gabrielle and Charlotte departed for Sedgemore Hall. And Augustus.

"Good *bye*, Governess Rushabout," he sneered. "Goodbye Dumb Charlotte." He looked at them both as if they were something nasty he'd trodden in.

Charlotte turned her back on her brother and marched out of the front door to the carriage.

"Goodbye, Master Sedgemore," Gabrielle said calmly, and smiled at the butler. "Goodbye, Penson."

"I trust you have a comfortable journey, mademoiselle," he replied.

Augustus climbed a few stairs and poked his tongue out at Gabrielle over the top of the butler's head.

Gabrielle pretended she didn't see him and soon she and Charlotte were safely inside the carriage and rolling away from Brighton.

They both peered out of the windows. It didn't take long for the buildings of the town to be replaced by a view of fields and hills.

"No more sea walks," Charlotte broke the silence. "No more ice cream. No more Augustus."

The unmistakable satisfaction in her last three words made Gabrielle smile.

"Will you miss the sea?" she asked. "We didn't get long to enjoy it."

Charlotte hummed thoughtfully. "It was interesting—but we didn't find any good snail shells. I think we will find more at Sedgemore Hall."

Gabrielle suspected there were just as many snails in and around Brighton. But there were also more people to wonder why a little girl and her governess were showing a strange and special interest in the creatures. Collecting snail shells would certainly be easier at Sedgemore Hall.

She felt a little wistful she was traveling away from Quin, but really Lady Henderson had inadvertently done everyone a favor. The only time Gabrielle had ever corresponded easily with her papa and Felix had been when she and Charlotte had lived at Sedgemore Hall in Lady Henderson's absence.

For a few weeks at least, she and Quin wouldn't need to employ anyone else's help in maintaining their correspondence.

To pass the time, Gabrielle got Charlotte to play the "I see a..." game in French. But after a few hours of describing the scenery, the game lost some of its charm. They'd stopped at a wayside inn to water the horses, but neither of them had alighted from the coach.

Charlotte stretched out her arms and legs and wriggled around. "We haven't walked *anywhere* today, mademoiselle," she grumbled. "My legs are tired." She kicked her feet up and down.

"They can't be tired, they haven't done anything," Gabrielle pointed out. "But I know what you mean. I'd like to get out and walk around too. Shall we stop and see what's in the hamper Mrs. Whittle gave us?"

The driver, an older man called Nedcott, halted the coach on the side of the road, next to an open gate. Gabrielle handed up to him a meat pie, a slice of cake and a bottle of ale.

"Miss Charlotte and I want to stretch our legs before we eat," she said to Nedcott. "I thought we might walk to that tree and back." She pointed to an oak growing in the field about fifty yards from the gate. "Can you see any reason that's a bad idea?"

From his position on the box, Nedcott's view wasn't impeded by the hedgerow bordering the field.

He stood up and looked around. "No people, and no livestock," he reported, resuming his seat.

"Excellent, come along, Charlotte." They walked briskly to the tree, but Charlotte dragged her feet when they turned to go back to the coach.

"Meat pie, cake *and* lemonade," Gabrielle encouraged her.

"Lemonade?" Charlotte perked up. "It's not as good as ice cream, but it's better than barley water."

The sun was high in a cloudless sky. Even their small amount of exertion had raised a sheen of perspiration on Gabrielle's face, and there was barely any breeze. It had been warm in the carriage this morning, and it was going to get hotter as the day progressed. Gabrielle was grateful she didn't have to sit outside like Nedcott.

Once they'd returned to the coach, he climbed down and sat near the horses' heads in the shade of the hedge to finish his cake and ale.

Gabrielle and Charlotte ate and drank too, and then it was time to climb back into the carriage. This section of the road seemed particularly uneven, and the wheels juddered over the winter ruts that had dried into rock hard ridges in the summer heat.

Charlotte scowled out of the open window. "I hope my snail shells don't get cracked."

"We packed them carefully," Gabrielle reminded her.

In another few miles, the road smoothed out, but the countryside also changed. Now the view from the window was full of yellow gorse and spindly trees and bushes.

They were crossing a heath, and soon the horses' hooves and the wheels threw up so much dust that Gabrielle had to close the windows.

"Now it will be even hotter," Charlotte complained.

"But at least we won't be choking on dust." Gabrielle replied. She could feel a fine layer of gritty sand sticking to her cheeks and taste it on her lips.

"I wish we were already there," Charlotte said. "I wish we were already there by the lake with the frogs."

"Me too. Why don't you lie down and try to sleep for a while?" Gabrielle suggested. "I'll fan you."

Charlotte heaved in a sigh that lifted the whole upper half of her body, then made a face and lay down with her head on Gabrielle's lap.

Gabrielle fanned them both as she gazed out of the window,

hoping the road would soon leave the open heath behind and enter the shade of some trees.

Instead, the sound of a gunshot jolted her from her half-dozing state a fraction of a second before the carriage rocked to a halt.

Chapter Twenty-Two

Gabrielle's heart thudded sickeningly against her ribs. For an instant she was back in France, fleeing the revolutionaries who wanted to send her family to the guillotine.

On another gasping breath she remembered she was on an English country road, and that meant this was a different kind of threat.

Charlotte had been fully asleep. Her wordless mutter as she woke, suggested she was more confused than alarmed by the rude interruption to their journey.

"Hush," Gabrielle whispered. "Be still, sweetheart."

The carriage rolled back a few inches and then forward. The closed windows muffled Nedcott's voice, but she could hear him alternately cursing the man who'd fired the pistol, and the horses as he tried to get them under control.

Gabrielle knew it wouldn't take him long. Once he'd done so, she would have to face the villain who'd waylaid them. An English highwayman, for sure.

The traveling blanket on the opposite seat caught her desperate eye. She grabbed it and cast it over Charlotte.

"Draw your feet up, and be still and quiet as a mouse," she whispered, moving so that the little girl's head no longer rested on her lap.

"Une souris," Charlotte whispered in a trembling voice.

"Une souris," Gabrielle agreed.

"You in the coach—show yourself or I'll shoot your coachman!" a rough voice demanded.

Gabrielle leaned forward and lowered the window with cold, unsteady hands. The first thing she saw was a man on horseback, the lower half of his face covered in a thick scarf, a pistol in both of his hands.

One of those pistols was already empty, she reminded herself, which was small comfort in the circumstances. Even as she watched, he shoved one of the pistols into a holster on his saddle and pulled another one from his pocket.

"Who else is there?" he demanded. His horse shifted restlessly beneath him, a sign his emotions were in a dangerous state of agitation. But his aim at Nedcott remained steady, and now Gabrielle could see the mouth of the pistol he was aiming at her.

"No one, sir," she replied calmly.

Here was the true wolf, she thought with dreadful clarity. This villain who might shoot all of them on a whim.

Before her family's escape from France, she'd given a lot of thought to how she should respond if she was ever directly threatened by the revolutionaries. This situation wasn't entirely the same, but she instinctively fell back on the plans she'd made then—to treat whoever threatened her with the same calm respect she'd employed with the wolf.

And do nothing to inflame his temper or aggression.

"Sir?" the highwayman repeated, with a harsh crack of laughter. "You have that right, yer ladyship. Funny how the Quality loses their airs and graces when they're on the wrong end of a brace of pistols. Get out of the coach and bring yer jewelry box with you."

Gabrielle picked up Mrs. Whittle's basket, opened the door, and scrambled awkwardly down onto the dusty road. She wanted to get the highwayman's attention away from the coach as soon as possible, so she moved a few feet from it, clutching the basket before her.

She didn't turn around to close the door. She didn't want the villain to think there was anything inside worth hiding.

"What's that?" he demanded. "Bring it here."

"It's a basket of food. It's the only thing I had in the carriage with me," she said, tilting it so he could see the contents. "There's not much cake left, but there's an excellent meat pie. Please—would you like the meat pie?"

"I want yer jewels!" he snarled.

"I don't have any jewels." Gabrielle heard her voice start to rise and took a shaky breath. "Truly, I have nothing of value with me except a few coins in my purse." She shifted the basket into one hand and lifted her reticule with the other.

"Hah! I'll bet yer husband gives you a big allowance." The highwayman stuffed one of his pistols back in his pocket and rode toward her.

Gabrielle held her ground as the horse swung broadside onto

her, enabling the highwayman to lean down and snatch her reticule. She was afraid of the rider, not his mount. For a few seconds the highwayman's booted foot was only inches from her hands. She imagined seizing it and flinging him backward out of the saddle.

But despite the mixture of anger and fear ringing in her ears, she didn't do anything. The element of surprise would be on her side, but success was far from assured. And even if he did fall, he'd still have his pistols. The last thing she wanted was to get shot by a highwayman because she'd hurt his dignity.

He used his teeth and his free hand to tug open the string that held her reticule closed, and dragged out the paltry contents.

"Pah!" He tossed it aside in disgust. "Have you gambled away your whole allowance?"

"Why are you so sure I've got money?" Gabrielle asked. "I haven't. I promise you, I haven't."

"Your carriage says otherwise," he said sarcastically. "If you don't want people to know you're rich you shouldn't ride around in a carriage with a great golden crest on the door."

He meant the Henderson coat of arms, Gabrielle realized, with a sinking sensation. If they'd been traveling in a less ostentatious coach, he might have let them pass by unmolested. She almost told him she was only the governess, not the lady he assumed her to be—but then he might wonder if there was a child in the carriage.

"Coachman, get those trunks down from the back," the highwayman ordered. "We'll see what treasures you've got in there."

His horse danced uneasily as he turned it toward the rear of the coach. He was getting frustrated, Gabrielle thought, and that might make him more careless—or more dangerous.

If only she had something of value to give him—

A shot shattered the afternoon air. The highwayman rocked backward, and his pistol fired harmlessly into the sky.

"*Mademoiselle!*" Charlotte screamed from inside the carriage.

Gabrielle's single focus was the threat the highwayman presented. She lunged forward, narrowly avoiding the horse's hooves, and grabbed his boot. Exactly as she'd earlier imagined, she heaved with all her might.

Chapter Twenty-Three

For an agonizing moment, the highwayman seemed glued to the saddle. Then he started to slip. The next instant he crashed to the ground. His horse plunged forward. Gabrielle stumbled back, but it galloped harmlessly away onto the heath.

She bent over, her hands on her knees, gulping in lungfuls of gritty air. Her heart pounded so hard she was afraid she might throw up. She stared blankly at a rut on the road, struggling to regain her composure, and Charlotte's terrified cries finally pierced her awareness.

She was about to call out a reassurance, when she remembered the highwayman still had one unfired pistol in his pocket. Renewed fear streaked through her trembling limbs. She lurched fully upright, determined to get to it before he did.

But another horse was approaching fast. The man riding it sprang down from its back almost before it stopped, and swiftly retrieved the loaded pistol from the motionless highwayman.

He straightened and looked up at her.

"Quin?" she gasped.

He met her gaze, a fierce, almost dangerous, expression burning in his eyes. She could see no hint of the mild-mannered man who studied moths by moonlight in the warrior standing before her. She had the dizzying realization that this was a part of his character she'd never before seen.

She was still trembling from her encounter with the highwayman, and the power of Quin's gaze locked her to the spot.

He took a stride toward her, then glanced sideways and his eyes widened. Gabrielle finally became aware of gasping sobs and running footsteps.

She turned as Charlotte cannoned into her. She'd had no time to brace herself for the impact, and they both ended up in a heap on the road.

"I thought he shot you! I thought he shot you!" Charlotte sobbed hysterically, latching her arms tightly around Gabrielle's neck.

"No, sweetheart, I'm not hurt. Nedcott's not hurt." Gabrielle glanced up at the coachman and saw his affirmative nod.

Nedcott's face was dead white, his expression tense from the aftermath of danger. But his walk was only slightly unsteady as he went to join Quin beside the fallen highwayman.

Gabrielle bent her head over Charlotte, hugging the small, weeping body tightly against her chest. Now the threat was over, her own limbs began to tremble so badly she doubted she could stand, even if she wanted to. It was a relief and a comfort to hold Charlotte close, and to know they were both safe.

"It's over, sweetheart," she murmured. "We're all safe. You

were so brave. I'm proud of you." She rocked them both back and forward as she spoke, hardly aware of what she was doing.

"I hid." Charlotte hiccupped. "I wasn't b-brave. I hid."

"I told you to hide," Gabrielle said. "You were a good girl to obey—"

"Until I thought he shot you and Nedcott!" Charlotte reared back to fix her tear-drenched eyes on Gabrielle's face. "I couldn't hide when I thought you were *shot*!"

"Of course you couldn't," Quin said, crouching beside them. "I'm proud to know two such brave and resourceful ladies." His voice was husky.

Charlotte clung to Gabrielle and peered past Quin to the highwayman. "Is he dead?" she demanded, her eyes still too big for her face.

"No," Quin replied, shifting slightly so it was clear he with speaking to both of them. "My shot hit him in the arm, and he seems to have struck his head when he fell, but he's still alive."

"I wish he was dead!" Charlotte said fiercely.

Quin nodded gravely. "I understand how you feel. But since he isn't dead, we are now obliged to act honorably, even though he didn't."

Charlotte wiped the back of her hand under her nose as she stared at Quin. "What's that mean?" she demanded.

He pulled a neatly folded handkerchief out of his pocket and gave it to her. As Charlotte blew her nose, Gabrielle realized her own appearance must be as disheveled and unladylike as her charge's—and her reticule was trampled into the road.

Embarrassment heated her skin, and she averted her face,

surreptitiously pressing her cheek against her shoulder and the fabric of her bodice.

Quin didn't say a word, but a moment later his hand covered hers as he gave her a second handkerchief.

"Thank you," she whispered. She kept her face turned away and one arm firmly around Charlotte, and blew her nose with as much delicacy as she could manage in the circumstances.

"We must hand the highwayman over to the nearest constable, and make a statement to the local magistrate," Quin explained to Charlotte. "Then he will be kept in jail until he's tried for his crime before a judge and jury. Now, ladies, I think it's best you don't sit on the road any longer. Will you permit me to carry you, Miss Charlotte?"

Without a word, she went into his open arms. He settled her comfortably against one shoulder, and offered his other hand to Gabrielle. She wanted to believe she took it from courtesy, and the comfort of having his fingers wrapped around hers. But when she tried to stand, she discovered she was still so shaken she needed to rely on his strength to gain her feet.

"I think that silver birch tree looks like a promising tree, don't you?" Quin said to Charlotte.

He released Gabrielle's hand but, to her surprise, he didn't offer her his arm. He put it round her waist instead and drew her close to his side.

It wasn't the easiest way to walk across the heath, but the comfort of being able to put one of her arms around Quin's back and the other around Charlotte was worth the awkwardness.

Quin had arrived when she'd needed him most. She'd allowed herself to hope he might visit as well as write to her at Sedgemore

Hall. But it hadn't occurred to her he'd be on the road behind her until she'd looked up and seen him.

There were no large trees on the scruffy heath, but they made their way between clumps of heather to the modicum of shade provided by the birch tree. The rich almond scent of the yellow gorse flowers hung heavy on the heat-saturated air. But then a light breeze gently rattled the drying seed heads and felt almost as welcome as a cool drink against Gabrielle's hot skin.

"Look, a butterfly," Quin said to Charlotte.

Gabrielle followed the direction of his nod to see a butterfly with wings of a beautiful violet blue hovering over the gorse bush, before alighting on the flowers.

"Many interesting plants and creatures make their home on heaths," Quin said.

"It's pretty," Charlotte said, sniffing.

"Yes, it is. Now, all you both need to do is rest for a little while," he said, when he was sure they were settled comfortably.

Gabrielle wanted to ask him what *he* was going to do next, but she could tell he was trying to distract Charlotte from their terrifying experience, so she didn't say anything.

"I wonder why Lord Quin is here?" Charlotte said, as they watched him stride back to the carriage. "Do you think he was looking for plants on the heath? Or was he following you, mademoiselle?"

"We'll ask him later," Gabrielle said.

Quin's gut churned with residual anger and fear. Not fear for himself. He'd never been in any danger. But from the moment he'd heard the shot echo across the heath and suspected the carriage had been held up, he'd had to maintain an unrelenting grip over his fear for Gabrielle.

There had been times on the expedition when his friends had been in great danger, but he'd never experienced such terror on their behalf.

But he loved Gabrielle. He'd willingly die for her—and the driving temptation to intervene had almost overwhelmed him. Somehow, he'd clung to the cool-headed, rational part of himself that served him best in hazardous situations, and used the tall gorse bushes as cover to make his way closer. It would have been unforgivable to do anything that might put Gabrielle in more danger, while the highwayman was still pointing his weapon at her.

When Quin had seen her leap toward the villain's horse, his heart had catapulted up to his throat. The highwayman had fallen, Quin had realized what she'd done—and he'd been torn by conflicting impulses to scold her for being so reckless, or praise her courage and quick wits.

She'd stayed calm, protected the child in her care, and acted in a split second the moment an opportunity arose. She was amazing. He wanted to sit beside her, hold her, and assure himself she really was unhurt.

But it was his job to make sure Gabrielle and Charlotte didn't suffer any more distress from their shocking experience, not laze under a silver birch tree assuaging his own agitated emotions.

"What are we going to do now?" Nedcott asked as soon as Quin rejoined him.

"Is he still alive?" Quin jerked his head toward the highwayman.

"Yes. I've bound his wound like you said. I reckon the ball is still lodged inside him, but nothing we can do about that here—even if I was inclined to help him." Nedcott's eyes burned with anger and contempt.

"No. We need to tie his hands and feet. Do you have rope?" Quin asked, more curtly than he'd intended. He realized the deliberate air of calm cheerfulness he'd assumed while he was with Gabrielle and Charlotte was slipping, and he took a moment to compose himself.

"Yes, sir."

"I'm Lord Hanwell." It belatedly occurred to Quin to introduce himself. "Both ladies know me."

A smile came and went across Nedcott's face. "Thought they might, my lord."

"I've known Mademoiselle Rousselle longer," Quin admitted.

His attention shifted to the prone highwayman. "Make sure you bind him tightly. I'm going to take Mademoiselle Rousselle and Miss Charlotte some water, and discuss with mademoiselle how we will proceed."

He went to his horse and retrieved the flask and traveling cup which had gone around the world with him. Then he strode back across the heath, the dry, dusty soil creating a film over his boots until they appeared gray, not black.

Chapter Twenty-Four

The water Quin brought them was very welcome. Charlotte gulped down a cupful without pausing to take a single breath. Gabrielle didn't realize how thirsty she was until it was her turn. When the first sip of water touched her tongue, it required all her self-control not to guzzle it as quickly as Charlotte had.

"Thank you. You always bring me something to drink when I need it most," she said to Quin.

"And I always will," he replied, a fiercely protective expression in his eyes. "Always." He poured some more water into the cup for them.

"Now," he continued. "We need to get to the next staging inn as soon as we can. Would you be agreeable to riding beside Nedcott, Mademoiselle Rousselle?"

"Yes, of course, but...why?" His suggestion puzzled her.

"I can't imagine either of you wishes to travel inside the coach with the highwayman," he said quietly, "and I want to deliver him to the local constable at the first opportunity. If you don't object, Charlotte can ride in front of me. I swear I'll take good care of her."

"I know you will," Gabrielle said, even as Charlotte sat up, interest dawning in her eyes.

"I can ride on your horse with you?" she said to Quin.

"Yes—if Mademoiselle Rousselle approves," he replied.

"Of course I approve," Gabrielle said. "But—"

"I'll be able to point out to Charlotte some of the interesting things we'll see along the way," Quin said. "One has a completely different view of the landscape from the back of a horse."

"We will stay close to mademoiselle and Nedcott, won't we?" Charlotte said. Her face was still streaked with tears and dust, but it was clear she was giving serious consideration to Quin's suggestion.

"Very close," he said at once.

"I will ride with you," she agreed.

"You're going to put the highwayman inside the carriage?" Gabrielle's mind didn't seem to be working as quickly as usual, but she'd belatedly guessed that was why Quin wanted her to sit beside Nedcott.

"Yes. He's securely tied up, and not yet conscious, so he's not dangerous. But I can't imagine either of you wants to travel with him," Quin said.

Gabrielle thought about it for a moment, and realized she wasn't comfortable with the notion that no one would be keeping an eye on the highwayman during their journey.

"I'll ride in the carriage with him," she said. "That way, if he wakes up and tries to escape, I can immediately shout a warning."

And perhaps, if she could do so when Charlotte wasn't listening, she'd ask Quin to lend her a pistol. "This is a case of preferring to keep my enemy where I can see him," she explained.

"No! No, no, *no*!" Charlotte seized Gabrielle's arm. "You're not riding with the bad man. No, mademoiselle, no!" New tears spilled from her eyes. "If you do, I will too."

"Neither of you are riding with the bad man," Quin said firmly. "Would you like to see for yourself that he's trussed up tighter than a chicken, Charlotte?"

She nodded warily, still clinging to Gabrielle with both hands.

"All right then, let's go and look at him."

"Gawk?" Charlotte sniffed. The handkerchief Quin had given her was lying in her lap. She picked it up and applied the crumpled linen to her eyes and nose.

"Gawk?" Gabrielle questioned.

"We're going to rudely gawk at the bad man because he rudely threatened us." Charlotte's voice was muffled by the folds of fabric.

"Let's immediately proceed with our rude gawking. Up you come ladies." Quin rose to his feet and offered a hand to each of them.

He'd taken off his gloves, and Gabrielle wanted to hold tight to his familiar hand. No, she wanted to fling herself into his arms and feel his embrace surround her. But this wasn't the time or place for such behavior.

He smiled at her, intimate, understanding warmth in his eyes. "We'll be safe and comfortable soon, dear heart," he said softly.

He guided them both back across the sunbaked heath. Charlotte walked between Quin and Gabrielle, holding both their hands. It was awkward to walk three abreast, but where the space between the bushes narrowed, Quin always went first.

Once they arrived at the coach, Quin looked inside and then stood back to let the others peer in.

It was the first time Gabrielle had seen the highwayman's uncovered face. His appearance was unremarkable except for a growing bruise on his temple. His eyes were open, but his expression was dazed and she wasn't sure he was entirely conscious. He did, indeed, seem to be securely tied up.

"You're evil!" Charlotte shouted at him. "Why haven't you tied something around his mouth?" She rounded on Quin.

"I don't want him to suffocate before we hand him over to the constable," he said. "It's our job to deliver him to the constable and the magistrate, so the law can deliver justice for his crime against you and mademoiselle and Nedcott."

"And then they'll find him guilty," Charlotte said.

"I expect so. The jury will decide on his guilt or innocence and the judge will decide his punishment," Quin said.

"*We* know he's guilty," Charlotte insisted.

"Yes, we do, and we will explain exactly what happened to the magistrate." Quin closed the carriage door. "Do you still want to ride with me?"

Charlotte looked from Gabrielle to him—and slowly nodded.

"I'll help mademoiselle onto the coach before we mount up," he said, and walked with Gabrielle the few necessary steps.

She turned to face him. There was so much to say, and yet she didn't know what to say. She just wanted—

He didn't speak either, just pulled her into his arms. She closed her eyes and leaned against him. He tightened his embrace. She could feel the strength in his body, and she'd seen him demonstrate his physical prowess more than once. But even though his strength was exhilarating, it wasn't why she felt safe with him. It never had been.

He stroked a comforting hand over her shoulder, released her and took a half step back.

She looked up at him and he brushed a light caress over her cheek with the back of his fingers. His eyes...his smile...he was saying so much to her without words, but all he said aloud was, "You must both put on your bonnets now you'll be traveling outside. Nedcott?"

To Gabrielle's surprise, the coachman produced their bonnets. The two men must have rescued them from the interior of the carriage before they dumped the highwayman inside.

"That's Charlotte's," she pointed to it as she claimed her own.

Quin took Charlotte's bonnet over to her. "Mademoiselle's mama explained to me that ladies should always wear some kind of headgear when you're out of the house," he said.

A memory of their happy, carefree days wandering the gardens of the château, rose so vividly in Gabrielle's mind she had to choke back a sob.

They were happy now, she reminded herself. They'd just had a bad afternoon—which hadn't turned out to be so bad after all.

She took Quin's hand and used his assistance to climb up onto the driver's seat beside Nedcott.

Chapter Twenty-Five

"There." Gabrielle finished tying the ribbon in Charlotte's hair into a bow and tapped her lightly on the shoulder. "All done. Turn around and let me see you."

Charlotte turned and stared at Gabrielle with huge, solemn eyes.

"You're as pretty as a picture." Gabrielle smiled and brushed one of Charlotte's curls back from her face.

Charlotte nodded, leaned in and put her arms around Gabrielle. Charlotte had never been much of a hugger. This was a new expression of her feelings. Gabrielle held her close, sharing the comfort of their embrace.

They were in a bedchamber of the posting inn they'd reached twenty minutes after resuming their journey. As soon as they'd arrived, Quin had bespoken a room for Gabrielle and Charlotte. Gabrielle had asked for their luggage to be brought up from the coach, and for plenty of warm water as well.

She didn't know how long they would be staying at the inn.

But she'd been certain she and Charlotte would both feel better after they'd washed off the dust and sweat covering their bodies and changed into new clothes.

For several long minutes, Charlotte continued to stand by Gabrielle's chair, leaning into their hug.

Gabrielle stroked Charlotte's hair and gazed out of the open window at a view of tree tops and blue sky. The light breeze from the open window carried the fragrance of the roses which clung to the inn wall. She could hear the sound of muffled voices, and the more distant lowing of a cow.

It was a typical, peaceful late afternoon in summer. And that's what she was going to focus on—not the mental image of the highwayman's pistol pointing at her.

The attempted highway robbery wasn't the only thing of note that had happened today. Gabrielle had gradually realized that Quin's miraculous intervention, combined with the way he'd treated her and Charlotte, would also have consequences.

He'd made no verbal claim upon her, but he'd held her in his arms in full sight of Nedcott and Charlotte. And he'd touched her in a way that revealed as much about their relationship as any words.

She didn't know what that would mean for their plans to maintain a discreet correspondence. Were they going to take Nedcott into their confidence? At least the coachman seemed well disposed toward Quin.

"Lord Hanwell seems to be a very competent and honorable gentleman," Nedcott had mused, when she was sitting beside him on the coach. "Have you known him long, mademoiselle?"

"Since I was thirteen and he was fifteen," Gabrielle had replied. "He's always been competent and honorable."

"Ah. Good thing for all of us he was in the neighborhood, I say." Nedcott had fallen silent and only spoken again to call for assistance when they arrived at the posting inn.

Gabrielle brought her attention back to the present. "The roses smell nice, don't they?" she said.

"Mmm." Charlotte straightened up and gave Gabrielle a small smile. "I like roses. Lord Quin likes roses, too. We talked about our favorite flowers. I like horse riding. He said he was following you."

"Oh." Gabrielle didn't know how to respond.

"He said he has a letter for you that's got pictures in it that we will both like to see," Charlotte continued.

"A letter *and* pictures?" Gabrielle's voice was husky.

"Mmm. He says the sketches aren't as good as yours would be, but he believes they show what he saw well enough. But he wouldn't tell me what's in the pictures." Charlotte frowned over that. "He said I have to wait until you open the letter. He said he's still not going to take you away from me."

"He has a very big heart." Gabrielle managed to smile.

"Don't cry, mademoiselle." Charlotte delicately touched Gabrielle's cheek. "I will *never* tell Mama or Augustus about Lord Quin. Never. Ever." She clamped her lips shut, the determined obstinacy in her eyes so fierce it seemed a tangible thing.

"Thank you, sweetheart." Gabrielle pulled her close and hid her tears against Charlotte's shoulder.

Charlotte patted Gabrielle's back as if she was the one offering comfort. "Lord Quin said you like horse riding, too."

"I do." Gabrielle raised her head. "Though it's been a long time since I've had the chance to ride."

Charlotte's tummy rumbled, and an odd combination of expressions danced across her face. She looked at the floor, and then sideways at Gabrielle.

"I'm hungry," she said gruffly.

"So am I." Gabrielle hadn't thought she was until that moment, but she realized she could eat. "Let's go and see if we can find Lord Quin."

That wasn't, and never had been, the correct way to address him, but Gabrielle was certain Quin didn't mind.

She stood up, sparkles of anticipation dancing in her veins at the prospect of seeing him again.

◦◦◦

"WE'LL BE REMAINING HERE for dinner at the very least," Quin said to the landlady. "But until I've spoken to Mademoiselle Rousselle, I regret I can't tell you what time—"

The landlady's gaze shifted away from him toward the stairs. He turned to look in the same direction and forgot what he'd been saying.

Gabrielle and Charlotte were coming down the stairs. They were both wearing different gowns, and they'd done up their hair. Gabrielle appeared as poised and fresh as if she'd spent the afternoon relaxing in a drawing room. Her beauty took his breath away.

But to him, she was always beautiful, whether she was sitting in a heap of dusty skirts in the middle of the road, or smiling up at him on Marine Parade.

The thought of what might have happened to her if he hadn't been riding so close behind their carriage made his stomach clench. Those fraught moments he'd been maneuvering into position to take action would take a while to fade from his memory.

He moved to stand at the bottom of the narrow stairs and smiled up at them. "Mademoiselle Rousselle, Miss Charlotte, I'm pleased to see you."

There was a window on the small landing at the top of the last flight of stairs, so the light was behind them as they began their last descent. It created an apparent halo of gold around Gabrielle's blonde hair, and even Charlotte's darker hair shimmered with strands of red gold.

Quin was so struck by the beautiful effect he nearly told them they looked like angels, but quickly changed his mind. Angels who descended from Heaven very soon returned to Heaven. In the current circumstances, that wasn't a comfortable thought.

He wanted both the young ladies coming downstairs toward him to continue enjoying the more prosaic delights of Earth for a long time to come—and have no more close encounters with pistol-wielding highwaymen.

By the time they reached him, the light from the open front door behind him made it easy for him to see their faces clearly. He was glad they were smiling at him, and the evidence of Charlotte's heart-wrenching tears had been erased.

"You both look refreshed and very pretty," he said gruffly. "I hope you're also feeling somewhat more the thing."

"Yes, thank you, my lord." Gabrielle smiled at him, and he wanted to kiss her. "Thanks to you, we are very well. Aren't we, Charlotte?"

"Yes." Charlotte took a small step to the side and sank into a curtsy so deep she nearly ended up sitting on the floor.

Quin seized one small waving hand and held it securely as she tried to regain her balance.

"I thought that deep curtsy was the one reserved for a marquess," he teased her gently, and then wished he hadn't made any comment, because he didn't want her to think he was laughing at her.

"I was trying to do the king's curtsy," she said, in all seriousness, tightening her grip on his fingers. "But I haven't practiced it much."

"I'm honored." Quin was touched by the sentiment that must have prompted her action.

"Hmm." Charlotte frowned with concentration, still wobbling in her awkward crouch.

Quin didn't want her to finish her grand gesture of thanks by toppling into an ignominious heap on the floor, so he claimed her other hand as well. When she looked up at him with a questioning expression on her face, he grinned. Then he pulled her up, hoisting her a foot off the ground before he lowered her again.

She rewarded him with a beaming smile of her own.

"We're hungry," she said.

"I was just discussing dinner with Mrs. Larkin," Quin told

her. "Mademoiselle Rousselle?" He looked at Gabrielle, his voice unconsciously softening as he met her smiling gaze. "Mrs. Larkin says she can serve dinner within the next thirty to forty minutes if that would suit you?"

"That would be wonderful, thank you," Gabrielle addressed the landlady directly.

"You're very welcome, mademoiselle," Mrs. Larkin replied. "I hope you and the young lady found everything to your satisfaction in your bedchamber?"

"Oh, yes, it's a very pleasant room," Gabrielle said.

"Let's go and sit in the private parlor I've reserved for us," Quin suggested. "Would you like some tea or anything else to drink while we're waiting for our dinner?"

Gabrielle agreed she would enjoy a cup of tea and Charlotte asked for milk. He relayed their requests to the landlady and then took them into the parlor.

Chapter Twenty-Six

"This is a very comfortable inn." Gabrielle looked appreciatively around the private room Quin had bespoken for them. "It seemed so small from the outside, I didn't expect it to be so well appointed inside." She sat down on the sofa near the unlit hearth, and Charlotte immediately sat beside her.

"I'm glad it is." Quin took the chair opposite the sofa. "It was a great relief to me when Nedcott assured us he's familiar with it. I don't want either of you to suffer any more discomfort or inconvenience."

'Inconvenience' was a mild description of what had happened. Quin had never been prone to dramatics, but today Gabrielle was certain he'd chosen that phrase for Charlotte's benefit as much as hers. Especially when she remembered the fierce, battle-ready light in his eyes after he'd shot the highwayman.

He'd comforted her beside the carriage. She suddenly wondered if he needed comfort or reassurance himself.

"You arrived to rescue us just like a knight in a story," she said. "Didn't he, Charlotte?"

"Just like a knight," Charlotte agreed. "Except he doesn't have armor or a lance, and he's an earl. But you galloped like a knight, and you rescued us better than a knight," she told Quin. "A lance wouldn't have been any good against the highwayman until you were right up close to him. Shooting him was better."

Despite her apparently prosaic words, Charlotte's face drained of color as she was speaking. She edged closer to Gabrielle until she could lean against her side.

Gabrielle put her arm around Charlotte's shoulders, kissed the top of her head, and smiled at Quin.

His color had heightened when she'd initially compared him to a story knight, but his visible self-consciousness was quickly replaced by concern.

"I know it was a deeply unpleasant experience for you, Charlotte," he said. "I'm sorry it happened, but you and mademoiselle are safe now. And soon we'll all have dinner."

"Where's the highwayman?" Charlotte asked, from her position tucked up against Gabrielle's side.

"Locked in one of the storage sheds until the constable comes to transport him to the local jail." An uncompromising expression appeared briefly in Quin's eyes, but his voice was as calm as if he was confirming the horses had been put in the stable.

"Can he escape from the storage shed?" Charlotte glanced uneasily at the door.

"No," Quin assured her. "Nedcott and two of the ostlers are guarding him until the constable arrives. I've already made it plain I don't want him to be kept in any part of the inn for any longer than necessary. Mrs. Larkin is in full agreement with me," he added.

Gabrielle imagined that was *very* true. If she was the landlady, she wouldn't want a villain locked in one of her storage sheds for any longer than necessary either.

She decided not to ask the other questions she had about the highwayman's injury, and what would happen to him, because Charlotte was listening.

"What are we going to do after we've had dinner?" she asked instead.

"That's what I wish to discuss with you both," Quin said. "We're still waiting for the constable and the magistrate. Nedcott and I need to give our statements to the magistrate and, unfortunately, we don't know how long it will be before he arrives."

"What about my statement?" Gabrielle asked.

"If you feel able to give it to him, I'm sure he'll want to hear it," Quin replied.

"What about me?" Charlotte said in a small voice.

"If you want to give him your account, I'll tell him, but otherwise I don't think you need to speak to him," Quin said. "Do you want to give the magistrate your account of what happened?"

Charlotte stared at him for a few seconds, then shook her head firmly.

Quin acknowledged her response with a quiet smile. "All right. Now, Nedcott has told me it's another hour and a half in the coach to get to Sedgemore Hall. Since we can't know how long we'll be waiting for the magistrate, I think it's probably best if we decide to spend the night here. That way, we can feel properly settled for the rest of the evening."

"Stay here tonight?" Gabrielle repeated. Quin's suggestion wasn't a complete surprise to her, but she'd assumed they'd make their final decision after they'd spoken to the magistrate.

"Yes," Quin said. "But only if you're both comfortable with that idea? If the magistrate arrives in the next few minutes and doesn't take long recording our statements, there'll still be time to reach Sedgemore Hall before it gets too dark to travel. But if we don't make plans now, we might spend all evening on edge waiting for him—which will be unsettling for all of us."

"Charlotte and I can share the room where we changed our dresses," Gabrielle said.

"That's what I thought. Are you happy with this idea, Charlotte?" he asked.

Gabrielle loved him for including Charlotte in the conversation. Although she was also certain he'd already made the decision, and was telling them as both a courtesy and reassurance.

"Good. I will arrange for a messenger to go to Sedgemore Hall to let them know you'll be arriving tomorrow." Quin stood up.

"I don't think you need to," Gabrielle said.

He gave her a questioning look.

"I doubt Lady Henderson sent any warning ahead that we're coming," she explained. "But it would be best to find out what Nedcott thinks as well."

"I see." Quin's expression relaxed. "You believe sending a messenger might create worry rather than allaying it?"

"Yes."

"I'll go and check with Nedcott before we have dinner. I won't be long. Ah." He paused and picked up two objects from the table. "This is for you." He handed Gabrielle a fat letter.

"And this is for you." He gave Charlotte a book. "Unfortunately, I couldn't find any useful references to snails in it when I checked yesterday, but I hope you may find some of it interesting."

"For me to keep?" Charlotte hugged the book against her chest.

"For you to keep," he confirmed.

He met Gabrielle's gaze, glanced down at the letter in her hand and back up to meet her eyes again. "It's very…dull and prosaic. I'm not a troubadour. You can…well…you can open it now." He flushed. "I won't be long."

He went out, closing the door quietly behind him.

Gabrielle and Charlotte looked at each other.

"I think he means he hasn't written you a love poem," Charlotte whispered. "Do you mind he hasn't written you a love poem?"

"No. What's the book?"

Charlotte lowered it and opened the cover to the title page.

"*The Natural History of Selborne*, by the Reverend Gilbert White," Gabrielle read out.

Charlotte carefully turned a few pages. "I can't read this, mademoiselle." She sounded upset. "It's too difficult."

"Let me see." Gabrielle took the book from Charlotte and read a random paragraph. "*It has been remarked that every species of bird has a mode of nidification peculiar to itself…*"

"What's nidification?" Charlotte asked.

"In French, nid means nest," Gabrielle replied, trying to work it out herself. "It must be something to do with nesting. Yes, I think it's saying you can tell which kind of bird made a nest just by looking at how the nest is constructed."

Quin came back into the room as she was speaking. He picked up a dining chair and moved it so he could sit directly in front of them. "That's what it's saying. I'm afraid you might find a lot of it rather dull, Charlotte."

Gabrielle flipped a few more pages, read the start of another paragraph, and her eyes opened wide.

"What?" he asked.

"Letter thirty-two," she said, handing him the book.

He scanned the text she'd mentioned and rubbed his temple with his fingertips.

Reverend White's book was presented as a series of letters in which it seemed he discussed anything that interested him. The letter Gabrielle had spotted began with the words, '*Castration has a strange effect: it emasculates both man, beast, and bird...*'

"Charlotte," Quin said. "This is your book. Some of it's very interesting—at least I found it so. Some of it you'll probably find dull or annoying, especially when he breaks into Latin. But I think it's best if you allow mademoiselle to guide which parts of it you read. It has got pictures," he added.

Gabrielle swallowed a laugh. Poor Quin. He'd tried to find a gift for Charlotte that respected her interests, and now he was afraid he'd chosen something improper for a child.

"It was written by a reverend," she reminded him. "There can't be anything too startling in it."

Quin's gaze slid sideways, then he looked at her straight on and grinned ruefully. "I hope not."

Charlotte was avidly watching their exchange. "You found a bit about mating, didn't you?" she said.

Gabrielle somehow managed to choke on her own saliva and started coughing.

"Would you like a sip of tea, mademoiselle?" Quin asked solicitously.

She pressed her handkerchief against her lips and shook her head.

He looked at Charlotte. "What led you to that conclusion?" he asked calmly, although Gabrielle could tell he too was fighting his amusement.

"Birds build nests to put their eggs in—and eggs don't hatch if there isn't a cock in the hen house," Charlotte explained. "The cock has to mount the hen to get chicks out of the eggs."

Quin nodded appreciatively. "An excellent piece of deductive reasoning. Have you and mademoiselle spent a lot of time looking for snails in farmyards?"

"Not as much as I'd like. The gardener's boy told us about needing a cock to get chicks. Did I guess right?" Charlotte stared at him. She was curious about the answer, but Gabrielle thought she was even more curious about *how* Quin was responding to her questions.

"Almost." He paused, clearly considering how to continue. "However, rather than being about a rooster, the letter mademoiselle noticed was mentioning ways in which the male of a species might be...um...discouraged from mating with the females."

"By shutting him out of the hen house," Charlotte said.

"That's certainly one method which can be attempted," Quin agreed. "And often is. Would you like to read your letter, mademoiselle?"

Gabrielle hadn't forgotten the letter on her lap. She'd half-hoped she might open it when two pairs of eyes weren't fixed upon her, but she couldn't leave Quin floundering under Charlotte's inquisition any longer.

She carefully broke the seal and unfolded both the surrounding letter, and a folded sheet of paper covered with small drawings.

"It's the transformation of a dragonfly from a creature that lives below the surface of a pond, to one that flies above it," Quin explained. "I've numbered the sketches, but I think the order of progression should be reasonably clear."

"Oh." Gabrielle's smile trembled as she flattened the sheet with careful hands. "Your drawing has improved so much."

"That's what Miss Trent said. As an artist, I can't hold a candle to you or Duncan, but I've tried to improve my ability to record scientific details."

The door opened as Quin finished speaking. "It seems dinner is ready." He sounded relieved. "Let's eat."

∽

IN THE BLINK OF AN EYE, or the crack of a highway robber's pistol shot, Quin had gone from being a single gentleman to being a man at the head of a small family.

And he liked it.

He enjoyed sitting down to dinner with his future wife and Charlotte.

He'd enjoyed his adventurous trip around the globe, too. But he'd gone on his travels to seek knowledge, not adventure for the sake of it. Now he'd returned to England, he was more than ready to set up his own household with its regular domestic routines. Being able to have breakfast every morning with Gabrielle would be the peak of happiness.

Especially if breakfast was preceded by a night of marital bliss in a well-appointed bedroom.

But that was for the future. Here and now, he was concerned about the continuing harm the highwayman's attack might have caused Gabrielle and Charlotte. Not physical harm, but the invisible kind which could linger in a person's memory or lower their spirits.

He considered it his duty to ensure his young ladies felt secure and content in their temporary surroundings. But sharing those teasing, laughing glances with Gabrielle, and chatting to Charlotte about Reverend White's book and dragonflies had soothed Quin's agitation too. The more he sensed his companions were truly relaxed and comfortable, the better he felt himself.

He'd expected Gabrielle to appear outwardly calm because that's how she'd been raised. But though Charlotte had conversed with him more than he'd expected on the ride to the inn, he'd wondered if she would withdraw into herself once she'd had more time for reflection.

She hadn't.

She'd curtsied to him as if he were a king, while explaining to him what she was doing. And later, she'd hugged Gilbert White's book to her slight body and smiled at Quin as if he'd given her a casket of precious rubies.

That gave him hope the highwayman's attack wouldn't be the setback to Charlotte's slowly growing confidence he'd feared it might be.

Of course, he should have obtained Gabrielle's approval of the book *before* he'd given it to Charlotte. Since he hadn't, and he didn't want to undermine Charlotte's trust in him by taking it back from her now, he hoped they'd be able to navigate awkward passages about castration, and such like.

Meanwhile, Charlotte told him all about her snail shell collection while they ate roast beef and mashed potatoes.

"Would you mind if a snail crawled on your bare hand, Lord Quin?" she asked.

"No." He smiled at Gabrielle's carefully bland expression.

"Or a slug?" Charlotte pursued. "What about a worm or a frog?"

"I can handle any of the creatures you've mentioned without anxiety," he said, blocking his mind to awareness that the creature he wanted to handle tonight was sitting across the table from him, elegantly consuming her dinner.

At the confectioner's yesterday, he'd teased Gabrielle under the table. Today he didn't have the self-control for such games. He wanted her too badly.

"However," he said to Charlotte. "In some parts of the world, there are frogs whose skin is so laden with poison that a single touch can prove fatal."

Charlotte gazed at him, her meal forgotten.

"Often they signal their toxicity by being brightly colored," Quin continued. "Vivid yellow or blue, for example."

"A blue frog," Charlotte breathed, entranced. "Did you see one?"

"Yes, when we visited Brazil. I was careful to keep my gloves on when we ventured into the forest."

A small movement from Gabrielle caught his eye.

"I'm safely home, dear heart," he said, guessing squeamishness was not the cause of her swiftly covered distress on this occasion. "And we have no blue frogs in England. Or wolves."

"I'd like to see a blue frog *and* a wolf," Charlotte declared.

"I completely understand your curiosity," Quin said. "But I think we should make a pact, you and I."

"Me and you?" Charlotte glanced from him to Gabrielle and back.

"Yes. I propose that while we're eating, we don't discuss anything which might interfere with anyone's relaxed enjoyment and digestion of their food," Quin said.

It was Gabrielle's turn to throw him an odd look.

"For mademoiselle's sake?" Charlotte said. "All right."

"Yours and mine too." Quin smiled at her. "While we've been talking, you've forgotten to eat."

"Oh." Charlotte looked down at her plate and cut off a piece of beef. "It's a very good dinner."

"Yes, it is."

"What can we talk about when we're *not* eating?" Charlotte asked.

"Anything you want. Well," Quin considered. "As scientists, we're naturally interested in a wider range of subjects than some other people. So, before we become too deeply engrossed in a topic, we should consider whether our companions are also likely to be interested."

"Mademoiselle is interested in everything," Charlotte claimed loyally.

"I know. It's a sign of her affection for you…and me. But we shouldn't take advantage of her generous nature."

"I love you both," Gabrielle said. "It makes me happy to hear you talking about anything…that makes you happy." Her voice wavered.

Quin put down his fork and reached out to take her right hand.

Charlotte's gaze tracked his gesture and then she looked into Gabrielle's face.

Gabrielle put down her fork and took Charlotte's hand, so she was connected to both her companions. "Let's talk about our favorite foods," she suggested. "That seems appropriate for dinner time."

Charlotte continued to stare at her. "You love me?" she whispered.

"Yes, I do."

"Mademoiselle." Charlotte blinked and her mouth worked, but she didn't burst into tears, the way she had earlier.

The clock ticked on the mantelpiece.

Charlotte returned her attention to her plate and pulled her hand away from Gabrielle's.

Quin squeezed Gabrielle's other hand, and she gave him a tremulous smile.

"I like ice cream," Charlotte said gruffly. "Am I truly a scientist?"

Chapter Twenty-Seven

Gabrielle didn't know why it had disturbed her when Quin mentioned the poisonous blue frogs. He was clearly sitting beside her in the peak of health and fitness.

But over the past few days, she'd experienced so many extremes of emotion from joy to sorrow and stark terror that her inner serenity was gossamer thin.

Quin lifted her hand and bent his head to kiss it. The firm press of his mouth against her skin sparked a breathtaking series of sensations deep inside her.

She clasped his fingers tighter, wanting—needing—to draw him closer.

"Dear heart." His voice was low and not quite steady. She saw his chest expand, and he gently placed her hand on the table.

"I like gooseberry pie," he said, as if there had been no interruption to the conversation, though his color was higher than before. "And Mrs. Larkin told me that's what we'll be having next. Yes, you can be a scientist if you want, Charlotte. Well," he amended, "I see no reason why you can't *study* scientific subjects. For example, a lady called Caroline Herschel is a notable astronomer. She works as an assistant to her brother, William, who is official astronomer to King George."

"Astronomer?" Charlotte's searching gaze had been darting back and forth between Gabrielle and Quin, but now settled on him.

"Someone who studies the stars and other celestial bodies in the sky," Quin explained. "Miss Herschel and her brother look at the night sky through the powerful telescopes he constructs. I believe Miss Hershel has discovered several comets herself."

"We don't have a telescope," Charlotte said.

"No, nothing like the powerful instruments the Hershels use. But I do have my folding magnifier with me." Quin pulled it from his pocket, unfolded the three small lenses and offered it to Charlotte.

"I gave you that!" Gabrielle's body was still tingling from Quin's brief caress, but she did her best not to reveal how much she wished they were alone together.

"You gave me that, and it's been all round the world with me." Quin smiled at her, and she could see he was wishing the same thing. But then he shook his head in an almost imperceptible gesture, briefly closed his eyes, and looked away.

"Um, Charlotte?" he said.

Her head was bent over, as she studied different items on her plate, and the weave of the tablecloth, but she raised it questioningly.

"I beg your pardon," Quin said. "I'm afraid I should have shown you the magnifier *after* we've finished our dinner, not in the middle. Be sure to follow mademoiselle's example when it comes to matters of etiquette, not mine."

"All right." Charlotte reluctantly handed it back. "Then can we look at a snail through it?"

"I don't think we should go in search of snails this evening," Quin said. "I hope we'll be able to do so tomorrow. But we could look at a rose or some other flower through it later, if you like."

Charlotte nodded.

"Mademoiselle used to have one of her own. Do you not have it anymore?" He looked at Gabrielle.

"Mademoiselle had to leave everything behind when she ran away from France," Charlotte said.

"I'll buy you another one." Beneath the table, Quin laid his hand on Gabrielle's knee. "For now, you and Charlotte can use mine when you're making detailed botanical illustrations."

"I have...missed the ability to check the finest details of some specimens." Gabrielle barely knew what she was saying. She was afraid she might actually have squeaked when Quin touched her —but only from pleasure.

The feel of his hand vanished from her leg.

"No," he muttered, and took a gulp of his hitherto untouched wine.

"No?" Charlotte repeated.

"No...it's...not acceptable that mademoiselle and you don't have the benefit of a magnifying device to enhance your drawings," he said thickly. "I'll make sure you both have one at the earliest opportunity."

Gabrielle struggled to suppress the giggles that wanted to erupt from her like effervescent champagne bubbles. She was sure his 'no' had been a verbal admonition to himself, not a comment about the magnifier.

"I can have one of my own?" Charlotte said.

"Yes..." Quin hesitated and looked at Gabrielle. "There's no reason why she shouldn't have a magnifier is there? I daresay it would also be helpful with embroidery and similar more typically feminine pursuits. Though the sailors sewed their own clothes during the voyage."

"Would you tell us some of your adventures?" Gabrielle asked.

"The ones that won't upset mademoiselle's digestion," Charlotte reminded him solemnly.

Gabrielle started to laugh.

Charlotte looked shocked, and that made her laugh harder, even though she also felt guilty.

"I'm sorry," she gasped. "I'm sorry. I'm not laughing at you Charlotte, or...or...anyone."

"We've had a very eventful day," Quin said. "I'll tell you the most tedious of my anecdotes to help you relax. So tedious you'll think the account of me wrapping and re-wrapping seeds was an exhilarating adventure and fall fast asleep from boredom."

Gabrielle managed to regain control. "You c-couldn't be boring if you tried."

"Not to you, perhaps. And for that I am forever grateful." Quin smiled into her eyes. "But I assure you, large swathes of people consider me exceedingly boring,"

"Only stupid people," Charlotte said.

They were halfway through their slices of gooseberry pie when the landlady came to inform Quin that the magistrate had arrived.

Even though this was the news they'd been waiting for, Gabrielle's stomach still gave a flip and Charlotte's expression grew pinched.

"Thank you, Mrs. Larkin, I'll come out to speak to him at once." Quin stood up. "Excuse me, ladies." He gave them both a small bow.

"Sir Ralph said he'd wait until you've finished your dinner, my lord," the landlady protested.

"That's courteous of him, but I'd prefer to conclude this business as quickly as possible. However…if you have any gooseberry pie left, perhaps you could offer him a slice?" Quin suggested. "Then I could bring mine with me."

"I'll do so directly, my lord." Mrs. Larkin hurried away.

Quin picked up his plate and smiled at Charlotte. "I haven't had gooseberry pie for years," he confided. "As I said, you should be guided by mademoiselle on all matters of etiquette, not me. Are you still agreeable to speaking to him?" he asked Gabrielle.

"I want to give him my statement," she said, even though the prospect made her anxious.

"Thank you. I'll speak to him first, and Nedcott will also need to give his own account. In the meantime…" He fished in his pocket and offered Gabrielle his folding magnifier.

She took it, a frisson of pleasure shimmering up her arm from where their fingers touched. "We'll enjoy looking at things through this after we've finished our dinner, won't we, Charlotte?"

Chapter Twenty-Eight

As soon as Quin opened the parlor door, he heard Gabrielle's voice.

"...so the prince swung his sword with all his might. He cut and hacked at the great thorny hedge until he was covered in scratches and panting for breath—but he couldn't make any progress."

Quin concluded they'd been left alone so long, the entertainment value of peering through his magnifying lenses had palled.

"When the prince couldn't see anymore because of all the sweat running in his eyes, and his muscles were as wobbly as Miss Bianchetti's jelly, he had to stop," Gabrielle continued. "He sat on the ground, took a long drink of water from his enchanted jug, and tried to think of a better plan."

"The prince is being very silly," Charlotte said.

"Why?" Gabrielle asked. "What do you think he should do?"

Quin had opened the door quietly to avoid startling Gabrielle and Charlotte. He hadn't intended to eavesdrop on their conversation. But now, despite the fact that the magistrate and Nedcott were standing behind him, presumably hearing everything he was hearing, he didn't walk straight into the room. He was intrigued to hear Charlotte's answer.

"The prince should go back and find the dissatisfied woodsman, of course," she said. "He should ask the woodsman to exchange his ax for the prince's sword, then they will both be happy."

"That's a very sensible and clever solution," Gabrielle said. "Unfortunately, the prince is not as wise as you, and—"

Quin pushed the door fully open and walked into the parlor.

"Good evening, my lord." The moment she saw him, a smile lit up Gabrielle's face, but her expression sobered when she noticed the other two men.

At the sight of the magistrate, Charlotte edged closer to Gabrielle on the sofa.

"I'm sorry we've kept you waiting, ladies," Quin said. "Mademoiselle Rousselle, Miss Sedgemore, this is Sir Ralph Edney. He's the magistrate dealing with the attack on your coach this afternoon."

"Good evening, ladies," the magistrate said. "I'm sorry to meet you under such unpleasant circumstances."

"We're glad you're here to assist us, Sir Ralph," Gabrielle replied.

Charlotte was staring at the magistrate, very much as she'd stared at Quin when she'd first met him. He thought it was unlikely she was going to volunteer a verbal greeting.

"Charlotte?" He waited until she was looking at him and

smiled reassuringly. "Sir Ralph agrees there is no need for you to speak to him—unless you wish to?"

She shook her head.

"No? Very well, then. Mademoiselle, are you ready to give a statement to Sir Ralph?" he asked.

"Yes, but—" She glanced sideways at Charlotte.

"Mrs. Larkin has kittens," he said, guessing the reason for Gabrielle's hesitation. "That's to say, her cat has recently had kittens. I've just been to see them myself, and they're the prettiest, fluffiest creatures I've ever beheld. Charlotte, would you like to go and look at them with Nedcott?"

"I'll try not to keep Mademoiselle Rousselle talking too long," Sir Ralph promised in a kindly voice.

"Lord Hanwell is right, the kittens are very fluffy," Nedcott said encouragingly. "I want to see them again myself. Shall we go and look at them, Miss Charlotte?"

Charlotte nodded, slid off the sofa and walked over to Nedcott, giving the magistrate the widest berth possible in the small room.

"I can't blame the child for being wary of strangers after what happened," Sir Ralph said philosophically, once Charlotte and Nedcott had left. "By all accounts you've both had a most unpleasant day, Mademoiselle Rousselle."

"Yes," she said simply, and invited the magistrate to sit down.

He took the dining chair closest to the sofa, and set out his ink well and papers on the table in front of him.

"I've already taken statements from Lord Hanwell and your coachman," he said briskly, "and they will probably be sufficient, but if you feel able to give me a full account of what happened, that will be very helpful."

"Of course," Gabrielle said calmly. "Shall I begin from the moment I heard the first shot?"

"That would be perfect, but I need to take down a few particulars first," Sir Ralph said.

Quin walked over to sit in the armchair opposite Gabrielle as she gave the magistrate her full name, her position as governess to the daughter of Lord and Lady Henderson, and her address.

"Charlotte and I were living in Brighton until this morning," she explained. "We're currently on our way to Sedgemore Hall in the country."

"I understand." Sir Ralph looked up from completing his last note. "Let us now continue from the moment you were surprised by the shot."

This was the first time Quin had heard Gabrielle's description of what had happened. Even though he knew the outcome, he had difficulty listening quietly to her unadorned statement. Part of him wanted to get up and stride about to relieve his tension, a larger part wanted to sit beside Gabrielle and hold her in his arms.

Since it would be highly inappropriate for him to do either, he rested his curled hand on his knee and hoped his simple presence was bringing Gabrielle some comfort.

He hadn't told Sir Ralph he'd been deliberately following the coach. Charlotte knew. Nedcott had probably guessed, but hadn't mentioned any suspicions to the magistrate.

In Quin's opinion, the reason he'd been so close behind wasn't relevant, especially since any suggestion he'd been planning a romantic tryst with Gabrielle could damage her reputation. Unfortunately, it was probable that gossip would ultimately be unavoidable.

For the most part, Gabrielle spoke in a quiet, steady voice, and needed few prompts. Only once or twice did her voice falter.

"It occurred to me that Charlotte was the greatest treasure in the coach," she said at one point. "I didn't want the highwayman to know she was inside in case he decided to kidnap her and hold her to ransom."

"A grim prospect," Sir Ralph replied. "Fortunately, I don't think that wretched fellow has the wits to concoct such a plan."

"I wished I *did* have a box of jewels," Gabrielle said. "I'd have given him anything to get him to go away without hurting any of us."

"Your coachman is full of praise for your calm courage," Sir Ralph said. "And you're giving me a clear, straightforward account of what happened this afternoon. You are an exceptional lady, mademoiselle. Lord and Lady Henderson owe you a great deal for your actions today."

Quin agreed wholeheartedly with the magistrate, though he couldn't predict how the Hendersons would actually react when they learned what had happened.

That was a problem for another day. This evening his priority was to ensure Gabrielle and Charlotte experienced the minimum of further agitation.

"Thank you, mademoiselle," Sir Ralph said at last. "All that's left to do now is for me to read your statement back to you. If you're happy it's an accurate record of what you've said, you must sign it. Then I'll leave you in peace for the rest of the evening."

"May I read it for myself?" Gabrielle asked, as he turned the pages back to the beginning.

"Certainly, if that's what you prefer." He handed her the sheets containing his neat transcript of her words.

A few minutes later, after Gabrielle had amended a couple of phrases where she'd recalled details more precisely, she signed her statement and returned it to Sir Ralph.

"Thank you, mademoiselle." He placed all the documents together and put them into his leather satchel. "You've both given clear, detailed statements. More than that, your actions have made the heath safer for anyone crossing it in the future. You both have my gratitude and respect for your actions. But I'm extremely sorry you've had to endure such an unpleasant experience in this county."

He rose to his feet and Quin immediately did the same.

"Thank you for coming to deal with this matter so promptly and efficiently." He shook Sir Ralph's hand.

"I'm pleased to get another of the villains who prey on innocent travelers into custody," Sir Ralph replied. "May I ask...am I correct in believing you're the gentleman who was part of HMS Wayfarer's scientific expedition, recently returned to London?"

"Ah...yes," Quin admitted. As part of his statement, he'd given Sir Ralph his full name, and reported he was traveling from his father's house in Brighton to Winchester on business.

That was a departure from the pure truth, but not by much. Sedgemore Hall and Winchester were both located in Hampshire, and Quin suspected he might end up in Winchester on his quest to find Lord Henderson.

What he hadn't done, was mention how he'd spent the last three years. But it seemed the magistrate had recognized his name.

"It's an honor to meet you, my lord," Sir Ralph said. "A great honor. I wasn't able to attend the lecture you gave last week in London. Will you be giving any more? I daresay it would be overstepping the bounds of courtesy to ask you to dine with me, but I'm greatly interested in hearing more of your discoveries. Very greatly."

It seemed, his official duty done, Sir Ralph was finally allowing himself to give voice to his personal interests.

Quin gathered his thoughts, which hadn't been on the expedition.

"Yes, Lord Duncan and I will be giving more public lectures about our discoveries soon," he said. "Lord Duncan Waring was the surgeon on the Wayfarer and also a very fine botanist, as I expect you know. Duncan and I are currently drafting a book giving an account of the voyage, which we hope to publish as soon as possible. I would be delighted to dine with you, but I'm afraid I can't arrange a specific date to do so this evening. My plans are currently somewhat unsettled."

Sir Ralph looked increasingly gratified by Quin's response. "I completely understand, my lord. You weren't expecting to encounter a highway robber on your way to Winchester—who you dealt with most expeditiously, I must say. I will write to let you know about the progress of the case. Perhaps we'll be able to make dinner arrangements then."

"I'm sure we will," Quin agreed. "Thank you again, Sir Ralph."

The magistrate took the hint and bowed to Gabrielle. "Mademoiselle Rousselle, your servant." He walked across the parlor, but then paused with his hand on the door handle to look back at her. "How is the prince going to get through the thorny hedge?" he asked.

Gabrielle blinked and then laughed. "Exactly the way Charlotte proposed, though not until he's done at least one other silly thing. But he mustn't do too many foolish things, or she'll decide he's too silly to hear about and demand a different story."

The magistrate grinned. "Miss Sedgemore is obviously a very discerning audience. Good evening to you both. There is no need to show me out. I'm familiar with Mrs. Larkin's establishment." With those words, he closed the parlor door quietly behind him.

Quin followed to press his hand against the central wooden panel. The door was securely closed. Beyond it, he could hear voices, but no sound of anyone else approaching the parlor.

He exhaled and turned to look at Gabrielle still sitting on the sofa.

He crossed to her in a few swift strides, seized both her hands and pulled her to her feet—and into his arms.

Chapter Twenty-Nine

Gabrielle hadn't expected Quin to advance on her with such focused intent, but she relaxed willingly into his embrace. It was exactly where she'd wanted to be since he'd helped her climb up to sit beside Nedcott so many hours ago.

She wrapped her arms around his waist and closed her eyes. He stroked her back and pressed his cheek against her hair.

She didn't know how long they remained like that as she soaked in all the comfort, reassurance...and more...that Quin's strong arms promised her. This was the man who was destined to be her lover, and that spark of awareness was present between them, even though they were standing quite still.

At last Quin lifted his head, his gaze searching her face. "My dear heart, are you well?"

She smiled up at him. "I'm wonderful."

"Yes, you are." He kept one arm around her waist. With his other hand, he caressed her cheek. "I ask myself—how am I so lucky that someone as wonderful as you chose me? Chooses me?"

"That's not what I meant." Her smile trembled and she tilted her face into his palm.

"I know." He bent his head and claimed her mouth with his.

Gabrielle abandoned any attempt to speak because kissing him—being kissed—was so much more satisfying.

She'd never kissed any other man. She didn't believe he'd kissed any other woman. This evening he was careful with her, but he wasn't tentative. His tongue explored her mouth and played with her tongue until her lips were tingling and swollen, and she was conscious of the swelling, aching need between her legs.

She pressed her lower body more firmly against him, and the hard pressure of his arousal sent a thrill of excitement through her veins.

"Hmm-hmm." Quin's hum could have meant anything, but she knew it was a signal they should exercise restraint.

He broke the kiss and smiled down at her. His pupils were huge, his lips as swollen and wet as hers.

"Does Charlotte know what it means for a cock to mount a hen?" he asked hoarsely.

"Does…?" Her mind was so hazy from his kisses that it took a moment to collect her thoughts. "I don't know. I don't know if she's just repeating what the gardener's boy told her."

Quin exhaled an odd huffing laugh, and leaned his forehead against Gabrielle's. "I want to mount you so badly, right now—" He froze, his whole body stiffening, and she was sure his groan was one of mortification. "With utmost delicacy…tenderness…"

He kissed her cheek, brushing her skin with soft, gentle caresses.

Gabrielle slipped her hand between them, pressing her fingers over his lips.

"I think—" She caught her breath as he sucked one fingertip into his mouth, feeling the sensual pull all the way to her core.

He smiled around it. "You think?"

"I think...if you're *too* delicate things...may not proceed quite...quite as we hope," she gasped.

Quin froze again—then hugged her close, rocking them both back and forward.

"Oh, my Gabrielle. Oh, my brave, practical—" He held her away from him, gazing down into her eyes. "I do love you. I'm not always easy with words, but I do love you. My Gabrielle."

"And I love you. I'm so lucky I found you before any other lady discovered what a treasure you are." She stroked his jaw. "And you're much better with words than you sometimes claim."

He raised a skeptical eyebrow, but then smiled. "I suppose it depends on the occasion and who I'm talking to. And we need to talk now, before we go and find Charlotte." He guided her to sit on the sofa and took the seat next to her.

She immediately twisted so she could see him more easily, her knee pressing against his thigh, her hand on his chest.

His lips twitched, and he covered her hand with his. She could tell he was remembering other times when they'd sat like this—and when she'd tempted his restraint.

"Am I a tease?" she asked, suddenly worried at the idea.

"No. Well...yes."

She tried to pull her hand away, but he tightened his grip and lifted it to kiss her palm.

"I like it, and you know I do." His breath was warm against her skin. "At least, I hope you do. And we managed well enough before I went away."

They'd teetered close to the edge, but they'd never fallen completely over. Gabrielle knew that was because of Quin's care, far more than hers. And on occasion, it had caused some tension between them.

She'd always been certain that neither her parents nor Quin's father had known the extent of their explorations. But now she wondered whether that's why he'd become more reserved.

"Did Papa ever speak to you?" she asked.

Quin shook with a silent laugh. "Your papa, your mother, *my* father, your papa's huntsman, Felix."

"*Felix?*" she gasped. "He was eleven the last time he saw you."

"He delivered his first lecture younger than that." Quin grinned. "Don't fret, dear heart, none of them were unkind to me. Mostly there was a great deal of emphasis on honor."

"Papa's huntsman, Michel Gresset? *He* spoke to you?" Gabrielle was startled that someone outside their family had taken it upon himself to lecture Quin.

"He saw us coming out of the maze one day and suspected we'd done more than get lost." Quin rested their linked hands on his upper chest.

"Ohh." There was one particular day in the maze that Gabrielle always remembered with a thrill of excited pleasure— and regret, because it was the closest they'd ever come to abandoning all caution. From then on, Quin had always been more restrained.

"Was it...*that* day?" she whispered.

Quin bowed his head a barely perceptible degree.

"Michel saw us? That's why you wouldn't do it again? Was he mean to you?" she asked.

"No, but he was the most direct. I knew we had to be more careful. I was older, so it was my responsibility."

"*I* was mean to you." She'd yearned so intensely for more of his kisses and intimate touches, and she'd been frustrated with him for taking several steps back.

"You weren't mean to me." He stroked a lock of hair away from her face with his free hand. "And who could blame you for pouting for a day, after I'd pontificated to you about a gentleman's honor in such a pompous way?"

"Only after everyone else had pontificated to *you*. Why didn't you tell me?" Of course, she'd been listening to her mama's strictures on behaving in a ladylike way all her life. She'd assumed Quin had received similar lectures from his father, but she hadn't guessed that *everybody* had been watching them so closely.

His smile was rueful. "I wanted to tell them all it wasn't their business—especially the damned huntsman! But I knew we were their business. And I didn't want our situation to degenerate into some kind of latter-day Romeo and Juliet, skulking around in secret."

"You were more...formal after that," she said. "For a while. I thought I'd shocked you. Later, when you were remembering what we'd done. Not at the time."

She was certain he'd been as engrossed as she'd been during

that breath-taking, exquisite time in the maze when he'd kissed her lips and her throat. Caressed her ankle and then slowly, gently stroked higher to the top of her stocking. The bare skin of her thigh. The throbbing, needy place between her legs.

His expression changed. His pupils expanded so much his eyes appeared almost black. He was remembering too, and it wasn't with disapproval.

Tension hummed between them...

He closed his eyes and dropped his head back against the sofa.

"I've *never* been shocked by you. But we have to *talk*," he muttered. "We have to make *plans*."

Happiness bubbled inside her like pure spring water rising from the ground. "Haven't you already made our plans?" she asked in an innocent voice.

Without lifting his head from the back of the sofa, he rolled it to one side and looked at her under his lashes. "Tentatively," he admitted. "But I'm lacking some important information."

"What information?"

He raised his head. "Why did Lady Henderson send you and Charlotte away this morning? Was it because we took you for ice cream yesterday?"

"Oh, no." Gabrielle blinked. "It was because...well, Lady Henderson said it was because of one thing, but I think it was another." She described her conversation with the viscountess the previous morning.

"Staring at naked male swimmers?" Quin raised his eyebrows.

"I didn't!" Gabrielle said indignantly. "You know you're the only naked male I'd like to see."

He grinned and laid a finger on her lips.

"Only you," she repeated in a whisper, even though she was certain no one else could overhear their conversation.

"When we go swimming together—naked or otherwise—we're not going to be anywhere near Brighton seafront," he said softly. "Do you suspect the viscountess does believe her son's accusation against you?"

"I don't know." Gabrielle was distracted by the idea of swimming naked with Quin. She recoiled instinctively from the idea of going into the sea, but being naked with Quin sounded wonderful. With an effort, she brought her attention back to his question. "Sometimes I'm sure she does. But she also knows how much Augustus dislikes me, so perhaps she does believe he made a false accusation to get rid of me."

Quin pressed his lips together. "I've never met the boy, but I'm already badly disposed toward him."

"Charlotte dislikes him intensely," Gabrielle said. "But most of the time, she's good at pretending he's not there. He stuck his tongue out at us when we left this morning, and she didn't react at all."

Quin frowned. "Didn't you say he's older than her? That's *not* how he should behave. Ever."

"No. We're not going to be able to have a discreet correspondence as we planned, are we?" Gabrielle adored the fact she was having a private conversation with Quin this evening. But what would happen when the Hendersons found out about the hold-up and Quin's part in the highwayman's capture?

Quin shook his head. "Not the way we discussed. The case will be tried at the next assizes. Even if no rumors circulate before that, it's likely to be reported in the newspapers at that time. A viscount's daughter in a waylaid carriage. Accompanied by an émigré duke's daughter now employed as a governess—"

"Saved by a dashing, handsome earl, already well-known for his daring exploits," Gabrielle inserted.

"Botanical discoveries," Quin corrected. "Not daring exploits. We can't hope to conceal this incident from the Hendersons or anyone else. Earlier, I decided not to send a message to anyone we know until I'd discussed it with you, but tomorrow we must."

"I'm worried about Charlotte," Gabrielle said.

"So am I." Quin began to play with Gabrielle's fingers in a thoughtful, but distracting way. "It would be ideal if we find Lord Henderson at the Hall when we arrive tomorrow."

Gabrielle felt a little jolt of apprehension at the prospect of explaining what had happened to either of Charlotte's parents, though she was more worried about Lady Henderson's reaction than Lord Henderson's.

"I've no idea if he will be," she admitted.

"If he isn't, I hope someone will know where I can find him," Quin said. "To all appearances, he seems to have abdicated responsibility for caring for his children—but he's the one who has ultimate authority over them. He's the one I need to negotiate with."

"To get what?" Gabrielle knew what she wanted, but she couldn't imagine how they could get it, or even if Quin would want it too. It was one thing for him to play father-figure for a child he'd only just met over the course of a single afternoon and evening. But would he want to do that for the next decade or more?

"I want what you want," he said. "But until I've met Lord Henderson and got the measure of the man, I don't know what's possible. But you and I protected his daughter from harm today. For her sake, it's right you remain with her, and for your sake it's right and fair that you're able to correspond freely with me, and meet with me regularly."

"What do I want?" Gabrielle watched Quin, her whole being filled with love for him.

"You want every dinner to be like the one we enjoyed today," he said. "Though probably without the snails and blue frogs, which I can't entirely promise because Charlotte and I—"

Gabrielle flung herself into his arms, ending up on his lap in a tangle of skirts as she covered his face with kisses.

He settled her more comfortably on his thighs and kissed her back, but then reminded her, "We have to go and collect Charlotte from Nedcott and the kittens soon."

"Yes." Gabrielle cupped his face with her hands. "There are beds upstairs, not haystacks."

He met her gaze, his focus sharpening, and she felt him suck in a breath.

"Once Charlotte falls asleep, she usually stays asleep," Gabrielle said. "I don't know if that will be the case tonight. I can't promise. But if she does...shall I...shall I come to you?"

Quin took another breath. She saw the need in his eyes.

"We can...practice together," she whispered.

"Are you sure, dear heart?" he asked hoarsely.

She nodded. "We're making many choices for Charlotte's sake. We can make this one for ourselves. And we don't need anyone else's permission."

Quin breathed out. A long, not quite steady exhalation. "Yes. Yes, I want you to come to me."

Chapter Thirty

Quin had never wished so ardently for another person to sleep well, but he did his best to tamp down his rising excitement.

He summoned the memory of Charlotte's distress immediately after the highwayman's attack. That sobering mental image acted as both a partial curb on his body's reaction to Gabrielle's offer—and a painful reminder of why Charlotte might not sleep soundly tonight.

He hoped she didn't have nightmares for her sake, as well as his and Gabrielle's.

The landlady had placed a basket for the mother cat and her kittens in a small room near to the kitchen. Quin had left Charlotte and Nedcott there earlier, and it was where he led Gabrielle now.

The door was a few inches ajar. He pushed it wider gently, not wanting to startle any of the room's occupants. A quick scan revealed everyone apart from Nedcott appeared to be asleep—

though the mother cat opened her eyes and raised her head when he and Gabrielle entered.

It was a storage room, with shelves up to the ceiling on every wall except for where the window and door were located. Folded blankets were stacked on some of the shelves, ready to go back into use when the weather turned colder.

Someone had put a couple of the blankets on the floor beside the cat basket, and Charlotte was curled up on them. Her eyes were closed. She appeared to be asleep, though one of her arms was stretched out toward the kittens.

Quin exhaled, relieved and cautiously optimistic—until it occurred to him that if she was woken now, so soon after falling asleep, she might not drift off again for hours. That would be worse than finding her wide awake now.

He wished they didn't have to disturb her. But they couldn't leave her on the floor of a storage room all night.

Nedcott was sitting on a straight-backed chair the landlady had brought in for him. Quin was glad to see the coachman's posture was more relaxed than it had been when he was giving his statement to the magistrate.

Gabrielle had remained calm while she talked to Sir Ralph, but Nedcott had nearly broken down. Quin had understood his distress all too easily. The coachman had felt responsible for the safety of the females in his care, yet it was Gabrielle who'd had to deal directly with the highwayman.

But Nedcott had managed to keep the horses under control throughout the hold up. The sound of Quin's shot, followed by Charlotte's piercing scream shortly after, had startled the horses as much as the highwayman's first warning shot.

In their agitation, they could easily have dragged the coach off the road, or overturned it and injured themselves and anyone in the carriage.

It was because Nedcott had kept control of the team that Charlotte had come to no harm when she'd tumbled out of the coach to race to Gabrielle.

Quin had told Nedcott that in the hope it would assure him he'd provided valuable service. Instead, all the color had drained from the coachman's face. He'd likely been imagining the injuries Charlotte might have sustained if she'd been pitched out onto the road.

Since Quin's attempt at verbal reassurance had been a dismal failure, he'd cast around for some other way to help Nedcott regain his equilibrium.

The kittens had been his salvation. The landlady had mentioned them to him earlier as a possible source of comfort and distraction for Charlotte. And when Quin and Nedcott had gone to see them, to make sure they were tame enough to tolerate the attentions of a little girl, Quin had immediately sensed an improvement in the coachman's spirits.

"They're so pretty." Gabrielle slipped past him to kneel beside the basket. "Sweet mama, may I stroke you?" She reached slowly into the basket. "How clever you've been. What beautiful babies you have."

Quin exchanged a glance of manly indulgence with Nedcott, although they'd both stroked the cat when they'd first seen it.

"Ma'm'zelle?" Charlotte roused slightly.

"Yes, it's me." Gabrielle switched to stroking Charlotte's hair instead of the cat. "It's time to go to bed, sweetheart. You must wake up enough to climb the stairs."

Charlotte gave a wordless murmur of protest, squirming onto her back and curling up into a ball on her other side.

Quin moved to crouch beside Gabrielle. "Charlotte, may I carry you upstairs?" he asked.

She opened her eyes and looked at him for a few seconds. Her features were relaxed, though not blank. He thought she was considering his suggestion, but he wasn't entirely sure. She nodded and raised her arms languidly toward him. He had a feeling if he didn't react immediately, she'd let them flop down onto the blankets and go back to sleep.

He lifted her carefully, one arm beneath her shoulders, the other under her knees, and rose to his feet. When he'd carried Charlotte across the heath, she'd put her arms around his neck and clung on tightly. Now she was just a bundle of sleepy, relaxed child. Quin dared to hope that augured well for the night ahead.

"We'll set off as early as possible after breakfast tomorrow morning," he said quietly to Nedcott.

"Yes, my lord. Goodnight, mademoiselle."

"Goodnight, Nedcott. Thank you for taking such good care of Miss Charlotte while I was speaking to Sir Ralph," Gabrielle said softly.

Nedcott retrieved the lantern, and they all exited the room, leaving the door ajar for the mother cat to get in and out.

Quin carried Charlotte up the stairs and waited for Gabrielle to open the door of their bedchamber. There was only one double bed in the room, which Gabrielle and Charlotte would be sharing.

Gabrielle hurried forward to pull back the covers and moved out of the way.

Quin laid Charlotte gently down on one side of the mattress. "Sleep well," he said softly. "You're safe, Charlotte."

He thought she hadn't heard his reassurance, but then her eyelids flickered, and half opened, and a tiny smile twitched her lips.

He felt a pang of emotion. It wasn't love. He'd only met Charlotte the previous day. But he did like her, and he wanted the best for her for her own sake, not just to please Gabrielle.

"Good night." He straightened and stepped back from the bed.

Gabrielle smiled at him.

"I'm in the next room," he said softly, tilting his head toward the wall, indicating which side.

She nodded. Her lips parted. He thought she was going to speak, but she glanced at him, then at Charlotte, and back to him.

She'd brought a candle up with them, and he saw the flutter of the modest frill on her bodice. She was nervous. So was he. And with Charlotte lying only a few feet away, he couldn't voice any of the thoughts at the forefront of his mind.

"Make sure you douse the candle, dear heart," he said.

"In a while. I must attend to Charlotte first. Good night, my lord." The expression in her eyes promised the same thing she'd promised aloud downstairs.

He shared a last, emotion-laden look with her, and retreated to the room he would be occupying for the night.

Once there, he stood still for several seconds, and then drew in a deep, shuddering breath. She would come. As long as Charlotte didn't wake, she would come.

He glanced around the room. It was small, but seemed clean and comfortable. He'd wanted to surround Gabrielle with every luxury when they took the next, irrevocable step in their courtship. But perhaps, in their current circumstances, a reasonable degree of privacy away from judgmental eyes was the greatest luxury they could have.

He was glad that before dinner he'd washed off the dust of the journey and changed his linen. That was simply good manners. He hadn't shaved, and he rubbed his chin. Would Gabrielle mind?

She hadn't minded downstairs, and shaving with cold water didn't appeal. Especially when she might appear at any moment. How long would it take her to settle Charlotte? The child was already asleep.

Stirred into action, he removed his coat and waistcoat, and sat down to pull off his boots. He set everything neatly to one side, and wondered if he should untie his neckcloth.

He didn't want to look as if he was ready to leap on Gabrielle the moment she came through the door—*if* she came through the door.

On the other hand, he didn't want to waste time on mundane activities, such as removing his own boots, when he could be removing Gabrielle's clothes. He supposed he would finally be able to see her fully unclothed—wouldn't he? Perhaps she wouldn't want him too.

His breath shuddered again, imagining the glory of seeing her naked breasts, holding them in his palms.

He'd felt more of her exquisite body than he'd ever seen because, even when his self-control had been threadbare thin, he'd known they might need to shake out her concealing skirts at a moment's notice.

And *where* his fingers had explored and played that one, glorious time, was rather more scandalous than a delicate kiss on her bosom—which he hadn't achieved with much greater frequency.

His cock was a steel rod, protesting against the confines of his breeches. Demanding attention *now*. Gabrielle's attention.

Gabrielle...what if she changed her mind? What if he couldn't please her?

He swallowed a groan and rubbed his hands over his head.

He was thinking, if not acting, like a fool.

Unless Charlotte woke, Gabrielle would come to him. They would both be the same people they'd been downstairs, when she'd sat on his lap, and he'd kissed her. Being with him made her happy. She'd told and shown him that so many times, both before he'd gone on his travels and since his return.

He could give her what she needed to be happy. He knew he could. He'd used his hand to bring her to ecstasy in the maze on his first attempt—even though that hadn't been his original plan for the afternoon.

He could begin there tonight. No, not begin there, it would be overbold. They would begin more circumspectly, with tender kisses, and progress to more intimate caresses until they achieved the ultimate union.

His heart thudded, sending his blood surging through his veins.

~

Gabrielle's body hummed with anticipation. The moment she'd dreamed about for so long was about to become a reality. Happiness encompassed her whole being, but she didn't want to communicate her mood to Charlotte.

She consciously slowed her breathing and kept her touch unhurried and gentle as she removed Charlotte's shoes.

"Ma'm'zelle?" Charlotte slurred.

"You can't sleep in your shoes and stockings," Gabrielle said softly.

Charlotte's stockings were already around her ankles, so they were easily dealt with, but Gabrielle decided not to try to get Charlotte into her nightdress. That much exertion might wake her properly, and Gabrielle desperately wanted her to go back to sleep.

"Are you scared of kittens?" Charlotte opened her eyes as Gabrielle pulled the sheet over her.

"No." Gabrielle smiled and brushed Charlotte's hair back.

Charlotte sighed and closed her eyes again. "What did the silly prince do next?"

Her question made it clear she wanted her usual bedtime story. There was a stool as well as a chair in the small chamber. Gabrielle placed the stool close to the bed and sat down. She didn't want to risk the mattress moving, and possibly disturbing Charlotte, when she stood up to leave.

"I'm going to tell you how the prince followed the advice of a clever little wren," she began. "Before I do, I just want you to know that after I've finished telling you the story, I'm going to go and speak with Lord Quin for a while before I come back to bed."

She held her breath for a few seconds, waiting for Charlotte's response. She'd debated with herself whether she should say anything to Charlotte about her intentions. But the last thing she wanted was for the little girl to wake and find herself alone in an unfamiliar place.

Charlotte was used to her governess sitting up longer to read or sew or talk to Mrs. Whittle. Gabrielle hoped she wouldn't consider there was anything unusual in her sitting up to speak to Quin.

Without opening her eyes, Charlotte gave a small nod, her breathing slow and even.

Gabrielle resumed her tale of the prince battling through an impenetrable hedge to get to his princess. He swapped his sword for an ax easily enough. But then he got stuck sharpening and resharpening the blade as he chopped his way through a hedge that had grown as wide as a forest.

Gabrielle was afraid Charlotte might have to provide the prompts for what would happen when the prince and princess finally met, because her imagination was conjuring activities that were completely unsuitable for a child's bedtime tale.

When she was sure Charlotte was asleep, she stood and took a moment to compose herself. All she needed to take to Quin was herself…and the candle…and the door key.

The last item gave her momentary pause. She wanted to lock the door so a stranger couldn't wander in on Charlotte, but it was essential she didn't lose the key. Another moment's thought and she had the solution.

Finally, it was time to go to Quin. The candle flame trembled when she picked up the holder. Was the flicker caused by a stray gust of air—or her own trembling anticipation?

She slipped out through the door, locked it behind her, and tiptoed the few steps necessary to scratch one finger on Quin's door.

Chapter Thirty-One

The door opened instantly. Gabrielle's heart leaped at the sight of Quin.

He drew her inside, and released her so he could lock his door.

She turned to face him, clutching the candle in one trembling hand and her door key in the other. He'd told her to douse the candle, but she hadn't.

"I wanted light. I want to see you," she said breathlessly.

"Then you shall." He smiled into her eyes. The connection between them filled her heart so full she was overflowing love like a brimful jug.

"Let me?" He took the candle from her and set it safely on a small table well away from the bed.

When he returned, she could see his breathing was as uneven as hers. She half-expected him to sweep her into his arms. Instead, he gently tapped the hand in which she was holding the key.

"Oh." She'd almost forgotten. "I put it on a ribbon. We mustn't lose it."

"No." He took the key from her and looped the ribbon over the door handle. Now her key dangled below the one in the lock. "Is Charlotte asleep?"

"Yes. I told her I was coming to talk to you for a while." Gabrielle could barely compose a coherent sentence.

"We can talk."

"I don't want to talk. I want...I want you," she ended on a whisper, warmth flooding her cheeks.

"And I want you." He put his hands on her upper arms. A simple touch, except her sleeves were short, so he was touching her bare skin, igniting a response deep inside her.

"Oh." She quivered.

He pulled her closer, his mouth descending on her parted lips. Passion swirled between them and around them. A kaleidoscope of vivid sensations, aching pleasure, and unfulfilled yearning. Intense, hungry need.

He covered her cheek and neck with greedy, open-mouthed kisses. She tugged at his shirt, desperate to feel his bare skin beneath her fingertips. She got her hands underneath the linen and flattened her palms against his back. His muscles were hard, his skin damp. His body curving and flexing as he bent to kiss her throat.

Her head fell back, and she arched her breasts toward him. She wanted his kisses *there*.

But she also wanted to feel and see him. She brought her hands around to his chest and pushed her hands upward. The front of his shirt bunched around her wrists and fell to her elbows. She could feel him, but she couldn't see him. She huffed with frustration.

He swayed backward, ripped his shirt over his head and dropped it on the floor.

"Oh, thank you." Thrilled with her new access, she caressed his chest, following the contours of his muscles, and then gliding her hands upwards to curve around his shoulders and down over his bunched biceps.

His breath came short and fast, but he remained still beneath her fascinated explorations.

She looked up into his eyes. "You're magnificent. So strong. So beautiful."

"Climbing the rigging." His voice was rough.

"I remember." She leaned forward to kiss his chest. His skin was damp, and she tasted salt. His chest hair tickled her cheek. She knew her nipples were sensitive, and she wondered if it was the same for him.

She kissed him there, enjoyed how it was making her feel, and followed up with an investigative lick.

He shuddered, groaned and cupped the back of her head. "Can we take off your dress? I feel I would like…to do the same thing to you."

She licked him again, loving the way she could feel how she was affecting him.

"Turnabout is…fair play," he rasped, and held her away from him. "How do we remove this?"

She fumbled at the small buttons closing the front of her bodice. A task she normally performed without a second's thought now seemed frustratingly difficult.

She tugged impatiently at the closure.

"No." His hands captured hers. "Don't tear it. We have to be able to put you back to rights by morning."

Giggles erupted out of her before she could suppress them.

He wrapped his arms around her, helping her muffle her ill-timed hilarity against his chest.

"I promise, my Gabrielle," he said against her hair. "I promise I will tear any item of clothing off you that you like—once we're safely under our own roof."

She'd felt, and seen, his strength in action. She knew he'd only use it in service of her, never to hurt her.

"Or you can tear something from me." He kissed her temple, and his hands roamed over her back, shaping the curve of her hips. "I would like that. Would you like me to rip off your clothes, one day?"

The suggestion that he'd let her tear off his clothes, or abandon his own self-control and allow himself to tear off her clothes, startled her—and then heightened her arousal.

She loved Quin's care and thoughtfulness. But the idea of them being swept away together on a tide of unfettered passion was intoxicating.

"Perhaps an old dress or nightgown I've grown tired of. It might be...exciting." She kissed and licked the base of his throat.

"Yes." His voice was thick. "We will aspire..."

He didn't explain what they were aspiring to, but eased back to cup her face in his hands.

"There will be no ripping tonight." His expression turned serious. "I don't want to hurt you."

"You couldn't—"

"I could. I would never mean to. Never. But I could." He stroked his thumbs over her cheeks. "You must tell me if I do anything that hurts you."

She gripped his wrists with her hands. "Some pain might be inevitable," she whispered. "At least, so I've heard."

"So have I. But also, that I can make it easier for you, if I take time to ready you, to…excite you…"

"You talked about me to someone else?"

"No." He began to unbutton her bodice. She could feel the gentle movement of his fingers against her skin through the fabric. Another inch, and his knuckles were achingly close to her breasts. "The buttons used to be at the back."

"I used to have a maid," she said.

He lifted his gaze from the buttons to her face. "You will again. Tonight, I will perform the duties of your maid."

He folded back the unfastened fronts of her bodice, baring the upper curves of her breasts. His chest expanded, his attention now fixed on what he'd revealed. Her short stays confined her breasts but also pushed them up a little.

Her pulse throbbed between her legs. She didn't think he was consciously trying to excite her simply by looking at her, but his enraptured expression was having that effect.

He ran one finger along the neckline of her chemise, a tantalizingly light caress, and not in the place she needed it most. Her nipples were hard, her breasts aching to be released into his palms. She whimpered and swayed towards him.

He froze, his gaze flying to her face, and then he smiled.

"You wore a gown this revealing one evening in France. I didn't dare look at you for fear I'd lose track of the conversation completely." He bent his head and kissed the top of her cleavage, caressing her delicate skin with his lips and tongue.

"You did look at me before you did *that* in France," she gasped, because he had snatched a few kisses from her that evening, and they hadn't all been on her mouth.

"I did. And caused myself much frustration."

"And me." She wriggled her arms out of the sleeves and felt a brief flare of relief once she was completely free of the dress.

For convenience, her short stays, like her dress fastened in the front. Quin's assistance was less considered as he helped her remove the stays, leaving her in only her chemise, stockings and shoes.

He put his hands on her waist. She saw his throat move as he swallowed, and glanced down at herself. Her erect nipples were now very obvious through the thin lawn of her chemise.

He moved his hands upwards, the soft material sliding and gathering over her skin, until he cupped the sides of her breasts. Gazing into her eyes, he brushed his thumbs over her nipples.

Her breath skittered and escaped her throat in a sigh that was almost a moan.

He did it again and her legs trembled.

"Can we take it off?"

She answered by raising her arms. He pulled her chemise over her head and tossed it onto the chair with her dress and stays.

"You're exquisite. The most desirable…the most ravishing." His disjointed praise made her feel beautiful in a way nothing else could.

For a few more seconds he simply looked at her, as if his need to see her couldn't be satisfied in such a brief moment.

Then he pulled her into his arms for more hot, feverish kisses. For the first time ever, her naked breasts pressed against his bare torso. As he moved, the hair on his chest teased her nipples. Her senses were overwhelmed with the taste and feel of him until he became her whole world.

She didn't realize they were moving, stumbling across the room, until her legs made contact with the side of the bed.

He seized the covers and hauled them out of the way. His urgency added to her own. She fell back onto the mattress, pulling him down with her.

He went willingly, but shifted his weight to one side, rather than sprawling across her.

She rolled over, reached for him, and realized he was still wearing his breeches. She ran her palm down his thigh, feeling the powerful muscles she still couldn't see.

"Take them off," she ordered, in a voice she didn't recognize as her own. "You can see all of me. I want to see all of you."

He hesitated a heartbeat, and then left the bed.

Gabrielle propped herself on her elbow, watching as he shucked the rest of his clothes to stand naked before her.

Every inch of him was lean, powerful masculine perfection, but it was the dark patch of hair at his groin, and the proud thrust of his erection that drew and held her gaze.

Her breath caught. Her pulse rushed in her ears. When he mounted her...when they made love...*that* would be inside her. It was momentarily daunting, but she knew perfectly well they were made to fit together.

She remembered the sound of the unknown couple making love on the other side of the wall the night of the ball. Even without having seen them, she was certain they'd been indulging in the full act of joining. And the lady had sounded as happy and satisfied as the man by their coupling.

This would work. Quin was the man she loved and passionately desired. She knew they would find ecstasy together, and she held out her arms to him.

He came to lie on the bed next to her. He rested one hand on her waist and leaned over to brush her lips with a soft kiss. As he did so, she felt the prod of his erection against her hip.

They were skin to skin, flesh to flesh everywhere. She tried to roll toward him and felt her heel catch on the sheet.

"What?" His breath was warm against her cheek.

"My shoes," she murmured against his mouth.

"I'll deal with them." He trailed kisses down her body, along the valley between her breasts, her stomach...

She squirmed at the delicious feel of his mouth on her lower belly, just above her mound. Of their own volition, her legs opened in a silent invitation—an invitation he didn't take. He skimmed his hand down her outer thigh, and shifted down the bed so he could reach her feet.

She propped herself on her elbows so she could watch him raise first one leg in the air, and then the other. He dropped her shoes over the side of the bed, and his heated gaze traveled slowly up the length of her body.

He was breathing heavily. In the candlelight she could see the sheen of sweat on his body. He was still gripping one of her ankles. When he lowered her leg to the bed, it was further from her other leg than it had been before.

His gaze settled on the blonde curls between her thighs. She'd never seen that expression on his face before. It was so intense she felt as if he was stroking her with his gaze, though in this instant no part of his physical body was touching hers.

Anticipation coiled so tightly inside her she could hardly breathe.

He began to crawl back up the bed.

"My stockings?" she gasped.

"I like them." He stroked the outer side of her thigh again.

She wriggled. She wanted him to touch the *inside* of her thighs.

Did she say that aloud?

Because he switched legs and began to trail his fingertips up the inside of her other thigh. Slowly, painting circles on her delicate skin, building the tension in her core.

She whimpered, her legs fidgeting, drawing together and then opening again.

"You make me…wanton," she half-moaned, sinking back onto the mattress.

"Good. It's your job to be wanton." He settled himself beside her again.

"It is?" She put her hand on his side, determined to tease him as much as he was teasing her. Besides, she was curious. She felt her way down his body, curving around until—

He caught her hand in his before she reached her intended destination.

"Yes." He brought her hand to his lips and sucked one of her fingers into his mouth. "Next time, you may touch me how you will," he said hoarsely. "But tonight, I must lead every step of our dance."

"Oh." She let him place her hand on her own stomach, even though her instincts rebelled against such passivity.

But he was doing everything for her, determined to make this pleasurable for her, even though they both suspected she would feel some pain. It was fair she allowed him to arrange things as he thought best.

He kissed her breasts in turn, closing his lips around one nipple and laving it with his tongue, while teasing the other with his fingers. She arched up into him, soft gasps and whimpers escaping her throat, though she tried to be quiet.

His hand slid down her body. There was a new unevenness to his movements, as if he was fighting his instincts to go faster. He cupped his hand between her legs. Her knees lifted, her hips rocked up toward him.

He groaned against her breast, the raw sound vibrating through her body. His fingers curled, separated her folds, delved deeper.

Her hips bucked.

"Wet." The single word rasped in her ears. Dimly she understood he was describing the part of her he was exploring. Her swollen, aching, slippery wet center.

He inserted a finger into her. His breathing was rough and uneven. Hers rushed in her throat. She writhed against his hand.

"Stay still...can you?"

She clutched his biceps and tried not to move.

He withdrew his finger and replaced it with two together. She could feel him stretching her.

He shifted so he could look into her eyes. His forehead was beaded with sweat, his muscles so taut he was almost trembling.

"We need to…try now. Yes?"

"Yes." She was panting, her heart pounding.

He settled over her, carefully aligning his hard, blunt tip with her opening. He pressed forward.

She gasped.

He stopped, his body vibrating with tension.

"Look at me," he ordered, his voice raw.

She hadn't realized she'd closed her eyes. She opened them and all she could see was him.

"Look at me," he repeated. "I need to see…"

"Not hurting," she promised. Perhaps it was a little, but she'd never admit that to him.

She smiled instead, instinctively raising her knees higher.

He sank deeper.

She caught her breath, and he went rigid.

"Go all the way," she begged. "All—"

He pushed again, the hardest part of him sliding deep into her.

"That's it," he grunted. She'd never seen such a strained expression on his face, but he held himself still. "Tell me…when I can move."

He closed his eyes for a moment, but only a moment. He was watching her, trying to judge her reactions.

The excited, anticipatory need that had earlier consumed her whole body had receded. It hadn't gone completely, and the sharpest discomfort was over, but she was still adjusting to the unfamiliar sensation of being filled and stretched by him.

"I love you," she whispered.

His lips were parted as he breathed through his mouth. His

eyes burned with emotion. But he was so tense from the control he was imposing on his body, that his answering smile was only a brief twitch of his lips.

"You can move." She flexed her hips, altering the angle of her pelvis.

He did. His first few thrusts were reasonably smooth. He withdrew too far and slipped all the way out, but then he was back inside her.

The discomfort disappeared. The rising pleasure she'd felt before returned. Now it was going to be like it had been in the maze, only better because they were truly making love together.

He pumped harder, faster...

A ragged groan tore from his throat. He shuddered, jerked, and she felt heat spurt inside her.

Oh, that meant it was over.

They were pressed belly to belly, but he was propped above her on his elbows. His head was hanging down, his chest rising and falling like a pair of bellows.

Surely she was allowed to touch him now? She lifted her arms to stroke his back. The muscles beneath her hands only seemed as tense as they needed to be to maintain his position without crushing her. He'd achieved most of what he'd hoped for this night, but she was certain he'd wanted her to experience the same moment of culmination he had.

"You're wonderful," she whispered. "No woman ever had a better, gentler lover. You're magnificent."

He raised his head. The strain was gone, replaced by an unmistakably rueful expression.

"I know you didn't," he said.

"I...how?" His hair was falling forward. She stroked it back from his face.

"I know how you sound and look when you do."

"You mean...in the maze?"

"That memory has been a joy and a torment to me for years." He lowered himself to kiss her, his tongue pressing between her parted lips in an imitation of the other way he was still inside her.

He raised himself again, this time with an expression of determination on his face. "We're not done yet." He shifted his weight onto one elbow so he could take hold of her right hand.

She didn't understand until he drew it down between their bodies, all the way to the place where they joined.

"You can, my bold, beautiful girl," he murmured, adjusting his position sufficiently that she could slide her fingers where his were before.

"Me?" she breathed.

"I know you can, my bold, adventurous, beautiful..." He kept praising her in that low, intimate voice.

The candle sputtered out, but the darkness wasn't complete because moonlight was coming in through a gap in the curtains.

She slipped her fingers into that private, secret place. The place that belonged to her and now she shared with Quin. Touching herself like this when he was still inside her, when his scent and his voice surrounded her was both unfamiliar, yet also like her nighttime fantasies.

But being with him was better than any fantasy. She stroked and rubbed, the coil of delicious tension building inside her faster than she'd thought possible.

He continued to praise her. She was so lost in rising sensation she couldn't distinguish the individual words, and she couldn't see him clearly in the shadows, but she knew his voice.

"Quin!" Her gasp turned into a long moan.

Her inner muscles spasmed around him, launching her into a glorious peak of ecstasy. Her body became a receptacle for deep, pulsating ripples of pleasure that overwhelmed her in the most wondrous way. Even her toes curled into the mattress.

He jolted, a startled, wordless sound escaping his throat. "I didn't know I'd feel it like that," he rasped. "You are wonderful…perfect…my Gabrielle."

Chapter Thirty-Two

Quin's muscles were lax with satiation, but his mood was a potent mixture of all-consuming love, exaltation—and relief. He hadn't failed Gabrielle. It was true he'd had to enlist her help at the end. But the fact that she'd trusted him, had allowed herself to be vulnerable to him in such an intimate way, humbled him, and heightened the passionate tenderness he felt for her.

"You are splendid," he whispered against her damp cheek. "Brave. The most beautiful..."

Her body was limp beneath his, her rapid breathing gradually returning to normal. She turned her head so his mouth brushed against her lips. He felt her smile, even as she sighed with deep satisfaction.

"You," she murmured. Her arm was still between their bodies, but now her hand was resting bonelessly on her belly. She roused herself enough to pull it out and put her arm around his back. "You're so clever."

That unexpected praise startled him into a brief chuckle.

Reluctantly, but carefully, he withdrew from her and shifted to lie by her side. She rolled with him, coming to rest with her head on his shoulder and her leg partially lying across his. He slid his hand down her side, hooked it under her thigh, and pulled her leg higher.

She wriggled, but only to edge nearer, and then she relaxed again.

They had things to do, for themselves and in preparation for what lay ahead tomorrow.

He wanted to tend to her on the most intimate level. Make sure he hadn't hurt her and that she was comfortable. But she wasn't giving any indication of discomfort now, and this moment was unique in their lives. No matter how many times they made love in the future, this would always be a vivid memory for them both.

The hand she'd pleasured herself with was now resting on his chest. He picked it up, brought it to his lips and sucked her index finger into his mouth. Her taste stirred his arousal.

"Oh." She lifted her head. He sensed he'd surprised her.

"Next time—or the time after, you must decide—I will go straight to the source," he murmured.

"The source...you'd kiss me there?" she whispered.

"Mmm. Only if you're willing. Why am I clever?"

"Clever and so generous." She settled down again.

He waited, one hand holding hers, the other drawing idle circles on her back.

"Because you had me maze myself." He could barely hear her soft words.

"Maze...oh, yes." He understood her reference and smiled in the darkness. "I hoped my own stamina would be sufficient. I tried...but in the end I did fall short."

"You did *not*," she lifted her head again. "You were perfect. *Perfect*. My assessment of your...your prowess is the only one that matters."

"Yes, it is." He grinned, overwhelmed with happiness. "Yours is the only opinion that matters to me. But I've had years to think and plan for this night. To imagine how I should proceed, how to give you the greatest pleasure I could."

"Did you... maze yourself...while you were imagining?" she asked breathlessly.

"Dear heart, I've been mazing myself when I think about you for years, long before I went on the expedition," he confessed.

"Oh." She hitched herself higher. "I mazed myself when I thought about you too. Pretending it was you. I always pretended it was you. You're not shocked, are you?"

He cupped the back of her head to hold her steady for his kiss. "I'm never shocked by you," he said against her lips. "I only care that we never make you vulnerable to the judgment or disapproval of other people. The likelihood of you being able to maze yourself was a factor in my anticipatory planning for our first time."

"I know that's not the real word," she admitted. "But I like it better."

"It's our code." He coasted his palm over her naked shoulder. "Are you cold?"

She shook her head. "You're keeping me warm. Truly."

It was a sultry night and she was wrapped around him, so he believed her.

"Let me tend to you, dear heart. I'm sorry the water won't be warm." He eased from the bed and used a dampened towel to clean himself and returned to gently do the same for Gabrielle.

As soon as he lay down again, she snuggled up to him the way she had before.

"We can't do this again—the full act—until we're married," he said quietly. "I should have pulled out, but that wasn't how I planned things. I always imagined we'd be married, or only days away from our wedding, when we took this step."

"It's my fault you went against your principles." She sounded subdued.

"Not principles, practicality. I'm the one who's debauched you, and I'm the one who's going to marry you. There's no conflict there. And precious little scandal if anyone found out we spent tonight in bed together and three weeks from now we're walking along Marine Parade as the Earl and Countess of Hanwell."

"It's because I want to stay with Charlotte. A governess can't be debauched by anyone, even an earl, and not lose her position. I'm sorry." Only moments ago, she'd sounded so happy, now she sounded sad.

"We don't know how things are going to unfold in the next few days," he reminded her. "I need to find and speak to Lord Henderson. The fact he takes such a lackadaisical approach to raising his daughter gives me hope he'll be open to negotiation."

"We can't risk talking to Lady Henderson," Gabrielle said. "She's volatile and spiteful. Although she did prefer to send me away from Brighton than engage with the possibility I've broken her rules, and I didn't expect that."

"Lord Henderson's the one with ultimate authority over his children, and he'll be easier for me, or Father or Marcus to deal with," Quin said.

He stroked Gabrielle's arm, and then patted it gently. "Though I would love it if you could, we can't remain like this all night, dear heart. You need to go and make sure all is well with Charlotte, and get some sleep before tomorrow."

"I wish I could stay here." She stroked his chest.

He swallowed. "So do I. But we'll need our wits about us tomorrow, and that means we need some sleep and time to compose ourselves. We know we've just had our wedding night. But at this point I think it's advisable nobody else guesses that."

Gabrielle hoisted herself higher over him. "I love you so much." She lowered to kiss him.

"I love you too." And he didn't want to let her go anywhere.

In a sinuous movement she changed her position so she could more easily caress his chest.

"Gabrielle?"

"You planned so well for this night." Her voice held a sultry note he'd never heard before, though he didn't believe she was deliberately adopting that tone. "You concentrated so hard on my pleasure, and wouldn't let me do anything that might interfere with the execution of your plans."

"I did," he agreed, amusement and rising desire coursing through his body.

"And you succeeded triumphantly." Her hand trailed over the ridges of his belly.

His stomach muscles jerked. He drew in a sharp, involuntary breath and his cock, which had already been half-hard, rose to full mast.

"Can I touch you?" she whispered. "Now you can relax and not make my pleasure your priority? Will you show me how to give it to you?"

He didn't say anything, torn between yielding to the need pounding through his body and determination to follow the path of discretion.

Her hand moved slowly, inexorably lower. He had the sense she was holding her breath, not afraid, but uncertain of his reaction.

He took her hand. She went completely still. He guided it lower until she wrapped her fingers around his cock.

She started to breathe again, though he could barely hear the quick, soft sounds over the thudding of his own heart.

She stroked, delicately explored his length and then gave him an experimental squeeze. He groaned, his hips jerking up toward her.

"Show me how," she said.

He did, and then allowed himself to be carried away on the tidal wave of the blissful release she gave him.

After that he cleaned himself up and caressed her intimately, but with great care because he was worried she was sore, until she experienced her own blissful release.

"I will always care about your pleasure," he said, when they could both speak again. "And with more practice, I'm certain we'll be able to synchronize. But now we really must set ourselves to rights before the sun rises."

Chapter Thirty-Three

Gabrielle gradually became aware of murmuring voices, followed by feet scampering across the floor toward the bed.

"Mademoiselle?" Charlotte whispered. A child's hand delicately stroked Gabrielle's cheek. "Mademoiselle, are you awake?"

Gabrielle smiled before she opened her eyes. "A little bit. Good morning, Charlotte."

"Good morning, mademoiselle." Charlotte's return smile was sunny. "Lord Quin gives you his compliments and hopes you slept well."

Quin.

Glorious memories of the night they'd shared flooded Gabrielle. She rolled onto her back, drew in a deep, luxurious breath, and raised her head. The door was open a crack, but not enough for her to see Quin on the other side. He was being discreet.

She let her head fall back. There was a mild, unfamiliar ache between her legs, but her body felt decadently relaxed and satiated.

"Please thank Lord Quin for his kindness and say I slept very well," she told Charlotte. "And give him my compliments, etcetera."

Charlotte hurried across the small room to deliver the return message.

Gabrielle smiled at the ceiling, listening to the low-voiced conversation.

Charlotte came back. "Lord Quin had a very good night too, and wants to know if it's all right for me to go for a walk with him before breakfast while you get ready?"

"But you—" Gabrielle broke off when she saw Charlotte was still wearing the dress in which she'd gone to sleep. She squinted at it. "I suppose you don't look too badly crumpled. Make sure you wear your bonnet. What about...oh, you've already put on your shoes and stockings."

"I did that already before Lord Quin knocked." Charlotte swung her bonnet on its strings. "We'll see you at breakfast, mademoiselle."

The door closed behind her and Gabrielle flopped back onto the mattress.

Quin was taking Charlotte for a walk in yesterday's clothes, before she'd even had her hair done, and Gabrielle was letting it happen. Her mother—Gabrielle's mother—would be horrified. Poor Mama. Gabrielle felt a pang of old grief. She wished her mother was still alive to see Quin's return and hear his adventures.

But a small, barely acknowledged, part of her also wondered

how easily her mother would have adjusted to their change of circumstances. The Duchess de la Fontaine had been a kind, gracious woman. But it was hard to imagine her living as the wife of a fencing master, even one as well-renowned as Papa had become.

No doubt Lady Henderson would also be horrified by Gabrielle's lax performance of her duties as Charlotte's governess. The thought sent a shiver of unease through Gabrielle.

She slid her hand down her body to rest it on her belly. After last night, she could be pregnant already. If she was, her choices would become even more restricted than they currently were— and might end with a betrayal of the promises she and Quin had made to Charlotte.

Disquiet chewed away at her relaxed mood. She could never regret her night with Quin, but he was right. In future they must do nothing that might risk her becoming pregnant while she was still employed as Charlotte's governess.

She wasn't even sure when they'd get the chance to share any degree of intimacy again. For her to keep her position, her conduct would have to appear impeccable.

Today, they would finish their journey to Sedgemore Hall. Quin was hoping Charlotte's father would be in residence. Gabrielle hoped for the same thing, even though it wasn't likely to be a comfortable encounter. Otherwise, there would be more waiting and uncertainty.

But before that, there was breakfast with Quin and Charlotte to enjoy. Gabrielle got out of bed and set about making herself look like a pattern-card of virtue, and not the wanton woman Quin had praised so lavishly in the darkness last night.

~

Gabrielle had been sitting in the private parlor for several minutes when she heard voices outside the door.

Quin and Charlotte had returned.

Her pulse quickened. She set her teacup down in the saucer, her gaze locked on the door.

It flew open.

"Mademoiselle, are you—yes, she's here, Lord Quin," Charlotte called over her shoulder.

"So I see." Quin met her eyes, a warm smile and a quiet question in his gaze. "Good morning, Mademoiselle Rousselle."

"Good morning, my lord." Heat scalded her cheeks. When he looked at her like that, all she could think of were the things they'd done together last night. She knew what his chest looked like under his tailored coat. Knew how his naked body felt when it claimed hers in the ultimate physical union of two people.

"It's a beautiful day, isn't it?" she said. "Do you…? I'm mean, would you like some tea?" She reached toward the teapot, but she was looking at Quin, and her hand didn't find its target.

"Yes, please." His attention switched from her face to her hand hovering over the table. Then he met her gaze again, and though his lips barely moved, she felt the warm, private smile he shared with her deep in her soul. He was remembering exactly the same things she was—secrets that belonged to them alone. Secrets they needed to keep private for Charlotte's sake.

"A cup of tea would be welcome, thank you," Quin said. "What would you like, Charlotte?"

"May I have some milk?" Charlotte pulled off her bonnet

with one hand, tossed it onto the sofa, and went to sit at the table beside Gabrielle.

"The milk and your breakfast will be brought out directly, my lord," Mrs. Larkin said, and for the first time Gabrielle realized the landlady had also come a short way into the parlor.

"Thank you." Quin's calm tone gave no hint he might be experiencing any heightened emotions—except his cheeks were a darker color than usual.

Gabrielle averted her gaze, wondering if the landlady had noticed the undercurrents swirling between them. Did Mrs. Larkin guess they'd been lovers last night? Would she, or the maid who changed the sheets, ever be called upon to give evidence against them?

No, that kind of lurid public testimonial was only relevant when a husband was suing his wife's lover for damages, or in divorce cases. There was no reason for either of Charlotte's parents to interrogate Mrs. Larkin or her servants.

"Dear heart?" Quin murmured, coming to sit beside her in the same place he'd occupied the previous evening.

"It's of no consequence. My imagination was running away with me," she assured him. "Did you have a good walk?"

"Very good," Charlotte declared. "We saw two creatures we're not allowed to mention at mealtimes, and we brought you some flowers." She held out the small bunch she was clutching in her hand.

"Thank you, sweetheart." Gabrielle took them and sniffed appreciatively. "They're beautiful."

"It was Lord Quin's idea." Charlotte fidgeted on her chair as if she was too happy to sit still. "It was a good idea, wasn't it?"

"A very good and lovely idea." Gabrielle shared a smile with them both, and something different about Charlotte's appearance caught her attention.

"Did you do your hair, sweetheart?" she asked.

"Lord Quin did." Charlotte wrapped her hands around the tumbler of milk a servant placed before her and took a long drink.

"Lord Quin?" Gabrielle threw him a bemused glance. "When did you learn how to do ladies' hair, my lord?"

"This morning," he replied.

Charlotte lowered the tumbler back onto the table and wiped her mouth on her napkin the way Gabrielle had taught her.

"He looked at me when I came out of our room and said that, even though *I* was as comely as ever, it was clear a naughty little bird had nested in my hair while I was asleep." Charlotte's eyes twinkled, as if she understood he'd been trying not to hurt her feelings while drawing attention to something he felt should be rectified.

"Some birds are partial to lining their nests with hair," Quin said.

"He said we should brush my hair so the little bird wouldn't come back and sit on my head while we were out walking." Charlotte broke into giggles. "Wouldn't that be funny, mademoiselle? If a little bird came and sat on my head while we were out?"

"Very funny." Gabrielle made no effort to conceal her own amusement.

"So Lord Quin got his brush, and we came in here to do it," Charlotte said. "He said he'd made lots of corn dollies in his time and he would apply the same prini...princi..." She frowned. "Do it the same way. Mrs. Larkin gave us the ribbon. Have you made corn dollies, mademoiselle?"

"Yes, but not as many as Lord Quin, I daresay, and none as fine." Gabrielle felt a pang as she remembered the last one he'd given her.

They'd been sitting in the shade beside a half-harvested wheat field. The sun had been warm and the sky a clear blue. Quin had worked swiftly to make her a beautiful, complex dolly from the wheat straw. She'd treasured it—but it had been left behind when they'd fled the château.

"I'll make you another one this harvest." Quin touched her knee under the table. She wondered if he'd noticed her momentary sadness, because his gesture seemed more designed to reassure than tease. "I'll make you both one. I'm sure I still have the knack."

"Thank you, my lord." Gabrielle smiled at him, and made a show of leaning closer to admire Charlotte's hair—and surreptitiously check what he'd done, and how hard it would be to undo. "What fine work."

"They're just braids." He sounded amused, as if he guessed her thoughts. "Easy to unravel when a more accomplished person takes command of the situation. But I thought we should make a good impression if we encountered any local inhabitants on our walk. I wasn't sure how long Charlotte's bonnet would stay on her head."

"That was very considerate of you." Gabrielle wanted to hug him, but she contented herself with a smile.

"I'm good at keeping my bonnet on," Charlotte said. "Except sometimes it comes off if I crawl under low branches. That's why we tie it so it'll easily come undone if it gets caught on something —not choke me."

"Not necessarily a problem all young ladies experience," Quin reflected. "But I believe I was present on the occasion mademoiselle learned that lesson."

Chapter Thirty-Four

Quin enjoyed breakfast with Gabrielle and Charlotte, but he gently encouraged them not to linger over the meal.

His conversation with Lord Henderson was going to be delicate under the best of circumstances. He didn't want it to be complicated by accusations he'd deliberately delayed reporting the highwayman's attack and subsequent events to the viscount.

Gabrielle and Charlotte went up to their room to make their final preparations for resuming the journey, while Quin sought out Mrs. Larkin to settle his account with her.

"Thank you for ensuring Mademoiselle Rousselle and Miss Charlotte have been so comfortable here." He handed over the full amount on the landlady's bill, plus a sizable extra sum.

She looked at the banknotes and then up at him, a question in her eyes. "I think you may have miscounted, my lord."

"No, I didn't," Quin said. "Both the young ladies had a great fright yesterday. Your hospitality has done much to help them recover their composure."

Mrs. Larkin's expression turned quizzical. "I would say it's your presence that's helped them most, my lord. Your timely arrival on the road yesterday was great good fortune for them."

Quin nodded. "I'm glad I could be of service to them." He was aware he was beginning to sound more stilted with every word, but this wasn't the kind of conversation he'd ever had to hold before.

The landlady had surely guessed that he and Gabrielle were more to each other than passing acquaintances. And if she didn't already know Gabrielle had spent part of the night in his room, she would by the time they were a mile or so down the road.

Quin wasn't going to discuss his private affairs with Mrs. Larkin, but he hoped she'd be more likely to exercise discretion if she formed a favorable impression of him.

"Miss Charlotte asked if she may see the kittens again before we leave," he said.

"Of course she can, and very welcome." The landlady smiled and tucked his payment into her pocket. "Next time you travel this way, I hope you'll stay here again."

"You may be sure I will." If Gabrielle ended up living at Sedgemore Hall for an extended period, Quin might find himself traveling frequently along this road when he visited her from Brighton.

A short while later, he escorted Gabrielle and Charlotte to the storage room for a last visit with the kittens.

Charlotte sat on the floor to play with them. She picked up

one wriggling ball of fluff and put it on her lap. "I wish I could take her with me," she said.

"She's too young to leave her mother just yet." Quin crouched down to stroke one finger across the kitten's head. "Her eyes are barely open. She won't grow into a strong, healthy cat if we take her away from her mother too soon." He waited a few moments and then said, "We need to leave now, Charlotte. Nedcott and the horses are waiting for us to depart."

A mulish expression appeared on her face. Quin thought she was going to rebel and prepared himself to enforce his command in a gentle, but firm manner.

But after scowling dreadfully at the floor for several tense moments—at least, they were tense as far as Quin was concerned, because he'd been thrown into deep water when it came to caring for a little girl—she nodded and gently put the kitten back in the basket.

"*Au revoir*, kitten," she said, and clambered to her feet.

Quin wondered if Charlotte had deliberately chosen a form of goodbye that meant 'until we meet again', and glanced questioningly at Gabrielle.

She smiled and gave a small shrug. Yes, she was expecting to hear more about the kitten over the next few weeks. Perhaps something along the lines of 'is it old enough yet?'. Quin had no doubts Charlotte was intelligent enough to wait on that battle until it was worth fighting.

So when they arrived in the coach yard and Charlotte stopped dead, stubbornly refusing to walk forward, it took him completely by surprise

"Is that your horse?" she demanded. "I thought you were coming with us."

"I am coming with you," Quin said. "I'll ride alongside or ahead of your carriage."

Charlotte didn't budge, even though the carriage door was now invitingly open.

"No, no, no." She shook her head vehemently. "I want to ride with *you*. I'm not going in the coach. I'm riding with you."

Quin wouldn't have minded taking Charlotte up before him again, but Gabrielle shook her head.

"You must ride in the coach today," she said, a discernible undercurrent of tension in her voice. "It's only in very unusual circumstances that a lady may ride on the same horse as a gentleman. Today everything is normal, and you must travel in the coach with me. Come." She took Charlotte's hand and gave it a gentle tug.

"*No!*" Charlotte wrenched away. "I'm not getting in the coach. I'm staying with the kittens." She spun around and ran straight back into the inn, dodging past a servant on his way out.

"*Charlotte!*" Gabrielle started to follow, but Quin caught her shoulders and held her still.

"Wait," he said. "Wait."

She looked up at him and he saw the distress in her face.

"I *can't* wait. I have to speak to her. We *have* to get in the carriage. We have—"

"Shush." Quin wanted to pull her into his arms, but there were too many witnesses to their conversation, so he made do with squeezing her shoulders comfortingly before he released her.

Something was upsetting both Charlotte and Gabrielle, and he needed to understand what it was without delay.

A few minutes ago, Charlotte had made a perfectly rational decision *not* to have a tantrum when he'd told her it would harm the kitten to take it from its mother. In fact, in the brief time he'd known Charlotte, she'd *always* behaved in a way that made sense to him. So there had to be a reason for her unexpectedly naughty behavior.

Nor could he believe Gabrielle was usually brought to the point of tears because of a battle of wills with Charlotte.

Over her head he saw the carriage, and Nedcott's concerned, tired face—and understanding dawned.

"You don't want to get in the coach either, do you, dear heart?" he said softly.

"I..." Gabrielle ducked her head, and he saw her swallow before she looked up at him again. "I wasn't concerned until I saw Charlotte's reaction, and that reminded me...I'm so sorry I'm being silly."

Quin shook his head. "You're not being silly." From the look on Nedcott's face, he suspected none of his three companions were eager to continue their journey in the carriage today, though there was no sign the coachman was going to balk at carrying out his duty.

"All right," Quin said, "we've established the problem. Now we just have to devise the solution."

Gabrielle rewarded him with a tremulous smile. "I'm so glad you're here this morning."

"So am I." He hadn't put on his gloves yet, and he couldn't

resist the urge to stroke her cheek. "May I help you into the carriage? Then I'll go and speak to Charlotte."

Chapter Thirty-Five

Gabrielle sat in the carriage, listening to Quin and Charlotte talk about hedges, of all things.

Quin had solved the apparent impasse by simply telling Charlotte he'd ride inside the coach with them. He'd even climbed in first and pulled Charlotte up after.

Gabrielle was certain Quin's decision would be thoroughly frowned upon by everyone who believed obedience was the paramount virtue a child should display.

She wasn't sure herself whether he'd been too indulgent—except *she* was glad he was sitting with them. Charlotte had still been visibly tense when they'd first left the inn behind, but she'd quickly relaxed.

"The prince can't get through the hedge," she explained to Quin. "He keeps chopping and chopping and sharpening his ax, but he can't get *through*." Frustration rang in her voice. "I even dreamed about him chopping and chopping and chopping...it's very annoying."

Gabrielle bit her lip. Charlotte must have heard more of the repetitive part of the story than she'd guessed, but she'd never expected it to invade Charlotte's dreams.

"That is annoying," Quin agreed cheerfully. "Poor prince. From the sound of things, he's encountered a trained hedge without realizing it and is trying the wrong technique to get through."

"A *trained* hedge?" Charlotte gave him a skeptical look. "You can't train a hedge."

"Yes, you can," Quin replied. "I'll wager many of the hedges we're traveling past today have been trained at one time or another."

Charlotte peered out of the window at the luxuriant hedge bordering the road. Pale pink wild roses grew profusely among the greenery. It was a pretty sight, though Gabrielle couldn't help wondering if there was another highwayman skulking behind it. She just hoped Charlotte didn't have the same thought.

"How do you train a hedge?" Charlotte looked back at Quin, her expression signaling both interest and continuing skepticism. She clearly suspected he was teasing her. "Do you have to give it a lesson in being a hedge every morning when it's a young hedgelet?"

"A hedge is a row of plants growing close together," Quin said. "Not one single entity. Sometimes those plants could grow into trees if they were planted alone. Hawthorn, for example."

Charlotte frowned out of the window at the hedge. "I knew that, I think. If they tangle their branches together, they become a hedge."

"That's it. And if you lay a hedge correctly—or train it—you can encourage that tangling together," Quin said.

Gabrielle imagined other things lying down and tangling together and slid a glance at Quin.

He caught it and a smile twitched his lips, but then he returned his full attention to Charlotte.

"I can tell you've never seen a skilled hedge-layer at work," he said to her. "The chore is done during the winter months. Each plant stem must be cut part way through near the base, and bent sideways…"

Gabrielle listened as he described inserting stakes so many yards apart for securing the living hedge plants. She tried to engage with what he was saying, but all she truly cared about was hearing his voice and knowing he was within touching distance. What would happen when they arrived at Sedgemore Hall?

"Different parts of the country have different hedge laying traditions," he said. "A laid hedge in Devon looks nothing like one in the Midlands. It's my guess that your story prince has the additional problem of dealing with a *magically* trained hedge. That hedge—" Quin pointed out of the window "—has been trained to keep livestock in. But I'll wager the hedge in your story has been specially trained to keep princes *out*."

Charlotte stared at Quin with a kind of awed excitement. "Mademoiselle, the prince is trying to get through a *magically trained* hedge." She bounced up and down on her seat as she shared the revelation. "No wonder his ax keeps going blunt!"

"No wonder," Gabrielle agreed. "Perhaps he needs a magic ax? What about the ax Jack the Giant Killer used to cut down the beanstalk? Was that magical?"

"Not that I'm aware," Quin shot her a grin. "And the one you're likely thinking of was also quite blunt. Now, as a plant lover and a man of reason, I'm not comfortable with all this random hacking and chopping at a hedge. After all, it's only doing what it's been trained to do. We need to come up with a better—" he broke off, turning his head sharply.

In the same instant, Gabrielle heard shouting outside the coach. Before she could distinguish the shouted words, Nedcott shouted back, and the coach juddered to a halt.

Charlotte gave a gasp of horror and twisted round to throw her arms about Gabrielle.

Gabrielle's own heart thudded sickeningly as she held onto Charlotte. All she could think of was the moment the highwayman had stopped them yesterday with a warning shot and shouted commands.

"Not again," she whispered. "Please, not again."

"I don't think so," Quin said, but he flipped open the bag on the seat beside him and Gabrielle saw the butt of a pistol.

"Is Miss Charlotte with you?" A man shouted. "Mademoiselle? Nedcott?"

"They're both safe in the coach, Roger," Nedcott shouted back.

Gabrielle closed her eyes, her shoulders sagging. She let her head drop forward until her cheek rested on the top of Charlotte's head. All the strength seemed to have drained from her body.

At the same time, Charlotte loosened her convulsive grip, though she didn't pull away. She too must have recognized the voice and realized her initial fears of another highway attack were unfounded.

"Roger is Lady Henderson's footman," Gabrielle told Quin, as a horseman rode up to the coach door.

"Mademoiselle? Miss Charlotte? Are you in there?" He bent from the saddle to peer through the window.

"Yes, Roger, we're here, and we're safe," Gabrielle replied unsteadily. "What are you doing here? Where's Lady Henderson?"

"Lady Henderson is in Brighton. She sent me after you yesterday with a letter, but when I got to Sedgemore Hall last night you weren't there! Steady...steady." The footman tried to calm his restive horse.

"Mademoiselle Rousselle and Miss Charlotte are both well, Roger," Quin said. "Please dismount and tether your horse securely so we may continue this conversation with more ease."

The footman threw Quin a startled glance that turned speculative by the time he rode away from the window.

"Wait here," Quin said to Gabrielle and Charlotte. He opened the door, jumped down, and closed it behind him.

"Why is Roger here?" Charlotte pushed back to look up at Gabrielle.

"He said he has a letter for me from your mama," Gabrielle replied, in the grip of a new wave of apprehension. Why had Lady Henderson written to her within hours of their departure yesterday?

Quin opened the door again. "Charlotte, will you come to me?" He held out his hand to her.

For some reason, his gentle question caused Gabrielle to feel a new surge of worry. Charlotte seemed to feel the same way, because her arms remained wrapped around Gabrielle as she peered at Quin over her shoulder.

"Why?" she said.

"So Mademoiselle can comfortably read her letter," Quin replied easily, raising the folded, sealed missive he held in his other hand.

Charlotte did not initially respond. Then she said, "I will sit beside her." She released Gabrielle and settled back in the seat, but she stared at the letter as warily as if it was a venomous creature.

"Fair enough." Quin got back into the coach and gave the note to Gabrielle.

She took it as reluctantly as if it was one of Charlotte's snail shells, and laid it on her lap while she pulled off her gloves. She knew removing them was an unnecessary delay, but she dreaded what might be in the letter.

Had harm come to Lord Henderson? Or—

Or to Papa or Felix?

The moment it occurred to Gabrielle the news might be about her father or brother, delay became abhorrent to her. She broke open the sealed letter with trembling hands, uncaring that she tore the paper.

Her emotions were in such a heightened state that, in her first scan of the short message, she only noticed it didn't mention any member of her family.

She read it again...and then again.

It was short, totally lacking in courtesy, and thoroughly bewildering.

"Mademoiselle Rousselle, Bring Charlotte back to Brighton at once. Livia, Lady Henderson."

The words 'at once' were underscored three times. There were also two large ink blots on the paper.

Gabrielle had no idea what to make of it. Had Augustus fallen ill? Or had Lady Henderson received bad news about her husband? The message gave no clue at all about the reason for Lady Henderson's order.

Gabrielle handed the unfolded letter to Quin, and looked down into Charlotte's worried face.

"Your mama wants us to return to Brighton," she said, as matter-of-factly as she could.

"Why?" Charlotte demanded.

"I don't know. I'm going to speak to Roger." Gabrielle leaned toward the door.

"Wait, I'll help you out." Quin returned the letter to her, jumped down a second time, and assisted her to descend.

Gabrielle kept hold of his hand for a few seconds, because her legs felt a little shaky. But then she smiled at him and went to speak to the footman.

Chapter Thirty-Six

"I don't want to go back to Brighton," Charlotte said. "I want to go to Sedgemore Hall and look for snails with you."

Quin gripped the door frame and looked into the coach at her.

"I'm afraid we must go back," he said, maintaining his calm demeanor with far more effort than usual.

Lady Henderson's rude message to Gabrielle had roused his ire as few things ever did. The viscountess must have known the mere fact she'd sent a message for Gabrielle so soon after her departure would be alarming, yet she'd written nothing to allay that alarm. Had not even bothered with a polite salutation, simply scrawled an order across a sheet of paper.

"Will you come in the coach with us all the way?" Charlotte asked.

"Of course I will," he said.

Charlotte slid off the seat to sit on the floor of the carriage in the open doorway, with her feet on the steps.

Quin suspected he ought to tell her it wasn't ladylike to sit on the coach floor, and remind her not to get her dress dirty, but he had a feeling there might be bigger battles ahead. He decided to let that one go.

"I *hate* the coach." Charlotte planted her elbows on her knees and her chin in her raised hands.

Quin looked up at Nedcott. "How much longer would it take to reach Sedgemore Hall?"

"Another forty minutes, maybe longer." The coachman sounded as disgruntled as Charlotte.

Quin nodded, easily able to see the weariness in the other man's face and bearing. Quin guessed the Hendersons' coachman wasn't often required to drive long distances on journeys lasting more than one day. Nedcott wasn't like the men who drove the mail and stagecoaches for a living—and yesterday he'd had the shock of a pistol being fired over his head. He must have been as eager to reach Sedgemore Hall as Charlotte.

"Where can you turn around?" Quin asked.

The carriage was currently sitting on the side of a long, straight road. That was good, because there was little risk of another vehicle dashing around a corner and crashing into them. On the other hand, there were hedges and ditches on both sides of the road, and not enough room for the horses to pull the coach around.

"A couple of miles ahead," Nedcott said, after thinking for a few moments.

"I hate Mama!" Charlotte burst out. "I don't want to go back to her. Don't take us back to her."

Quin's gut clenched. "I have to take you back to her. She's your mother and I have no authority to take you anywhere else."

Charlotte stared at him.

It belatedly occurred to him he should probably have reprimanded her for saying she hated her mother, but he instinctively recoiled from telling her how she felt.

"Do you *want* to take me back to Mama?" Her voice wobbled.

He took a breath and released it slowly. "No. I'd rather end our journey in forty minutes' time and help you find snails."

"Truly?" Her expression was stark with longing.

"Yes."

"But you can't run away with me and mademoiselle because you're honorable, so we have to go back to Mama." Charlotte turned her head to the side and rubbed the back of her hand over her eyes.

"We need to go back and find out what your mama wants—and then I'm going to find your papa," Quin said.

Charlotte's gaze flew to his face. "Papa? He doesn't care about me."

"That's a painful thing for you to believe," Quin said. "I care about you. Mademoiselle loves you."

Charlotte rocked back and forward, rubbing her hands up and down her shins in what he was certain was an unconscious gesture. "Mademoiselle loves me. I love mademoiselle."

"So do I...love mademoiselle." Quin hesitated. "Why did you stop talking?" As soon as the words were out, he wished them back. This wasn't the time or place to ask, and he didn't know what misguided instinct had prompted the question.

He was half afraid Charlotte would either ignore him or retreat into silence again.

A small flock of twittering sparrows darted in and out of the hedge. A robin sang somewhere nearby—and Quin's heart thudded heavily behind his ribs.

Charlotte stared straight ahead. "Mama screamed at me to shut my howling mouth."

Quin eased out a breath. "So you did?"

Charlotte looked up, a strange mixture of hope and defiance in her eyes, and nodded.

According to what Gabrielle had told him, Charlotte had stopped speaking soon after the death of her nurse. She'd most likely been crying with grief and in desperate need of comfort, not callous impatience. It was probable she'd been treated unkindly on other occasions.

"And your mama has never rescinded her instruction?" Quin asked.

Charlotte's brows drew together. He guessed she didn't understand what he'd said.

"Your mama never took her order back?" he clarified.

Charlotte slowly moved her head sideways in a negative motion.

Quin began to fear he'd pushed her back into silence. Damn it, why had he asked the question now?

"All right," he said. "If mademoiselle or I ever tell you to be quiet, there will be a very good reason, and we won't expect you to be quiet for longer than necessary."

"Mademoiselle told me to be quiet as a mouse yesterday," Charlotte said.

Relief washed over Quin at the sound of her voice. She was still talking to him.

"But I wasn't quiet when I thought she'd been shot!" Charlotte suddenly lost her remaining color, her focus turned inward, and a sob wracked her body. It was evident she was reliving that moment of utmost terror and despair.

"What happened next?" Quin asked. "Charlotte, what happened next?"

His question jolted her into looking up at him, a tear trickling down her cheek.

"What happened next?" he repeated in a less compelling tone.

"We cried...and...and hugged...m-mademoiselle and me," she whispered.

"Mademoiselle hugged you tightly, didn't she? And you knew she was safe. And you were safe. What happened then?"

"You carried us over the heath and gave us w-water."

"Was the water good to drink?"

Charlotte nodded and rubbed her cheek.

"Was the rest of yesterday good?"

She lifted her gaze and smiled at him. It wasn't the full beam he knew she was capable of, but it was a far cry from her distress when she'd remembered the highwayman's attack.

"You gave me a book about bird nesting and mating," she said.

Quin heard a quiet snort from the carriage, and remembered Nedcott had been a silent witness to their entire conversation.

"The Reverend Gilbert White's *Natural History of Selborne*," he said, for Nedcott's benefit more than Charlotte's. "Unfortunately, he didn't have much to say about snails."

He looked up and saw the coachman was watching him with a kind of interested respect—and something else, which probably had a great deal to do with what he'd just heard Charlotte reveal about Lady Henderson.

Quin couldn't talk about the man's employer with him. He'd had to walk a fine line with what he'd said to Charlotte, because he wasn't willing to make any promises to her he couldn't guarantee keeping.

Their short, intense conversation had been one of the most demanding he'd ever had. Though he'd tried to keep his posture easy, his muscles had knotted, and he was sweating despite the fact the morning hadn't yet heated up. He knew he didn't have his father's easy address, but he hoped he hadn't fallen too far short in finding the right things to say to Charlotte.

"My mama died when I was a baby," he said.

"Oh." Her lips parted, and she looked sad.

"I don't remember her at all," he continued swiftly. "What I meant to say is that when I was a little boy, I had a lady who was to me what mademoiselle is to you."

"You had your own mademoiselle?" Charlotte's expression cleared. "As kind as my mademoiselle?"

"They're the same in kindness. Her name's Miss Trent."

"Miss Trent?" Charlotte shaped the words.

"Yes. When I was younger than you are now, Miss Trent told me that if I remembered a bad or scary thing, I should keep remembering what happened next until I got to a good memory," Quin said. "And if I was worried or scared about something that might happen in the future, I should consider if there was anything I needed to be scared about right now."

Charlotte looked around. A sparrow fluttered down to peck at something in the grass verge, then flew away again.

"Everything's all right now, because you're here," she said.

Quin's heart contracted. How the hell was he going to make sure everything stayed all right for Charlotte and Gabrielle?

Yes, Quin's father was a marquess and his cousin a duke. But Charlotte's situation could get a lot worse if Lord Henderson decided to metaphorically lock his daughter in a tower and throw away the key for the next fourteen years.

"They're coming back. I don't like Roger," she muttered.

Nedcott shifted on the box. Quin looked up and the coachman gave him a small head shake.

It seemed neither of his companions liked the footman.

Gabrielle was walking one pace ahead of Roger. At first glance she seemed serene, but Quin detected hints of frustration and worry when she met his gaze.

"I've given Roger an account of what happened yesterday, and that it was our good fortune you were on your way to Winchester and were able to intervene, my lord," she said.

"I've sent word to my associate in Winchester that I've been unavoidably delayed," he lied.

An unmistakable smirk flickered over Roger's face—and faded when he met Quin's eyes.

"Mademoiselle Rousselle, are you satisfied your conversation with Roger is complete?" he asked.

"Yes, he's been helpful." Her words were polite, but he

sensed they were as much a lie as his claim to have an associate in Winchester.

"In that case, Roger, please return to Sedgemore Hall and reassure everyone there that Miss Sedgemore, Mademoiselle Rousselle and Nedcott are all safe and well," he ordered.

Roger didn't move. "By your leave, my lord, my lady told me to return to her as soon as I've delivered her message."

"Lady Henderson wasn't aware of the full circumstances when she issued that instruction," Quin said. "You left a household of people in a state of great anxiety this morning. She would certainly expect you to alleviate their worries as soon as you're able to do so."

Roger looked up at Nedcott, at Gabrielle and back at Quin.

Charlotte stood up on the coach steps.

"Roger, *I* am a *Sedgemore*," she said imperiously. "I *order* you to go and tell everyone at Sedgemore Hall that we are safe."

Roger's shocked expression was almost comical. He climbed up on his horse and turned it to face the direction he'd come from.

Gabrielle and Quin stepped aside as he rode past the coach.

"Clippety-clop," Charlotte said.

Chapter Thirty-Seven

Gabrielle bit her lip to keep from laughing and Nedcott seemed to have developed a cough.

No one spoke as they watched Roger urge his horse into a trot back the way he'd come.

"I sounded just like Augustus, didn't I?" Charlotte said gleefully.

Nedcott guffawed and hastily converted it into another cough.

"That's not usually something I would commend you on." But Gabrielle couldn't help smiling. "Yes, you did."

Charlotte's proud expression faded. "We have to get back to Brighton before Roger does. He'll tell Mama tales about Lord Quin being with us."

That was Gabrielle's worry too—but even if they beat Roger back to Brighton, they couldn't control what he said to Lady Henderson.

"We can't keep my existence a secret from your mama, Charlotte," Quin said. "But I agree it would be best if we get back to Brighton as fast as we can. Everybody into the coach so Nedcott can take care of getting us there."

Charlotte scrambled back inside, and Quin offered Gabrielle his hand.

"I don't know why Lady Henderson sent the message," she said softly. "Roger told me she went to Donaldson's Library yesterday. He wouldn't say anything else—but he knows something else."

Quin nodded. "Charlotte warned me she didn't like him. Let's make a start, dear heart."

Once they'd turned around, they made good time back to the posting inn where they'd spent the night.

Mrs. Larkin was surprised to see them, but happy for Quin to hire one of her men to sit beside Nedcott for the rest of the journey back to Brighton.

"He'll act as a guard, and also blow the horn whenever we're approaching a tollgate," Quin said to Charlotte.

"So the gatekeepers will open ready for us?" Her eyes shone with excitement.

"That's the idea." Quin winked at Gabrielle.

It was a sufficiently unQuin-like gesture that it distracted her almost as much as the horn-blowing guard sitting beside Nedcott was distracting Charlotte.

But not for long, and with Charlotte sitting with them she couldn't openly share her concerns.

The first time Charlotte heard the horn, they both had to keep hold of her as she peered out of the coach window to see what was happening.

"Mama and Augustus have a horn when they travel, but *we* never do," she said, sitting back on the seat. "We always travel with the other servants. But we're properly important now we've got a horn. That's right, because you're an earl. Is your papa's horn louder?"

Gabrielle carefully avoided looking at Quin.

"Because he's a marquess, you mean?" He took the question in his stride. "No, I don't think so, and he doesn't always have one blown when he's traveling. I only arranged for it today because it will likely save us some time on the journey."

The light went out of Charlotte's expression. "I don't want to arrive. We have to beat Roger—but I don't want to arrive."

"I know." The understanding look Quin gave Charlotte tugged at Gabrielle's heart.

"Can't we just keep going and going...and going?" Charlotte asked.

"We'd end up in the sea," Quin said.

"We could go in a boat. We could go in a boat to where the giant snails are?"

Quin smiled, but shook his head. "I only just came home. My papa will be sad if I go far away from him again so soon."

Charlotte's mouth wobbled.

Quin stretched out his hand to her. After a moment she laid her much smaller hand on his palm, and he closed his fingers around it.

"I have to take you and mademoiselle back to your mama today, Charlotte. We will decide between us whether or not I should come in with you when we arrive. And once you are settled, I will find your papa."

"I told you he doesn't care about me."

"If he really doesn't care, that might make things easier," Quin replied.

Gabrielle's throat was so tight she was afraid a sob would escape if she tried to speak. It seemed that while she'd been having an unsatisfactory conversation with Roger, Quin and Charlotte's talk had covered much more serious ground.

"Maybe Papa will say it's all right for me and mademoiselle to stay at Sedgemore Hall all the time," Charlotte said, after a few moments. "And you could come and visit us. We could bring mademoiselle flowers, and you could help me look for snails."

Gabrielle swallowed. "Quin...Lord Quin has to write his book with his friend," she managed.

"Giant Duncan? He can visit too. You and Giant Duncan can stay at Sedgemore Hall to write your book." Charlotte's head bobbed rapidly. "There are lots of big tables you can put your papers on."

Gabrielle didn't know what to say. It was clear Quin didn't either.

"I can lay the fire for you, so you don't get cold," Charlotte said desperately. "I can't lay hedges but I'm good at laying fires, aren't I, mademoiselle?"

"Very good." Gabrielle blinked tears. She'd discovered Charlotte's fire-making skills one morning when no one had come to tend the nursery hearth. She'd been trying to remedy the matter herself, and then Charlotte had taken over to show her how to do it properly.

By the time they'd finished, they'd both been dirty, warmed by their physical activity, and basking in the pleasure of success.

"You know how to lay a fire?" Quin said.

More violent head bobbing. "Tessie taught me. I know how to clean out the old one and lay a new one. Someone else has to light it. If you keep me, I'll lay all your fires for you." By the end of her promise, she was crying.

"We want to keep you, sweetheart." Gabrielle wrapped her arms around Charlotte. Her eyes met Quin's over the top of the little girl's head.

His expression was full of compassion when he looked at Charlotte, and his gaze was perfectly steady when he met Gabrielle's—but she could see the conflict in his eyes.

"Who's Tessie?" he asked.

"My old nurse." Charlotte's voice was muffled against Gabrielle's shoulder. "She taught me to lay fires and darn stockings. I'm good at darning, too, aren't I, mademoiselle?"

"Very good." Gabrielle kept hugging Charlotte until the carriage wheels jolted over a particularly large rut and Charlotte's head banged into Gabrielle's chin.

Charlotte sat up, rubbing her hand over her crown. "Stupid rough road."

"Why don't we go back to seeing if we can solve the prince's problem with that annoyingly trained hedge?" Quin suggested.

For the rest of the journey back to Brighton they didn't discuss any serious matters. Charlotte's interest in the prince seemed to have waned, so Quin told them about some of his adventures, and then they all played the "I see a..." in French game.

When they stopped for the last time before they reached their destination, Quin asked Gabrielle, "What do you think best, dear heart? Should I come in with you—or not?"

She bit her lip, and slowly shook her head. "I told Roger you were escorting us to Sedgemore Hall as a disinterested kindness to my papa. Once we're safely in Brighton, you probably consider your duty done and you can go about your own business."

A grin briefly lightened Quin's expression. "That's not how my father raised me, and well you know it."

"You didn't escort us all the way home after ice cream," Charlotte reminded him.

"No, we didn't. For the same reason I'm going to let mademoiselle's wishes prevail now. I'll tell Nedcott I want to alight when we turn onto the Steine," Quin said to Gabrielle. "And I'll arrange for our guard to take his leave of us now. No need to draw attention by arriving in Brighton in a grander state than you departed."

Then he looked directly at Charlotte. "I'll find and speak to your father," he said. "I promise."

Chapter Thirty-Eight

The carriage came to a halt outside the house. The front door opened, and a footman came out past the butler to unlatch the coach door.

Gabrielle's breathing was tight, her stomach gripped with nausea, but she murmured her thanks to the footman and accepted his assistance to the ground.

"Come, Charlotte." She walked up the shallow steps, hearing the scuff of small feet on the ground behind her.

Under other circumstances, she would have reminded Charlotte to carry herself with ladylike poise, but not today.

"Good afternoon, Mademoiselle Rousselle, Miss Charlotte. I hope your journeys to Sedgemore Hall and back were pleasant." Beneath Penson's professionally composed demeanor, Gabrielle sensed he was ill-at-ease.

"We were shot at by a highwayman," Charlotte said flatly.

The butler's shocked gaze swiveled down to Charlotte and back up to Gabrielle.

"On the outward journey," Gabrielle said. "No one was hurt."

"Except the highwayman. He's in jail now."

"Awaiting trial at the next...Assizes? I believe that's what the magistrate told us," Gabrielle said. "Nedcott will remember better than I do. I'm not fully familiar with the English justice system."

She wouldn't have chosen to announce they'd been held up the moment they crossed the threshold—but at least it meant no one could accuse her of trying to conceal the information.

Penson looked out at the carriage and then at Gabrielle. "I'm relieved you're all safely home, mademoiselle," he said faintly.

"Thank you, please have some milk and buttered bread sent up to the nursery," Gabrielle replied. "Charlotte, go up and wait for me, please. Is Lady Henderson in the drawing room?"

"No, mademoiselle, she's in her sitting room. She's waiting for you..." Penson's voice dropped lower "...impatiently."

"Thank you. I will go up to her." Gabrielle's mouth was almost too dry to speak, and her heart was in her throat.

She followed Charlotte up the stairs at a more measured pace and, with no one to see, ran her tongue over her lips.

She wasn't afraid on her own behalf. Unless Lady Henderson delivered bad news about her father or brother, there was nothing the viscountess could do or say that would hurt Gabrielle herself. But there were many things she could do that would hurt Charlotte.

Gabrielle did her best to assume an air of composed obedience, and quietly entered the sitting room.

Her trepidation grew when she discovered Augustus was

sitting with Lady Henderson. As soon as he saw her, he smirked triumphantly.

Gabrielle's pulse beat in her throat, but she moved smoothly across the carpet and curtsied to her employer.

"Good afternoon, my lady, Master Sedgemore," she said.

"Where's Charlotte?" Lady Henderson demanded.

The question momentarily wrong-footed Gabrielle. In the two years she'd worked for Lady Henderson, the viscountess had rarely shown any particular interest in her daughter besides making the occasional slighting comment.

"I sent her to the nursery to rest," Gabrielle said. "It's been a long day, and Charlotte is tired."

"No matter." Lady Henderson flicked her hand dismissively. "We don't need Charlotte until tomorrow morning, anyway."

"*Need* her?" Gabrielle's shoulders tightened. "What do you mean?"

"For your usual walk along Marine Parade," Lady Henderson said. "Only tomorrow, Augustus and I will accompany you."

"You urgently summoned Charlotte to return so she can go for a *walk* with you?" Gabrielle stared at the viscountess in disbelief.

"Don't be impertinent, you wretched girl," Lady Henderson snapped. "It's *your* fault I looked like a fool yesterday. But fortunately for you, I've seen how I can make use of your licentious behavior."

"My what?" Gabrielle could make no sense of what she was hearing, but Augustus's odious sneering reminded her he'd witnessed her clandestine return to the house after the masquerade. "My lady," she began, without any clear idea how to end her sentence.

"Spare me your excuses," Lady Henderson spat. "I know Lord Appledrum is your lover—"

"*What?*" The accusation was so unexpected, so ridiculous, it robbed Gabrielle of breath. "No, my lady, that's *not* so—"

"Don't waste time denying it," Lady Henderson said impatiently. "I know you left the house to meet a man the other night. And when I discovered Lord Appledrum stopped to speak to you on Marine Parade the following morning, I knew it must be a lovers' assignation."

"No, madam—" Gabrielle checked herself. She had to be calm, as outwardly calm as she'd been when she faced the highwayman.

The highwayman had wanted money. She still wasn't clear what Lady Henderson wanted, but Augustus was vibrating with spiteful pleasure at her discomfiture. She wouldn't give him the satisfaction of gloating over her confusion.

"I did not have an assignation with Lord Appledrum," she said evenly. "I had no idea he would be taking a walk at that hour."

"There's no other reason a man in Appledrum's position would waste time acknowledging a penniless chit like you," Lady Henderson retorted scornfully. "He can blather on all he likes about you being the daughter of his old friend, but that just means he has an advantage when it comes to setting you up as his mistress. Hasn't he offered you your own establishment yet?"

"I've spoken to the marquess once in the last two years,"

Gabrielle said. "Your suspicions are doing his lordship a grave injustice."

"Take my advice and make sure you entice Appledrum to give you plenty of jewels before he tires of you." Lady Henderson almost sounded magnanimous. "Men are fickle creatures. But first you're going to write a note to him, asking him to meet you on Marine Parade tomorrow morning. He must still be in the besotted stages of your affair, so I'm sure he'll be eager to comply."

"He's going to buy *me* an ice cream tomorrow," Augustus crowed, from his position beside his mother.

Gabrielle's mind raced. She couldn't possibly admit to having an affair with Quin's father. The idea was abhorrent on every level. But how could she persuade Lady Henderson she was mistaken?

"If you refuse to coax Appledrum into showing us favor, I'll make sure news of your liaison with him is the biggest item of gossip in Brighton by tomorrow evening," Lady Henderson warned viciously. "Your reputation will be in shreds. When the marquess casts you off, you'll never get another position as a governess."

Never, at any point over the past two days, had it occurred to Gabrielle that she'd be threatened with the public exposure of her non-existent affair with Lord Appledrum, if she didn't prevail upon him to buy Augustus an ice cream!

The whole thing was so preposterous a small, disbelieving laugh escaped her lips.

"You think your situation is funny?" Real enmity blazed in the viscountess's eyes.

"No, my lady. It's not funny at all." As Gabrielle's thoughts settled, anger rose within her. "Your words are an insult to me—and to Lord Appledrum. The marquess is an honorable man. He would never take advantage of me in the way you say,"

"Very prettily said, but don't waste your energy on playacting," Lady Henderson ordered contemptuously. "Sit down and write a charming note to him. I have the pen and paper ready on the table for you."

"I cannot." Gabrielle didn't move from the spot. "Lord Appledrum's eyes would start from his head if I sent him a letter asking for an assignation."

No sooner had she spoken, than she was assailed by doubts. Lord Appledrum knew Quin planned to marry her. Perhaps if she wrote the marquess an innocuous note, he would show it to Quin and both men would realize something was seriously amiss. But where would that end?

"It was entirely by chance that Charlotte and I met Lord Appledrum on Marine Parade the other day," she said.

Quin had engineered their 'chance' meeting, but Lady Henderson hadn't mentioned Quin, so Gabrielle didn't either.

Lady Henderson's eyes narrowed. "Then who did you have a tryst with the other night?"

"No one." A tryst was surely something prearranged. Gabrielle hadn't arranged to meet Quin at the ball. She'd simply hoped he'd be present.

"Stop playing the innocent, girl." Lady Henderson's voice scraped on Gabrielle's nerves like a knife scraping on a plate. "I know you left this house to meet a man! Who is he?"

"I left to go dancing." Gabrielle strove to keep her own voice steady.

She couldn't deny leaving the house, because Augustus had seen her return. She was willing to confess to her longing to dance. She'd been in breach of the viscountess's rules when she'd left the house without permission, but dancing at a ball was not a crime by any standards.

"Dancing?" the viscountess repeated. "Where? That was the night of Lord Appledrum's masquerade. There was no public assembly at the Castle or the Ship—" she broke off, breathing heavily. "Lord Appledrum's ball. Is that where you danced?"

"Everyone wore masks." Gabrielle felt light-headed, as if nothing around her was quite real. "It was the perfect opportunity to dance a few sets without anyone recognizing me. I left the house without your permission, yes. But all I wanted to do was dance."

"You attended Lord Appledrum's masquerade? And now you have the gall to pretend he's not your lover?" Scorn dripped from Lady Henderson's words.

Augustus watched avidly, seeming bloated with vindictive delight.

"He isn't!" Gabrielle insisted. "His lordship did speak to me briefly, but I'm sure he didn't recognize me behind my mask."

"What was your costume?" Lady Henderson demanded.

"Cinderella." Gabrielle saw no point in prevaricating on that issue.

"The girl with ashes on her miserable dress? You danced with me!" Lady Henderson exploded. "Were you laughing behind my back at how cleverly you were deceiving me?"

"I have never laughed at you behind your back." At no point had Gabrielle ever been amused by anything the viscountess said or did.

"Because you think you're so refined and possess such exquisite, aristocratic manners?" A truly ugly expression appeared on Lady Henderson's face.

"I've done with you, you stupid, wretched girl." She made a slashing gesture with her right hand. "If Lord Appledrum is not your lover, you're of no further use to me. You're dismissed. Leave this house immediately."

"No!" Charlotte's anguished shriek reverberated around the drawing room.

Chapter Thirty-Nine

Charlotte's scream was just as hair-raising as it had been the previous day, when she'd thought Gabrielle was dead. But this time Gabrielle guessed what would happen next, and she managed to keep her balance when the small body thudded against her.

"*You're not leaving me!*" Charlotte's arms clamped around Gabrielle, and she buried her face in the fabric of Gabrielle's gown.

Her own heart breaking, Gabrielle hugged Charlotte close. This was the outcome she'd desperately wanted to avoid.

Quin was going to find and speak to Lord Henderson, but Gabrielle had no idea how long that might take, or what concessions Lord Henderson would make.

"My lady, please..." She was willing to beg to retain her position. She'd made promises to Charlotte, and she'd do everything in her power to keep them.

"Charlotte, cease your hideous caterwauling and get out,"

Lady Henderson shouted. "God knows why I had to be saddled with you."

"Yes, stop caterwauling, stupid, dumb Charlotte!" Augustus jumped up. He ran over and started pulling at Charlotte's arms, trying to drag her away from Gabrielle. "Too dumb to speak. All you can do is scream and cry."

His sharp tugs, combined with Charlotte's limpet-like grip, forced Gabrielle to take a half step forward to stay on her feet.

Charlotte continued to sob. Augustus continued with his verbal mockery, though he changed his physical tactics. Instead of pulling at his sister, he began striking her with his clenched hands, and some of the blows fell on Gabrielle.

She gasped as one of Augustus's pointy fists landed on her side.

"Stop, Augustus!" she cried.

Earlier she'd felt as if she was being physically battered by the viscountess's verbal attack, but now she was at the center of a maelstrom of genuine physical violence. "Lady Henderson, stop your son!"

But the viscountess did not intervene, and Gabrielle didn't dare take her eyes off of Augustus. No one had ever hit her before. Her papa might be a master swordsman, but he'd never taught her how to withstand a flurry of blows or return a punch.

Every blow that landed added to her shock and distress. She tried to protect Charlotte's head while also struggling to seize Augustus's arms—or at least ward him off.

Charlotte suddenly relaxed her grip and turned to fight back.

"Boy, stop!" Quin thundered.

His compelling command cut across the childish shrieks

filling the room. Both children fell into a startled, motionless silence as Quin stepped across the threshold.

Gabrielle turned toward him with a sob of relief. She didn't know how he came to be present, but it didn't matter. He was here, and the expression on his face told her he was furious.

"Do you know who I am, fellow?" Augustus recovered some of his customary, obnoxious self-importance.

"I don't care who you are." Quin's damning gaze passed over Augustus. "An honorable man *never* abuses females."

"My father is—"

"Irrelevant to this conversation. I'm judging you on your behavior, not his, and *your* conduct is inexcusable. What's happening?" Quin turned to Gabrielle.

"I've been dismissed," she said.

"No!" Charlotte twisted around and locked Gabrielle in another fierce embrace. "You're not leaving me."

"Why have you been dismissed?" Quin asked. "Your devotion to Charlotte can't be questioned."

Gabrielle was too shaken by the events of the past few minutes to do anything but provide a garbled version of the truth. "Because she thought I was your father's mistress. She wanted me to coax him to buy an ice cream for Augustus. But I'm not, so I can't—and that means I'm of no further use to her."

"Your father? You...you're *Lord Hanwell*!" The viscountess lunged to her feet. "Lord Appledrum's *son*. Welcome, my lord. I can't think why the butler didn't announce you properly, but I'm sorry you walked in on such an unedifying scene. Mademoiselle Rousselle, take Charlotte to the nursery at once."

"No." Quin's icy tone froze the viscountess in her tracks. "Mademoiselle Rousselle is no longer in your employ and not obliged to obey your orders."

Without waiting for the viscountess's reaction, he looked down at Charlotte and smiled. "Miss Sedgemore, my father has invited us to have dinner with him. Let's go to his house straight away."

Charlotte stared up at him, tears streaking her cheeks. "Are you…taking me?" she asked.

"Yes, I'm taking you. Both of you." He flashed a look at Gabrielle, but most of his attention was on Charlotte.

He held out his hand to her, and offered his elbow to Gabrielle.

"I need but a minute to put on my bonnet," Lady Henderson said.

Quin turned his head to look at the viscountess and raised one eyebrow. Gabrielle had never before seen an expression of such supreme hauteur on his face.

"You're not included in the invitation, Lady Henderson," he said. "Nor are you," he added as his gaze fell upon Augustus. "Mademoiselle Rousselle, Miss Sedgemore, let us depart."

As soon as Gabrielle turned toward the door, she saw they had an audience, but none of the servants tried to interfere as she and Charlotte left the room with Quin.

She even saw Mrs. Whittle among the group. The housekeeper gave Charlotte a concerned look, but then she smiled, gave Gabrielle an encouraging nod and stepped backward.

They began to descend the stairs. Quin set an almost stately pace and the area between Gabrielle's shoulders was soon a knot of tension. At any second she expected Lady Henderson to start making demands or, at the very least, call Charlotte back.

But the whole household seemed to be in the grip of a stunned silence. Except, as Quin's little party turned to go down the last flight, Gabrielle saw a maid on the ground floor come dashing out of the back of the house with a man's hat and a lady's bonnet in her hands. She gave them to Penson and disappeared back the way she'd come.

Quin came to a halt in front of the butler.

"Your hat, my lord." Penson presented it to Quin with professional aplomb. "Miss Charlotte, your bonnet."

Gabrielle had never removed her own bonnet. At least she was appropriately dressed to go out onto the crowded Steine.

"Thank you, Penson," she said, and took the bonnet from him.

Charlotte's eyes were huge, her gaze riveted to Gabrielle's face. Gabrielle's trembling fingers fumbled the ribbons, but then she managed to tie a loopy bow under Charlotte's chin.

"Ready, ladies?" Quin asked. "Thank you, Penson."

With those quiet words he escorted Gabrielle and Charlotte out into the late afternoon sunshine. As they descended the two front steps, Gabrielle heard the butler close the door behind them.

Her legs turned shaky. She put her hand through Quin's arm and held on tight. Several people were promenading nearby, and she didn't want to fall down in front of them.

Quin responded by pressing his elbow against his side. A reassuring gesture that seemed to claim her hand, and provide her with extra support.

He'd put his arm around her on the heath, but she didn't want him to do that when so many eyes were watching them.

She leaned forward so she could look past Quin at Charlotte, and winced as she saw the little girl wipe the sleeve of her free hand over her tear-stained face and rub it under her runny nose. She needed to give Charlotte a handkerchief straight away—

And involuntarily clutched Quin's arm as she realized she couldn't give Charlotte a handkerchief, because she didn't have her reticule.

"Do you have—?" She looked up at him.

"A handkerchief? Yes. Let's go and look at the sea for a few moments while we compose ourselves." Quin led them across Marine Parade to the railings overlooking the beach.

"Can we go a bit further?" Gabrielle murmured. She meant away from the Hendersons' House.

"I'll point out the fish market where Mrs. Whittle helped me make a purchase yesterday morning." Quin guided them a few more yards along the railing, and then produced a handkerchief for Charlotte.

"You know Mrs. Whittle?" Charlotte asked.

"Not as well as you and mademoiselle. But well enough that I went around to the back of the house to pay my respects to her, while you two went in through the front door."

"I thought you left us to find my papa," Charlotte said.

"I am going to find your papa. But I didn't want to go too far away from you until we found out what kind of bee your mama had got in her bonnet." Quin lightly touched the brim of Charlotte's bonnet. "But she wasn't wearing anything on her head at all. Do you like honey?"

Charlotte nodded.

"My niece is fond of honey, too, so I'm sure my father will have plenty in the larder. A few slices of bread and honey will be just the thing to set us to rights after the busy day we've had. Are you ready, dear heart?" He looked at Gabrielle.

She didn't trust herself to speak, but when Quin smiled at her, she could tell he didn't need a verbal response.

Chapter Forty

Quin's mood swung between euphoria that he had Gabrielle and Charlotte safely in his care, fury at what he'd witnessed in Lady Henderson's sitting room, and guilt that he'd allowed his girls to enter the house unprotected.

Though the analytical part of him was also aware that the ugly episode should give him an advantage when negotiating with Charlotte's father.

His immediate goal, however, was to bring Gabrielle and Charlotte to the sanctuary of his father's house.

The mansion Marcus had leased for the season was nearer. In fact, they walked past it as they crossed the Steine. But Charlotte had never met Marcus, and he might be out. When Cecilia was in good health, Quin was sure she'd respond with unruffled kindness to the arrival of two unfamiliar, agitated young ladies. But Cecilia's difficult pregnancy was taking a heavy toll from her, and Quin wouldn't lay an additional burden on her.

So he walked steadily on, grateful he hadn't made any new

acquaintances in Brighton who wanted to greet him. Although he could sense they were attracting attention from the early evening promenaders.

"I believe moths may also be an important pollinator of some plants," he said. "Just the other evening, I was studying some honeysuckle and noticed how interesting it was to moths."

"I'm very fond of honeysuckle," Gabrielle said.

"Me too." Charlotte was clinging to his fingers tighter than any climbing vine, and walking close to his side.

Her current demeanor was nothing like that of the bright child who'd ranged around him picking flowers on their pre-breakfast walk.

It was an immense relief to Quin when they came to a halt at the front entrance to his father's house.

"May I knock, dear heart?" he said to Gabrielle.

"Of course." She sounded confused. "Oh...we're holding your arms prisoners." She let her hand fall with a wobbly laugh.

"My arms are always at your service." He rapped sharply on the brass door knocker. "Good evening, Tredworth. I've brought Mademoiselle Rousselle and Miss Sedgemore to visit us. Please come in, ladies."

The butler's eyes opened wider, but he stepped back and held the door for them. "Good evening, my lord. Good evening, Mademoiselle Rousselle, Miss Sedgemore."

Quin put his arm lightly around Gabrielle's shoulders and then, with Charlotte still clinging to his other hand, he walked into the house.

"Where's my father?" He looked back as the butler closed the door.

"He's in the library, my lord," Tredworth replied. "In fact—"

The library door opened, and Lord Appledrum emerged.

"Who...? *Harlequin!*" Lord Appledrum's exclamation held all the familiar warmth and pleasure Quin always heard in his father's voice when he welcomed him home.

The worst knots of tension within Quin immediately eased. He knew he'd have his father's unconditional support in whatever difficulties lay ahead.

"And Gabrielle!" the marquess continued, in the same warm tone. "Phillipe, it's Gabrielle!"

Another man emerged from the library—

"*Papa!*" Gabrielle dashed across the hall to throw herself into her father's arms.

"Gabrielle." The Duke de la Fontaine enfolded her in his embrace. A smaller version of the duke appeared beside them, reaching out toward Gabrielle in his turn.

Quin felt Charlotte's grip on his fingers tighten even more. He smiled reassuringly at her.

"That's mademoiselle's papa," he said, "and her brother, Felix."

Charlotte nodded, but there was an uncertain, bereft expression on her face when she looked at Gabrielle, who was completely preoccupied with greeting her family.

Quin crouched down beside Charlotte so they were more-or-less on eye level. The little girl's face was blotchy from her tears, and her nose had started to run again. Quin's anger reignited, but he suppressed it.

"Mademoiselle hasn't seen her father and brother for many, many months," he said gently. "She hasn't forgotten us, but they've missed her as much as you would miss her if she'd been away from you. They're still caught up in the first excitement of seeing each other after that long absence."

Charlotte nodded again, but she didn't return Quin's smile. "Are you keeping me?" Her voice was thready.

"Yes, I'm keeping you—and mademoiselle." Even if he did have to pile them onto a ship and take refuge in another country. Though he sincerely hoped it wouldn't come to that. Gabrielle was already in exile from her own country. He didn't want her to be exiled again.

Charlotte stared at him as if trying to plumb the depths of his soul. Then a tiny smile curved her lips and her hold on his fingers lessened.

"But now you should rest and refresh yourself after our long journey," he said. "You don't need to wear your bonnet indoors. We're not going out again tonight."

She looked around the large entrance hall and back at him. "You should take off your hat, too."

"I should, shouldn't I?" He lifted it from his head and held his arm out to the side without looking.

"Thank you, my lord." The butler took it.

"Thank *you*, Tredworth. I'm glad you were nearby. Otherwise, I would have looked very silly."

"We will endeavor to avoid that occurrence, my lord," Tredworth said gravely.

Quin smiled at Charlotte. "You should go upstairs now and refresh yourself. Here is Miss Trent, my mademoiselle, come to help you. Do you remember her?"

"Keep going to happy memories," Charlotte whispered, and

edged closer to him, as if she was afraid he might just hand her off to Miss Trent.

Her action made his heart ache for her. He put his free hand on her shoulder—and saw a flicker in her eyes, almost as if she was in pain.

He was momentarily confused, because he knew he'd only touched her lightly. But then he understood.

"Did that boy hurt you when he hit you?" His rising anger made his tone rougher than he intended.

She sucked her lower lip deep into her mouth and gave a small nod.

If Charlotte was hurt, then Gabrielle might be hurt.

Quin stood up, looking around for her. She was already coming toward him, a beaming smile on her face, her eyes shimmering with happy tears. Her father and brother were on either side of her.

"Did that boy hurt you?" he demanded, barely acknowledging the duke and Felix.

"Who...? Oh, Augustus." Concern replaced her smile. "He hit Charlotte most often. Did he hurt you, sweetheart?"

"A bit," Charlotte mumbled.

Gabrielle's eyes narrowed as she flexed her shoulders, her attention clearly focused inward. "Yes, he does have sharp little fists, doesn't he? I might have a bruise or too," she admitted.

"Someone *hit* you?" Her father's expression darkened. "*Who* hit you? I will deal with him immediately."

"No, Papa." Gabrielle put a restraining hand on the duke's arm. "Augustus is a little boy. I think I may have a few bruises from his flailing arms. But he struck Charlotte many more times."

"Why don't you both come upstairs with me," Miss Trent interposed calmly, before Gabrielle's father could express his anger more vehemently. "We'll see what we can do to make you both comfortable. We thought you'd gone to Sedgemore Hall," she added. "Have you come all the way back today?"

"Yes." Quin gently encouraged Charlotte to go with Gabrielle and Miss Trent. "These ladies were bounced around in the coach for hours yesterday, and again today. I think we would all like to rest quietly for a while, and have something refreshing to drink. Wouldn't we, Charlotte?"

She gave him a tiny smile.

"Is there any lemonade left over from the ball?" he asked.

He saw Miss Trent exchange a glance with his father and then Lord Appledrum said, "Tredworth will instantly dispatch Thomas to buy some from Miss Bianchetti. Also, some ice cream and jelly for our dinner."

Since Thomas was standing a few feet away, all Tredworth had to do was open the front door for him. Meanwhile, Lord Appledrum directed his next comment to Charlotte.

"Miss Sedgemore, it's a pleasure to see you again. I'm looking forward to catching up on your adventures since we last met—after you've taken Mademoiselle Gabrielle upstairs, so you can both refresh yourselves, of course."

Charlotte straightened her posture, gave him a solemn nod, and made him the curtsy she considered suitable for a marquess. Lord Appledrum responded with an equally courteous bow.

Then Charlotte took hold of Gabrielle's hand and pulled her toward the stairs after Miss Trent.

As soon as the three ladies departed, the tension drained from Quin's body. He released a deep breath, ran his fingers through his sweat-dampened hair—and looked up to find himself the focus of three pairs of intent male eyes.

"You're keeping Charlotte Sedgemore?" Lord Appledrum raised a brow.

"Lady Henderson did nothing to stop her son attacking Gabrielle and Charlotte. Indeed, her expression suggested she derived some pleasure from the spectacle," Quin replied tautly. "So yes, I'm keeping them both."

"All right," his father said. "Raise the drawbridge, Tredworth. Lower it again for Thomas to bring in the lemonade and other essential supplies. But otherwise, we're only at home for family."

"Thank you, sir." The weight on Quin's shoulders eased. "I'm sorry, your grace, I've not greeted you properly." He turned to the duke, belatedly realizing he probably shouldn't have made such a bald claim he was keeping Gabrielle, without even acknowledging her father's presence.

"Monsieur Rousselle," Gabrielle's father corrected him calmly. "I only use my title now for advertising purposes." He raised an arm to flourish an imaginary sword.

Quin didn't know what to say to a man who'd lost everything to the relentless forces of revolution. Words of sympathy seemed uncomfortably trite, so he didn't utter any.

"I owe you a debt of gratitude, sir," he said instead. "Having trained with you was a considerable advantage to me. I practiced regularly with some of the naval officers on the expedition. They greatly appreciated I was able to share your lessons with them."

The former duke smiled and inclined his head. "You were an excellent student. I look forward to crossing blades with you again soon."

"Yes, sir." Quin instinctively braced himself for the encounter.

Monsieur Rousselle laughed. "For entertainment only, as when I practice with your father." His laughter faded. "Now I want to hear more about this assault on my daughter."

"So do I." Felix's hands were balled at his sides.

"Come into the library." Lord Appledrum laid his hand on Quin's shoulder. "Have a glass of brandy and give us a full account of what's happened."

"I'd rather have a cup of tea," he said.

"All the tea you can drink, dear boy." His father's grip on his shoulder tightened. "All the tea you can drink."

Chapter Forty-One

Miss Trent took Gabrielle and Charlotte upstairs to a suite of rooms on the second floor.

"This is the nursery," she said. "Lord Hanwell never slept here because he was already too old by the time this house was built, so it's only been used by guests."

"It's lovely." Even at first glance, Gabrielle could tell this accommodation was far superior to her quarters for the past two years.

But the last time she'd stayed in this house she'd been a pampered guest, not relegated to the nursery. Was this an indication the housekeeper no longer considered her worthy of being more than a governess?

"Apart from this parlor, there are two bedchambers." Miss Trent opened the door to one and then crossed the parlor to reveal the second bedroom.

"They're charming, aren't they, Charlotte?" Gabrielle said.

Miss Trent gave her a questioning look, as if she'd detected

Gabrielle's uncertainty. Then she smiled, untrammeled warmth in her expression.

"This set of rooms will make it easy for you and Charlotte to be close to each other, yet also have a degree of privacy," she said. "Tomorrow we can discuss other arrangements, but I thought this would be best for tonight."

Her gaze lowered to where Charlotte was still holding Gabrielle's hand.

"I'm sorry, of course it is." Gabrielle was both relieved and embarrassed the other woman had noticed she'd needed the reassurance.

Still smiling, Miss Trent shook her head. "You've had a tumultuous few days. You and Charlotte are both welcome here, and we'll do everything we can to make you feel comfortable."

Charlotte craned sideways to peer into both bedrooms, then she tugged on Gabrielle's hand.

Gabrielle bent down to hear, but their bonnets bumped into each other.

"Let's take them off." She untied the bow beneath Charlotte's chin and removed her own bonnet.

With no further impediment, Charlotte whispered in her ear, "Lord Quin said he's keeping us."

"Did he?" Gabrielle was startled.

"Very clearly." Miss Trent sounded both amused and satisfied. "While you were still greeting your father and brother. He told Charlotte he was keeping her—and you. I hope that meets with your approval, Mademoiselle Rousselle."

"He just said it? Without even...?" Tears flooded Gabrielle's eyes, even as joy filled her heart, and she smiled at the housekeeper.

"I assume you already knew that was his intention?" Miss Trent said.

"Yes, but..." Gabrielle glanced down at Charlotte. What would happen when Quin finally spoke to Lord Henderson?

"In my experience, when Lord Hanwell sets out to do a thing, the thing gets done," Miss Trent said. "And he can call upon both his father and his ducal cousin to exert their influence if necessary."

Charlotte's shoulders settled. She gave Gabrielle a small smile, sniffed, and looked around again.

"Are we going to live here?" she asked.

"For tonight, and probably the next few nights," Gabrielle replied. "I don't know where Lord Quin will want us to live in the future, but it will always be a safe and comfortable place."

"You won't have to sleep with my snail shells anymore, mademoiselle." Charlotte sniffed again.

"Neither of us will have to sleep with your snail shells."

The collection would have been delivered to Lady Henderson's house, along with the rest of their luggage. Considering how they'd left, Gabrielle wasn't sure if they'd see any of their belongings again. But Charlotte could begin a new collection tomorrow. "Are you still holding Lord Quin's handkerchief, sweetheart?"

Parts of the crumpled cloth were extending out of the fist Charlotte had made of the hand she hadn't used to hold on to first Quin and then Gabrielle.

"Yes." Charlotte applied the damp handkerchief to her eyes and blew her nose.

"Thank you," Gabrielle said to Miss Trent. "We'll be very comfortable here."

The housekeeper smiled. "Warm water is being brought up for you. I have new hairbrushes, nightdresses, other necessities. The nightgown will be too long for Charlotte, but we can cut off the bottom. I can lend you a couple of gowns, mademoiselle, but we don't currently have any dresses in Charlotte's size."

She gave Charlotte a thoughtful look. "I have some spare dress lengths. We can use the dress you're wearing for the pattern, and make up a new one for you by tomorrow."

Charlotte's mouth fell open. "Are you a fairy godmother?"

Miss Trent laughed. "I'm a housekeeper."

"You're a very pretty housekeeper," Charlotte said. "You were Lord Quin's mademoiselle. Will you tell us stories about him when he was a very little boy—before mademoiselle knew him?"

"Yes, but not this evening. Ah, here is the warm water. Set it over there please," Miss Trent directed the two maids who'd brought it. "I'll leave you to rest and settle in."

"Miss Trent?" Gabrielle waited until the maids had left before she continued. "I think it might be a useful precaution if you're able to act as a witness. If we have any visible bruises from when Augustus hit us."

Charlotte hunched in on herself. "I never want to see him again."

"Nor do I," Gabrielle admitted. "But do you remember how Lord Quin, Nedcott, and I all had to give statements to Sir Ralph yesterday evening about the highwayman? I think it might be helpful if you and I write down an account of what Augustus did to us today."

"So Sir Ralph can put him in jail?" Charlotte brightened up.

"I don't believe Sir Ralph's jurisdiction extends this far," Gabrielle said. "But I thought it might make it easier for Lord Quin to keep us if we explain clearly why he took us away."

"Highwayman?" Miss Trent appeared concerned.

"Lord Quin shot him and now he's in jail," Charlotte explained. "And he gave us good water to drink and a good dinner and showed me his magnifying lens. Which is also good, and I want to look through it again. All the good things were Lord Quin."

"Lord Quin has always been a good thing," Miss Trent said. "I'll gladly be witness to any bruises you sustained, ladies."

Chapter Forty-Two

Quin sat down in a leather-backed armchair and accepted some brandy from his father.

After a couple of sips, he set the glass down on the small table near his right hand. "This is vastly superior to what we had on the expedition."

"I should hope so," Lord Appledrum said. "Since I'm giving it to men of impeccable taste. After Lady Henderson exiled Gabrielle and Charlotte to Sedgemore Hall, we assumed they'd be there for some time. What changed?"

"I don't know." Quin rubbed both hands over his face. Even though he'd ridden inside the carriage today, he could feel fine grit on his skin. He needed to wash and change before dinner too, but not until he'd given the others a brief account of what had happened.

"Lady Henderson sent Gabrielle a rude message ordering her to bring Charlotte back to Brighton immediately, but with no explanation. All the footman would tell Gabrielle was that the viscountess had gone to the library yesterday. But he knew something, smirking blackguard." Quin glowered and drank some more brandy.

"She came here," Lord Appledrum said grimly.

Quin frowned at his father. "What did she want?"

"Me to take her son to Bianchetti's for an ice cream."

"What? Why on earth—" Quin cut himself off, because something about that sounded familiar. But why?

"Apparently he's an exceptional child, far more intelligent and charming than Charlotte," Lord Appledrum said dryly. "And in transports of joy at the idea of meeting me."

"He's an exceptionally self-important and spiteful child." Quin's anger stirred again. "When I ordered him to stop hitting our girls, he demanded to know if I knew who his father is? As if I give a damn. Lady Henderson found out about our trip to Bianchetti's, I take it?"

"From gossip at the library. I imagine her nose was somewhat put out of joint. She came to gush her thanks and flatter me into giving her son the same favor," Lord Appledrum said. "I should probably have been less brusque—but I disliked her excessive fawning, and I didn't want to spend any more time alone with her than I had to."

As long as Quin could remember, his father had been ruthlessly defending his single status. On one notorious occasion, he'd even stepped back and allowed an elegantly swooning lady —who'd had aspirations to be his next marchioness—to end up in a heap on the stony ground rather than catch her in his arms.

Marcus, a fully-fledged duke long before he'd reached

manhood, had taken Lord Appledrum's advice on avoiding unwanted entanglements even more to heart than Quin.

As a married woman, Lady Henderson was no threat to Lord Appledrum's single status. He just didn't like her.

"I should have been more conciliatory," he said now. "Knowing that she was Gabrielle's employer. But she put her hand on my arm—so I told her I had an urgent appointment with my boot maker."

"But why did she want Gabrielle and Charlotte to come back to Brighton?" Felix asked.

"Because..." Quin hesitated, reluctant to repeat what he remembered Gabrielle saying to him in Lady Henderson's drawing room.

"Because?" Lord Appledrum prompted him.

Quin mentally braced himself and said, "She'd somehow taken the notion that Gabrielle is your mistress. Gabrielle was supposed to coax you into buying her son an ice cream."

Gabrielle's father swore in French, and Felix jumped up and began raging around the room.

"She's an evil, despicable woman! She can't be allowed to blacken my sister's name."

"Gabrielle will be my wife, as soon as I can make her so," Quin said. "That's one of the good things to come out of this mess. But I'm sorry she and Charlotte were abused before I brought them out of the house."

"I'm not clear on the sequence of events," Lord Appledrum said. "I know you wouldn't have allowed that if you'd been with them throughout."

"Gabrielle thought it would be more discreet if she and Charlotte arrived alone to find out what the viscountess wanted," Quin explained. "I decided to visit Mrs. Whittle. I was talking to her in the kitchen when we heard Charlotte scream upstairs." He rubbed his hands over his face. "She sounded the way she did when she thought Gabrielle had been shot—"

"Shot?" Gabrielle's father repeated.

Quin had been reliving the heart-stopping moment when he'd heard Charlotte scream. Now he was wrenched straight into a different emotional challenge.

"Damn it." He closed his eyes, put both hands on top of his head, and sucked in a deep breath. The sudden silence in the library reverberated with tension.

He opened his eyes to find everyone staring at him.

"She obviously wasn't shot, Phillipe, because she ran and hugged you and laughed with joy a short while ago," Lord Appledrum said.

"I apologize." Quin lowered his hands to the arms of his chair. "Sincerely, I apologize. Their carriage was held up by a highwayman yesterday afternoon. I was close enough behind to intervene. But when I shot the bastard, Charlotte thought Gabrielle had been hit. She screamed and came flying out of the coach. It's not a sound I'll easily forget. Thank you, Tredworth, I will really appreciate a cup of tea."

The butler had brought in the laden tray himself. "It seems so, my lord. If I may ask, what happened to the highwayman?"

"The bullet went through his arm. He's in the county jail now, awaiting trial at the next assizes. Unless his wound festers. Would anyone else like some tea?" Quin lifted the pot. "Anyone?"

Lord Appledrum stirred himself. "I'll have a cup. Do you have any other dramatic, hazardous events to regale us with?"

"I don't think so. Oh, I did give Charlotte Gilbert White's book on Selborne because I thought it would likely interest her. But when Gabrielle glanced through it, the second passage which caught her eye was about castration. So that didn't go as I anticipated."

Monsieur Rousselle choked on his brandy.

Quin briefly closed his eyes again, because perhaps he should have mentioned that in front of Gabrielle's father, either.

"We never actually got as far as Sedgemore Hall, because we had to wait at the inn for the magistrate to come and take our statements. However, in the interest of ensuring everyone enjoys their dinner, I've suggested to Charlotte we don't talk about subjects such as snails or blue frogs—or any frogs, for that matter—while we're at the table." He picked up his teacup and sat back.

"I don't know why Gabrielle is so squeamish about snails," Felix said. "I always thought they were quite tasty."

"Perhaps don't mention that to Charlotte," Quin suggested. "She has mixed feelings about thrushes because they eat snails. In the story she told me this morning, Lucy Ladybird is acting as lookout to warn Susan Snail if there are any thrushes or other mollusk-eating creatures in the vicinity." He swallowed some tea. "What?"

"Two days ago, you'd never met the child," Lord Appledrum said.

"Gabrielle loves her," Quin said. "It behooved me to get to know her. I must admit, I didn't anticipate I'd be stealing her from her home two days later."

"This is the first time I've ever thought it fortunate that kidnapping is only a misdemeanor, not a felony," his father mused. "Unless Henderson decides to accuse you of stealing the clothes his daughter was wearing when you walked out with her, the worst criminal punishment should be a fine. But we don't know what line the viscount will take when he finds out what's happened."

"I'm sorry," Quin said. "Not for taking Charlotte. In the coach, she promised she'd lay all our fires for us if we'd only keep her. But for the trouble this is going to cause you."

Lord Appledrum shook his head. "Any trouble you've caused has always been worth making. I'm proud to call you my son."

"Or son-in-law," Gabrielle's father said quietly.

"Brother-in-law," Felix added.

"You've done your duty by us," Lord Appledrum said. "I'm sure we'd all like a fuller account of some of your adventures but, for now, I recommend we pause your inquisition so we can all dress for dinner."

Chapter Forty-Three

In the end, Gabrielle and Charlotte didn't have to go to dinner in their travel-stained clothes. While they were with Miss Trent in the nursery, Mrs. Whittle and one of the Hendersons' maids delivered some of their luggage, including Charlotte's shell collection.

Miss Trent slipped out to confer with the footman who'd carried up the bags, and then returned.

"They weren't able to carry everything," she reported. "But Penson—I think he's the butler? He's locked your remaining bag in his pantry, mademoiselle."

"That's so kind of them." Gabrielle's throat clogged up, and she abruptly sat down on the end of the bed. "I don't know what I would have done without Mrs. Whittle's help these past two years."

"She left you her good wishes, but she didn't think it wise to spend too long away from her post this evening," Miss Trent said. "I'll contact her tomorrow and make arrangements to collect your bag. Do you have any other belongings in the Hendersons' house?"

"Augustus will spoil anything he finds." Charlotte tenderly unwrapped her shell collection and set it on the table. "Like my first snails. Are you nervous of snails, Miss Trent?"

"No. That's a splendid set you've got." Miss Trent admired the collection. "Has Lord Hanwell seen them?"

Charlotte shook her head.

"Then that's something he'll definitely be looking forward to," Miss Trent said. "He's always been fascinated by all types of collections. Have you made spore prints of mushrooms yet?"

"No." Charlotte looked intrigued.

"I'm sure he'll help you with that. But mind—" Miss Trent's tone and expression became serious "—I'm going to give you the same rule I gave Lord Hanwell when he was young. You may study all kinds of things to your heart's content—but do *not* eat anything unless it's served to you on a plate by an adult."

Charlotte nodded. "Mademoiselle reminds me about that rule often. I think I should only eat what a good adult gives me. I wouldn't want to eat anything the highwayman gave me." She shivered.

"Nor would I." Gabrielle held out her arm and Charlotte went over to receive a hug.

"I'm glad to say our chef is both a good man and a good cook," Miss Trent assured them. "Thomas was also able to fetch some ice cream and jellies to make your first meal with us more special. I'll leave you to finish your preparations for dinner. When you're ready, I'll escort you to the drawing room."

"I'm hungry, mademoiselle," Charlotte said when they were alone.

"So am I. Let's get ready as quickly as possible." Excitement hummed through Gabrielle's veins. In a few minutes she was going to see her papa, Felix—and Quin—again.

She was overjoyed to be reunited with Papa and Felix, but she also longed for a chance to speak privately with Quin. So much had happened since he'd left the carriage when it arrived in Brighton. And they'd not had any opportunity to be alone since he'd rescued them from the Hendersons' house.

"There you are." She set the hairbrush aside and smiled at Charlotte.

"Are we going to have dinner with *everyone*?" Charlotte chewed on her lower lip.

"I think so, but we already had ice cream with Lord Appledrum and Lord Quin," Gabrielle reminded her. "That was a comfortable occasion, wasn't it?"

Charlotte tipped her head on one side, considering—and then nodded.

"My papa and Felix are very nice, too," Gabrielle said. "I don't know if anyone else will be present, but if there is, I'm sure they'll be nice as well."

She felt a flutter of nervousness behind her own ribs. It seemed a very long time since she'd dined in a formal setting. She'd changed her dress, but it was still one suitable for a governess, not for dining with a marquess. Except, this marquess wasn't one to nitpick about such things, and his son would care even less.

She opened the door and a moment later saw Miss Trent coming toward her.

"You both look charming, ladies," the housekeeper said. "The gentlemen have gathered in the drawing room. I'll show you the way."

They went down to the first floor. Gabrielle could hear men's voices and laughter coming through a partially open door.

Her heart sang with excited anticipation.

Miss Trent pushed the door open wider, walked into the room, and stepped aside for Gabrielle and Charlotte to enter. "My lords, here are Mademoiselle Rousselle and Miss Sedgemore."

"Come in! Come in!" Gabrielle heard Lord Appledrum's welcoming voice, even before she saw him.

All the men were on their feet, but Gabrielle's gaze unerringly locked onto Quin. Their eyes met and her pulse quickened. She didn't notice anyone else. At first it seemed her feet were rooted to the carpet—but then she wanted to run to him.

His arms were by his sides, but his palms turned toward her, almost as if he was instinctively expecting her to do just that.

"Mademoiselle Sedgemore." Her papa stepped forward, partially blocking her view of Quin. "It's a pleasure to see you again. We weren't properly introduced earlier. I am Mademoiselle Rousselle's papa."

"The duke." Charlotte's voice wobbled, but she took a pace toward him and dropped into a curtsy.

Gabrielle's papa responded with an equally formal bow.

"And this is my son, Felix," he said.

Gabrielle couldn't see Charlotte's expression, but she was surprised when the little girl's only response was to turn her head toward Quin.

"Marquess," he said with a quiet smile.

Charlotte immediately curtsied to Gabrielle's brother.

Gabrielle realized two things simultaneously: she adored Quin more with every breath she took—and she'd done too good a job of drawing Charlotte's attention to the degrees of the nobility.

She'd hoped it would please Lady Henderson, but the viscountess hadn't noticed her daughter's efforts to learn. Now it was time to guide Charlotte toward not categorizing every new acquaintance out loud before greeting them.

Felix just smiled and bowed as elegantly to Charlotte as Papa had done.

But unlike his father, he stepped forward and took Charlotte's hand.

"Enchanté, mademoiselle," he said, and kissed the back of her fingers.

"Enchanté, monsieur," she stammered. "I see brown hair," she added in French.

Felix straightened up, his eyes wide with surprise, but then his obvious confusion disappeared.

"I see a pretty pink dress," he said, also in French. "What else can you see, mademoiselle?"

And Gabrielle remembered she'd mentioned the 'I see…' game in one of her letters to Papa and Felix.

Charlotte looked around. "Four gentlemen and two ladies… and bits of me." She stuck her hand out in front of her.

"A very precise answer." Lord Appledrum grinned. "If you were tall enough, you'd be able to see more of yourself in the mirror on the wall. Ladies, Tredworth mentioned just before you arrived that dinner is ready, so I propose we go downstairs directly. Charlotte, may I escort you to dinner?"

Charlotte looked at him, at Gabrielle and Quin, and back to Lord Appledrum.

"I understand your snail shell collection has been returned to you," Lord Appledrum said. "I trust it's all in order? Tomorrow we can look to see what we've got in the garden."

He strolled toward the door. After another glance at Gabrielle, Charlotte fell into step beside him. "I think we can talk about snails while we're *going* to dinner." Her whisper carried across the room. "But Lord Quin says we're not allowed to talk about them at the meal table."

Once they were out in the hall, her voice drifted back into the drawing room at its normal volume.

"Or frogs," she continued. "But I'm not sure if that's just blue frogs because they're poisonous, or all frogs."

"We'll err on the side of conversational caution and not talk about frogs of any complexion," Lord Appledrum assured her, his voice fading as they descended the stairs. "What shall we talk about instead?"

"Gabi!" Felix rolled his eyes at her.

"Don't tease your sister," her papa ordered. "Lead the way to the dining room, if you please."

Miss Trent followed them out, and suddenly Gabrielle was alone with Quin.

She hadn't seen him move, yet he was right in front of her.

"We must go…" she began.

He cupped her face in his hands, searching her eyes. "Are you well, dear heart?"

"Yes." How could she be anything other than well when he was with her and so were her family and Charlotte.

He moved his hands to her shoulders and then coasted them gently down her back. "Does it hurt when I touch you?"

"Never…oh…no." She realized what he meant. "We checked for bruises, and we did find a few. I asked Miss Trent to be our witness, in case we need a statement like we gave to Sir Ralph."

He brought his hands back up to her shoulders. "That was very practical and clear-thinking of you. I'm sorry. I should never have let you enter that house alone." She could see the self-recrimination in his eyes.

"You couldn't have guessed. I never imagined anything like that would happen. And it gave you excellent grounds to take us away." She stroked his cheek.

"Perhaps. Charlotte seems to have recovered her spirits?" His expression lightened but was still questioning.

"You told her you're keeping us," Gabrielle said simply.

"I'm going to—even if we all have to run away to the land of giant snails." He smiled.

"What?" Gabrielle ran her finger along the line of his brow. "Why there?"

"Because that's where Charlotte asked me to take us all while you were talking to Lady Henderson's insolent footman." Quin caught Gabrielle's hand in his.

"You had a very serious conversation with Charlotte in those few minutes, didn't you?" she said. "What else did you discuss?"

"I'll tell you later. Now we must go to dinner." But he bent his head and kissed her first.

Chapter Forty-Four

Quin held Gabrielle's hand all the way downstairs and into the dining room on the ground floor. He was grateful for the few private moments they'd shared, and he was determined to have more time alone with her, later in the evening. But he knew Gabrielle would love to enjoy a meal with her family, and so would he.

But when they entered the dining room, he saw someone he didn't expect. His stride checked momentarily as he saw his father holding a chair for Agnes to sit at the foot of the table.

The idea of eating with her wasn't strange to him. During the years when he'd still been under Agnes's direct care, his father had come to the nursery several times a week to dine with them both. Quin hadn't realized how unusual that was until he'd been much older.

And since he'd returned from his travels, Agnes had been sitting with them at breakfast. But this was the first time she'd ever come to join them for dinner.

What did it mean?

Was there some secret he hadn't been told?

His grip on Gabrielle's hand involuntarily tightened, and she squeezed back.

Monsieur Rousselle, Felix and Charlotte had already taken their seats. Monsieur Rousselle and Felix look quite at their ease, while Charlotte was sitting very straight, obviously on her best behavior.

Tredworth and various other servants were standing by.

His father looked at him. "Harlequin?"

Quin couldn't quite read the expression on his father's face, but somehow, he knew how he reacted now mattered a great deal. To his father, and to Agnes.

"Nancy told me you're teaching her to call me Harlequin, sir," he said. "Only it sounds more like Uncle Haquin, doesn't it, Miss Trent?"

"It does." Agnes sounded a little less assured than usual. "But I'm sure she'll soon master the extra syllable."

"Certainly, I'm teaching Nancy to use your full name, Harlequin." His father touched Agnes's shoulder so discreetly Quin almost missed the gesture. Then he walked to the head of the table. "It's a *magnificent* name. I don't know why you're so reluctant to use it."

"It is a magnificent name." Quin held the chair next to Charlotte for Gabrielle. "Most colorful and flamboyant. It's just..." He sat down between Gabrielle and Agnes "...I'm not a very flamboyant person. I would say I'm more of a steady, plain, perhaps even workaday man—why are you all laughing at me?"

Gabrielle leaned into his side. "We aren't laughing at you. We love you."

Quin kissed her, which was easy, and then shot a furtive glance around the table at the grinning faces.

"I love you all too," he said, which was a lot less easy. He cleared his throat. "I'm looking forward to dinner, especially the ice cream."

Under the table, Gabrielle put her hand on his knee. Not exactly comforting him, because he didn't need comforting, but silently telling him she understood how awkward he was feeling.

Extremely happy—but very awkward.

"There's also a gooseberry tart." Agnes smiled, but it was a tense facsimile of her true smile.

Quin hated to see her discomfort. She should never be tense because of him.

"My favorite." He tried to convey with his own smile how pleased he was to be sitting beside her. "You've always spoiled me, Miss Trent." He lowered his voice. "I wouldn't be the man I am today without you."

Then he turned his attention to his soup, to give himself time to regain his inner composure.

"Now you're back in Brighton, you can play on my cricket team tomorrow, Harlequin," his father announced.

Quin groaned. "No, sir! That's to say, thank you for the honor, but no. I haven't touched a cricket bat for years. But I will escort Gabrielle and Charlotte to watch your team and Marcus's battle it out on the cricket pitch tomorrow."

"Do not expect to remain sitting on the sidelines for the

entire summer," his father warned him. "But you may be excused tomorrow. Do you enjoy cricket, Charlotte?"

"I don't know," she said cautiously. "But I'm sure it will be very nice to watch *you* play it."

"Nancy has her own small cricket bat." Quin leaned back in his chair so he could see Charlotte. "If you feel you would like to try playing, I'll have one made for you. Have you ever played throwing and catching a ball?"

She shook her head.

"You don't have to if you don't want to." A thought struck him. "Have you ever played ball?" he asked Gabrielle.

Laughter lit up her eyes as she too shook her head.

"Oh." Mildly flummoxed, he frowned back at his childhood memories. "I distinctly remember Cecilia playing ball with us."

"Cecilia, Lady Daubney, is Harlequin's cousin," Lord Appledrum explained to Charlotte. "And Nancy's mother. I think the difference might be that Marcus and Cecilia are closer in age, Harlequin. And Ceci wanted to be like her brother, whereas Gabrielle was already a young lady when you met her."

"And Nancy kept picking up sticks or even her grandmother's fan, pretending they were cricket bats until her uncle had a small one made specially for her." Agnes's smile was the same, composed and quietly amused one that Quin knew well.

"A lace and ivory fan is not ideally suited to whacking a cricket ball," Lord Appledrum observed.

"Gabi, I failed you," Felix said theatrically. "I never taught you how to throw and catch a ball."

He was eight years younger than Gabrielle. And as long as

Quin could remember, his ambition had been to become a master swordsman like his father, not a cricketer.

"You don't have to learn to play ball if you don't want to," Quin said to Gabrielle.

Then he thought of the balls he did want her to play with. Balls she'd spent some time delicately exploring the previous night, before proceeding to bring him to a state of physical bliss. Because she was looking at him, he saw the moment the same memory occurred to her.

She blushed adorably, but managed to say, "If Miss Nancy likes playing cricket, I daresay it would be a useful skill to know how to throw balls to her."

Quin started to laugh for no particular reason. Except that the erotic memories filling his mind had no place being there when he was sitting across the table from Gabrielle's father.

Luckily, his own father picked up the conversational baton.

"In Nancy's case, the requirement is to roll the balls over the grass toward her rather than throw them," Lord Appledrum explained calmly. "Sometimes she hits them, sometimes she doesn't. Either way, she runs to fetch them, so you'll roll again. You'll both meet her tomorrow, if you come to watch the cricket. It should be a splendid day. Dare I say it, even a *spectacular* day."

"From your brief description earlier, I've no doubt it will be spectacular." Monsieur Rousselle smiled at Quin. "Your father has retained the town crier to open the proceedings, because it will be the first game of the season. The event promises to be as magnificent as your given name."

"The town crier?" Quin repeated. "That didn't happen at the last game I attended."

"Those were early days." Lord Appledrum waved his hand in an expansive gesture. "We've grown in splendor since then, haven't we, Tredworth?"

"Yes, my lord," the butler said. "It will be a very grand affair. And may I say that every man on your team is eager to help you to victory over the Duke of Candervale's team."

"Tredworth and Thomas are our best batsmen," Lord Appledrum explained to Charlotte and Gabrielle. His gesture encompassed both the butler and the footman who'd gone to fetch the ice cream.

"Second to yourself, my lord," Tredworth said deferentially.

Lord Appledrum grinned and shook his head. "Unfortunately for us, no one is the equal of the Duke of Candervale on the cricket pitch, and he has a strong team. But we've had some notable victories in the past. And we're aiming to have another one tomorrow, aren't we, Tredworth?"

"Yes, my lord."

"Are you sure you don't want to be part of the spectacle?" Monsieur Rousselle asked Quin.

"Not tomorrow. I'd rather watch and cheer both teams on with exquisite impartiality," Quin said.

"The stands have already been erected for the spectators," his father said. "And there will be refreshments part way through the day, including ice cream."

"I'm looking forward to it very much," Felix declared.

After that, the discussion moved away from cricket. Quin listened more than he spoke, allowing the others to direct the conversation.

His heart was full, but there were too many questions in his mind regarding Charlotte's future for him to truly relax.

He might not want to pick up a cricket bat himself, but now he'd returned to Brighton in time, he did want to support his father and cousin at their first match. On the other hand, watching a game of cricket wasn't going to get him any closer to finding Lord Henderson.

Meanwhile, his father occasionally brought Charlotte into the conversation. He'd just asked her if she'd ever ridden on a donkey, when a footman came into the room with a silver card tray.

By some kind of butlerish sleight of hand, Tredworth passed the bottle of wine in his hand to the footman closest to him, and went to confer with the newly arrived footman.

Charlotte demonstrated how sensitive she was to changes around her, because she faltered in her account of riding on Quin's horse with him.

Quin couldn't see her face, but he could hear the worry in her voice.

"I'll go for a donkey ride with you, Mademoiselle Charlotte," Felix said. "I'll walk at the donkey's head and hold the leading rein, so you'll be perfectly safe."

Tredworth carried the small silver tray over to Lord Appledrum.

Lord Appledrum glanced at it, looked at Quin and inclined his head slightly toward the door. He picked up the card and stood.

"Please excuse us, ladies and gentlemen," he said. "We'll be back shortly. Monsieur Rousselle, I appoint you host in my temporary absence."

"Then I'll claim your chair as well as your duties, my lord." Gabrielle's father promptly moved to sit at the head of the table. "That is only fair, is it not, Mademoiselle Charlotte? Now I have been given the responsibilities of a host, should I not sit in the chair of the host?"

"Thank you, monsieur," Quin said, and followed his father out of the dining room.

"Who is it?" he asked, once they were alone in the large, marble-floored hall.

In answer, his father handed him the card.

"Lord Henderson?" Quin lifted his eyes to meet his father's gaze. "I didn't think anyone knew where he was."

"Apparently, he's in our drawing room. Do you know what you want to say to him?"

"I know the outcome I want to achieve," Quin replied. "What I say is going to depend on him. But I don't want Charlotte's situation to become fodder for the gossip mill or the courts."

"No." Lord Appledrum's smile was uncharacteristically grim. "You have me and Marcus at your back. I'm not aware Henderson has any allies of similar stature. Let's see what he has to say for himself."

Chapter Forty-Five

They discovered Lord Henderson standing with his back to the unlit fire. Marcus had told Quin the viscount was in his thirties, but he appeared older, though perhaps that was the effect of his obvious fatigue.

"Lord Appledrum," he said, when he saw them. "I apologize for intruding upon you. But...is my daughter here?"

"Yes. We were in the middle of dinner when your card was brought to me," Quin's father replied.

Lord Henderson stared as if he couldn't make sense of what he'd been told. "Your butler told me you were at dinner. Where is Charlotte?"

"At the dining table," Lord Appledrum said.

"She's eating with you?" Lord Henderson appeared to struggle with the notion.

"My father doesn't expect his guests to sit and watch him eat," Quin said curtly.

Lord Henderson turned to him. "You...you must be Lord Hanwell?"

"I am. I'd intended to find and speak to you at the earliest opportunity," Quin replied. "I had no idea you were already here, in Brighton."

"I wasn't, until a short while ago," the viscount said.

"Take a seat, Henderson." Lord Appledrum's tone conveyed his words were an order as much as an invitation. "Would you care for some brandy or port?"

"Thank you, my lord. Brandy would be welcome." The viscount lowered himself into an armchair, his shoulders slumped forward. When he took the glass, he swallowed several quick mouthfuls before lowering his elbow to rest on the arm of his chair.

When he saw Quin was watching him, his complexion turned a dull red, though perhaps the brandy was also contributing to his heightened color.

"I'm not entirely clear on everything that's happened," he said. "But I believe I owe you a debt of gratitude for intervening when the coach carrying my daughter was held up yesterday."

"Mademoiselle Rousselle, Nedcott and I all gave full statements to the local magistrate, Sir Ralph Edney," Quin replied. "After that, it was too late for Mademoiselle Rousselle and Charlotte to continue to Sedgemore Hall yesterday evening. This morning, under my protection, they resumed their journey—until we crossed paths with your wife's footman. Lady Henderson's note ordered Mademoiselle Rousselle to bring Charlotte back to Brighton, so we came back." Quin made no effort to soften his tone. His anger at Lady

Henderson had increased, not diminished, since he'd first read her note.

"I'm sorry you've been put to so much trouble on behalf of my family," Lord Henderson said stiffly.

"Mademoiselle Rousselle is my fiancée. I will go to any amount of trouble to ensure her comfort and peace of mind," Quin said.

"Your fiancée. I had no idea." Lord Henderson raised his glass for another swallow of brandy. "I suppose she would have immediately resigned her position as Charlotte's governess in any event."

"No, that wasn't her intention," Quin said.

"No?" Lord Henderson's brows drew down. "But..."

"Mademoiselle Rousselle and I discussed the situation. She made it clear that her love and sense of duty toward Charlotte, compelled her to remain your daughter's governess." Quin's anger rose close to the surface.

Lord Henderson gaped. "She'd rather be a governess than your countess?"

"Mademoiselle Rousselle doesn't give a damn about being a countess. She *does* care about being my wife. But she wasn't willing to risk causing more pain and damage to a child's fragile heart." Quin checked himself before he let his outrage get the better of him.

"I was present at the moment when Charlotte realized my son Harlequin was her mademoiselle's 'Quin'," Lord Appledrum said. "I have never seen such an expression of fear and devastation on a child's face, as when Charlotte thought Mademoiselle Rousselle would be leaving her."

"Mademoiselle Rousselle has been—" the viscount began.

"And then I heard my son promise Charlotte he would not take Gabrielle away from her." Lord Appledrum ruthlessly cut across Lord Henderson's stumbling reply. "And I saw Mademoiselle Rousselle struggle to maintain her composure, because her heart was being cut in two by the situation."

"I don't know what to say..."

"You're in a difficult position, no doubt," Lord Appledrum said. "But I want you to be fully cognizant that my son and Mademoiselle Rousselle were willing to delay their marriage indefinitely for your daughter's sake. I'm unaware of anyone else willing to make such a sacrifice on her behalf."

"I'm not even sure she is my daughter. Livia said..." The rest of the viscount's words were lost in his brandy glass.

Quin's heart thudded in his chest. He hadn't realized until he'd heard the fury in his father's voice, how strongly his father felt about the situation. So many people had been hurt because of Lady Henderson's casual cruelty.

"She's certainly not Harlequin or Gabrielle's daughter," Lord Appledrum countered. "But she's a child who deserves care. One who bears your name."

Lord Henderson rubbed his hand across his brow. "I arrived at Sedgemore Hall this morning, so I knew something about the attack on the carriage yesterday. But it's not entirely clear what happened in my house here in Brighton a few hours ago."

"The most important thing you need to know, is that I was speaking to Mrs. Whittle in the kitchen when I heard Charlotte screaming 'no'." Quin tensed at the memory of the jagged alarm that had lanced through him at that moment. "I ran upstairs to discover your son hitting Charlotte and Mademoiselle Rousselle as hard as he could—"

"*Hitting* them?" The viscount looked genuinely aghast.

"And taunting Charlotte with insults," Quin continued grimly. "Your wife was doing nothing to stop him. Indeed, she had a most unpleasant expression on her face while she watched."

Lord Henderson closed his eyes and drew in an unsteady breath. "Are they hurt?" he asked. "Charlotte and Mademoiselle Rousselle?"

"I don't believe they've suffered lasting physical harm," Quin replied. "After we arrived here, I happened to rest my hand lightly on Charlotte's shoulder, and she flinched, so some harm was done. Before we went down to dinner, Mademoiselle Rousselle told me a lady of this household has seen their bruises, and made a written account of them."

Lord Henderson's eyes widened. "Are you going to charge my son with assaulting your fiancée?"

Quin was about to deny any such intent, but then decided not to allay the viscount's concerns immediately.

"Charlotte wants to remain with me and Mademoiselle Rousselle—we will soon be married. And that's what we want too."

"You barely know her," Henderson exclaimed.

"I know her well enough, and Gabrielle loves her. Charlotte is a clever, generous-hearted child—"

"She's dumb!"

Quin gripped the arm of his chair. "Charlotte stopped talking because your wife told her to shut her howling mouth."

Lord Henderson's stricken expression reminded Quin of

Charlotte. In fact, the longer Quin talked to the viscount, the more similarities he noticed between their features. Not that such similarities were conclusive proof of paternity.

"How...how do you know?" Lord Henderson asked.

"She told me, and I see no reason not to believe her. It seems she communicates with silence—or honesty."

"And you're willing to include her in your household? Under what terms?"

"As our foster daughter. We won't expect her to lay our fires for us every day as a condition of keeping her," Quin said.

Lord Henderson frowned in obvious confusion.

"That's what she offered us in the carriage on the way back to Brighton," Quin explained.

Lord Henderson flinched.

"Do you agree to Charlotte living with my son and his wife as their foster daughter?" Lord Appledrum asked.

An oddly desolate expression flickered on the viscount's face. "I have no other way to provide for her. She was happy when Tessie cared for her. I remember her laughing."

"Tessie was her nurse who died," Quin explained to his father. "She was the one who taught Charlotte to lay fires, but Charlotte hasn't mentioned anything else about her. We don't want to deny you access to her, Henderson. She doesn't think you care about her, but she's not actively hostile toward you."

"I agree...I agree to what you suggest," the viscount said thickly.

"We'll consult our lawyers on Monday to ensure everyone's interests are protected," Lord Appledrum said. "My son isn't concerned about financial compensation for taking Charlotte into his household. But it would be appropriate for you to make provision for her living expenses. It will be something positive for her to know about you."

"The money we have came with my wife," Lord Henderson said. "It's appropriate for some of it to provide for her daughter."

"Charlotte might be your daughter too," Quin said. "I've spent a great deal of time over the past two days talking to her, and now I'm sitting across the room from you. I see similarities. Unless you know for sure she's not your child, I believe she could be."

Lord Henderson went still. "You think Livia lied to hurt me?"

"I've met her once, very briefly. I cannot comment on that. Let's draw up a short statement of our agreement now." Quin stood to go over to the writing desk.

"Have you eaten?" Lord Appledrum asked the viscount.

"No?" His reply was so hesitant it was almost as if he didn't know the answer. "No," he repeated, more firmly. "I haven't." He shook his head, appearing oddly forlorn. "It's no matter, I will go to...to the Castle after I leave here."

"I'll have a tray sent up for you." Lord Appledrum walked across the room, but he paused and turned toward the viscount before he opened the door.

"There's one thing I wish to make plain, Henderson." His voice hardened. "Your wife and your son are likely to be angry and resentful at what they'll consider to be unfair favor shown to Charlotte. I will not tolerate any intrusion into my house by either of them. And I will take action if they circulate slanderous gossip against me or my family."

Lord Henderson stared into Lord Appledrum's implacable face—and abruptly lowered his gaze. "I'll remove them from Brighton."

"I've no interest in your marital arrangements," Lord Appledrum said. "But, in my opinion, there is little point dedicating yourself to improving your estates, if they are to be inherited by a spoiled, malicious brat. Instead of making sure you are always somewhere your wife is not, perhaps you should consider whether raising a son you can be proud of would be a better legacy?"

Chapter Forty-Six

Gabrielle and her family tried to continue a normal conversation after Lord Appledrum and Quin left the dining room, but it was obvious Charlotte was too worried to let herself be distracted.

"You're safe, ma coccinelle," her papa finally said to Charlotte, abandoning any attempt to pretend the situation was normal. "We won't allow any harm to come to you."

Charlotte looked at him. "A duke is more important than a marquess."

Gabrielle's papa smiled wryly. "Not always, and we are in England. An English marquess is much more powerful in England than a French duke who lost his estates and fortune. And the Marquess of Appledrum is a very important man. But I am a better swordsman," he added, with a gleam of humor.

"I'm *learning* to be a great swordsman," Felix announced. "But when I meet your brother, I'm going to challenge *him* to a bout of fisticuffs."

"You are?" Charlotte gazed at him in amazement. "Why?"

"Because he is a poltroon who attacked my sister and you," Felix said, smoldering anger in his dark eyes. "He's a boy, so papa can't challenge him to a duel, but *I* can be your champion."

"A champion—like a story knight?" Charlotte asked.

"*Oui*." Felix drew himself up proudly.

"Oh." An unreadable succession of expressions flickered over Charlotte's face. Then she slid off her chair and came close enough to Gabrielle to whisper in her ear.

"Should I give him one of my hair ribbons as a favor?" she asked.

Gabrielle swallowed an unexpected urge to laugh. "I'm sure he'd appreciate that."

"All right. Will you take one out for me?" Charlotte asked.

So Gabrielle carefully removed one of Charlotte's hair ribbons. "You'd probably best walk around to bestow it upon him," she recommended.

Charlotte nodded, took a deep breath, and marched around the large dining table to stop beside Felix.

"Sir Knight, here is my favor!" She thrust her clenched fist at him and opened her hand. A startled Felix only just managed to catch the falling ribbon, while Charlotte ran all the way back around the table to Gabrielle's side.

"Very well done, Mademoiselle Charlotte," Gabrielle's papa praised her.

Charlotte was bright red and didn't quite manage to meet anyone's gaze. She didn't seem to notice when Miss Trent quietly left the table.

"Did you call me a ladybird before?" she asked Gabrielle's papa.

"I did." His eyes twinkled. "Would you prefer to be something else? A dove or a cabbage, perhaps?"

She gave him a skeptical look, her nose not exactly wrinkling, before she produced a polite smile. "Thank you. I think I'd rather be a ladybird than a cabbage. A dove is nice too, but I like the pretty red ladybirds."

Miss Trent returned to her seat, and the servants began to clear the table.

Charlotte looked dismayed and leaned toward Gabrielle. "Lord Quin didn't finish yet."

"Don't worry, I would never allow either of my lords to go hungry," Miss Trent assured her. "Would you like some ice cream now?"

Charlotte moved her head from side to side. "When Lord Quin comes back."

"He's only upstairs," Miss Trent said. "He'll be down to join us again soon, I'm sure."

A footman came into the room and approached Gabrielle's papa. Despite his magnificent livery, Gabrielle recognized him as Thomas, the one Lord Appledrum had claimed was an excellent cricketer. She wondered what he wore on the cricket field. Presumably not his grand livery.

"Monsieur, Lord Appledrum presents his compliments and requests you join him in the drawing room," Thomas said to her papa.

"Intrigue," Papa murmured, getting to his feet. "Don't worry, ma coccinelle, you are surrounded by allies."

He left the dining room, and Thomas turned to bow to Charlotte.

"Lord Appledrum's compliments, miss. He says he's looking forward to talking further with you about those things which aren't to be mentioned at the meal table." The footman's expression was professionally bland, but Gabrielle could see the curiosity burning in his eyes.

Miss Trent started to laugh. "Snails, Thomas. My apologies, mademoiselle, I hope you don't mind me explaining. Lord Hanwell has decreed we're not allowed to talk about snails and frogs when we're eating."

"I see." Thomas's curiosity seemed partly appeased, but not entirely. Probably snails and frogs weren't a regular topic of conversation at Lord Appledrum's dinner table.

"I collect snail shells." Charlotte expanded the explanation. "Only when no one's living in them anymore—except sometimes they aren't empty after all."

"Very inconvenient, miss," Thomas said.

"Yes, because I have to put them back outside. Do you like snails?"

"My mother swears they're good for the lungs," Thomas replied. His gaze flicked to Miss Trent, and he added, "I collected frog spawn sometimes when I was a boy."

"I've never done that." Charlotte twisted toward Gabrielle. "Do you think Lord Quin will let us collect frog spawn?"

"I'm sure he will," Gabrielle said.

"Aren't you scared of frogs?" Charlotte whispered.

"No, only snails and similar creatures make me uncomfortable," Gabrielle said. "I don't like the idea of them touching me."

"I won't let them touch you, mademoiselle." Charlotte patted her arm. "Never, ever."

"I know you won't, sweetheart." Gabrielle put her arms around Charlotte and hugged her. Not conventional behavior at a nobleman's dinner table, but this meal had become far from conventional. She knew Charlotte was scared. She wasn't exactly scared herself, but she was worried.

What was happening that required both Lord Appledrum and Quin's presence *and* her papa's?

"We aren't usually in Brighton during the spring," Miss Trent said, "but there are always tadpoles at Appledrum. Lord Hanwell had a special, glass-sided tank when he was a boy, so he could view the growing tadpoles from all angles. We'll find it in time for next spring."

The door opened and Lord Appledrum entered in, followed by Quin. Gabrielle's papa wasn't with them.

Her pulse quickened, and she felt Charlotte stiffen in her embrace. Where was Papa?

Quin walked across the room and sat down at the head of the table, but Lord Appledrum remained close to the door.

"Miss Trent, Felix, please join me. We're enjoying our after-dinner tea in the library this evening," he said.

Quin didn't move as the dining room emptied, but he did reach out and take one of Charlotte's hands. He was holding a document in his other hand, which he placed gently on the table.

The door closed behind the last servant.

Charlotte looked between Quin and Gabrielle. Gabrielle could feel her trembling.

"Charlotte, your father has agreed you can live with us," Quin said.

Charlotte stared at him, twisted to peer up at Gabrielle, and turned to stare at Quin again. "He says you can keep me?" she whispered.

"Yes, we've signed an agreement." Quin pushed the document across the polished table so that it was within Gabrielle's reach.

"Agreement made this day of our lord, Friday, the eighteenth of July, seventeen hundred and ninety-four between Harlequin..." She read aloud Quin's full name and title and Lord Henderson's, saw her own name a few words further on and read silently and impatiently to the end.

"Your papa has given you over into my care, Charlotte." She lowered the paper. "And once Lord Quin marries me, we'll both be in his care. He's promised to look after us both."

She smiled at him over the top of Charlotte's head, her vision misty with tears. Quin's promise to care for them wasn't only intended for Charlotte's papa, it was for her papa as well.

Papa and Lord Appledrum had signed the document as witnesses to Quin's and Lord Henderson's agreement. In fact, the four signatures took up almost as much space on the page as the agreement itself.

"We'll be talking to lawyers next week to refine the details," Quin said. "But I wanted the basic agreement drawn up today. I have a copy and Charlotte's father has one."

"I told you Papa didn't want me," Charlotte said in a thin voice.

Gabrielle hugged her tighter.

"I'm not sure that's true," Quin said. "I don't think he knows how to look after you, but it seemed to make him sad when he realized that."

"He never tried." Charlotte wasn't crying, but Gabrielle's tears spilled over onto her cheeks. She kissed the top of Charlotte's head.

"People have to show us they care before we believe they do," Quin said, "and he never showed you, did he?"

Charlotte shook her head.

"Mademoiselle shows you every day," Quin said. "And you show her."

"And you'll keep taking care of us," Charlotte said.

"Yes. I don't know much about little girls, so I'll probably get things wrong sometimes. But then you must tell me." He smiled at her and then lifted his gaze to meet Gabrielle's eyes.

"I love you," she mouthed at him.

"I love you too," he said aloud.

Charlotte went so still Gabrielle thought she'd even stopped breathing. "Will you…will you love me too…one day?"

Quin looked at her, smiled and nodded.

She wriggled in Gabrielle's embrace, and when Gabrielle released her, she threw herself into Quin's arms and burst into tears.

Gabrielle shifted along into Charlotte's seat and rose enough so she could lean over and kiss his cheek.

"This has been a very eventful day," he said. "It's not surprising we're all feeling overwrought."

Charlotte's crying bout didn't last long.

"Let mademoiselle set you to rights," Quin said. "Do you have…?"

Gabrielle produced two handkerchiefs from her reticule and gave him a watery smile.

"Ah, that's good. I need my own handkerchief for myself." He openly dabbed his own eyes.

Charlotte blew her nose. "Why are ladies' handkerchiefs smaller than gentlemen's?" she asked. "Mademoiselle's nose is almost as big as yours."

Gabrielle and Quin looked at each other, and then they both started laughing.

"Dear heart, your nose is as dainty as…the daintiest thing you can imagine." Quin pressed his hand across the lower half of his face, but his eyes continued to laugh at her.

"But why?" Charlotte insisted. "I could blow my nose more times on your handkerchief before there were no more dry bits than on mine or mademoiselle's."

"You've raised what seems to me to be a valid question," Quin said. "We should discuss it in more depth with mademoiselle soon, but perhaps not this evening."

"Charlotte wanted to wait to have her ice cream until you came back." Gabrielle dried her own eyes and tried to blow her nose as delicately as possible.

Quin grinned at her and then looked at Charlotte.

"Your papa is still here," he said. "He was having his dinner in the drawing room. I think he'd like to see you."

"Do I have to?"

"No. I told him it would be your choice," Quin replied.

Chapter Forty-Seven

Charlotte stared at her shoes for several seconds. Then raised her head, a resolute expression on her face. "All right."

"Do we all feel ready?" Quin looked at Gabrielle.

She nodded, though she couldn't help feeling an inner qualm. There had been so many emotional reversals today. They were ending the evening in a state of joy, not despair, but she didn't have many reserves left to deal with an unpleasant encounter.

But if Charlotte was willing to see her father, Gabrielle could do no less than summon the same resolution.

Quin walked them upstairs, holding each one by the hand.

A footman opened the drawing room door for them, and they went inside.

The moment Lord Henderson saw them, he leaped to his feet.

Gabrielle had only met the viscount on a few occasions.

While trying not to be rude, she couldn't help studying him curiously.

His clothes were travel stained. There was still dust on his boots, and he seemed weary and dejected. She didn't feel sorry for him, but some of her anxiety that he might create a scene receded.

"Mademoiselle Rousselle, Charlotte, good evening," he said jerkily.

"Good evening, my lord." Gabrielle didn't curtsy to him, but Charlotte took a half step forward and bobbed him a small curtsy, nothing like the deep curtsies she'd given to Lord Appledrum or Gabrielle's papa.

"I…um…I deeply regret any mistreatment you suffered under my roof, mademoiselle," Lord Henderson said.

Gabrielle had no idea what to say to that, so she said nothing at all.

Lord Henderson scanned her face and Charlotte's and seemed to withdraw into himself.

Gabrielle couldn't see Charlotte's expression, but she knew what it was like to be on the receiving end of the little girl's blank stare. Was that how she also appeared? No wonder Lord Henderson was struggling.

"Thank you for allowing me to continue to care for Charlotte, my lord," she said. "I…Lord Hanwell and I, will always do our best to ensure she feels happy and secure."

Because Charlotte had taken a small step forward to curtsy, Gabrielle only had to look sideways to see she was still clinging to Quin's hand. She saw Lord Henderson notice that, too.

His smile was sad. "I have no doubts."

"Shall we all sit down?" Quin suggested.

He and Gabrielle sat on the sofa with Charlotte between them. She hadn't said a word, and Gabrielle wondered if she would.

"Do you like snails?" Her voice was as croaky as a frog's, but Gabrielle understood her question.

Lord Henderson gaped at her.

"For their interesting shells," Quin clarified. "Charlotte enjoys adding new, empty, snail shells to her collection."

Lord Henderson closed his mouth. But he continued to stare at Charlotte for a few more seconds before shifting his attention to Gabrielle.

She smiled at him. "Charlotte is exceptionally observant. She's very good at noticing subtle variations in their patterns."

"That's..." Lord Henderson swallowed. "I'm glad to hear you're observant, Charlotte. I'm afraid I've never paid any attention to snails."

She kicked a foot forward and then tucked it back under the sofa. "What about frog spawn?"

"Frog spawn? You're talking to me!" His bewilderment transformed into belated realization.

Charlotte ignored his startled comment. "Lord Quin kept tadpoles in a tank to look at when he was a little boy. Did you have tadpoles?"

"In a bucket, one year." Lord Henderson passed an unsteady hand over his thinning hair. "I remember watching their legs appear as they changed into tiny frogs."

Charlotte leaned against Quin. Much as she loved him, Gabrielle might have felt a pang at the way Charlotte was favoring him after only two days. Except Quin was the one with the power in the room, and Charlotte knew it.

"Maybe you can come and see our tadpoles next year," she said. "But don't bring Augustus. We don't want Augustus."

Lord Henderson visibly flinched. "I'm sorry he hurt you."

"He broke my first snail shells. That's why we have to keep them in the bedroom, even though mademoiselle is scared of them. That's how I know she loves me."

The clock ticked. Lord Henderson stared at Charlotte, then at Gabrielle, and then he closed his eyes.

Quin reached his arm behind Charlotte to put his hand on Gabrielle's shoulder. She didn't think he'd known they'd kept the snail shell collection in their bedroom, not just in the nursery.

"I'm sure we'll be able to find my old fish tank. If not, we'll have a new one made," he said. "Perhaps we can prevail upon mademoiselle to make a series of detailed sketches of the tadpoles transforming to frogs?"

"Of course I will." She'd do anything for him.

Quin lowered his hand to wrap his arm around Charlotte's shoulders. "It seems we can look forward to renewing our acquaintance with frog spawn next year, Henderson. And this evening, I believe we can also look forward to ice cream in the library. I don't think Charlotte would mind if you join us."

∽

WHEN QUIN HAD GONE to the fish market the previous morning, he'd feared it would be years before he could claim Gabrielle. The best he'd hoped for was that he and Gabrielle would be able to meet frequently, and correspond easily with each other.

Now here he was with everything he'd wanted within his grasp. He could barely believe his good fortune.

He hadn't expected his bride would come to him with a foster daughter. He knew Charlotte's presence would make some aspects of their married life more complicated, but he'd exerted himself to keep her, not just for Gabrielle's sake but for Charlotte's, and even his.

What he now wanted more than anything was to find a quiet private place with Gabrielle—preferably containing a bed—and celebrate and discuss everything with her.

Instead, he invited Lord Henderson to join them all in the library and hoped he hadn't made a mistake.

"After you, my lord," he said to the viscount.

Lord Henderson preceded them out.

Charlotte took Quin's hand again. He didn't believe she would always be so clingy. But if he yearned for some quiet time to reflect on everything that had happened, Charlotte likely felt the same.

He couldn't imagine the turmoil of emotions that coming face-to-face with her father had stirred inside her. He needed to talk to Marcus. His cousin's early childhood hadn't been directly parallel to Charlotte's. Nevertheless, Marcus might have insights Quin lacked.

With Charlotte holding his hand, Quin's opportunities for a romantic interlude with Gabrielle were limited. But...

"Damn it," he muttered and put his free hand on her arm to halt her. When she turned around with a question in her eyes, he cupped the back of her head and kissed her.

It wasn't a long or passionate kiss. He could feel the promise of passion rising in his veins, but he lifted his lips from hers before he forgot their other obligations.

She sifted her fingers through his hair. "Thank you," she whispered.

"For ice cream? Let's hope there actually is some." He kissed her cheek and then laid his hand on her back to guide her to the door.

Lord Henderson was looking at them. Quin couldn't read the expression on his face, but he didn't think it was disapproval.

Lord Appledrum welcomed them warmly into the library, and Quin was relieved to discover there was ice cream and lemonade for Charlotte.

"Lord Quin didn't get his gooseberry tart, either, Mademoiselle Trent," she said politely.

Quin wondered if anyone had called Agnes 'mademoiselle' before. Charlotte presumably knew Agnes wasn't French. But Quin had described her as his 'mademoiselle', so perhaps that's why Charlotte had used the term.

No one corrected her.

"Nor did you." Agnes smiled. "Would you like some along with your ice cream?"

Charlotte nodded.

Agnes went to confer with Tredworth. Gabrielle and Charlotte sat together on a sofa, with Quin sitting in a chair at right angles to them.

Lord Appledrum introduced Felix and Agnes to Lord

Henderson, providing only Agnes's name, and no explanation of her role in the household.

Agnes gave the viscount a cup of tea and he sat down in a chair a little removed from the others. He didn't look at ease, but he also seemed content to sip his tea in melancholy silence.

Every few minutes, Charlotte threw him a glance that suggested she didn't know what to make of him, or how to feel about his presence.

The ice cream and gooseberry tart were welcome. Quin was still hungry, and Lord Appledrum and Gabrielle's papa were also served the portions they hadn't been able to enjoy at the dinner table.

Monsieur Rousselle distracted attention by praising Lord Appledrum's cook for the gooseberry tart. Then he launched into a discussion about whether Italians did make the best ice cream.

Charlotte looked at Quin, and he was pleased to see mischief dancing in her eyes. She leaned closer to Gabrielle to whisper something.

Gabrielle laughed.

Quin raised his eyebrows at her.

"She says it's much nicer having fruit tart with ice cream," Gabrielle explained.

Charlotte dipped her chin and didn't exactly shake her head when she looked at Quin under her brows.

He grinned. "Mrs. Larkin's gooseberry pie did taste nearly as good, but it didn't look as beautiful," he said.

"This tart is very, *very* beautiful," Charlotte said emphatically. "And very tasty. I never had such a nice dinner." Then worry flickered over her face. Quin guessed she was wondering whether she'd upset him by hinting that today's dinner was better than yesterday's dinner at the inn.

Quin smiled. "Tomorrow, I hope we'll be able to enjoy dinner together without me having to jump up and attend to business halfway through."

Meanwhile, the others had been talking about their favorite ice creams and cricket. Quin suspected Gabrielle's papa and brother hadn't often enjoyed ice cream during their exile, if at all, when they weren't guests of his father.

At first glance, Phillipe Rousselle didn't appear much altered from when he'd been the Duke de la Fontaine, but Quin was sure there were scars hidden beneath his debonair appearance.

How could there not be, when Phillipe had gone from being the master of a grand château in the French countryside and an elegant house in Paris, to becoming a fencing master, earning his living through his prowess with a sword?

The dishes had been cleared, and Quin was wondering how much longer people would linger chatting, when Felix asked, "Gabi, how did Quin propose to you?"

"Um..." Gabrielle hesitated and looked at Quin. "It was... um...very romantic."

Quin became aware that everyone in the room was staring at him. When he looked at Gabrielle, he could tell she was remembering their conversation in the moonlit hayfield. Neither of them wanted to recount every detail of what they'd said then—or why.

"I didn't ask her...exactly," he prevaricated. "I suppose we could say I told her to marry me."

"You told her?" Felix exclaimed.

"In a very romantic way." Gabrielle smiled at Quin, even as she was biting her lower lip. He thought…hoped…she was trying not to laugh. There really hadn't been anything romantic about the way he'd told her they should marry immediately.

"He ordered you?" Felix turned to Quin, an expression of manufactured indignation, at least Quin hoped it was manufactured, on his face. "You *ordered* my sister to marry you?"

"He didn't order me," Gabrielle defended Quin. "And I told him I couldn't…not yet. But I can now," she added hastily. "Because he's sorted everything out."

Charlotte glanced at her father. Quin automatically followed the direction of her gaze and noticed Lord Henderson's countenance appeared more animated than it had during the previous half hour. Was the viscount going to renege on their agreement because he misinterpreted Felix teasing them?

Chapter Forty-Eight

Though it didn't seem likely Lord Henderson would change his mind, Quin's gut tightened at the possibility. He took a breath and turned to Gabrielle.

"The simplest solution is for me to ask you now, in front of all these witnesses," he said.

Her eyes glowed with love—and understanding. She knew how uncomfortable he was becoming. It had been natural and easy to tell her he loved her in front of Charlotte, but he felt much more awkward speaking of his feelings in front of so many extra people—especially Lord Henderson. But Lord Henderson was the one who particularly needed to hear this proposal, so he'd best continue.

"All right," Gabrielle said softly. "I love you."

Her words and her tone steadied him.

"Gabrielle," he began, "will you..."

From the corner of his eye, he saw Charlotte shaking her head

His stomach jolted. "What's wrong?"

"The prince in mademoiselle's story got down on his knees to propose to the milkmaid," she whispered loudly.

Quin's whole body relaxed. All he had to do was focus on Gabrielle and Charlotte, and all would be well.

"I thought the prince was still stuck behind the trained hedge," he said. "When did he get through it?"

"That one's still stuck. This is a different prince," Charlotte explained. "But if a prince is supposed to get down on his knees, shouldn't an earl do so too?"

Quin grasped the arms of his chair and pushed himself forward on the seat, ready to kneel at Gabrielle's feet. Then a question occurred to him. "How many knees?" he asked.

Gabrielle gave a choke of laughter and pressed the fingertips of both hands against her lips.

"It's a serious question," he said, adopting a serious mien. "Would you like me to kneel on one knee or both knees, dear heart?"

He could hear her little bursts of silent laughter behind her hands, but she didn't speak.

"Two knees suggests an attitude of supplication," Lord Appledrum mused. "Suitable perhaps, for a suitor who feels he needs to beg forgiveness before making his proposal. Possibly appropriate in this case, since apparently you forgot to propose in the first place…"

Gabrielle shook her head and held up one finger.

"One knee is more in keeping with a dashing knight, confident in his ability to perform great deeds of valor," Lord Appledrum continued.

Quin ignored his father. "One knee?" he said to Gabrielle.

She nodded and lowered her hands to her lap. "You are our valiant, steadfast knight."

Quin's breath hitched at the love in her eyes. But he couldn't remain perched on the edge of his chair forever. He had to get this proposal over with so they could have some time alone together. He began to rise—

"Flowers," Gabrielle's father said. "As a botanist, my lord, it's surely expected you will give my daughter flowers when you propose to her?"

"Flowers," Quin repeated. "Yes, sir." He stood up and instinctively started patting himself, even though he knew he didn't have his pocketknife anywhere in his evening attire. He walked over to the desk and inspected the objects on it.

"What are you looking for, Harlequin?" his father asked.

"A penknife, so I can go and cut some flowers." Quin heard the sound of soft movement and looked up to discover there were more people in the library than before. Tredworth and several footmen were easing through the door to line up by the bookshelves.

He threw his father a suspicious glance, but Lord Appledrum was sitting back at his ease, grinning at him. Agnes was on her feet, but Quin was sure it was his father's idea to invite the whole household in to watch him fumble his proposal.

He gave Gabrielle an apologetic look and went back to searching for the penknife. He'd just spotted it when there was a loud knocking on the front door.

Quin tensed. Impatient knocks were rarely a good thing this late in the evening.

The nearest footman hurried to open it. Quin couldn't see who'd arrived from his present position, but he heard Nancy say, "Hello, Gerald, we've come to see Uncle Appdrum."

"Good evening, Miss Nancy," the footman replied. "Your grace."

Quin stared at his father.

"I invited Marcus to join us this evening so he could hear about your betrothal in the peace of our home," Lord Appledrum said, "not in public at the cricket match tomorrow. I didn't anticipate you'd be in the middle of rectifying your failure to propose to Mademoiselle Rousselle at the moment he arrived."

Marcus strode through the library doorway with Nancy sitting on his arm.

"His grace, the Duke of Candervale, to see you, my lord," Tredworth announced sonorously. "And Miss Nancy."

Marcus set Nancy's feet gently on the floor and she rushed across the room to Lord Appledrum. "Uncle Marcus goes faster than a donkey."

Lord Appledrum scooped her up and sat her on his knee. "If he ever gets into a race with one, I'll know to wager on him. Why aren't you in bed?"

"I wasn't sleepy. Hello, Uncle Haquin." She looked around. "There're new people here."

"Yes, there are," Lord Appledrum agreed. "And I'll introduce you soon. But now we all need to be quiet, so Uncle Harlequin can propose to Mademoiselle Rousselle."

Marcus gave his hat to Tredworth and cast Quin a puzzled glance, but didn't ask any questions.

"Someone will explain while I go and cut some flowers," Quin said. "Gabrielle, everyone, if you'll excuse me for—"

"Quin." Agnes was coming toward him, drying the stem of a single flower with her handkerchief. He glanced past her and realized she'd taken it from one of the flower arrangements in the room.

"Will this suit?" She offered the beautiful bloom to him, just as she'd been offering him loving care ever since he was three years old.

"Yes. Thank you, Miss Trent." His throat was tight as he gave her a one-armed hug and accepted the flower.

He went back to Gabrielle and was about to kneel before her, but then he hesitated. "Is anyone going to tell me I need anything else?"

"A ring?" Felix suggested, grinning.

"No," Quin said firmly. "I mean, yes, of course I'll give you a ring, dear heart. As many as you like. But I'm sure you'd prefer to choose them for yourself."

He dropped onto one knee before her, and the rest of the room receded from his awareness. He was about to simply hold out the flower to her. But then it occurred to him he was probably supposed to make some kind of grand romantic gesture with it. His gaze locked with hers. He brushed the petals across his lips and offered her the flower.

She reached out, her fingers lightly caressing his before she gripped the stem and lifted the flower to her own lips.

He took her other hand in his. He could feel the love flowing between them from his heart to hers, in a continuous loop through their clasped hands, and the warmth in her eyes.

How could he be so lucky that she was his? For long moments, he lost himself in the connection between them, until he heard his father say softly, "She can't answer if you don't speak."

He blinked and wondered how long he'd simply been gazing at her.

"Mademoiselle Rousselle." His voice was husky. He swallowed. "Gabrielle...my dear love." He hesitated, suspecting he should expound more on that, but there were no other love words he was comfortable saying to her before an audience.

She squeezed his fingers. It was a secret communication shared only between them.

"Will you marry me?" he asked.

"Lord Hanwell...Harlequin...my darling Quin," she smiled at him, more radiant than any sunrise he'd ever seen. "I love you so much that even if..."

It was her turn to pause. He wasn't sure if it was for effect, or because she'd lost track of what she was saying with her voice, because her eyes were saying so much more.

"Even if...?" he prompted her.

"Even if you said we'd have to live in the land of giant snails *forever*, I'd marry you in an instant. Yes!"

He stood, pulling her up into his arms in one continuous move, and kissed her.

He was distantly aware of cheering, but he was too busy enjoying the taste of Gabrielle's lips and the feel of her body against his, to pay any attention.

"Where's the land of giant snails?" Lord Henderson asked in the background. "Is it in fairyland?"

"I believe it's in Africa," Lord Appledrum replied. "Bring the champagne, please, Tredworth. Harlequin, allow me to introduce Nancy to Gabrielle. Harlequin!"

Quin lifted his head. Gabrielle smiled at him. She only had one arm around his neck because she was still holding the flower.

"I'm going to paint it." She touched it gently against his cheek. "And then you can help me preserve it."

"Anything you want, dear heart," he promised. "Anything you want. Now I must introduce Nancy to you."

Chapter Forty-Nine

Quin was alone in the library.

Marcus and Nancy had left first, because Nancy had been falling asleep in Lord Appledrum's arms.

"Come on, Nan, you'll be so grumpy if you fall all the way asleep and have to wake up to go home." Marcus had reclaimed her and departed.

Miss Trent, Gabrielle, and Charlotte had been the next to retire, followed by Gabrielle's brother and father.

Lord Henderson hadn't moved, or shown any sign of moving, until Quin's father had started making pointed statements about how he needed a good night's sleep before the cricket match tomorrow.

Much as Quin had wanted to go and find Gabrielle, he'd stayed because Lord Henderson was his problem more than his father's.

Lord Appledrum came back into the library after showing the viscount out.

"I was beginning to think we'd have to use Henderson as a paperweight and tell the maids to dust around him," he said.

"He didn't want to go home."

"Who would to that house? I need to cultivate his acquaintance—but that's for another day." Lord Appledrum went over to the brandy decanter. But then he replaced the stopper without pouring any, and turned to lean against the edge of the desk. "I have a question for you."

"Yes, sir?" Quin came alert. Something in his father's voice told him this was an important question. But so much had happened over the past few days he couldn't guess what it would be about.

As the silence lengthened, his tension grew.

"What did you do with my ladder?" Lord Appledrum asked.

"Your *ladder*?" Air gusted from Quin's lungs. He stared at his father. "What lad—you mean the ladder Gabrielle used to climb over the wall?"

"That ladder." Lord Appledrum nodded. "I went to fetch it the morning after the ball, but it was nowhere to be found."

"I thought it belonged to the hay makers. I carried it over to lean against one of the haystacks when I returned." Quin was dumbfounded. "You mean *you* concocted the plan for how Gabrielle could attend the masquerade?"

"No." Lord Appledrum came to sit in the chair opposite Quin. "Mrs. Whittle and Agnes hatched that scheme between them. I only discovered the details when I went looking for Agnes one evening, and found her sitting on top of the orchard wall."

Quin was fascinated by that revelation. But what struck him

most was that, instead of referring to her as Miss Trent, his father had called her Agnes. He'd never before spoken of her in such informal language. It meant something important.

"You found Miss Trent on top of the wall?" he said.

"She wanted to be sure a lady would be able to implement their scheme," Lord Appledrum explained. "At the moment I found her she was trying to pull the ladder up to lower it over the other side."

"I imagine that was rather…surprising," Quin said carefully.

"I told her if she wanted to escape that desperately I'd open the front door for her," Lord Appledrum said. "No, I didn't really think she was trying to escape. But I'd never found her on top of a wall before so, as you say, it was surprising."

"I knew Mrs. Whittle and Miss Trent were conspiring on our behalf behind the scenes, but I didn't realize you were actively involved." Quin couldn't get over the idea.

"Agnes explained it all to me. She began befriending Mrs. Whittle as soon as we learned Gabrielle had joined the Henderson household, by the way."

"Two years ago?" Quin exclaimed. "That's—I must thank her. She's been watching over Gabrielle from afar all this time." Love and gratitude expanded within him at learning the effort Agnes had made on Gabrielle's behalf.

"She likes Gabrielle, but she did it for you," Lord Appledrum said. "At least, in the beginning. Agnes never came to France with us, so she's had few opportunities to meet Gabrielle. But Agnes knew you loved her, so she did her best to extend her mother's wings over her."

"I...will thank her." Quin's throat was too tight with emotion to say anything further.

His father nodded. "It takes time to establish trust in a new friendship. Agnes only recently learned that Mrs. Whittle has remained in her post through loyalty to Lord Henderson—and Charlotte. I don't know what choices Mrs. Whittle will make now, but Agnes has told her that we'll have employment for her if she seeks a change of position. And if you set up an independent household, you'll need a good housekeeper."

Quin took a breath. "Gabrielle and I haven't talked about where we'll live after our marriage," he admitted. "We've barely had a moment for private conversation all day."

"You walked Gabrielle and Charlotte out of Lady Henderson's house, brought them here, and arranged to foster Charlotte —all without discussing any of it with Gabrielle?" Lord Appledrum raised an amused eyebrow.

Quin rubbed his temple. "We did talk about what she wanted yesterday evening—but I never suspected I'd be able to make it happen so rapidly."

"And you truly never proposed to her until today—even before you went off on your travels?"

Quin shook his head. "We talked about marriage. She wanted to marry me and come on the expedition with me! But you know why I didn't seek a formal betrothal between us."

"In case she found another man she preferred to you. Wouldn't you have fought for her?"

"Yes, if I'd been here," Quin replied. "And I didn't want to wed her, be married for a few months, leave her, and perhaps come home to find a two-year-old child I'd never met. I mean, I wanted the first part of that, but not the second."

He glanced at his father, and then away.

"No," Lord Appledrum said quietly. "I imagine you'll stay close by Gabrielle's side when she begins increasing."

"I will." There was no need for Quin to explain further. His mother had died shortly after giving birth to him.

Lord Appledrum hadn't lost the love of his life when his young wife had died, because theirs had been an arranged marriage. But he had been fond of her and perhaps, if they'd had more time, a deeper love would have grown between them.

The lingering consequence of that shared loss on both men was their awareness that childbirth could be a dangerous business for a woman. It had been unthinkable to Quin that he expose Gabrielle to that risk, and then sail off with the expedition, unable to support her if she had fallen pregnant.

"Your courtship of Gabrielle may not have followed a conventional path," Lord Appledrum mused, "but the bonds between you are unmissable. Mrs. Whittle reported that when Gabrielle saw your message for her in the newspaper, she jumped up and danced with joy. A masquerade ball meant she'd be able to attend at least part of it without risk of recognition."

Quin blinked at the implication of that comment. "You made it a masked ball for Gabrielle's sake, not mine?"

His father lifted one shoulder. "I thought there might be more chance of you enjoying yourself at a ball in more anonymous circumstances, but primarily it was for Gabrielle's sake. After you disappeared into the garden, I did think there was a possibility you'd come across each other out there and never make it into the ballroom."

"I only recognized her as she finished dressing. That is, she was already dressed and masked when she came over the wall," Quin added hastily. "She just changed her shoes and gloves. That feathery thing on her head was very distracting."

"Turban." His father grinned at him. "You're probably correct to leave the choice of ring to her."

"Gabrielle believes Mrs. Whittle went out earlier to leave the ladder in the right place." Quin suddenly recalled how this conversation had started.

"I thought Mrs. Whittle would be accompanying her," his father said. "That she'd hand the ladder up to Gabrielle, when it was time to lift it over into the orchard. That's how I practiced with Agnes."

Quin shook his head. "Gabrielle would never have left Charlotte alone."

"No, and she managed by herself very well. I'll tell the gardener to buy a new ladder. That wasn't the question." Lord Appledrum's tone changed abruptly.

"It wasn't?" Quin sensed a re-emergence of the same underlying tension in his father that he'd noticed when he'd dithered about pouring himself a glass of brandy.

His father never dithered. The muscles in Quin's belly tightened in anticipation of hearing what his father really wanted to ask.

"It was *a* question. But not the most important one." Lord Appledrum glanced away before returning his gaze to Quin.

A trickle of apprehension invaded Quin's body. Not because

he was afraid of his father, but because he was afraid he wouldn't respond correctly to whatever he was about to hear.

"Agnes won't marry me without your approval," Lord Appledrum said. "I've told her that I'm forty-three years old and don't need my son's permission to wed but...she won't proceed without it."

Part of his comment was almost flippant, but there was nothing flippant about the unguarded expression in his eyes.

Quin would have agreed to any request his father made. And though he hadn't expected this one, the answer was easy to give.

"Yes," he said. "Yes, a thousand times. Yes."

It was only when the tension left his father's body that Quin realized he'd been braced for a different answer.

"You couldn't have thought...how could you have thought I'd disapprove." The idea deeply troubled him.

"I didn't—until you seemed shocked when you saw Agnes at the dining table tonight."

"I wasn't. I'm sorry. She was where I didn't expect her to be, but I was happy she was there." Quin wished he was better at expressing the nuances of emotion. "She's the core of our family."

"Yes, she is. It was an impulse to ask her to join us for dinner this evening," Lord Appledrum said. "She was hesitant. But there have been so many occasions when I've had to recount to her afterward what happened on some special occasion. I wanted her to be present for your first meal with Gabrielle and her family. If I'd known you were going to make Gabrielle such a romantic proposal, I'd have been doubly insistent."

"She...Miss Trent...played a crucial part in it," Quin said. "I'm so glad she gave me the flower I gave to Gabrielle."

Candlelight reflected in the shimmer in Lord Appledrum's eyes. "For a plain, workaday fellow, you have a fine instinct for romance. Agnes helped me be a true father to you—and that meant I had some idea of how to help Marcus and Cecilia when I became their guardian. So yes, for me, you and Agnes are the core of my family, with my sister's family only a hair's breadth removed."

Quin sat silently as his memories and understanding rearranged themselves, and the foundation of his life shifted from something he instinctively felt, to something that had now been made explicit.

"How long?" he asked.

"How long since the first time I proposed to her?" his father interpreted the cryptic question. "Or the most recent?"

Quin raised his head, surprised again that his father might have asked Agnes to marry him more than once.

"I never went down on my knee either," Lord Appledrum said. "Perhaps that's where I went wrong. You were twelve the first time."

"Twelve?" Quin rocked back. "That's...that's half my lifetime!"

"No need to make me sound like Methuselah, dear boy. You're only three years past your majority."

"But..." Quin remembered how he'd felt when he'd thought he might have to wait eight or nine years for Gabrielle. His scattered thoughts coalesced into one vivid certainty.

"I was going to speak to the vicar tomorrow about having

our banns read, but your wedding should take precedence. We have Charlotte safely here, we can wait."

Lord Appledrum shook his head, but his face was full of unhidden love and appreciation. "No, I'd prefer your marriage to take place first. The step from nurse to marchioness was too long for Agnes. From housekeeper to marchioness is still daunting. If we set love aside—which I don't—she has all the graces and practical knowledge to take her place by my side in our world. But she wasn't born into it."

"You fear society will treat *your* wife unkindly?" Quin was indignant at the idea.

"I think they'll be beside themselves with curiosity when I finally tie the knot—having been infamous for my fierce resistance to marriage for so long," Lord Appledrum said. "We might have to retire to the country for the next few years until the gossip dies down."

"You want Gabrielle and me to draw the gossip mongers' fire," Quin realized.

"No, I don't want to put you in the firing line," his father said. "I know how much you'd hate being the center of that kind of attention."

"But not as much as Miss Trent because, when all is said and done, I *am* the Marquess of Appledrum's son," Quin said.

His father laughed. "Yes, you are. One I'm proud of. Now, I'm sure you have things you'd prefer to be doing—books you could be writing, for example—so I'll see you in the morning. Make sure you cheer loudest for my team tomorrow. And you're on notice that you can't sit out every match for the rest of the summer."

"I won't, but I need some practice first." Quin frowned. "I wonder where Duncan is? We can't finish our book until we spend some time together. I've been absent these past few days, so I don't fault him, but I want to introduce him to Gabrielle."

Lord Appledrum grinned. "He sent me a message apologizing for his absence at dinner. He was busy helping Miss Bianchetti make ice cream for tomorrow."

Quin's jaw dropped.

"I suspect Thomas brought us a portion of the supply she intended to sell at the cricket," Lord Appledrum said. "And Duncan's helping her replenish her stocks. She's short-handed while her parents are still away."

Quin closed his mouth. "I look forward to meeting her tomorrow."

"Most likely you'll also have an opportunity to meet the lady who's been occupying your cousin's thoughts as well," Lord Appledrum said.

"Marcus is interested in a lady? Why am I only now hearing about this?" Quin demanded.

"Your romance was not the only one facilitated by my masquerade ball," his father said proudly. "I consider it a spectacular success. Now we must hope the other couples will achieve the same happy understanding with each other that you have with Gabrielle."

At any other time, Quin would have had a host of further questions to ask. But this evening, he was too impatient to find Gabrielle, so he bade his father a warm goodnight and went in search of her.

Chapter Fifty

Gabrielle put the finishing touch to her painting, rinsed her brush in clean water and laid it down.

Tonight, she hadn't used the detailed style she'd developed to produce botanically accurate pictures for Quin. Instead, she'd allowed the watercolor to flow from her brush in a much looser style. Partly because she didn't have the patience for fine details this evening, but mostly because she'd tried to capture the deep, glowing joy of love represented by the flower.

The exact shape of the petals wasn't important, but the love in Quin's eyes when he'd held the flower to his lips before giving it to her was transcendentally important.

And she didn't only feel profoundly loved. While she was working on her painting, she'd gradually become aware that she felt safe, too. Not so much physically safe—she'd been nervous when they'd fled France, but the only time she'd ever been in true physical danger was when the highwayman had threatened to shoot her yesterday.

She felt safe on a deeper level, as if she was finally standing on firm ground. In a secure place where she could start making plans with Quin for their longer-term future with Charlotte, not just planning the next day's lessons—

A soft knock on the door brought her to her feet and across the room almost before she was aware of the interruption.

She opened it, and there was Quin.

Happiness dancing in her veins, she seized his hand, pulled him into the nursery and threw herself into his arms.

With a soft grunt of surprise, he welcomed her into his embrace, but then lifted her as he took a couple of steps backward.

She wanted to kiss him, and she put her hands behind his head. Then she belatedly realized he was trying to nudge the door quietly closed with his shoulders.

"Dear heart," he murmured against her cheek. "I shouldn't be here. Let me shut the door, my wanton dream."

"I am wanton." She stroked the nape of his neck. "I want you so much. I love you so much."

"Yes." His voice was thick. "Charlotte?"

"She's asleep."

"Thank God. Which is your room?" With the door closed, Quin swept Gabrielle up into his arms.

"That one. I love your arms. I love everything about you."

"I love everything about you too. Bring the candles." He turned so she could pick up the candelabrum from the table.

"I should paint the flower again in daylight," she mused. "But tonight's was painted in the light of love, and that's so bright. So glorious. It lights every cell of my body. I'm vibrating and glowing with love."

Quin set her on her feet by the bed, retrieved the candelabrum and placed it down on her dressing table. He closed the bedroom door, locked it, and came back to her.

"Have you been imbibing extra champagne since you retired, dear heart?" His smile brimmed with loving amusement.

"No. I'm only intoxicated by you. And I feel safe." She began untying his neckcloth. "I'm overflowing with love and happiness—and now you're back I feel safe."

His brows lowered. "Did you never feel safe in the Hendersons' house? That's—"

She pressed her fingers against his lips. "I misspoke. Until today I never felt in physical danger there. And even today it was more the shock of being hit by a little boy, not actual danger."

"He's not that little." Quin was still scowling.

She stroked his brow in an effort to soothe his mood as well as the visible furrows.

"I meant I feel safe to plan for the future," she explained. "You're with me now. We'll talk about what we want to do." She tossed aside his neckcloth and unbuttoned his waistcoat. He wasn't wearing his coat, so it was easy to rid him of the waistcoat, especially with his cooperation.

She tugged his shirt out of his breaches and pushed it up his body. The heat of desire flowed through her veins. She could feel the dampness and the throb of arousal between her legs. Her breasts ached for his touch.

He glanced past her to the bed, where she'd already pulled

back the covers. When his gaze met hers again, his eyes were hooded and dark with passion.

"I take it you have immediate plans for us?" He pulled off his shirt, revealing his muscled torso.

"To maze each other." Gabrielle barely recognized the sultry tone in her voice as she shaped her hands over the hard planes of his chest. "We can, can't we?"

His breath caught. When she rested her palm over his heart, she could feel it racing.

"Yes." He swallowed. "We have so much to discuss—but we can talk later."

It was his turn to make quick work of freeing her from her garments. Soon she was standing before him in only her stockings.

"You like my stockings?" She kissed the center of his chest, and stroked his back from his shoulders to the taut buttocks still encased in his breeches.

"Seeing you wearing them and nothing else inflames me even more," he confessed. "I don't know why. Sit." He backed her up until her legs were against the edge of the mattress.

As she sat, he went down on both knees before her. She hadn't expected him to do that, but her momentary surprise evaporated when his lips closed around her nipple.

His arms curved up around her back, providing her with the support she needed to arch into him.

Her legs fell apart, and he settled closer between them, kissing and sucking her breasts until she was whimpering with pleasure and need.

A shimmering thought reminded her this was supposed to be

a mutual mazing. She was allowing Quin to give her all the pleasure, and she wanted to give him equal pleasure.

She could feel the hard ridge of his erection pressing against her through the fine cloth of his evening breeches, but she wanted them to be skin to skin. She gasped, moaned and fumbled to undo the buttons keeping him confined.

Before she'd made any progress, he laid her back onto the mattress, still lavishing attention on each of her breasts in turn, and then her stomach...

Desire rippled across her tender belly. The swollen throbbing between her legs intensified.

"My sweet Gabrielle." His breath was warm against her skin. "Beautiful Gabrielle." He settled back.

A tiny zephyr of breeze from the window heightened her tingling awareness of the skin his kisses had dampened. His hands rested on either side of her hips. Then his thumbs gently stroked the creases at the top of her thighs.

She quivered, panting and squirming beneath his touch. His thumbs brushed over the top of her soaking wet curls.

"My Gabrielle, I'm going to kiss you now," he said hoarsely.

He parted her intimate folds before she'd understood his meaning. She lifted her head from the mattress in time to see his dark head lower to the juncture of her thighs.

He stroked her plumped, soaking flesh with his thumbs and her breath fluttered in her throat. Her head fell back onto the mattress. She tried to rock her hips from side to side, because he wasn't caressing the place that ached most for his touch.

"My beautiful Gabrielle." His voice was rough with passion. "Pearl beyond compare."

She felt his breath against her, and then he was giving her the most intimate kiss she could imagine. He sucked on—

Was that what he meant by calling her a pearl? Then every coherent thought whirled away in a haze of delirious pleasure. He teased her with his tongue until she was panting and whimpering. Until the coil of anticipation inside her was so tight she trembled with need—

Until the almost unbearable tension flew apart in glorious cascades of ecstasy. Her inner muscles clenching in spasms of rippling pleasure that rolled out through every part of her quivering body.

Satiated, she sank into the mattress, her heart racing, her breath ragged, and her limbs now so languid they were almost too heavy to move.

Quin's hands rested on her thighs. "You're magnificent," he said.

"It's you. Always you. Only you." Her reply was little more than breathless, barely coherent gasps.

He stood, and she rolled her head to one side to watch him remove his breeches. He was still rampantly aroused.

She pushed herself up onto her elbows. "I'll maze you now."

A slight smile quirked his lips as he returned to her.

"That's not what you call it, is it?" She found the energy to shift herself back to make space for him, and rotate so she was lying on the bed in the usual direction.

"Not until last night." The mattress dipped as he lay beside her. "But I like our code word. You've been amazing me ever since we first met. It's only fitting you maze me as well." He cupped her breast, his hold light but possessive.

She put her hand on his side, relishing the taut muscular tension beneath her palm. He was a virile young man in the peak of his perfection. "I'll love you just the same when we're both old and perhaps need walking sticks to get about," she whispered.

Even though it was obvious he was in the grip of fierce arousal, his expression softened. "I love the heart of you…your soul…more than your gorgeous body, my Gabrielle."

She rolled more toward him, lifting her head so she could kiss his chest, while her hand moved purposefully over his damp skin.

He drew in a shuddering breath. "A moment…a moment ago you were as…limp as a strand of silk. I thought—"

Her hand closed around him. "What's this?"

"My cock," he gritted out.

"And here?" She stroked down to cup him lower.

"My balls," he choked, every muscle in his body strung as tight as harp strings. "As you know, dear wanton…" His breath hitched "…witch."

Love was a joyful upswelling of happiness and laughter. She caressed his inner thigh and then wrapped her hand around his cock and stroked him from root to tip.

He jerked beneath her ministrations. He was breathing heavily, but let her explorations continue without interference.

"Tomorrow, you're going to teach me ball games we can discuss at dinner without blushing," she said.

"Yesssss." The word was hissed between his teeth. "Dear heart—" He groaned, his whole body shuddering as his release spurted from the head of his cock.

Excited, fascinated, aroused, she kept working him until he

relaxed back onto the mattress, all the tension drained from his muscles.

She raised herself to smile down at him. "Now you're the one as limp as a strand of silk," she said smugly.

He gave her a lazy grin. "I am. A moment, my dear wanton witch, then we can be limp strands of silk together."

He rolled from the bed, retrieved a handkerchief from the pocket of his breeches and wiped away the evidence of his explosive release from both of them. Then he lay beside her and pulled her against him.

She relaxed with her head on his shoulder.

"I didn't know I was so wanton," she mused, absently toying with the hair on his chest.

"I like it, and mine is the only opinion that counts on the matter." He cupped her head. "Your hair's down. It looks beautiful. I did notice earlier, but I was too preoccupied to say."

She smiled. "I took a moment to brush it before I finished my painting. I didn't know how long you'd be."

Quin's groan wasn't one of raw desire, but rather remembered frustration. "I thought Henderson would *never* leave. And we need to treat him with respect. He's given us his daughter and I don't want him to have any reason to change his mind."

"No. There's so much to talk about...but I'm so tired," she admitted.

"I know. We've had a string of short nights and exceptionally exciting days," he agreed. "Nights and days that have given me my heart's desire." He kissed the crown of her head. "But we do need some sleep before we face the cricketing extravagance that awaits us tomorrow."

"Don't you like cricket?" She closed her eyes, content to breathe in his scent and listen to his voice.

"In my opinion, it's more entertaining to play than watch." He laughed ruefully. "And a week tomorrow, you *will* be watching me play. Before then I'll need to get in some more rigorous practice than rolling a ball to Nancy."

"I'm sure you're wonderful at it," she murmured.

"Are you falling asleep on me?" he asked.

"No." But her hand went still on his chest as drowsiness crept over her.

"Don't fall asleep yet, dear heart. I have two important things to tell you before I leave," he said.

"I don't want you to leave." She snuggled him closer. "No one knows you're here."

"I'm quite certain Father knows exactly where I am right now." Quin's muscles remained relaxed but there wasn't a trace of doubt in his tone.

Gabrielle's eyes popped open. "Did you tell him?"

"Of course not—but he knows." Quin's chest lifted in a sigh. "I hope your papa is less knowing, but we still need to be discreet."

She raised herself up to look into his face. "Papa loves you," she said firmly.

"He holds me in high regard," Quin agreed. "But he's not what I need to talk to you about now."

"What?" She wasn't nervous because Quin was so relaxed, but she was curious because she heard an odd note in his voice she couldn't decipher.

"After Henderson left, Father asked for my permission to

marry Agnes Trent," he said.

She blinked, her sleepy mind trying to make sense of that unexpected statement. "Your permission?"

"Not really." Quin smiled at her. "He said Agnes wouldn't proceed without it. I think it's more that they both want my acceptance of their marriage."

Gabrielle's confusion cleared. "I forgot. She was with us all evening, acting in every way the lady of the house. I forgot she's your papa's housekeeper. I suppose I didn't forget, exactly. But she gave you the flower to give to me, just as if she was your mother. She rescued you from our papas' teasing. It was so lovely."

Remembering that moment brought emotional tears to Gabrielle's eyes.

"I know. I will forever regret my momentary hesitation when I walked into the dining room and saw him holding the chair for her." Quin's expression was troubled. "It wasn't because I disapproved, only that I was surprised. But I worried him. I wish I could go back and redo that moment."

Gabrielle cupped his cheek and raised herself to kiss his lips. "You've no need to reproach yourself," she whispered. "I'm sure your papa doesn't."

Quin kissed her back, supporting her in his strong arms, but stopped before passion reclaimed them.

"Father told me the first time he asked Agnes to marry him, I was twelve years old," he said.

"That's…that's so long ago." Gabrielle was dumbfounded.

"I know." Quin threaded his fingers gently through her hair.

"It's longer than I thought I'd have to wait for you if you couldn't leave Charlotte till she was seventeen or eighteen."

"I'm so glad you didn't have to wait...*we* didn't have to wait," she whispered. "I love you so much that you were willing to—but it hurt knowing I was hurting you."

"You weren't hurting me," he corrected. "The situation you were in caused us both distress—but now we've resolved it."

"Because of you." She kissed him.

"Father and Agnes helped," he said a short while later. "Apparently he found her sitting on top of the wall one evening, testing whether a lady would be able to use a ladder to get over it."

"Miss Trent and your father put out the ladder for me?" Gabrielle was astonished. "I thought it was Mrs. Whittle."

"As I understand it, Agnes and Mrs. Whittle conceived the scheme between them, Agnes wanted to test its feasibility, and Father took over part of its execution." Quin grinned up at her. "He asked me what I did with his ladder this evening. I told him I carried it over and leaned it against a haystack. He's going to buy a new one."

"Oh." Gabrielle's smile was misty. "Your father is wonderful. I'm not even sure if my papa would have done that, and I love him with all my heart."

"I suspect it's hard for a man to allow his daughter the same freedoms he allows his son," Quin said tactfully. "My father wasn't willing to let Agnes carry the ladder about the place, and he thought Mrs. Whittle would be going with you to the orchard wall."

"The ladder wasn't too heavy," Gabrielle said. "It was only awkward because I'd never done anything like that before."

"If I'd known it was you and not a lady burglar I'd have rushed to help," Quin assured her. "And now we need to help Father and Agnes."

"Of course. What are we to do? Are they worried people won't accept Miss Trent as Lady Appledrum?" Gabrielle asked. "I saw this evening that your father's household already treats her as if she is. But society can be less forgiving."

"Father won't care for himself, but he will care for Agnes. I think he's been waiting for her to overcome her reservations," Quin said. "He described it as a long step from housekeeper to marchioness."

"And she started as your nurse." Anyone meeting Miss Trent for the first time now at a society ball or one of the public assemblies wouldn't question her suitability to attend such events. But plenty of people would be aware of her current role in Lord Appledrum's household, and perhaps more of her history as one of his servants.

"Every woman who was anxious to become the next Marchioness of Appledrum, or ambitious for their daughter to become your father's next wife, will be ill-disposed to the lady he does marry," Gabrielle said. "The gossip and the false tales about them will sweep through the drawing rooms and salons of London."

Quin winced. "I hope most people will not be unkind. I don't know why anyone derives pleasure from treating others badly."

"They don't have your generous heart." Gabrielle caressed his chest. "Or your ability to accept people as they are, not as society expects them to behave. I don't know any other man who'd have the patience to sit and talk to a little girl about snails."

"My father would. And Marcus. Duncan too, most likely. I'm sorry you haven't met him yet. Apparently, he's making ice cream with Miss Bianchetti. But we're straying from the point—"

"Giant Duncan you're writing your book with is making ice cream with Miss Bianchetti?" Gabrielle interrupted.

"He's not a giant. Father suspects we ate some of her supplies for tomorrow and Duncan is helping her replenish them. Focus, mademoiselle." Quin tapped her lightly on the nose. "We need to discuss our marriage."

"Oh, I want to talk about that too. Can it be soon? Tomorrow? Oh, no, we have to watch cricket tomorrow. The next day?" she asked hopefully.

"Not unless I pile you into a carriage this minute and we rush to Scotland—and I doubt we'd make that journey in two days."

"And it would only make a scandal. I don't think that would benefit your father and Miss Trent." She sighed.

"My original plan was to speak to the parson tomorrow and see if the first set of banns could be called this Sunday," Quin said. "Then we could marry in three weeks' time—"

"I like that plan."

"So do I, but I think we need to be a little more conventional. Send a formal notice to the newspapers, attend balls as a betrothed couple...do whatever else betrothed people do. I'm probably supposed to take you driving. Do you need to buy new clothes? A trousseau?"

"I don't have much money, and I'm not sure how much Papa can afford." Gabrielle felt sadder on her papa's behalf than her own.

"I have a generous allowance. And once Duncan and I have finished our book, I need to turn my attention to learning estate management," Quin said. "Whereupon I'll start earning my allowance. I don't know how much a trousseau costs, but I imagine I can afford whatever you want to buy."

"I won't be extravagant," Gabrielle promised. "I think Papa will want to pay as much as he can. I'll speak to him. If we're not getting married in three weeks' time, when shall we set the date?"

Quin drew thoughtful circles on her shoulder with his fingers. "Early September?" he suggested. "That's less than two months away, but not an unseemly scramble."

"September is a beautiful month." Ecstatic he wasn't making them wait any longer, she leaned over to give him a kiss that quickly turned heated.

"You were falling asleep a few minutes ago." His lips moved divinely over her mouth.

"You woke me up again."

"As it happens, you've woken me up too." He rolled them over so he was on top.

She wrapped her arms around him, sighing with appreciation at the feel of his hard body pressing her into the mattress. "I like you here."

"I like being here too. If you're agreeable, I'm going to try pulling out this time." He nuzzled her cheek, her throat and the side of her neck, arousing the most delicious sensations within her.

"I'm agreeable to anything you want," she breathed. "My love. My darling Quin."

Chapter Fifty-One

"Dear heart, I must return to my own room now." Quin kissed Gabrielle's cheek and got up to dress.

"I wish you didn't have to leave," she said drowsily.

"I know, but I must. Go back to sleep." He made quick work of getting into his clothes, partly because there was only one burning candle left in the candelabrum. Navigating an unfamiliar room was a lot easier if you could see enough not to stumble over unexpectedly placed furniture.

He leaned over the bed to kiss her again. "I'll see you in the morning, dear heart." Then he picked up the candelabrum, unlocked the door and slipped into the adjoining sitting room—which wasn't empty.

Surprise trapped his breath in his throat, but the figure trying to open the curtains was far too small to present a threat.

"Mademoiselle?" Charlotte turned toward him. "Lord Quin?"

"Hello, Charlotte." His mind went blank. To give himself

time to think, he quietly closed Gabrielle's bedroom door. "It's not morning yet. I mean to say, why are you opening the curtains?"

"I'm thirsty. Did you come to kiss mademoiselle awake, like a prince?" Charlotte gave the curtain another tug.

"Ah, yes, but she's sleeping so peacefully I don't have the heart to wake her." It wasn't exactly a lie, it just missed out everything that had happened while Gabrielle was awake.

"There it is!" Charlotte exclaimed.

"What?"

"The water jug. And it's nearly full." She padded over to the sideboard.

"You were opening the curtains to let more light into the room." Quin belatedly understood.

"The moon is still quite bright." Charlotte poured water into a glass. "Have you ever been out in the moonlight?"

"Yes." Quin rubbed his free hand over his face.

"It must be pretty. It's probably best you didn't wake mademoiselle. She hasn't been sleeping for a hundred years like story princesses. Would you like some water?"

At Quin's best guess it was about three o'clock in the morning. Not the time a little girl and her new guardian should sit down for a social call over a glass of water. On the other hand, it had been an unusual day for everyone, including a child who usually slept through the night.

"Yes, please." He spotted an unlit candle on the mantelpiece and quickly touched the wick to the guttering candle in the candelabrum. "Why are you awake?"

"My thoughts woke up and they were very noisy, and then I

was thirsty." Charlotte emptied her glass of water in one go, sighed with satisfaction, and sat down on one of the chairs.

He thought that was another hint she wanted to talk to him, so he sat down on the sofa and stretched out his legs. "Thinking can be thirsty work," he agreed. "Sometimes, when my thoughts get noisy, but I know I should really be sleeping, I recite multiplication tables to myself. It's so boring and familiar I usually fall asleep."

"I'm still learning mine." Charlotte pulled her legs up onto the chair and tucked her feet under the hem of her nightdress.

It was a warm night in the middle of summer. But she was small, and small bodies cooled quicker than large ones. Quin assumed the same rule applied to children as to volumes of water. He wasn't wearing a coat, so he couldn't give it to her, but he spotted a shawl draped over the back of another chair. He got up and laid it gently over Charlotte. She didn't say anything, but she smiled.

He went back to the sofa, wondering if she was now falling asleep, but her eyes were open, and she seemed to be thinking.

"We're going to have hot chocolate in the morning," she said.

"I know. Do you like hot chocolate?" He sipped his water.

"I'm not sure. I've never had it before. It's exciting." She snuggled the shawl closer around herself and gave him a sideways look. "Are we always going to live in this house?"

"Probably not all year around. But wherever I am, you and mademoiselle will be, too," he said. "Or perhaps I should say, wherever mademoiselle and you are, I will be too."

"Forever?"

"Until you're much older than you are now. When you're grown up, you might find a prince of your own."

Charlotte narrowed her eyes. "Can a lady go in search of a prince instead of waiting for him to come to her?"

"Hmm." Quin took a moment to consider the question. Gabrielle had climbed over the wall instead of waiting, but he wasn't sure if that was something he should share with Charlotte. "I see no reason why a *story* princess shouldn't go in search of a suitable prince. When the prince has solved the problem of the trained hedge, why don't you make your next story about a princess?"

"He's already solved the hedge." Charlotte yawned.

"He did? How?" Quin had feared they might be battling the hedge for a long time to come.

"He got down on both knees and begged for its forgiveness for attacking it with a sword and an ax," she said. "Then he explained how important it was for him to get through so he could wake up the princess, and he begged it to make a little opening for him to crawl through."

Quin did his best to divert his thoughts from those euphoric minutes when he'd gone down on both knees for Gabrielle in the privacy of her room.

He drank some more water and asked, "What happened after the prince crawled through the hedge?"

"He found the princess, kissed her awake, and a fairy godmother conjured delicious ice cream for them to eat," Charlotte said.

"What are they going to do next?"

"Live in the castle and order ice cream for everyone every

Wednesday. I think the next story should be about a princess who goes to the land of giant snails?" There was a definite question in Charlotte's voice, a suggestion that someone else might have to contribute to the story, perhaps with details about the land of giant snails.

"We can collaborate on that, if you like," Quin said easily.

She shot him a glance.

"Collaborate means work together," he clarified.

She nodded. "My papa looked sad."

"Yes." Lord Henderson had given the impression he was sinking into an apathetic melancholy. If so, Quin hoped it would be a temporary state. He wondered if spending several hours in her father's company was why Charlotte's sleep had been disturbed.

"I don't mind if he visits sometimes," she said. "But only if you're right there at the same time."

"Me especially?"

She gave a single, sharp nod. "Mademoiselle is good and brave, but she doesn't have power."

"Ah, I see. She'll have more power when she's my wife," Quin pointed out.

"She'll be a countess, and my mama's only a viscountess. My mama will have to curtsy to mademoiselle." Charlotte sounded grimly pleased about that.

Quin hoped such encounters were an infrequent occurrence.

"But mademoiselle will never have as much power as Lord Appledrum or Duke Marcus." Charlotte frowned. "That's not what I should call the duke, but I don't remember his whole name."

Quin cast his mind back. "I think the only time it was used yesterday evening was when Tredworth announced him. It's Marcus, Duke of Candervale."

The door to Gabrielle's bedchamber opened. He looked around to see her standing there, her glorious hair around her shoulders, a dressing gown hastily dragged on over her nightgown, a befuddled expression on her face.

"What's happening?" she asked.

"Lord Quin came to kiss you awake, but you were sleeping so peacefully he didn't want to disturb you," Charlotte explained. "And I was thirsty."

Gabrielle blinked at them both.

"Now we're discussing hot chocolate, power and princesses." Quin held out his hand to her. "I'm not sure how much more conversation there is. Would you like to join us?"

"I heard voices. It was confusing." She came to sink onto the sofa beside Quin.

He put his arm around her and kissed her temple. "I know. Charlotte, strictly speaking, my father and my cousin, Marcus, both have more power than I do in terms of worldly influence. If, for any reason, I'm not with you, you'll always be safe with them. But I'm not planning on going anywhere."

"Lord Quin says he'll go wherever we go, mademoiselle," Charlotte said. "But aren't we just going to stay with him?"

"That's my plan," Gabrielle said. "I think it's an excellent one, don't you?"

"Yes, mademoiselle." Charlotte smiled, yawned again, and closed her eyes.

"Quin?"

He woke to the sound of a familiar voice, gently rousing him to consciousness, and the smell of hot chocolate.

"Trentie?" His voice was thick with sleep, and he spoke before he opened his eyes.

Agnes was standing in front of him, smiling at him with the same loving tenderness with which she'd woken him when he was a young child in a different nursery.

The past receded, and the present rolled forward to claim him. Charlotte was still curled up in the chair, fast asleep.

Gabrielle was a warm and relaxed armful at his side, equally fast asleep. Both his female companions were dressed in their night attire. Thankfully, he was fully and respectably clothed.

Agnes looked as if she was trying not to laugh.

"Of course I approve." He said the most important thing first. "It fills me with happiness for you and Father to find joy with each other."

Agnes's smile trembled. "I don't know why…" She paused to take an unsteady breath. "I don't know why you doubt your ability to say the right thing. You've never failed me yet."

Gabrielle must have woken because she untangled herself from him. He stood and hugged the only mother he'd ever known.

"What am I going to call you?" he asked. "When Miss Trent is no longer appropriate?"

"Agnes. Call me Agnes." She touched his cheek.

In her chair, Charlotte yawned and stretched, and the shawl fell off. "Is it time for hot chocolate?"

"Yes, it is." Agnes's smile was a little damp, but full of mischievous humor when she looked at Quin. "The maid who brought up the chocolate told me the nursery was full of sleeping people, so I had to come and see for myself. Lord Hanwell's hot chocolate is waiting for him in his room."

"I'll retire there now." Quin could take a hint. "And later we'll all go to watch the cricket."

Chapter Fifty-Two

On a warm September morning, Gabrielle stood in the church vestibule with her papa and her bridesmaids.

A broad beam of sunlight streamed in through the open church doors behind her. Within the church, organ music was being played to entertain the waiting congregation.

Papa peeped around the curtain. "Half the population of Brighton has come to see you wed," he reported, his eyes twinkling.

Anyone could attend the church service, while the invited guests would enjoy the wedding breakfast that would take place at Lord Appledrum's house.

Papa scanned his three companions and smiled. "You're all looking beautiful, ladies. Nancy, please don't kick that flagstone with the toe of your dainty shoe."

"It is dainty, isn't it?" She stuck her foot out to admire it.

"Yes, but it won't remain dainty if you keep kicking things with it," he said.

"But the stone's sticking up, Uncle Philp."

"So I see. Now you've drawn attention to the raised edge of the flagstone, after the service, I will mention to the vicar that it needs to be leveled. Will you remind me, ma coccinelle?" He looked at Charlotte.

She gave him a flustered nod, and took Nancy's hand. "I'm sorry. I am minding her, I promise."

"It takes a whole battalion to mind Mademoiselle Nancy," Papa said cheerfully. "We're all doing very well."

Charlotte nodded.

Papa turned to Gabrielle, and his expression became infinitely tender. "Your mother would be proud of you," he said softly.

Her mouth trembled and tears beaded on her lashes. "I wish she was here. I'm so glad you're here. I'm proud of all of us today," she whispered.

She knew her father carried a deep wound of regret that he hadn't made better preparations before their flight from France.

Two days after their arrival in England, she'd had a heart-wrenching conversation with him. She'd seen him cry in grief when her mother had died, but his tears in Brighton had been because he'd failed to make adequate provision for his children.

She could still remember the broken sound of his voice when he'd confessed that Lord Appledrum had advised him months earlier to transfer money into an English bank.

"But I was distracted by your mother's failing health, and negligent, and now you and Felix are paying the price." He'd been full of self-recrimination.

But by the next morning, he'd packed away all his regrets and sorrows, and focused on making a new life for himself in England as a renowned fencing master.

He had paid for her wedding dress, but he hadn't covered the whole cost of her trousseau. After a quiet—and private—conversation, they'd agreed Papa needed to maintain and build his reserves to pay for Felix's school fees and other expenses.

Felix didn't know. Gabrielle suspected he'd be indignant at being favored in such a way. Right now, he was sitting in a church pew, waiting for their entrance.

And Quin was waiting at the altar for her!

"I'm proud of you, Papa," she said again. "I'm proud of all of us. We all look wonderful. Nancy, please walk behind me beside Charlotte, the way we practiced. Are we all ready? Let's go in."

She took her papa's arm, and they began their slow march toward the altar—toward Quin.

She heard the ripple of awareness through the congregation as she passed between the rows of pews, but the only face she saw was Quin's.

He was smiling at her, undisguised love in his eyes—and the awareness of a shared secret.

Two weeks ago, she'd confessed to him she thought she was already pregnant, most likely from their first night together. The night she would always think of as their true wedding night.

He'd been both thrilled and chagrined. "I shouldn't have risked it, even once. But, oh my dear heart, as long as you're happy, I'm happy."

"I'm happy." She'd kissed him. "I'm so happy. And I can't wait to make love, now you don't have to be so careful anymore."

He'd more than risen to that challenge, and their secret

shared knowledge was in his eyes as he took her hand in his. Tonight, as an officially married couple, they would make love again.

But first they would say their vows before the vicar, so the whole world knew they were married.

∼

Hello!

You probably won't be surprised to learn that Cinderella was my starting inspiration for Quin and Gabrielle's story.

In particular, I focused on the grand party my heroine would attend, and what she would wear. It seemed to me that knowing the source of my heroine's ballgown would tell me a great deal about her character.

Since I'm writing a historical romance series without any fantasy element, no benevolent character with a magical wand could appear—or even a household of mice skilled in the art of dressmaking.

In the end, I decided to go with the idea that the dress already belonged to the heroine, a leftover possession from her former life. And that's how Gabrielle, a noble exile from the French Revolution, came to life.

I saw her climbing a ladder to get into Lord Appledrum's grand masquerade ball. And that was the first scene I wrote.

But wait, who's the man hanging out in the orchard when Gabrielle's feathered turban appears over the top of the wall?

Clearly, he's the hero, but why is he fascinated with honeysuckle and moths?

Ah hah! He must be an eighteenth-century botanist, naturalist and explorer. A man who is more comfortable with the idea of confronting a burglar than navigating the hazards of a ballroom.

One of the most famous of those real-life gentlemen scientists and explorers was Sir Joseph Banks, who traveled with Captain James Cook on his first voyage of discovery.

But Quin's adventures and his personality are entirely his own.

And I confess, I have no idea why the Royal Navy and the Royal Society decided to launch the scientific expedition I invented for Quin and his friends. But I'm sure they had a good reason to send HMS Wayfarer around the globe so Quin could encounter giant snails and tigers on his travels.

When I started writing Quin and Gabrielle's story, I didn't anticipate how important Lord Appledrum's masquerade ball would be in the romances of other characters.

But then Meg fell over during the cotillion and Marcus took her out into the garden to help her regain her composure. They started talking about Meg's quest to find a husband during her stay in Brighton, and Marcus turned out to be very interested in that conversation!

And poor Duncan came down the stairs wearing a Minotaur mask, feeling like a bull in a china shop.

(His family crest includes a bull's head, but it turns out wearing a papier-mâché bull's head on your shoulders when you're already 6'5" isn't such a good idea, after all).

In his efforts to avoid the ballroom, Duncan ended up in the same chamber where Maria Bianchetti was struggling to do the work of three people because of a family emergency. Duncan was so happy to offer his assistance.

Oops, getting a bit ahead of myself here...

The next story in the Brighton Seasons Series will be Meg and Marcus's – *The Best Bride for the Duke*.

Duncan and Maria's story will follow, most likely titled *Lord Duncan and the Sweet Maker*.

There are more characters hanging about in my mind, waiting to make their appearances.

I've got a spreadsheet to keep the timelines of the different, overlapping stories straight...

Happy reading, wherever your mood takes you next.

Evie

https://www.eviefairfax.com/

About the Author

Evie Fairfax writes Georgian and Regency era historical romance. She's always loved learning about how people lived in the past, and she loves reading romance, so it felt natural for her to write in the historical romance genre.

If she's not writing, she's likely to be reading. She's also had many different crafty hobbies over the years including knitting, cross stitch, woodwork and even soap-carving—but she doesn't do that last one anymore because the soap dust makes her sneeze.

She enjoys walking in the countryside, photography, and watching birds through her window while she's thinking about her stories.

To find out more about her books or sign up for her newsletter, visit https://www.eviefairfax.com/

Printed in Great Britain
by Amazon